They have just one desire — to win the…

Heart of a Hero

Three dramatic and intense romances from
three fabulous Mills & Boon authors!

Heart of a Hero

ANNE MARIE WINSTON
LORETH ANNE WHITE
LYN STONE

MILLS & BOON

All the characters in this book have no existence outside the imagination of the author, and have no relation whatsoever to anyone bearing the same name or names. They are not even distantly inspired by any individual known or unknown to the author, and all the incidents are pure invention.

First published in Great Britain 2011
Harlequin Mills & Boon Limited,
Eton House, 18-24 Paradise Road, Richmond, Surrey TW9 1SR

HEART OF A HERO © Harlequin Enterprises II B.V./S.à.r.l. 2011

The Soldier's Seduction, The Heart of a Mercenary and *Straight Through the Heart* were first published in Great Britain by Harlequin Mills & Boon Limited.

The Soldier's Seduction © Anne Marie Rodgers 2006
The Heart of a Mercenary © Loreth Beswetherick 2006
Straight Through the Heart © Lynda Stone 2006

ISBN: 978 0 263 88339 8

05-0211

Printed and bound in Spain
by Litografia Rosés S.A., Barcelona

THE SOLDIER'S SEDUCTION

BY
ANNE MARIE WINSTON

RITA® Award finalist and bestselling author **Anne Marie Winston** loves babies she can give back when they cry, animals in all shapes and sizes and just about anything that blooms. When she's not writing, she's managing a house full of animals and teenagers, reading anything she can find and trying not to eat chocolate. She will dance at the slightest provocation and weeds her garden when she can't see the sun for the weeds any more. You can learn more about Anne Marie's novels by visiting her website at www.annemariewinston.com

Dedicated to the memory of those animals who perished when they were left behind during Hurricane Katrina and with warmest thanks to every rescuer and animal lover who responded and saved so many others.

One

It wasn't what he'd expected.

Wade brought the rental car to a halt along the curb and simply absorbed the sight of the modest, cozy home nestled in the small-town neighborhood. Phoebe's home. Phoebe's neighborhood.

He cut the ignition and eased himself from the car, taking in the pretty autumn wreath on the front door, the carved pumpkin on the second of the brick steps leading to the porch, the fall flowers in bright shades of rust, burgundy and gold that brightened up the bare spaces in front of the small bushes along the foundation.

He'd assumed she would live in an apartment. He didn't really know why he'd thought that, but every time he'd pictured Phoebe since he'd learned she had moved away, he'd imagined her living in an apartment or a small condo. Nothing so…permanent, as this house appeared to be.

He'd gotten quite a shock when he'd finally returned home, eagerly anticipating his first sight of her—only to learn that she'd left California months earlier. He didn't even want to think about the bleak misery that had swept through him, the letdown that had been so overwhelming that he'd just wanted to sit down and cry.

Not that he ever would. Soldiers didn't cry. Especially soldiers who had been decorated all to hell and back.

Living at home had been difficult. Only two short months before he'd been injured, he'd gone home on leave for his mother's funeral. While he was recuperating, his father made valiant attempts to keep things as normal around the house as possible. But without his mother, there was a big hole nothing could disguise.

He made casual inquiries about where Phoebe had gone, but no one seemed to know. By the time he was home for a month, he was desperate enough to start digging. The secretary of her high school graduating class had no forwarding address. A light Internet search turned up nothing. He finally thought to call Berkeley, the university she'd attended, but they wouldn't, or couldn't, give him any information.

He was about ready to consider hiring a private investigator when he thought of calling June, the only girl other than Phoebe's twin sister Melanie who he could really remember Phoebe hanging around with in high school. Geeky little June with her thick glasses and straight As. Someone Melanie wouldn't have been caught dead hanging out with, but as he recalled, a genuinely sweet kid.

They really had seemed like kids to his four-years-older eyes back then. But by the time the twins had graduated from high school, those years had no longer seemed to be of much consequence.

Getting in touch with Phoebe's old friend was a stroke of luck. June had gotten a Christmas card from Phoebe four months after she'd moved. And God bless her, she'd kept the address.

That address had been quite a shock. She'd gone from California clear across the country to a small town in rural New York state.

Ironically, it was a familiar area. Phoebe's new home was less than an hour from West Point, where he'd spent four long years in a gray uniform chafing for graduation day, when he could finally become a real soldier.

He wouldn't have been so impatient for those days to end if he'd known what lay ahead of him.

He climbed the small set of steps carefully. His doctors were sure he'd make a full recovery—full enough for civilian life, anyway. But the long flight from San Diego to JFK had been more taxing than he'd anticipated. He probably should have gotten a room for the night, looked up Phoebe tomorrow when he was rested.

But he hadn't been able to make himself wait a moment longer.

He knocked on the wooden front door, eyeing the wavy glass diamond pane in the door's upper portion. Although it was designed to obscure a good view of the home's occupants, he might be able to see someone coming toward the door. But after a few moments and two more knocks, nobody showed. Phoebe wasn't home.

Disappointment swamped him. He leaned his head against the door frame, completely spent. He'd counted on seeing her so badly. But…he glanced at his watch. He hadn't even considered the time. It was barely four o'clock.

The last time he'd seen her, she was a year out of college with a degree in elementary education, and she'd been teaching first grade. If she still was a teacher, she might soon be getting home. She probably worked, he decided as relief seeped through him.

If she wasn't married, he thought, trying to encourage himself, it stood to reason she'd need income. And June hadn't heard anything about a husband. If she had married, she hadn't taken his name, which didn't really fit with the quiet, traditional girl he'd known so well. And he knew she hadn't taken anyone's name because he'd checked the local phone book and found her there: P. Merriman.

Fine. He'd wait. He turned and started for his car, but a porch swing piled with pillows caught his attention. He'd just sit there and wait for her.

If she'd been married, he wouldn't be here, he assured himself. If she'd been married, he would have left her alone, wouldn't have attempted to contact her again in this lifetime.

But he was pretty sure she wasn't.

And despite the good reasons he had for staying away from Phoebe Merriman, despite the fact that he'd behaved like a jerk the last time they'd been together, he'd never been able to forget her. Never been able to convince himself that being with her had been a mistake. He'd thought of little else during his long months of recuperation and therapy. He'd nearly reached out to her then, but some part of him had shied away from a phone call or an e-mail.

He wanted to see her in person when he asked her if there was any chance she'd let him into her life again. Sighing, he dragged one of the pillows up and leaned his head against it. If only things hadn't gotten so screwed up at the end.

It had been bad enough that Phoebe's twin Melanie had died because of him. Indirectly, maybe, but it still had been his fault.

He'd compounded it in the biggest damn way possible when he'd made love to Phoebe after the funeral. And then he'd run.

Phoebe Merriman jumped when the mobile phone in her minivan began to play the jazzy tune she'd programmed into it. That phone hardly ever rang. The only reason she had it, really, was so that Bridget's babysitter could always reach her in case of an emergency.

Alarmed, she punched the button to take the call. A quick glance at the display had the dread in her stomach lurching uncomfortably. Phoebe had good reason to fear unexpected phone calls. And just as she'd feared, it was her home number. "Hello?"

"Phoebe?" The babysitter, Angie, sounded breathless.

"Angie. What's wrong?"

"There's a man sitting on the front porch. In the swing."

The news was almost anticlimactic, considering that she'd been fearing a high fever, blood or broken bones.

"Sitting? And what else?"

"Nothing else." Phoebe realized Angie wasn't breathless; she was whispering. "He came to the door but I didn't answer, so he sat down on the swing and I thought I'd better call you." Her voice quavered a little.

Phoebe remembered how young her sitter was, newly graduated from high school and still living with her parents on the next street over, taking evening classes at a local community college. Phoebe had met Angie's mother in her Sunday-school class and had felt lucky to find Angie.

"You did exactly right," she assured the younger woman. "If all he's doing is sitting there, just stay inside with the doors closed. I'm only a few blocks from home."

She pulled into her driveway a few minutes later, the cell phone's line still open. There was a gray sedan with a rental tag parked in front of her house. Maybe it belonged to whoever was waiting on her front porch.

"Okay, Angie," she said. "I'm home. You stay right where you are until I come inside."

She took a deep breath. Should she call the police? Common sense told her whoever was waiting on her porch probably wasn't a criminal. Otherwise, he wouldn't be here in the middle of the day, unconcerned about the neighbors taking down his license plate or identifying him. She positioned her keys between her fingers with one key thrust outward, as she'd learned in the self-defense class she'd taken when she'd first started college. Then she pivoted on her heel and headed up her front walk.

She started up the porch steps, unable to see the swing because of the trellis of roses blooming across the front of the porch. She knew from experience that a person sitting there on the swing could see out much more easily than anyone could see in.

As she reached the porch, a very large man came into view. Adrenaline rushed through her as he began to rise from the swing. She angled her body to confront him.

"What are—*Wade!*"

As the man's identity registered, a wave of shock slammed into her. It couldn't be.

Wade was dead.

Her knees felt as if they might buckle and she groped for the railing behind her. The keys fell to the floor with a loud jangle. "You—you're Wade." An inane statement. Of course it was Wade.

He was smiling but his eyes were watchful as he took a step forward. "Yeah. Hi, Phoebe."

"B-b-but…"

His smile faded as she took a step backward. One eyebrow rose in a quirk as familiar to her as her own smile in the mirror. That quizzical expression had been only one of the things she'd loved about Wade Donnelly. "But what?" he asked quietly.

"I thought you were dead!" She blurted out the words as her legs gave way and she sank to the top step, dropping her head onto her knees as incredulity warred with a strong desire to cry hysterically.

Footsteps rang out as Wade crossed the porch and then the boards of the top step depressed as he sat down beside her. One large hand touched her back. "My God," she said, the words muffled. "You really are here, aren't you?"

"I'm really here." It was definitely Wade, his distinctly masculine tone one she would recognize anywhere. He touched her back again, just one small uncertain touch, and she had to fight the urge to throw herself into his arms.

He never really belonged to me, she reminded herself.

"I'm sorry it's such a shock." His voice was quiet and deep and rang with sincerity. "I *was* presumed to be dead for a couple of days until I could get back to my unit. But that was months ago."

"How long have you been home?" He'd been deployed right after Melanie's funeral. The memory brought back others she'd tried to forget, as well, and she focused on his answer, trying to ignore the past.

"About five weeks. I've been trying to find you." He hesitated for a moment. "June gave me your address and she knew I survived. I assumed she— or someone back home—had told you."

"No." She shook her head without lifting it. She'd stopped reading the news from home the day she'd read his obituary. And though she'd sent June a Christmas card this year, they hadn't exchanged more than signatures since she'd moved.

Silence fell. She sensed that he didn't know what to say any more than she did—

Bridget! Shocked that she could have forgotten her own child for a moment—particularly this moment—Phoebe leaped to her feet, ignoring Wade's startled exclamation. "Just—ah, just let me put my things inside," she said. "Then we can talk."

Her hands trembled as she turned away from the man she'd loved throughout her adolescent years and into young womanhood. The keys were slippery in her sweaty grasp and she dropped them again. Before she could react, Wade came to her side and stretched down for the keys.

"Here."

"Thank you." She took the keys carefully, without touching his hand, fumbled the correct one into the lock and opened her front door.

Reality hit her in the face again. Wade Donnelly was alive and waiting to talk to her. And she had to tell him she'd borne his child.

Angie rushed forward as Phoebe came through the door and closed it firmly behind herself. Before the sitter could speak, Phoebe put her finger to her lips to indicate silence. She walked through the front rooms toward the back of the little house and dropped her things onto the kitchen table. "Listen," she said to Angie in a quiet tone, "there's nothing to worry about. He's an old friend I haven't seen in a long time. Can you stay a little longer in case Bridget wakes up?"

Angie nodded, her eyes wide. "Sure."

"We're going to talk outside. "I don't—I'm not inviting him in and I don't particularly want him to know about Bridget, so please don't come out."

Angie nodded, an uncharacteristically knowing smile crossing her face. "No problem. I wouldn't want to cause trouble for you."

Phoebe paused in the act of walking back through the living room. "Cause trouble for me?"

"With people back where you came from." Angie gestured vaguely. "I mean, I know everybody has babies without getting married these days, but if you don't want anyone back home to know, that's your business."

Phoebe felt her eyebrows rising practically to her hairline. She opened her mouth, then closed it abruptly before hysterical laughter could bubble out. Dear innocent Angie thought she was hiding Bridget because she was ashamed of having an illegitimate child. If only it were that simple!

She swallowed as she slipped through the front door again, closing it securely behind her. Wade was standing now, leaning against one of the porch posts, dwarfing the small space. Lord, she'd forgotten how big he really was.

She drank in his appearance, trying to reconcile the grief she'd carried for the past six months with the reality of seeing him alive and apparently well. His dark, wavy hair was conservatively short compared to the out-of-control locks he'd sported in high school, but quite a bit longer than the last time she'd seen him, when he'd had a high and tight military cut that had stripped every bit of curl away. If he weighed an ounce more than he had then, it wasn't noticeable; his shoulders were still wide and heavily muscled, his hips narrow and his belly flat, his legs still as powerful looking as they'd been when he'd been a running back for the high school football team. That had been almost a dozen years ago, and she'd been a silly middle-school teen at the time, already pathetically infatuated with her older, totally hot neighbor.

Then she realized he was watching her stare at him, his gray eyes as clear and piercing as always beneath the black slashes of his eyebrows. She felt her cheeks heat and she crossed her arms over her chest.

Taking a deep breath, she voiced the question burning in her mind. "Why were you reported dead if they weren't sure?" Her voice shook with the remembered agony of learning that Wade was gone forever. "I read about your funeral…" The sentence died unfinished as she realized she'd read about the *plans* for his funeral. In his obituary.

Wade blinked, but before his gaze slid away from hers, she caught a glimpse of a haunting pain. "Battlefield mistake," he said. "They found my dog tags but not my body. By the time the mistake was corrected, word had already gone out that I'd been KIA."

She put a hand to her mouth, fighting the tears that desperately wanted to escape. All these months she'd thought he was dead....

"I was injured," he said. "In the chaos that followed the explosion, a friendly Afghani hid me. It took the guy three days to make contact with American troops, and it wasn't until then that the mistake was caught. The fellow who died whom they'd assumed was me had already been shipped to Germany for autopsy. They'd have caught the mistake eventually, but I sure gave a lot of people a shock. And just for the record," he added, "Mom and Dad didn't actually have a funeral. It was planned, then canceled. I guess you didn't attend or you'd have found out."

She opened her mouth, then closed it again and simply shook her head. She still wanted to cry. Badly. *I was having your baby at the time* was so not the thing to say.

She risked a glance at him and was almost undone by the pain in his eyes.

Unable to bear being the cause of that pain, she said, "I couldn't come back for the funeral." She turned away and settled on the porch swing. "It took every penny I had to move here." *Well, that wasn't a lie.* She'd been lucky to find this place, luckier still that, although she had few assets, her credit history was good and with the teachers' credit union behind her, she'd been able to qualify for a mortgage. It hadn't hurt that the cost of living in California was so much higher than it was here. She'd never have been able to afford even this modest little home if she'd stayed on the West Coast.

"Why did you move?" he asked suddenly. "All the way across the country? I know you don't have any family to keep you in California, but that's where you grew up, where your roots are. Don't you miss it?"

She swallowed. "Of course I miss it." *Terribly. I miss the cobblestones on the beaches and the freezing cold water, the balmy days and cooler nights that rarely vary. I miss driving down to Point Loma, or over to Cardiff, and watching whale migrations in the fall. I even miss the insanity of driving on the freeway and the fire danger. Most of all, I miss you.* "But my life is here now."

"Why?"

She raised her eyebrows. "Why what?"

"What makes rural New York state so special that you have to live here?"

She shrugged. "I'm a teacher. I'll have tenure in two more years and I don't want to start over again somewhere else. The pay is good here and the cost of living is more manageable than in Southern California."

He nodded. "I see." He joined her on the swing, sitting close but not touching. He placed an arm along the back of the swing and turned slightly toward her. "It's good to see you." His voice was warm, his eyes even more so.

She could barely breathe. He was looking at her the way she'd dreamed of for years. Years when he'd been too old for her to do more than dream of, years when he'd been her sister's boyfriend, more recently when she'd thought he was dead and she was raising his child alone.

"Wade…" She reached out a hand and placed her palm gently against his cheek. "I'm so glad you're alive. It's good to see you, too, but—"

"Have dinner with me tonight."

"I can't." Fear infused her voice with a touch of panic. She started to withdraw her hand but he covered it with his, turning his face into her palm, and she felt the warmth of his lips whispering against the tender skin.

"Tomorrow night, then."

"I—"

"Phoeber, I'm not taking no for an answer." The silly childhood nickname gave the moment an even deeper intimacy. "I'm not leaving here until you say yes."

She stepped back a full pace as he finally released her hand. Dinner was a bad idea, given the way her heart still pounded at the mere sight of him.

She'd grown up in the months since she'd become a parent. She no longer believed in the kind of love she read about in romance novels. At least, not mutual love that was returned. And she'd stopped allowing herself to believe that what had happened between Wade and her that day at the cabin had been anything but his reaction to the shock of her sister's death.

Now Wade was here, back from the dead, untying every neatly packed-away detail in her memories. Confusing her, rousing feelings she hadn't let herself feel in more than a year, the warmth of possibilities in his eyes scaring her to death.

She wanted to go back an hour, to come home as always to an empty porch and no tough conversations.

But she had to tell him about Bridget.

It was the last thing she wanted to do, but she had to. A few weeks before she thought he had died, she'd realized she couldn't keep Wade's child from him. Telling him in an e-mail or on the phone was unthinkable, however. She'd been planning to visit him, wherever he was stationed, as soon as she could travel again, and a promise was a promise. Even if it was only to herself.

But not yet. She could hardly just invite him in, not with the bassinet and high chair, the board books and infant toys, unmistakable signs of a baby in residence. And anyway, Angie had class tonight so she wouldn't be able to stay much longer. Phoebe needed to get rid of him, plan the best way to tell him of his fatherhood.

"All right," she finally said. "Dinner tomorrow night because I have something to tell you." The words nearly choked her.

Wade raised an eyebrow in question, but when she didn't elaborate he made no comment. All he said was "Shall I pick you up at seven?"

"I'll meet you," she said quickly. "Are you staying in town?"

As it turned out, he was staying at a hotel on the other side of town. Attached to it was a restaurant that she knew had somewhat secluded booths along the walls, so she suggested they meet there. Then she stood on the porch and watched as he walked to the gray sedan.

He smiled at her over the roof of the car before he climbed in. "See you tomorrow night."

She nodded, her heart stuttering at the warmth

in his eyes, even though she reminded herself it wasn't anything more than friendship she saw there. "See you then."

But as she watched him drive away, she wondered if it wouldn't just be easier to vanish, the way people in the witness protection program did. Anything had to be easier than telling Wade he was the father of a child. Her child.

Memories bombarded her....

She was twelve. Her twin sister Melanie perched beside her on a pink bike exactly like Phoebe's purple one, and they both watched the neighborhood boys playing baseball on the local park's grassy ball field.

"I'm gonna marry Wade when I grow up," Melanie announced.

Phoebe frowned. "He's going to be grown up before we are. What if he marries somebody else?" The thought of Wade Donnelly marrying anybody made her feel all twisted up inside. Wade lived across the street from them, and he was four years older than they were. Phoebe had had a crush on him since before she could remember.

"He won't marry anybody else," Melanie said confidently. "I'm going to make him love me."

And she had.

When they were seniors in high school,

Melanie had initiated her move. Phoebe went to the prom with Tim DeGrange, a friend from her Latin class. Melanie had asked Wade, even though he had just graduated from West Point that year, and to Phoebe's shock he had said yes. Prom night had been long and miserable. Melanie had clung to Wade all evening. He'd looked so handsome in his brand-new dress uniform that he'd made Phoebe's heart hurt, and she'd been suddenly so shy she could barely force herself to talk to him.

That had been the beginning. Melanie and Wade had dated through the early summer until his leave had ended and he'd headed off for his first assignment at a training school. It had been hell for Phoebe, seeing them together. But it had grown much, much worse when Melanie had begun seeing other guys while Wade was away....

"We're not exclusive, Phoebe." Melanie's voice was sharp as she responded to the censure in her twin's eyes.

"Wade thinks you are." Phoebe was certain of that. She'd been all too aware of Wade's devotion to her sister throughout the early weeks of the summer.

"I'm sure he doesn't expect me to just sit at home while he's gone," Melanie said. "It's not like he's on a short vacation. He's in the army."

"If you're going to date other people, you should tell him."

But Melanie hadn't listened. Which was nothing new. Melanie had never listened to Phoebe's words of warning since they'd been very small girls.

It hadn't taken Wade long to realize that Melanie's affections for him were…something less than he clearly wanted. And it had wrung Phoebe's heart when he'd come home on leave to find that Melanie wasn't waiting for him. The two had had fight after fight. They'd finally broken up for good a year and a half later, after Christmas of the girls' sophomore year in college. Phoebe only knew the details from a distance, since she'd gone to school at Berkeley, hours north of their home in Carlsbad, California. Melanie had stayed closer to home and, although the sisters had stayed in touch largely through e-mail and instant messaging, Melanie hadn't volunteered much about Wade. Phoebe, always terrified her attraction to him would be noticed, had never asked.

After Wade and Melanie had broken up, Phoebe had noticed Wade came home less and less often over the next few years. His parents, who lived two doors down the street, had occasionally mentioned his travels to her mother, but they never shared enough information to satisfy Phoebe's hungry heart. And after her mother had passed away at the end of her junior year at Berkeley, she'd heard even less.

Then came her high-school class's five-year reunion. Melanie had invited Wade…and everything had changed forever.

Two

The following evening, Wade was ready a full fifteen minutes early. He went down to the bar in the restaurant and took a seat facing the door. And barely ten minutes later, Phoebe arrived. Also early.

He took the fact that she was early as a good sign. Did she still want to be with him the way he wanted her? Yesterday's conversation on her porch had been confusing. One moment he'd have sworn she was about to fall into his arms; the next, she seemed as distant as the moon, and only slightly more talkative.

How had he missed seeing how beautiful

Phoebe was all those years they'd been living on the same damned street?

Wade knew the answer as he watched her come across the room toward him.

Both Merriman sisters had been pretty, but Melanie's dramatic coloring had always drawn more attention. Melanie had been a strawberry redhead with fair, porcelain skin, and eyes so blue they looked like a piece of the sky. Phoebe's darker, coppery curls and deeper blue eyes were equally lovely but her quiet, reserved personality kept her from joining her exuberant, vivacious sister in the limelight. Which wasn't a bad thing, he decided. Melanie had been volatile, her moods extreme, her desire for attention exhausting sometimes. Hell, most of the time, if he were honest.

She had had a sunny, sweet side and, when she was in a good mood, she was irresistible. But she'd always been excited about something, always looking for something to do.

Phoebe was calm and restful. And capable. She had always seemed very self-sufficient to him. If Melanie had had a problem, Phoebe had been the one to whom she'd turned.

Melanie. He'd successfully avoided thinking about her for a very long time. It seemed inconceivable that she wasn't leading some man in a merry dance somewhere in Southern California. Instead, she was locked forever in his memory at the age of twenty-three.

The same age Phoebe had been when he'd realized he had been chasing the wrong twin for several years.

As she drew near, he drank in every detail of her appearance. Her hair was longer than it had once been, and she wore it up in a practical twist. She had on a khaki-colored pencil-slim skirt with a sweater set in some shade of a pretty green-blue that he didn't even have a name for. Although she probably thought it was a modest outfit, the skirt ended just above her knees, showing off her slender, shapely calves and ankles, and the sleeveless top beneath the outer sweater clung enticingly to her curves. Tendrils of curls had escaped from the twist and danced around her face in the light breeze.

She was looking down at the floor rather than at him and he had a sudden moment of doubt. She'd been all he'd thought about since the last day he'd seen her. Even when he'd been in combat, or leading troops, he'd carried the memory of her deep in the recesses of his mind, where everything he couldn't afford to think about in the heat of battle lived.

Guilt—and being deployed halfway around the world—had kept him away from her in those months after the funeral, but nearly losing his life in the mountains of Afghanistan had made him realize how sorry he would be if he walked away from the possibility of a life with Phoebe.

Had he waited too long? It had been fifteen months since the fateful class reunion that had changed their lives forever, since Melanie's death and their unexpected intimacy after the funeral.

Did Phoebe regret that? Or even worse, did she blame him for Melanie's death? That niggling little fear had lodged in his brain months ago and, despite the memories of Phoebe's shining eyes at the reunion and the sweet way she'd kissed him a few days later, he couldn't shake his worry. It didn't help that deep down, he knew he *was* to blame. He'd been Melanie's date that night, he'd known how possessive she could be and yet, when he'd taken Phoebe in his arms on that dance floor, he'd forgotten everything but the wonder of what had suddenly flared between them.

After her initial shock had faded yesterday, she'd been a little too distant for comfort. She'd always been reserved, but never with him. He'd enjoyed drawing her out and making her laugh, even when they'd been young, but he'd never realized just how much he took it for granted that she relaxed around him.

On her porch last afternoon, she hadn't been relaxed.

Maybe she had a serious relationship, even though she wasn't married or engaged. He knew because one of the first things he'd done was check out her ring finger. And besides, her name hadn't changed. She had been listed as Merriman in that phone book. *I have something to tell you,* she'd said. It had sounded ominous and he'd had to struggle not to react. He sure as hell hoped she wasn't going to try to brush him off for some other guy. He'd been a clueless idiot when they were younger, had failed to realize what a treasure she was. But he knew now, and any man who thought he had a claim to Phoebe could think again.

She was going to be his.

"Hello," she said. "Is my lipstick smeared or something?"

He jolted and smiled wryly. She'd caught him staring. "No," he said honestly. "I just couldn't take my eyes off you."

Phoebe blushed as he rose and came around the table to seat her. To his astonishment, her entire pretty face turned pink.

Returning to his seat, he said, "You look beautiful. That sweater makes your eyes even bluer."

Her face was still chair. "You don't have to say

that," she said. "Melanie was the beautiful one in our family."

"One of the beautiful ones," he corrected, studying her expressionless face. "Melanie drew attention to herself and people noticed her. You did the exact opposite and managed to make yourself practically invisible most of the time. Quite a feat for a woman as beautiful as you are."

Her gaze flew to his. Finally. "Thank you," she whispered. And when their eyes met, he felt again that sudden shiver of knowledge, a "we are meant to be" moment unlike anything he'd ever felt with any other woman. He'd felt it yesterday when she'd first noticed him; if he hadn't, he wouldn't have been here now.

He could remember the first time he'd experienced it as clearly as if it *had* been yesterday. Funny that he and Phoebe had grown up in the same neighborhood, had known each other all their lives, but suddenly one night, everything had clicked into place, and he'd recognized the woman he wanted to spend forever with….

He stood by the bar and finished his soda, watching his date. Melanie sat at a table across the room on some guy's lap. She was shrieking with laughter and as Wade watched, she tilted a glass to her lips and drank. She listed to one side and nearly fell off the man's lap, and Wade suddenly realized how drunk she was. Why had he ever thought she was what he wanted?

Because you were listening to the brain in your pants, dope.

He'd been stupid to say yes when Melanie had asked him to accompany her to her first class reunion. He knew her well by then, well enough to know that Melanie didn't really want him so much as she wanted the effect she had on people when she walked in with a man in uniform. It didn't bother him anymore the way it once had, but he wasn't going to stick around here and wait for her for the rest of the evening. Phoebe had driven Melanie to meet him here, so he wasn't obligated to get her home.

He raised his glass and finished the drink, then straightened and headed for the exit.

"Wade! Wait!"

He turned at the sound of the husky female voice, his irritation fading. "Hey, Phoeber," he said. "I'm heading out. Melanie's going to catch a ride with someone else."

"You're leaving?" Her dismay was plain.

He nodded. Over the beat of the music, he said, "Yeah. I'll see you before I leave again. Promise."

"But…" Phoebe's eyes were fastened to his and he thought for a moment that she was fighting tears. Had someone hurt her feelings?

Behind her, the band segued into a familiar slow song and couples began flocking to the dance floor.

Phoebe swallowed and licked her lips. "I was hoping you'd dance with me tonight."

Because it was Phoebe, and because he sensed she wasn't very happy, he turned away from the exit. "All right." He took her hand and began to draw her after him to the dance floor. Whatever had upset her, he could worm it out of her while they danced.

He pulled her into the middle of the crowded area and turned to draw her into his arms. There were so many people they were literally pushed together.

Phoebe's slender body slid against his and settled as if she'd been made just for him. He realized suddenly that he'd never danced with her before. Never.

Would it have been like this between them before now if he'd been smart enough to dance with her? His heart began to pound and arousal began to stir. Automatically, he began to move to the beat of the music, and she moved with him, her soft curves a shocking temptation beneath his hands.

It was heaven. He turned his head slightly and breathed in her scent, and his entire body tightened.

What the hell… This was Phoebe. His little neighbor.

Not so little anymore. She was the same age Melanie was, though he'd bet his paycheck she was far less experienced. Stunned, confused, he actually stopped dancing right there in the middle of the crowd.

"Phoebe?" He pulled back far enough to see her face, wondering if she was feeling as overwhelmed as he was.

She tilted her head back and her entire face was shining as if someone had lit a lantern inside her. "Yes?"

When she met his eyes, something clicked into place. Something precious and irreplaceable, something that filled a spot inside him that he hadn't even realized was empty. He forgot everything he'd been going to say, everything in his head, everything in the world. Nothing else mattered because everything he needed was right here in his arms, her eyes telling him that she felt the magic they were making together as well as he.

"Never mind," he said at last. He pulled her close again, then grasped her hands, which had been resting on his shoulders, and slid them up behind his neck. The movement increased the intimacy of their position and he had to fight the urge to shift his hips against the soft body plastered to his. This was crazy. *He* was crazy. Crazy about a woman he'd known most of his life without really knowing her at all.

Phoebe made a small sound and turned her head toward him, nestling against his chest. He bent his head to hers and set his lips against her ear. "The rest of the evening."

A shiver rippled down her spine and he delighted in the knowledge that she was as aroused as he was. Her head came up and their lips were a whisper apart. "What?"

He smiled and dropped his head farther, then brushed his nose lightly across hers. He wanted to kiss her worse than he'd ever wanted anything, including his first brand new bike and his ranger tab. But when he kissed Phoebe for the first time, he didn't want an audience, and he didn't want to have to stop. "You're dancing with me for the rest of the evening."

She shot him a glowing smile, and he swore there were stars twinkling and sparkling in the depths of those blue eyes. "All right."

* * *

Dinner was the most nerve-racking experience Phoebe had ever had in her life. In the back of her head a steady cadence hammered: *I have to tell him I have to tell him I have to tell him.*

It was so insistent that she couldn't relax and enjoy these moments she'd thought were gone forever. But she couldn't tell him here, not in a restaurant.

Fortunately, Wade didn't seem to want to discuss serious topics, either. He asked about her teaching job and seemed honestly interested. He asked questions about the little house in which she lived and how she'd found it. He asked about New York and how it was different from California, but he didn't ask her why she'd moved. Thank heavens. Maybe he simply assumed that she'd wanted to get away from all the memories.

He told her a little bit about where he'd been and what he'd done. A lot of it was classified, but he could share generalities.

They didn't talk about anything important. Neither of them mentioned the reunion, or the magical moments they'd shared, or what had occurred between them after the funeral.

And they didn't talk about Melanie.

Melanie, for whom Wade had cared deeply for years before one evening of dancing…

"Phoebe, you'll never guess who's coming to the reunion with me."

"I give." She smiled as Melanie breezed into the living room of her small apartment on the weekend of their first class reunion. It had been nice to move away from home and get away from her sister, but it also was nice to see her from time to time. Melanie was lovable; she was just…too much sometimes. "Who?"

"Wade!"

Phoebe froze. She'd been expecting her sister to name a classmate, probably a male one, knowing Melanie. "Wade didn't graduate with us," she said carefully.

"I know, silly." Melanie shook her head in exasperation. "I invited him."

"But…"

"He's going to wear his uniform." Melanie waved a hand as if she was fanning herself. "I can't resist a man in uniform."

Neither could Phoebe, if that man was Wade. But she couldn't say that to Mel.

The doorbell rang then, saving her from making

a response. Melanie said, "That must be Wade. Let him in, will you? I've got to finish getting ready!"

Phoebe resisted the temptation to salute as she reluctantly moved toward the door and opened it.

"Wade." It wasn't hard to smile as she lifted her arms. It was much harder not to appear too thrilled. "It's great to see you."

"You, too." Wade's arms came around her and he kissed her lightly on the cheek before she backed away. "How've you been, Phoeber? You look terrific."

He released her and stepped back a pace. "Seriously terrific," he added, as he scanned the simple navy-blue dress she'd chosen.

"Thank you." She knew she was blushing, and not just because of the admiration in his eyes. The feel of his hard arms around her had been overwhelming to senses that had been starved for even the sight of him. To suddenly be in her version of heaven was too much. She took a deep breath. "You look good, too. The army's agreeing with you?"

He nodded. "And you're enjoying teaching." It wasn't a question; they had stayed in loose touch by e-mail once or twice a month since she'd graduated from high school and headed off to Berkeley. As badly as she longed to hear from him, Phoebe always forced herself to wait at least a week before e-mailing him back. The last thing she wanted was for Wade to realize how she felt about him.

She nodded. "I think I told you I'm switching from first grade to fourth next year. It'll be an interesting change."

He grinned. "Yeah, the boys will have gone from being mildly annoying to thoroughly bratty."

She laughed. "Hmm. Sounds like personal experience speaking."

"Fourth grade was the year I got sent to the principal's office for putting a tadpole in Miss Ladly's Thermos of iced tea."

"I've heard that story before. Guess I'll be checking before I take a sip of anything."

They smiled at each other and a companionable silence fell for a moment. But then she broke the mood. "How long are you home for, and where do you go after that?" He probably had no idea that she could recite every move he'd made in the nine years since he'd graduated from high school.

Wade's face suddenly seemed guarded, his gray eyes darkening. "I have a few more days left of my two weeks' leave and then I'm being deployed to Afghanistan."

Afghanistan. The fear she'd always lived with rose, almost choking her. "Oh, God, Wade."

"I'll be back," he said. "Who would come around to bug you once in a while if I didn't?"

She forced herself to smile. "Just be careful."

He nodded, reaching out a hand and rubbing her arm. "Thanks. I will."

"Hey there!" Her sister's voice singsonged a flirtatious greeting Phoebe had heard her employ dozens of times before. And just like many of those other times, Wade's head swiveled around and Phoebe was instantly forgotten.

Lowering her eyes, she stepped away and busied herself gathering a few items for her evening bag while Melanie threw herself into Wade's arms and gave him a loud kiss.

For the rest of the evening, she avoided looking at Wade and her sister as much as she could. It was just too painful.

Not long after they arrived at the reunion, she lost herself on the other side of the crowd. Her best friend from high school, June Nash, had come. June still lived in town. She'd married a former classmate and was expecting her first child. Phoebe felt conspicuously alone as she looked around. Everyone seemed either to be married by now or to have brought a date.

But June was genuinely delighted to see her, and they spent the mealtime catching up on the years since high school. Although they faithfully exchanged Christmas cards, their e-mails and phone calls had gradually slowed as their lives took different paths.

"So you're teaching." June smiled. "I bet you're fantastic with children. I still remember how great you were when the student council helped with Special Olympics."

Phoebe shrugged. "I enjoy it." And the school district in which she taught was far enough from where she'd grown up that few people knew her as "the quiet twin."

"That's good." June nodded her head in the direction of another group. "I see Melanie and Wade are an item again. I thought that ended a couple of years ago."

Phoebe winced. "It did. But we've all stayed friends and Melanie invited him as her date tonight."

Thankfully, the band began to play at that moment and she was spared any more discussion. June wasn't dancing since her first child was due in less than two weeks and she said she felt like a hippo in a mud hole. But a group of girls Phoebe had known when they were all in the marching band dragged her up to the dance floor with them, and Phoebe decided she was going to enjoy what was left of the evening. She danced with a group of her classmates until the first slow song and then moved to another table to visit, forbidding herself to look around the room for Wade.

An hour later, she'd had enough. She'd seen the people she'd wanted to see, had danced and laughed and done her best to give the impression that life was treating Phoebe Merriman well. Melanie, as always, was the life of the party. She had abandoned Wade for a guy Phoebe barely remembered, and the two of them were knocking back drinks with a like-minded group.

This time Phoebe did look for Wade. He was standing alone by the bar and, as she watched, he set down his drink and approached Melanie. After a brief exchange, Melanie laughed and Wade turned and walked away.

When she realized he was heading for the door, she panicked. Plain and simple, she couldn't bear the thought of Wade leaving without at least speaking to him one more time.

"Wade!" she called out. "Wait!"

Two little words. She could still remember them. Two little words that had altered her life. And not just hers. Three lives had been altered by that evening, four if you counted Bridget. If Wade had left the dance when he'd intended to, Melanie might still be alive. If Melanie were still alive,

Phoebe and Wade would never have walked up to that cabin, would never have…and Bridget would never have been conceived.

Try as she might, Phoebe couldn't regret those stolen moments of heaven she'd experienced with him. Nor could she imagine her world without her beautiful baby daughter in it.

"Would you like to go to a movie when we're finished eating?" Wade smiled at her across the table. A movie. With Wade.

There was a time when she would have given an arm for that invitation. But things were different now. What she wanted and what was reality were two very separate things.

"Thank you, but no," she said. "I have to get home pretty soon."

He looked taken aback and, as she watched, the warmth in his eyes drained away. "All right."

"Wade." She leaned forward and took an irrevocable step. "I'd like you to come with me. There's something I have to tell you."

"You mentioned that yesterday," he said, but she noticed he seemed to unbend a little. "Sounds scary."

She couldn't even smile. "I hope not."

They left the restaurant and he followed her minivan directly back to her house. She'd offer him a glass of wine first, she decided, and then…

then she'd have to decide how to tell him. But none of her opening lines sounded good. And now she had a new worry.

What if Wade didn't want to be a father? What if he rejected Bridget and didn't want to be part of her life?

Since yesterday, Phoebe had been trying to brace herself for sharing Bridget with her father when he came East. Which could be quite infrequently. After all, the man was probably going to be out of the country most of the time. If Wade didn't want anything to do with them, their lives wouldn't change appreciably.

But it would break her heart if he didn't find Bridget as miraculous and irresistible as she did.

He followed her into the house at her invitation.

And it was then that she realized the flaw in her plan. Duh. How could she possibly explain the presence of a nanny?

Angie rose from the couch and gathered up her schoolwork. "Hi, Phoebe. Give me a minute to get organized and call my brother. I have an econ test tomorrow."

Phoebe managed a smile. "Do you think you're ready?"

Angie shrugged. "As ready as I'll ever be."

She glanced at the ceiling. "Everything went fine this evening."

Phoebe was having trouble getting out words. Her chest felt like there was an enormous weight bearing down, preventing her from taking one good, deep breath. "Good."

Angie nodded and went to the phone. A moment later, she said, "He's on his way."

"I'll walk out with you." One more minute. Just one more minute to plan what she was going to say. Her hands were shaking as she followed the sitter to the end of her driveway. Angie's brother was already rounding the corner and walking toward them, and Phoebe returned his wave as Angie moved away.

Then she took one last stab at a deep breath and turned toward her home again.

Wade stood framed in the doorway. His face was in the shadow, and golden light from her cozy little home streamed around him, illuminating the tall, unmoving figure. It looked right, she thought. Then she immediately censored the notion. There was no point in wishing for the moon.

Phoebe mounted the steps and he moved aside to let her enter. His brow furrowed as he watched her close the door behind herself. "You have a housekeeper?"

"No." She took a deep breath. "No, I don't. Angela is my nanny." It wasn't, perhaps, a perfect opening line, but she might as well jump in. She had to get this over with.

She watched the expressions move swiftly across his face: simple acceptance of an answer, then shock, and a growing incredulity as he took in what she had said. "Why do you have a nanny?" He looked around as if to confirm the obvious conclusion, but the books and toys had been put away in the large basket beneath the window, so there was no obvious evidence of a child in residence in the living room.

"I have a daughter."

"I see." His expression had gone so noncommittal she wondered what in the world he was thinking. Of all the reactions, calm acceptance wasn't the one she'd anticipated.

"Wade?"

To her shock, he had started for the door. "This was a mistake," he said. "Goodbye, Phoebe."

"Wade!"

He stopped halfway to the door without turning around. "Yeah?"

"Don't you even want to know about her?"

There was a long moment in which she held her breath. Then he turned around and in his eyes she saw a sadness so deep she couldn't fathom what was wrong. Surely the existence of a child couldn't be that terrible, could it? Maybe it reminded him of what he would never have with Melanie—

"No," he finally said. "I don't."

"But—"

"What we did—after the funeral—meant something to me."

And she had known it would. He'd had a sense of honor a mile wide as long as she'd known him. It was one of the reasons she had been so loath to tell him she was pregnant. Even after she'd gotten past the hurt and the anger that he'd never contacted her after what they'd shared, she'd feared his reaction. She knew Wade well. He would have felt obligated to ask her to marry him.

The last thing she wanted was a man who felt forced into a loveless marriage with his child's mother. But dear Lord, if he'd asked her to marry him then…she wasn't sure she'd have had the strength to turn him down.

"I assumed it meant something to you," he added.

"It did!" He was the first and only man she'd ever been with. He couldn't possibly know what that meant to her.

"But you've moved on." He laughed, but it wasn't a sound of humor. "You've moved on in a big way."

She couldn't follow…. "I didn't have a choice," she said.

"Is the father still in the picture? I presume you're not married or you wouldn't have gone out with me tonight. I hope," he said coolly.

She blinked, completely thrown off stride. He thought she'd—he thought Bridget was—"No," she said. "You don't understand. There is no other man."

"Maybe not now, but—"

"She's yours."

Three

Wade froze, his face a classic mask of disbelief. Finally, as if he were sure he hadn't understood what language she was speaking, he said, "What?"

"She's your child," Phoebe said. She probably should have been angry at his initial assumption that there'd been another man, but he looked so totally poleaxed now that she couldn't summon much outrage.

"Are you kidding me?" He sounded as shocked as he looked. "We only—that one time—"

She nodded sympathetically, understanding his shock. "That's how I felt when I found out, too."

"When you found out." He pounced on that like a cat waiting for the mouse to come out just far enough, shock morphing into anger right before her eyes. "Just when in the hell *did* you find out? And why didn't you bother to tell me?"

She forced herself not to stammer apologetically. Instead, she indicated the couch. "Would you like to sit down? I'll explain it all."

"Hell, no, I don't want to sit down!" The words exploded with fury. "I just want to know why you didn't tell me you were going to have a baby!"

She wanted to shrink into a little ball and hide beneath the furniture, exactly like a frightened mouse. The guilt she had lived with since his death flared to life. "I don't know," she said in a quiet voice. "At the time, it seemed like the thing to do. Now— for some time now—I've known it was wrong."

"So why didn't you look me up and tell me?"

"You were dead! At least, I thought you were."

He fell silent, clearly taken aback. "I keep forgetting that," he said in a slightly milder tone. Then his eyes narrowed. "But I wasn't dead when you found out you were pregnant."

She had to look away. "No," she said, "you weren't."

Silence fell. She wrapped her arms around

herself and turned away, feeling the rage crackling in the room behind her.

"I want to see her," he said.

"All right." She swallowed. "Tomorrow after school—"

"Now." The word was a whip and she jumped as it lashed her ears.

"She's asleep," she said protectively. But Wade's face was stony and unmoved when she looked back at him. "All right." She blew out a breath of nerves and exasperation, realizing she'd been stupid to imagine she could tell Wade about his child without letting him see her for himself immediately. "I'll take you up to see her if you promise not to wake her."

There was another tense silence. Finally, Wade said, "So let's go."

She turned on her heel and walked to the stairs on shaking legs, leaving him to follow.

She was extremely aware of his large presence at her back as she went up the steps and down the hall. At the door of her daughter's room, she paused. Her chest felt as if someone were sitting on it and she couldn't get enough air. She'd swear she could feel Wade's breath on the back of her neck and she didn't have the courage to turn around. Over her shoulder, she whispered, "Her name is Bridget. She's six months old."

The door was open just a shred, and she grasped the knob and carefully pulled it wide, then stepped aside and gestured. "Go ahead."

Wade nodded once, a sharp jerk of his head, and she watched from the doorway as he took slow, almost hesitant steps toward the crib against the far wall.

He stood there for a long, long time, looking down at the sleeping baby in the low light she'd switched on. He didn't move to touch her, didn't glance around the room at the charming wallpaper border with the red-and-blue alphabet-blocks motif she'd found, the gingham curtains or the shelves filled with board books, stuffed animals and toys to stimulate a growing baby. He just... stood.

Finally, she entered the room and went to his side.

"Is she really mine?" His low voice was wondering and she understood he wasn't trying to offend her.

"She's really yours," she assured him softly. "You can touch her." His big hands were still, grasping the rail of the crib. He made no move but Phoebe could practically feel the longing radiating from him. Finally, she couldn't stand it. She took his hand, and when he didn't resist, she lifted it and tugged him forward so his palm rested flat against Bridget's small back.

Phoebe found she had a lump in her throat. Her daughter's body looked so tiny and fragile with Wade's hand covering her whole back.

Her own hand tingled where she'd touched his skin. It wasn't fair. Even an innocent touch like that set her pulse racing. In the years before and after Wade, she'd never met another man who could affect her so effortlessly. She doubted he even knew he'd done it.

But she knew. For the rest of her life, she'd always be comparing any man she met to Wade. She hoped to marry someday, but she was realistic enough to know that she wasn't going to be able to offer a man the kind of all-consuming love she felt for Wade. She also knew she could never pretend to care for someone just to get a ring on her finger, and she feared that there might be many lonely years in her future, broken up by the joys of motherhood.

She was distracted from her morose thoughts by movement. Bridget had squirmed and twitched in her sleep, and Wade had automatically soothed her with gentle circles on her back. The baby gave a sigh and stopped moving, but he didn't. He extended his index finger and very, very lightly brushed it over the smooth petal softness of his daughter's cheek. He stroked it back and forth over the wild red curls that sprang from her tiny head. Then his hand moved to touch her much smaller one.

And Phoebe thought her heart might break when Bridget grasped one big finger and held on for dear life, still sound asleep. A lump rose in her throat and she fought not to sob aloud at the tenderness of the moment.

She swallowed hard several times until she felt she had enough control not to cry. Then she opened her mouth to whisper an apology, but when her gaze landed on his face, the words dried up in her throat.

Wade had tears on his cheeks. Silvery in the moonlight, they made gleaming trails where they fell from his eyes and rolled down his face. He didn't even seem to notice them, not even when one fat tear dripped from his jaw onto the back of the hand that still clutched the side of the crib.

His sorrow hit her harder than anything in the world had since the news of his death. And guilt was right on its heels. *She* was the cause of this agony. *She* was the source of the sadness that gripped him. She hadn't told him about her pregnancy when she'd had the chance, and then she'd lost the chance, she'd thought, forever.

Wade turned away from the crib and made his way from the room slowly. She followed him equally slowly, her own battle with tears completely lost. As they moved down the hallway, she swallowed the sob that wanted to surge up and said, "Wade, I—"

"Don't." He held up one large hand in a gesture of denial without even turning around. "I can't talk to you right now," he said as he started down the steps.

Shaken by both his tears and the controlled ferocity in the low tone, Phoebe stopped talking.

And watched, stunned, as Wade walked out the front door of her home without another word.

Wade knew she went to work the next day because he was sitting in his parked car down the street, waiting for her to come home. When she emerged from her little minivan, she walked around to the passenger-side sliding door and unloaded what looked like a fifty-pound satchel, presumably full of work to be graded.

The sight of Phoebe lugging that obviously heavy load up her front steps aroused two emotions in him. The first was an instinctive protective urge. She shouldn't be lifting things like that. The second was another blast of the anger that had consumed him since last night, when it had fully begun to sink in that he had a child—and had missed more than half a year of her life because Phoebe had chosen to deny him the knowledge of his fatherhood. He didn't even know his child's birthday but he could guess approximately when she had been born.

God, if only Phoebe had told him when she'd learned she was pregnant…it might have made all the difference in the world.

He'd have married her. Hell, he'd known he wanted to marry her since they'd danced together at her class reunion and he'd realized what had been right under his nose for years. But then Mel was killed and things had gotten more and more out of control after that.

She'd been extremely drunk and upset that night and it had been his fault. The thought would haunt him forever, and he knew it had to have occurred to Phoebe. He could have stopped her from drinking so much. He could have gone after her faster. God, was it any wonder Phoebe hadn't wanted to contact him when she'd found out she was pregnant? If she blamed him for Melanie's death, how must she feel about having slept with him the very day of her twin's funeral?

He took deep, calming breaths as he got out of his

rental car and strode along the sidewalk to her house. A twinge in his hip reminded him that he wasn't quite as healthy as he wanted to be just yet. He had to get a grip. Yes, she'd been wrong, but shouting at her wasn't going to help the situation any.

Even if it would make him feel one hell of a lot better.

The door had barely closed behind her when he turned into her walk and bounded up the steps. He rapped briskly on the door.

Phoebe pulled it open a moment later. "Yes? Wade!" She clearly hadn't expected it to be him. Maybe she'd thought he'd gone back to California. *Think again.*

He stepped across the threshold, forcing her to step back. Her babysitter was just getting ready to slip out the door but she paused, brown eyes alight with interest.

"Bye, Angie." Phoebe held the door open and waved a hand, ushering the younger woman out. "See you Monday. Have a good weekend." The nanny was barely through the door when Phoebe closed it behind her. Then she turned to face him. "Hello. Would you like to come in?"

He snorted at her sarcasm, but he'd been thinking all night and he wanted to get things straight right from the get-go. "Okay. The way I see it, we have two choices. We go back to California, or we stay here."

Her blue eyes widened to the size of saucers. "*We? You* can do whatever you like but—"

"I'd like to take my daughter back to California to meet her only surviving grandparent," he said harshly.

Her lovely face registered horrified shock. "You can't just take off with my child."

"No, but I can take off with my child," he said.

He could see the moment that his earlier words registered. Phoebe's forehead wrinkled and her eyes widened as she said, "One grandparent? Wade, has one of your parents passed away?"

"My mother." Anger was preferable by far to the grief that still gripped him at unexpected times. "She died seven months ago."

"Oh, my God." Phoebe looked stunned. Her eyes filled with tears. "I need to sit down." Her voice was faint and she stepped backward until the couch hit the backs of her knees. Then she collapsed onto the cushion, her hands clasped together so tightly he could see her knuckles whiten. "Oh, Wade, I'm so sorry. What happened?"

"She had a stroke," he said flatly. "Ten months ago. It was terribly debilitating and she didn't want to live. Three months after the first one, she had another." *But if she'd known she'd had a grand-child, things might have been different.* He could see in Phoebe's horrified eyes that the thought had occurred to her as well.

She pressed the heels of her hands hard against her eyes, elbows resting on her thighs. "I am so sorry," she said in a muffled voice.

He knew she wasn't offering condolences. No, she was apologizing—again—for not telling him he had a child. "I want Dad to meet Bridget," he said, "before much more time passes."

"But…I can't just quit my job and go off to California."

"I didn't ask you to," he said evenly.

Phoebe's face lost what little color it still had. "Are you…are you going to fight me for custody?"

He took his time answering, finding himself a seat in the comfortable armchair angled close to the sofa. "Are you going to force me to?" He waited until she met his gaze. "I want to get to know my daughter. I want to be with her every day—I can't get back all the time I missed but I sure as hell don't want to miss any more." He closed his eyes against the surge of anger that shook him and waited for her to argue.

"Okay." Her voice was small.

He was startled. "Okay?" The Phoebe he knew

might be quiet and calm, but underneath she was a fighter when she believed in something.

But she nodded. "Okay." She swallowed. "I was wrong not to tell you as soon as I found out, Wade. I'm sorrier than you'll ever know."

He didn't know what to say to that. She was right—she had been wrong. Because she'd chosen not to tell him, his mother had died without ever knowing she had a grandchild.

He simply couldn't utter the words to accept her apology yet. He liked to think he was a big enough man that he'd soon be able to forgive her... but he didn't feel that magnanimous right now. Instead of answering, he stood and went out the front door to his car.

When he returned, Phoebe was still sitting on the couch with her hands clasped. She jumped up when he walked back in without knocking and dumped his duffel on the floor inside the door. There were tears on her face, which she hastily wiped away, and then she did a double take.

"What are you doing?" She already knew, and she was aghast.

"Moving in." He shrugged. "It's the only way to really get to know Bridget without taking her away from you."

She nodded as if she saw the logic, but a

moment later, she shook her head vigorously. "Wait! You can't just move in here!"

"Why not? You and I have always gotten along well. We probably know each other better than a lot of couples do. And you have an extra bedroom. I saw it last night. I'll pay rent."

She opened her mouth, then closed it again and shook her head helplessly. Finally, she said, "This is outrageous. So how did you just make it sound so utterly logical?"

He grinned, feeling a lot more relaxed now that she hadn't kicked him out first thing. "I'm gifted that way." He'd hoped her obvious guilt would help sway her to his point of view and, apparently, it had worked.

Suddenly, he realized she hadn't spoken. She was staring at him as if he'd grown a second head. "What?"

She shrugged. "That's the first time I've seen you smile since you got off that swing yesterday."

"I haven't had much to smile about," he pointed out.

Instantly, the angry tension was back in the room, humming between them like a downed electrical wire. He was about to speak again, to get more answers to the questions she'd never given him a chance to ask, when an odd whispering sound filled the air.

It was barely audible, but Phoebe reacted instantly, a blinding smile lighting her face. "Bridget is awake."

His body reacted to that smile. But—

"A-ba-bah-bah-ba," It was a little louder now. Wade glanced around the room and spotted a baby monitor on one end table. Aha.

Phoebe started for the stairs. "If I don't get her fast, they'll hear her down at the end of the street. I'll be back in a minute."

Wade smiled to himself as she took the steps two at a time. Bridget was six months old. That had to be a bit of an exaggeration—

"A-bah-bah-BAH-BAH!"

Whoa. His kid had a set of lungs on her like Pavarotti.

"Bridget." Phoebe's voice was a gentle singsong. "How's my girl? Did you have a good nap?"

The baby gave a delighted squeal that just about split his eardrums. Did Phoebe have that monitor turned up too high?

"Hello, my sweet baby girl." No, the monitor wasn't too loud, because Phoebe's voice sounded normal. "How was your nap? I've got somebody downstairs who wants to meet you." He heard her chuckle. "But first we'd better change your diaper or he's liable to keel over."

He listened to the rustle of the plastic diaper and the baby cooing, to Phoebe talking and singing little nonsense verses. It sounded surprisingly *right*. But he shouldn't be surprised. Phoebe had always had a sensible, motherly streak. Years ago, if someone had asked him if he could envision her as a mother, he wouldn't have hesitated for an instant before saying yes.

A wave of intense sadness swamped him. And now she was the mother of his child. If he hadn't been determined to find Phoebe, he'd never even have known he had a daughter.

Footsteps on the stairs alerted him that they were coming, and he shook off the moment of melancholy and braced himself for his first clear sight of his daughter. He knew from what he'd seen last night that her hair was some shade of red, but the low light of the nursery hadn't yielded much more.

Phoebe's legs came into view, and then the rest of her appeared. She was carrying a baby girl with the wildest red hair he'd ever seen in his life. Quirking in ringlets all over her head. Even at this young age, Phoebe had pulled the front of it atop her head with an elastic hair tie. Bridget's hair was much lighter than Phoebe's, and far more vibrant than Melanie's pale strawberry had ever been. His kid's hair looked like a live flame.

Her face was a pretty little oval with a slightly more determined chin than was probably good, her eyes blue and sparkling as they found him. His heart skipped a beat. He actually *felt* it trip and miss, and he took a deep breath. God, she looked a lot like Phoebe.

His throat closed up and he just stood there as they approached. Phoebe was talking to the baby as if she could understand every word she said, telling her about a friend of Mama's from far away who was coming to stay with them for a little while.

A little while? Ha. She might not choose to accept it, but he was here for good.

He swallowed the thick knot clogging his voice. "Hi, Bridget," he said. He was at a loss. What did you say to somebody this size?

The child grinned, a wide smile that sent a cascade of drool down her chin and showed him two tiny pearly white teeth on the bottom. Then she turned her head abruptly into her mother's shoulder.

Before he could figure out what to say, Phoebe saved him. "Daddy," she told his child. "Bridget, this is your daddy."

The baby peeked out at him with one blue eye, then grinned before hiding her face again.

"Flirt," said Phoebe. She walked across the room and expertly unfurled a large baby blanket while still holding the child on her hip with the other hand. Then she set the baby in the middle of the blanket.

Bridget wobbled for a moment, then seemed to find her balance and sit straighter. "She just started sitting up by herself two weeks ago," she told Wade over her shoulder. "Why don't you come sit down and play with us? She's not usually shy and she should get used to you quickly."

"All right." He strove for a normal tone although his heart felt as if it were going to fly right out of his chest.

He joined them on the brightly colored blanket. Phoebe was building a tower of blocks. Every time she'd get three or four stacked up, Bridget swiped her hand and knocked them over, squealing and chortling. Once, when Phoebe stopped for a moment, the baby smacked her little hands together and yelled, "Ack!" in a tone that left no doubt what she wanted.

Wade hastily reached for another block. "Way to get what you want, kid."

Phoebe chuckled. "She has a mind of her own. And if she doesn't get her way, she lets me know about it."

"Reminds me of Melanie." He'd said it without thinking. The moment the words hit the air, he knew they'd been a mistake.

The happiness drained out of Phoebe's eyes, leaving them guarded and sorrowful. "Yes," she said quietly. "Bridget does seem to have a stronger personality than I ever had."

He wanted to protest. There was nothing wrong with Phoebe's personality. Just because Mel had been more vocal about everything under the sun didn't mean Phoebe's personality was any less pleasing. She just wasn't loud and attention-grabbing, that was all. But he didn't know how to say that in a way that made much sense, and he could almost feel the resistance in the air. She didn't want to talk about Melanie, that much was clear.

A pang of guilt shot through him, tempering the anger that still simmered. He was blaming Phoebe for not telling him about the baby...but he'd been responsible for her sister's death. No wonder she hadn't told him.

The baby had grabbed a board book and was busily manhandling the sturdy pages. As he watched, she put it in her mouth.

"Here, honey." Phoebe extended a brightly colored set of rings and confiscated the book. "We don't chew on books."

Wade looked at the frayed corners of the one she held. "Apparently, some of us do."

She smiled, and abruptly it felt right between them again. "I'm working on it," she said wryly. Then she glanced at her watch. "It'll soon be dinnertime. Would you like to stay and eat with us?"

He raised one eyebrow.

"Are you planning to stay here *tonight?*"

"That's the plan." He stood and folded his arms. "If you spend the weekend teaching me how to take care of Bridget, then I could keep her while you work."

"Don't you have to work or something?" she asked in an exasperated tone.

"Or something," he agreed.

"So you have to go back to California." It wasn't a question.

"No. I'm pretty sure I'm retiring from the service."

She looked shocked. "But that's what you've always wanted to do. To be. A soldier."

"I'm not physically able to perform on the battlefield to the army's satisfaction anymore," he said quietly. "And I'm not interested in a desk job staring at a computer monitor all day. So I'm taking early retirement."

"But what will you do?"

He shrugged. "I'm checking out a number of options. One of them is with a freelance security firm out of Virginia. I'd be establishing a West Coast office."

"So you'd be going home?"

He noted with satisfaction that she still referred to California as home. But all he did was nod. "That would be the plan." He shrugged. "But now, everything has changed." He looked down at his daughter, who had rolled onto her stomach and was making swimming motions as she tried valiantly to get to another toy just out of reach. "Everything."

Four

Phoebe still sat on the blanket at Wade's feet and he reached down, putting his hands beneath her elbows and lifting her to her feet.

Her eyes were fastened on his face; her hands fell to rest against his chest for a moment before she moved away. She cleared her throat. "I understand it's going to take some time to get used to being a father," she told him, indicating the baby playing at their feet. Her voice was huskier than normal.

His body was having no trouble understanding that the woman he'd dreamed of for months—hell, years—was standing practically in his arms. *The mother of his child.* The anger he'd been hiding couldn't be summoned. Instead, he found the thought surprisingly arousing. Here, right before them, was something they'd made together during those wild, impossibly wonderful moments they'd shared in the cabin.

He exerted a little pressure until she stopped resisting and let him draw her forward. "It's amazing that we created that."

She nodded, looking straight ahead at his throat rather than tilting her head back. "It's a miracle."

He pressed a feather light kiss against her temple and felt her body shudder. "I'm still pissed at you. But thank you."

"I, ah—I don't think—"

"Don't think," he urged. "I won't if you won't."

He wanted to kiss her. He'd dreamed of it for so long that he could hardly believe this was real. Releasing her wrist, he put one finger beneath her chin and lifted her face to his. "Kiss me," he said. "Relax and let me—ahhh." In unison, they made an involuntary sound of pure pleasure as his thighs pressed into the cradle of her hips and his hardening body nudged the tender flesh between her legs.

He couldn't wait anymore. He dropped his head and fastened his mouth on hers, kissing her hard and deep, pouring all the longing and frustration of the past two years into the embrace. He felt her hands clench on his shoulders, but she wasn't pushing him away. Oh, no. He felt the way she melted against him, the way her fingers dug into his flesh and he knew she was going to be his again. But this time, he promised himself, he wasn't going to be a cad, wasn't going to leave her without a word.

This was a dream, Phoebe thought. It had to be. She'd imagined Wade kissing her so many times in the past year that it felt unreal to have him here, holding her against him. His tongue demanded her response, his big arms molded her close to the lean strength of his body. His state of arousal was impossible to miss, plastered against him as she was.

And memory rushed in, recalling the other time they'd been in this kind of embrace....

She was in heaven.

Phoebe nestled her face into Wade's throat and felt him shudder as they danced. This was a dream. It had to be. But oh, what a dream. She never wanted to wake up.

"Hey, you." She felt Wade's lips move against her forehead.

She lifted her head and smiled up into his gray eyes. Even in the low light on the dance floor, they seemed to blaze with heat and desire. For her? She was definitely dreaming.

"I want to take you home tonight." His voice was rough. "But I can't. You've got the car."

"You can drive," she offered. "Since we're practically going to the same place."

"I wish we were going home together," he said. "I'd like to hold you all night long."

His frank words were shocking, in a knot-in-the-belly exciting kind of way, and she knew her eyes widened.

"I don't want to rush you," he said quickly. "I realize this is new—"

"It's not new for me," she broke in. She reached up and placed a soft palm against his cheek. "Wade, don't you know I've—" loved you "—wanted this for a long time?"

He placed his hand over hers, holding it in place as he turned his head and pressed a hot kiss into her palm. He closed his eyes briefly. "I'm a dope. I never realized—"

"Shh. It's okay." She didn't want him to feel bad, or awkward, about anything. "Let's just start from this night."

"That sounds like a solid plan to me." He

smiled. Then his hand slid down, freeing hers as he cupped her chin and lifted her face to his.

She caught her breath, sure he was about to kiss her. Oh, God, she would melt right into the floor if he did—

"What's going on here?" The voice was strident, female, furious—and familiar.

Phoebe jolted, tearing herself free from Wade's arms.

Melanie stood in front of them, hands fisted on her hips. "Thanks for taking such good care of *my date,* sister dear," she said in a taut, sarcastic voice.

"Back off, Mel." Wade's voice was cool and commanding. "You didn't even notice I was leaving. Why the scene now?"

"Wade." Melanie turned luminous blue eyes on him and, instantly, the anger vanished and tears welled. "You—you brought me to the reunion. Why would you treat me this way?"

Wade shook his head. "Save the act for somebody who buys it. You couldn't have cared less what Phoebe and I were doing—"

"Phoebe and you." Anger distorted Melanie's pretty features and she tossed her long, shining hair back. Her eyes narrowed as she focused on Phoebe. "Sneaking around behind my back. My own sister. My twin. You've always wanted him, haven't you?

You've been in love with him the whole time, but he was mine."

"That's enough." Wade took Melanie's elbow, but she shook him off. Around them, people had stopped dancing and were staring openly, watching the drama unfold.

And Melanie loved it, Phoebe knew. She was the quintessential drama queen. This act was perfect for her.

"No," Melanie said, and her voice grew shrill. "That's not nearly enough. I will never forgive you for this, Wade. And you." She stabbed an angry finger in Phoebe's direction. "I wish I never had to see you again!"

And with one final toss of her bright tresses, Melanie whirled and stomped away, fury radiating from every move. The only thing that spoiled it was that she'd had far too much to drink and she staggered as she headed for the door, jostling a gaping group of classmates. "Get out of my way," she shrieked. She had worked herself into a sobbing fit of tears by that time.

Wade turned back to Phoebe. "We'd better go after her. She's had way too much to drink."

"Yes." She nodded. "It's a good thing she doesn't have a car."

"Come with me." He held out a hand.

She shook her head, her throat clogged with sobs. "No. She'll be impossible if she sees me. You know she'll calm down if she doesn't see us together."

Wade nodded, letting his hand drop to his side as he acknowledged the truth of her statement.

She turned and walked to the table where her small evening bag lay. "Here." She extended her car keys. "You take her home. I'll catch a ride later."

Wade took the keys. Then he caught her hand with his free one, bringing it to his lips for a moment. "I'll call you," he said.

Her heart leaped at the tender gesture. Could he really mean it? Could this evening, the moments between them on the dance floor, really be the day she'd dreamed of since she was old enough to feel her heart beating faster in his presence?

She offered him a shaky smile. "I'll look forward to it," she said, clutching the promise to her heart as he started away.

Just then, they heard tires shrieking in the parking lot.

"What the hell…?" Wade began to run full-out.

Phoebe rushed after him. She reached the door just in time to see her car flying out of the parking lot and down the road, and she knew immediately what had happened. Melanie knew Phoebe kept a spare key in a magnetic box in the wheel well. She'd taken the car.

Phoebe tore her mouth from Wade's. "This isn't— we can't do this." She was embarrassed that she was practically panting. And then she realized that she had a death grip on his wide shoulders. And worse, she'd made no move to separate their bodies, which were stuck like two slices of the peanut butter bread she often slapped together for lunch.

Wade's eyebrows rose. There was a glint in his eye that looked almost dangerous. "We just did."

"Anymore," she tacked on belatedly, removing her hands and stepping back, forcing him to release her.

"Ever?"

"Ever."

"Because…"

"Because your life is in California—" she spread her hands "—or wherever, and mine is here in New York now."

"Mine won't be wherever anymore," he informed her. "I'm going to live here if that's where you two will be. It's not half-bad."

"It gets really cold in the winter."

"I lived at West Point for four years, remember? Believe me, I know how cold it gets here."

"You always said you wanted to live somewhere warm," she reminded him.

"Being around for my daughter is a lot more important than worrying about the temperature. So your reasoning doesn't hold. What else is bothering you?"

"Well… It isn't fair of you to spring this on me without giving me a chance to think about it." *I can't get involved with him.*

Why? He wanted you after the funeral. And before, at the dance.

Wanting isn't love.

It's a start.

No false hope, she lectured herself. *He wanted to teach Mel a lesson at the reunion. It wasn't his fault she'd flown off the handle and everything had gone so horribly wrong. And the other… What guy's going to say no when a woman pretty much tears his clothes off and has her way with him?*

"Take your time. I'm listening."

But he wasn't. His eyes were on Bridget, watching her every move with an intensity that was painful to see. It was obvious he'd forgotten all about the kiss.

Bridget was happily oblivious. She was still lying on the floor with the toy she'd finally managed to snag. She rolled over on her back and was vigorously shaking it so that a musical chime sounded inside.

"She entertains herself well for her age." Phoebe glanced at her watch, trying to keep her voice from quavering. It tore at her heart to see Wade so desperately interested in his child. "But any minute now she's going to realize that it's snack time."

Friendly. Neighborly. That was the ticket. She could ignore her temporary lapse in judgment if she just concentrated on remembering Wade several years earlier as he'd been before—before anything had happened. They'd been friends. No reason they couldn't continue to be friends.

Wade still wasn't looking at her although she had a feeling he knew exactly why she'd changed the subject. But he didn't object, merely followed her cue. "Won't a snack spoil her dinner?"

"Not if it's a small snack like a cracker. And we don't usually eat until close to six." And then they'd sit down to dinner together, just like a real family.

A real family? What was she thinking? They were *not* a family. They were two people who had known each other for a long time and who now shared a child. But they hadn't shared most of the other basic details that members of a real family would have.

And they might not be a real family, but they certainly were going to be doing many of the things that families did. Her best bet, she decided, was to treat him as a tenant. Or no, maybe a boarder… he'd already announced he was moving in, so they were going to have to handle all the dumb little details, like meals and who bought toilet paper.

And there was the fact that they hadn't really talked about custody or visitation or any of the much bigger issues that had been haunting her all day. "I have to get dinner organized," she said, knowing she sounded less than gracious. "Nothing fancy, just a roast I put in the Crock-Pot this morning."

"I love red meat. It doesn't have to be fancy." He said it with a straight face and perfectly innocent eyes. Was she only imagining the double entendre?

She felt her face slowly heating and she turned away before he could see her blushing. "I'll make dinner if you'd like to play with Bridget."

"What do you do with her when you're alone?"

"She comes into the kitchen with me. I used to put her in an infant seat and sing to her but recently I've been able to lay a blanket down and let her roll around on it."

"She looks like you." He was watching Bridget again.

"Until she decides she wants something. When she's determined, she sets her jaw the same way you do, and her eyes get that intense look."

"I do not set my jaw."

Phoebe smiled. "Okay. I must have imagined it about a million times in the last twenty years."

He had to chuckle at that. "You know me well." The amusement faded from his eyes. "And that's another reason I need to be in Bridget's life. She deserves to know how her parents met, that we grew up together."

How her parents met? He made it sound as if they were an old married couple. That thought hurt. Hurt enough that she couldn't face him anymore, and she walked away without looking back. But when she reached the kitchen door and she did glance his way again, Wade was still standing there eyeing her with a speculative expression that made her very, very wary. She knew what he'd said about not fighting over Bridget... but could she trust him?

She watched him walk over and lower himself to the floor, tailor-fashion. He was incredibly limber for such a big man. Any man, really.

Bridget turned toward him with a delighted smile as he picked her up and set her in his lap. She promptly grabbed his finger and dragged it into her mouth.

Wade looked at Phoebe over his shoulder with a pained expression. A chuckle bubbled up and nearly escaped, and she couldn't help smiling as she moved into the kitchen. He was the one who'd wanted to get to know his daughter.

But she sobered rapidly as she checked the roast. Dear heaven, what was she doing? She couldn't just give in and let Wade live in her house!

But she didn't have a choice. If she didn't let him have free access to Bridget, he'd go to a lawyer.

In her heart, she knew she could never fight him on the issue, anyway. She felt terrible for keeping her pregnancy from him, worse that she'd never told him about his child. Guilt would kill her if she denied him one moment of time with his child.

And she'd never forgive herself for not telling him—or his family, when she'd thought he was gone forever—and letting his mother die without ever knowing she had a granddaughter.

Even if he'd been dead, as she'd assumed, she should have gone to his parents. She knew it, and she knew it was part of the anger that leaped in his eyes each time he dropped the carefully friendly facade.

She shivered as she assembled ingredients for biscuit dough and got out broccoli. He would never forgive her for that. Never.

The kid was a ball of fire. He sat on the floor of his daughter's bedroom later that evening, listening to the sounds of her bath progressing. He wondered who was wetter, Phoebe or the kid. Bridget made noise nonstop, giggling, squealing and occasionally shouting. In the background, intermittent splashing indicated that the bath wasn't quite over yet.

A few moments later, he heard Phoebe's footsteps in the hallway. She stopped in the doorway to the bedroom, the baby in her arms.

Bridget was wrapped in some kind of white towel with a hood, and she sent him a cheery smile that showed her two front teeth. Phoebe set her down beside him, and her diaper made a funny plastic hiss when she plopped down on the carpet. She immediately began waving her little arms, opening and closing her fingers, her babbling beginning to escalate in pitch until Phoebe snatched up a book and thrust it into her hands. Bridget squealed, a sound so high-pitched that it made him wince.

Yep, definitely a ball of fire.

And he meant that almost literally, Wade decided, eyeing the brilliant curls, still damp from her bath, that peeped out from beneath the edges of the white terry cloth on her head.

"Time to get you into your pajamas, little miss." Phoebe came over and sank down beside them holding a set of pink pajamas. "Here," she said to

Wade. "If you want to keep her next week, you'd better start practicing how to get baby clothes on and off. Sometimes I think the manufacturers sit around and brainstorm ways to confuse parents. Hey, c'mere, you." She deftly snagged the baby, who had begun to roll out of reach. "Oh, no you don't. It's bedtime."

Bedtime.

If someone had told him he'd be sleeping under the same roof with Phoebe two days after he'd flown east, he'd have figured they were nuts.

Bedtime. Phoebe.

How the hell was he going to sleep knowing she was right in the next room?

His daughter screeched as Phoebe set her in front of him again. "Go for it," she said, smiling.

"You're going to enjoy this, aren't you?"

"Oh, yeah." She chuckled. "I had to learn by doing, so it's only fair that you have the same experience."

"Thanks." He picked up the pajamas. There were snaps in places he didn't even know snaps could be sewn. And his hands were about twice the size of the little piece of clothing. This was going to be interesting. To his relief, Phoebe returned to the dresser from which the pajamas had come and began putting away items from a clothes basket set atop it.

Twenty minutes later, he breathed a sigh of relief. "There. I think that's it."

She came over and knelt beside him to look, then raised her gaze to his and nodded. "You got it. You pass Clothing the Baby 101."

He snorted. "What's 102?"

"Well, 102," she said, "is the class where you learn the Murphy's Laws of Childrearing. Like, 'a child does not have to go to the potty until after you have completely zipped, buttoned and snapped every loose fastener on a snowsuit.'"

"Sounds like you already know them."

"Teaching," she said, "has taught me at least as much as I've taught my students. Which reminds me, no school tomorrow. It's Saturday," Phoebe said. "Bridget's not much for sleeping in so we'll be up anytime after six or so."

"Six! You're kidding. I'm on leave."

She shook her head. "No such thing when you're a parent."

"I'll get up with her if you'd like to sleep in."

Phoebe looked at him as if he'd spoken another language. "You'd do that?"

"Well, sure. It must be tough being the one on call every minute of every day."

"It's not so bad." Her tone was stiff, as if he'd offended her. "You're welcome to get up with us," she said, "but until you learn your way around the kitchen and our morning routine, it's probably best if I get up."

"Phoebe." He rose and stopped her with a hand on her arm as she moved by him. "I am not trying to take your role in her life away, and I wasn't trying to slam you again for—I just want to learn everything there is to know about her."

She nodded, although she wouldn't look at him. "I'm sorry for getting prickly." The air of tension left and her shoulders sagged. "This is going to take some getting used to."

That it was. He watched as she bent over and picked up a discarded shoe and sock. She'd changed from the neat skirt and blouse she'd worn to school that day into a pair of faded jeans and a T-shirt, although she'd neatly tucked the shirt in and added a belt. Probably her version of hanging-around slob clothes.

Her backside was slim and rounded beneath the jeans. Damn, but he was annoyed with himself. He had a lot more important things than sex to think about tonight, and yet every time he looked at Phoebe all rational thought fled and he became one big walking male hormone.

Bridget let out a squeal and he came back to earth abruptly. Phoebe scooped the baby into her arms. "What are you fussing about, you silly girl?" she asked. "Would you like your daddy to read you a story?"

The kid couldn't exactly answer yes, but Phoebe motioned him over to the big maple rocker and set Bridget in his lap anyway. She came to him as if she'd known him all her short life, settling easily into his lap, then popping her thumb in her mouth. He read the story but after just a few minutes, her little head nodded against his chest and the thumb fell from her slack lips. Glancing down, he realized she'd fallen asleep.

His throat was tight and his chest ached; she was so precious! It was almost too much to believe, that this beautiful child was his.

He wanted to snuggle her against him but he was afraid if he moved she'd wake up. And so he sat with Bridget in his lap until Phoebe stuck her head around the corner of the door frame. "Is she asleep?" she asked in a hushed tone.

He nodded.

She came into the room and knelt at his side, lifting the baby into her arms. As she transferred Bridget's weight, the underside of her breast pressed against his arm for a moment, and her warm, intoxicating, feminine fragrance teased his senses. Instantly, awareness rose, and with it arousal. He wanted to kiss her again. Hell, he wanted to do a lot more than that. He watched silently as she rose to her feet with his child in her arms, and the knowledge that they had made this precious little person together was, oddly, a whole new kind of aphrodisiac. Their daughter had been conceived that day in the hunting cabin, and it didn't take much effort at all to recall the sweet, sizzling passion that had bound them together in far more than just a physical way.

Then Bridget's tiny arms hung limp and her head fell onto Phoebe's shoulder as Phoebe lifted her into her crib. She brushed a kiss across the fiery red curls as she laid the child down, and he swallowed hard, another emotion joining the riot of sensations rushing through him.

How was it possible to go from not even knowing his child existed to loving her more than he loved his own life in less than a day? He didn't even know her, really. And yet…he did. And he would. Another shock jolted him as he realized he could imagine her five years from now—because he'd known her mother at that age as well.

Phoebe turned and left the room on nearly silent feet, and he slowly pushed himself upright. He walked to the crib and gazed down at his daughter for a long moment. *I promise to be the best daddy I can be,* he vowed silently.

Then he followed his child's mother out of the room. They needed to talk about the changes that were about to occur in their lives.

Five

Phoebe was already at the table in her small dining room when he came down the stairs after unpacking his duffel, removing papers from her satchel and making neat piles carefully spaced on the table. She glanced up and sent him an impersonal smile. "Time to grade math tests."

He walked through the living room to her side, looking down at the work she was spreading out before her. "You do this often?"

"Just about every night." She smiled wryly. "The kids complain when I give them assignments, but I really should be the one whining. Every assignment they hand in multiplies my work by twenty-four students." She shrugged her shoulders as she pulled out her chair and took a seat. "It's going to get even more interesting when I start my next class. I'm taking a children's lit class that begins in January."

"I thought you already had a degree."

"Yes." She pulled out an ink pad and a stamp with a smiley face on it. "But in order to keep my teaching certificate I have to do continuing education every so often or work toward my master's degree. The specifics vary from state to state, but the general concept is the same. You probably have to do the same thing—keep your skills current, I mean."

"Yeah. Except now, if I were to stay in the Army, I'd be stuck behind a desk. My ability to hit a target dead center fifty times in a row isn't quite so critical anymore."

She bit her lip and he could see the moment when she realized that she'd reminded him of his forced change of career. Still, she continued to stare up at him, concern in her face. "Will you tell me what happened to you?"

He felt the muscles of his face tightening with the effort to keep a casual expression in place. "I have a piece of shrapnel in my leg. It's too risky to remove." He tried to smile. "Plays hell with airport security."

She didn't return the smile. "I meant how it happened."

He turned away, heading for the living room where he'd laid his book and reading glasses down. "One of my buddies stepped on a mine."

Out of the corner of his eye, he saw her flinch. "Did you see it?"

He nodded. A lump rose into his throat and refused to ease.

"I'm sorry," she said softly.

He managed a nod. "Yeah, me, too."

"You always wanted to be a soldier, didn't you?" A fleeting smile crossed her face. "I remember when Mel and I were about eight, you and the Paylen boys from down the street recruited us to be the enemy."

The lump in his throat dissolved as memory came flooding back, and with it came an irresistible urge to laugh. "Only that didn't last very long once my dad found out we were launching rocks at you out of that homemade catapult." He shook his head ruefully. "He always did have eyes in the back of his head."

Phoebe snorted. "He did not. Melanie ran and told on you."

"That twerp." His tone was fond. "I should have known. She ran and left you there alone. You were picking up the rocks and throwing them back. I never knew a girl could throw that hard, especially one your size."

She smiled smugly. "That's what the other softball players used to say when I was in high school."

Memories of Phoebe as a child, of himself during those same carefree years before the world had demanded its pound of flesh, came flooding back and he returned her grin. "We're lucky, aren't we, to have such good memories? I'd love to go back and be that age again."

To his surprise, her smile vanished. "I don't. You could not offer me anything to live my child-hood over again." There was a grim, flat note that he'd never heard before in her voice that told him he'd struck some nerve.

His interest sharpened immediately. "That surprises me," he said.

"Growing up without a father in the picture wasn't always easy."

Now that he thought about it, he could recall occasional unkind comments about the twins' illegitimate birth. But… "You and Mel seemed pretty happy to me."

Her face softened, the line of her mouth relaxing

as her lips curved up the tiniest bit. "We were," she said softly.

He chuckled, determined to get her to relax her guard again. "Happiest when you were tormenting the poor boys in the neighborhood who were all fighting over you."

"You're confusing me with my sister now. I never tormented anybody. All the boys I knew had the hots for Melanie."

"Not all." He said it quietly, but the instant he spoke, the atmosphere changed. Electric awareness sparked and crackled as her gaze flew to his.

But she looked away again immediately. "You, too," she said, and in her face he saw her determination to keep things light between them. "When she and I were seniors, she chased you until you caught her, remember?"

He smiled wryly. "I remember. Are you going to hold it against me forever? I was a teenage boy. And God knows boys that age are helpless against an attractive female who's as determined as Melanie was."

To his surprise, she chuckled. "She *was* determined, too. All she talked about that summer was you. What to wear so that you noticed her, where to stand so that she just happened to be where you were headed. You told her once that she looked good in pink so we shopped for pink for the next three months. Have you ever tried to find a good shade of pink for a redhead to wear?" She shook her head, still smiling. "You didn't stand a chance."

He didn't stand a chance now, either. Did she know how desirable she looked? Her eyes were soft and faraway, her body relaxed where she'd angled herself toward him. Her lips looked so soft and inviting as they curved with happy memories….

They *were* soft and inviting. His entire body revved for action as the memory of the afternoon's kiss leaped into the forefront of his mind again. All he'd wanted to do was sink into her sweetness, live the dream he'd kept in his head during terrifying moments of hiding when he'd been sure he would be discovered any minute. Make love to her for real, not just in his imagination while he lay in an American military hospital in Germany. He'd wanted her so badly he'd nearly forgotten the child playing on the floor mere feet away.

And when he'd remembered, it had taken every ounce of self-control he possessed to look away and focus his attention on his daughter.

"Is it really that bad an idea?"

Her unusually timid tone dragged him out of his introspection. "What?"

She was regarding him with thinly veiled curiosity. "A penny for *those* thoughts. I said you're welcome to invite your father to visit for a few weeks if you like. He might enjoy the chance to get to know Bridget."

"What?" he asked again.

"I said—"

"I know what you said! I guess I'm just…surprised at the offer. Are you sure you want my father underfoot?"

She smiled. "I always liked your father. Unless he becomes a werewolf at the full moon, or has some really weird habits I don't know about, it would be fine with me."

"Or we could take Bridget to California to visit him. He's not a young man anymore, and he's never been on a plane in his life."

A fleeting expression crossed her face so quickly he wasn't even sure if he'd seen it or imagined it. Had it been panic? Dismay? "You could fly home and then come back with him," she said. "You know, so he wouldn't have to fly alone."

"I could." He spoke slowly, watching as she twisted her slender fingers together in a sure sign of nerves. But what the hell was it that was making her so uptight? "Don't you want to come home? See the old neighborhood? You could manage one long weekend, couldn't you?"

Her fingers were practically tied in knots. "I…I guess so." Although, she sounded so reluctant he nearly let it drop. But his curiosity was aroused. She didn't seem to care if she ever went back. Why not? She'd grown up there; her family was buried there. "We can visit Melanie's and your mom's graves, and I can show you where my mother's buried."

"All right." Her voice was quiet. "Let me check the calendar and see when we could go."

Had she really agreed to go back to California with Wade? Phoebe wanted to slap herself silly. He'd been in her life again for just two days and already he was turning her world upside down. She should boot him out.

But she knew she never would. Keeping Bridget's existence a secret had been more than a mistake, it had practically been criminal. And she deserved his anger. She'd really been like that overused cliché—an ostrich with its head in the sand. But at the time, it had been so much easier simply to cut her ties with her old life.

If only she had told his parents about Bridget when she first realized she was pregnant. Or… even after she'd thought he was dead.

But other people would have found out eventually. She could hear them now.

Just like her mother.

At least she knows who the father is. She and her poor sister didn't even have that.

Oh, yes. She knew how small towns could be. At least, the small town where she had grown up. Vicious gossips. Not everyone, of course. She'd known many sweet, wonderful people in her hometown. But she'd known more than she liked of the kind who didn't want to let their daughters come over to play with Phoebe and Melanie.

As if illegitimacy was catching.

If she was thankful for anything, it was for the fact that the world had changed since her own childhood. There were families of every kind out there today, and a child without a father wasn't treated any different than a child with two mothers, or a child who shuttled back and forth between her mother's and father's homes in the middle of the week.

She sighed as she looked at her calendar. She had two days off in October, and if she took off another day, they could go to California for a long weekend and make it back without being so pressed for time that it wasn't even worth the flight. She wasn't sure her courage was up to the task of introducing Wade's father to a grandchild he didn't even know existed, but she could tell that Wade wasn't taking no for an answer.

* * *

"Are you sure you'll be okay? Angie is just one street over if you need her," Phoebe told him for at least the tenth time on Monday morning.

"We'll be fine," Wade said. Again. "I'll call Angie if I need anything. And if anything happens, I'll call you immediately."

"All right. I guess I'll see you this afternoon."

"Bye." He held the door open for her. "Don't worry."

She stopped on the verge of descending the porch steps and looked back at him, a wry expression on her face. "I'm a mother. It's in the job description." Then she heaved a sigh and headed for the car as he closed the front door.

It had taken some fast talking on his part, but yesterday she'd agreed to let him keep Bridget this week without anyone stopping by to check on him. And even better, she'd informed him that she'd worked out her schedule so that they could go to see his dad in just a few weeks. She had to clear it with the principal of her building, but she hadn't anticipated any trouble. So he'd make the plane reservations as soon as she came home and gave him a green light tonight.

His dad. How in hell was he going to explain this to his father? From the time he'd entered adolescence and his dad had sat him down for their first big "talk," the watchwords of the day had been *responsible behavior* and *protection.* Not to mention *morality.*

He'd never mentioned his feelings for Phoebe to his parents, never really had the chance, given what had happened with Melanie's death. And then, after the funeral, after things had gotten so wildly out of control, he hadn't had the chance. He'd had to leave the next morning. And Phoebe hadn't answered her phone, although he'd tried half the night to contact her.

He could have simply walked down the street and banged on her door. Should have, he amended. But he'd known she was grieving, and he'd felt he had to respect that. And he'd felt guilty, taking advantage of her trust when she'd been so vulnerable. He should have stopped her.

In the end, he'd given up, promising himself that he'd get in touch with her in a day or two. But he'd been deployed to Afghanistan earlier than expected, with barely twenty-four hours to prepare and he hadn't had time or opportunity to do anything more than think about her.

A month or two later, he'd learned from his mother that she'd left town, that no one seemed to know where she'd gone. The East Coast, someone thought, so he'd made up his mind to visit her the next time he came home. He'd e-mailed her at the same address he'd used for years now—and to his shock, it was returned as undeliverable. And then his mother had had the stroke and all Wade's phone calls and e-mails with his dad had been filled with medical concerns. He'd only been home twice during that hectic time, once not long after his mom's first stroke, the second after her funeral.

He'd come home for that on a three-day leave and gone right back again afterward. He wouldn't have had time to look up Phoebe if she'd just moved to the next town, much less across the continent. Just days after that, he'd watched one of his buddies die when he'd stepped on an unexpected land mine. Others had been dragged away by insurgents operating out of the Afghanistan mountains. He'd barely been able to conceal himself, but he'd managed it. And then unexpected help in the form of an Afghan villager had saved his life and gotten him back to his own troops. On a stretcher, but alive.

He'd had plenty of time to think about her then, while he'd been recuperating. He'd needed her, had finally admitted to himself that he wanted to see if there was any chance that they might have a future together. He'd considered trying to find her, but he didn't really want to call her and tell her he was lying in a hospital bed. So he'd waited until he was well enough to look for her in person.

But he'd never stopped thinking about her, about any of the all-too-brief time they'd spent together. The revelation of his feelings—and hers, he was pretty sure—at the dance. Which had promptly been put on indefinite hold when Melanie had been killed.

And then Melanie's funeral. Or more specifically, what had occurred right afterward. God, if he'd relived that once he'd been through it a thousand times. And that was probably a conservative estimate. He would never forget making love to Phoebe for the first time, no matter the circumstances....

"Are you okay?"

Phoebe looked up, clearly surprised. She'd been sitting on the swing under the rose trellis at one side of her uncle's home. Just sitting and staring.

Her eyes were red and puffy as she looked at him, and Wade realized what an inane question it was.

"I mean, I know you're not okay, but I didn't want to... I couldn't leave without talking to you."

Her nod seemed to take enormous effort. Slowly, she said, "I just needed a break from it." Her voice trembled. "I can't go back in there and talk about her anymore."

The graveside service was complete; Melanie's family and friends had gathered at her mother's stepbrother's home to console each other, to share memories and simply to visit. It was a terrible thing that it took a funeral to bring everyone in a family together again. Phoebe's father had never been in the family picture, as far as Wade knew. And her mother had passed away the second year the girls were in college. Mrs. Merriman's two stepbrothers lived in the same area, although Wade had never heard either Phoebe or Melanie talk much about their extended family; he'd gotten the distinct impression at the funeral that the family hadn't really approved of Phoebe's mother.

He looked down at Phoebe and a fierce wave of protectiveness swamped him. God, what he wouldn't give to go back to the night of the reunion. He'd almost said no to Mel when she'd asked him to go. If he had, they might not be sitting here today.

But if he hadn't, he might never have realized or appreciated his feelings for Phoebe.

Wade cautiously sat beside her, waiting for her to tell him to get away from her. When he'd first gotten the news about the accident, he'd waited for his doorbell to ring. Waited for Phoebe to come scream at him for sending her twin sister off in such a rage that she'd wrapped her car and herself around a tree as she'd sped away from the reunion.

But Phoebe hadn't come. She hadn't called. And he hadn't dared to contact her. He could hardly move beneath the weight of the guilt he felt; if Phoebe piled more on him, he might just sink right into the ground.

His mother had heard about the funeral arrangements before he had. And it never occurred to her that he might not be welcome. Wade didn't have the heart to explain it all, so he'd gone with his family to the service and tried to stay as far away from Phoebe as he could. God, she must hate him now.

Still, when he'd seen her alone, he'd known he had to talk to her, no matter how she felt about him.

But she didn't seem to hate him. Instead, she leaned her head against his shoulder. "I wish it was last week again." Her tone was forlorn.

"Me, too." She felt as fragile as she sounded. He put an arm around her.

Phoebe sighed and he felt her warm breath through the thin fabric of his dress shirt and t-shirt. "Could we take a walk?"

He nodded. "Sure."

He rose and held out a hand. When she curled her small fingers around his much larger ones, he

felt like bursting into song. Entirely inappropriate—
and insensitive—under the circumstances.

He led her through the apple orchard and into the
forest above the house, following a well-worn path
that both wildlife and human had helped to create.
They simply walked for a long time. When the path
narrowed, he helped her over roots, up steep rises
and around boulders, and across a small creek.

They came to a small cabin, a tiny rustic structure. "What's this?" he asked.

"My uncles occasionally use it when they
hunt up here."

Along one side was a large pile of wood that
looked to him like a grand place for snakes to be
hanging out. When Phoebe started forward, he
stepped ahead of her, scanning the ground. Most
Californians went their entire lives without seeing
a rattlesnake; he'd just as soon be one of them.

He pushed open the door of the cabin and
stepped inside. When Phoebe followed him, there
was barely room for two people to stand in the
small space. It held a woodstove, an ax in surprisingly good shape, two wooden chairs and a tabletop that folded flat against the wall, a bunk bed
with a mattress nibbled to shreds by squirrels or
mice, and two shelves above the table. One shelf
was crammed with an assortment of canned goods

and a couple packs of matches. The other held a kettle, a large pot and a scant, mismatched pile of dishes with a few spoons and forks thrown in. There was no electricity, no light. An oil lantern and a bucket hung from pegs on the bunks.

"Wow," he said. "I guess this is just for emergencies. But it's got everything you'd need." Indeed, he'd seen much worse in some of the homes in the Afghan villages he'd been through.

"They come up here and clean it out before hunting season each year. They stock it and add a couple of towels and blankets." She rubbed an absent circle in the dust on the table. "We used to play up here. Thought it was the best playhouse in the world."

We, he knew, meant she and Melanie. He imagined to two little girls it had seemed pretty grand. But he didn't know what to say now that she was talking about her twin again, so he didn't say anything.

"One time Mel got her finger pinched pretty badly by a big crawfish we found in the stream," she said, pointing through the open door down the hill to where the pretty little brook wound its way through the dappled shade and rushed over the rough rocks. "And I saw a snake on that rock another day." She smiled a little. "I don't know who scared who more. I screamed. He couldn't move out fast enough."

She stepped back a pace, forcing Wade to move back against the bunks. Even so, her body brushed lightly against his and he was annoyed with his instant reaction. *Relax,* he told himself. *This is not the time to be thinking of sex.*

Phoebe didn't seem to notice that he was getting hard just being close to her. She was looking at the back of the door. When she went still, he put his hands on her hips and moved her a shade to one side so he could see what she'd been looking at.

There, cut into the scarred wood on the old door, were initials. PEM. MAM. Phoebe Elizabeth and Melanie Adeline. He almost smiled thinking about how much Mel had hated that middle name. She'd always complained that Phoebe got the pretty one.

"We did that," she said softly, "when we were about ten. I remember how daring we felt. It was Melanie's idea, of course." She reached out and traced a finger over the rough-hewn initials. "I never told anybody, and I don't think she did, either. It was our big secret." Her voice wavered. "We said we would bring our daughters up here someday and show them."

Her breath began to hitch, and his desire died instantly, submerged beneath concern. He turned her around, and she immediately wrapped her arms around his waist, pressing herself against him like a little animal burrowing into a safe place as she started to sob.

"Hey," he said softly. "Phoebe. Honey." Finally he gave up and just stroked her hair as she cried. His own eyes were a little damp. He'd known and loved Melanie, too. Even though she'd been a brat occasionally, she'd been a part of his life since he was just a kid. She'd been more important than anything else in his life for a short while, until he'd realized that they had very little in common, that he'd never be happy with her. So he'd cut the strings.

He never should have agreed to go to the reunion, but he'd thought it might be fun. Instead, it had been…a revelation. He hadn't anticipated what had happened with Phoebe that night.

How the hell could he have missed it? For so many years, she'd been right next door…and he hadn't seen that the woman of his dreams was right under his nose. No, he'd even dated her sister and still he hadn't realized that Phoebe was the right one for him.

He'd figured it out that night at the dance. Unfortunately, so had Melanie.

Mel hadn't been unkind, he reflected. Just self-absorbed most of the time. She would never have reacted so badly to the sight of Phoebe and him if she hadn't been drunk. He should have realized how out of control she was. But he'd been too wrapped up in Phoebe to care.

And her death was his fault.

Phoebe stirred then, lifting her head. She pressed her mouth to the base of his throat and he felt the moist heat of her breath sear him.

"Hey," he said. A guy could only take so much and he had just reached his limit. He doubted if she even realized how erotic the action had been. He took her arms in a light grasp and tried to step back. "Maybe we should head back."

"I'm in no rush." She spoke against his skin and, this time, she pressed a very deliberate open-mouthed kiss in the same spot. And holy sweet hell, her arms were still around his waist, holding him tight against every soft inch of her.

"Phoebe?" His voice was hushed. "Ah, this isn't such a good idea—"

She kissed the underside of his jaw and then his chin. As she strained upward on her tiptoes, her full weight slid against him. He exhaled sharply. He wasn't going to look down at her. If he did, there was no way he'd be able to keep from kissing her. And if he kissed her, he wasn't going to be able to stop with just a few kisses. Not the way he felt.

He stared straight ahead and set his jaw—

And then she sucked his earlobe into her mouth and her tongue played lightly around it. He dragged in a rough breath of raw desire.

And looked down.

Six

Holy hell.

Wade realized he was still standing at the front door. Which, thankfully, he had already closed, since no one passing by could possibly miss his body's reaction to that memory in the clinging sweatpants he wore. He shook his head ruefully. His system had been at full alert ever since he'd seen Phoebe standing in front of him on her porch Wesnesday afternoon.

It had only been five days ago that he'd found her, he realized with a jolt, and only two since he'd moved in. And yet in some ways it felt very familiar, very comfortable, as if they'd been together a long, long time. Pretty weird considering that they'd never really even dated, much less lived together.

But that was going to change.

He didn't do such a bad job for a novice on his first day alone with Bridget. Phoebe had shown him the whole diapering deal, and had prepared bottles and baby food for lunch. She'd told him that Bridget did well as long as she was kept to a reliable schedule, so he made sure he followed the instructions she'd left for him.

He'd gotten up early with Phoebe and they'd eaten breakfast while she went over the directions she was leaving for him. And then she'd left.

He knew it had been hard for her to walk out the door and leave them alone. If she'd said, "Call me at school if you have any problems," once, she must have said it ten times.

He took Bridget to a park at the end of the street in the morning, then brought her home and gave her a bottle. He didn't even have to rock her, just laid her down in her crib, since her little eyes were practically shut already. Then, while she was sleeping, he opened and dealt with a large envelope of mail that he'd brought with him in case he had time to kill sitting in a hotel room.

Bridget woke up again about two hours later, so he laid a blanket on the living-room floor and played with her there until time for lunch. Phoebe had told him he needed to feed Bridget promptly if he didn't want her to get cranky.

God forbid the kid should get cranky. He'd hate to have to call Phoebe for help. So he heated the mushy-looking stuff Phoebe had left in a small dish and opened up some pureed apricots to mix in with the cereal Phoebe had left out, all of which Bridget devoured as if she hadn't had a square meal in a month. Which he knew was a crock because he'd watched her tuck away a similar mushy mess for breakfast. Not to mention the bottle he'd given her before her nap.

After lunch, he walked around the yard with her in his arms, and they played a little more before she went down for her afternoon nap. When she awakened, he brought her out to the backyard to play until Phoebe got home.

"Hello there!"

Wade glanced away from the sandbox. An elderly woman in a faded brown dress covered by a stained gardening smock stood at the fence between the two yards. She resembled a tiny elf, with white hair twisted up in a messy bun and twinkling eyes that crinkled as she smiled at him.

"Hello." He got to his feet, lifted Bridget from the sandbox and covered the few steps to the fence with his hand outstretched. Before he could elaborate, the elf clasped his hand in a surprisingly firm grip and pumped his arm up and down in vigorous welcome.

"It's so nice to meet you, Mr. Merriman. I'm Velva Bridley, Phoebe's neighbor. She's a dear, dear girl and that little one is too sweet for words." She poked a gnarled finger into Bridget's tummy, eliciting the now-familiar squeal. "Phoebe's never talked much about you. Are you back for good now?"

"Ah, yes. I was in the army in Afghanistan. But yes, I'm here to stay." He figured he'd better get a word in edgewise while he had the chance. Later he could decide whether or not it had been the right word.

"That's wonderful! Just wonderful. Bridget's really at that age now where she needs to have her daddy around. I bet it about killed you to be overseas when she was born. I know it would have done me in for sure, if my Ira had missed an important event like that. Here." She reached into the basket hooked over her arm without even taking a breath and came up with a handful of some kind of pink flowers. "Last snaps of the season. I was going to bring them over after Phoebe got home but you can take 'em in and set 'em in water. Might earn you some points, you know?"

"Snaps?" She'd lost him a few sentences back.

"Snapdragons. I always start mine indoors. Never bring 'em out until the twentieth of May on account of late frosts, my daddy always said, so I start 'em in the house and set 'em out bright and early on the twentieth. Got the first ones in the neighborhood, and the last ones, too," she added proudly. "Mine are hardy."

"That's, ah, that's nice." He cleared his throat. "So you've known Phoebe since she moved in?"

She nodded. "Sweet, sweet girl. I brought her my raisin cake that I always take to new neighbors, and we hit it off right away. I was a teacher a long time ago, before I married my Ira, and my goodness, it's amazing how things have changed in fifty years."

He smiled. "You sound just like my father. He'd happily go back fifty years to what he calls 'the good old days.'"

"Not me!" Velva shook her head. "Give me the age of technology any day. I love being able to instant message my grandchildren and find out what they're up to right that minute."

He almost laughed aloud. As it was, he couldn't

hide his grin. "Computers sure have made communication easier."

"My great nephew is in Iraq," Velva told him, "and getting e-mails a couple times a week really helps his wife to stay strong. I guess you and Phoebe know all about that, though."

"Hello there!"

Wade spun around. Phoebe stood on the back porch of her little house. "Hey," he called back. To Velva, he said, "It was nice to meet you, ma'am. I hope to see you again."

She looked amused. "Well, I expect if you're living next door, you're gonna see me from time to time. Now go greet your wife the way you want to."

Oh, boy. The lady had no idea what she was suggesting. He strode through the yard with Bridget and stepped up onto the back porch. Phoebe stood there in the navy skirt and the matching sweater with crayons on it that she'd worn to work.

"Hi," she said. "How did it—mmph!"

The sentence stopped abruptly as Wade hooked an arm around her waist and brought her up against his free side, setting his mouth on hers at the same moment.

He sought her tongue, sucking lightly and then probing deeply as he felt her body yield to his, her tension evaporating. She had put her hands up and clutched his shoulders when he'd grabbed her, and after a moment she flattened her palms, smoothing them over his back and up to his neck. Kissing Phoebe was like a drug, he decided, juggling the baby so that he could pull her closer. Addictive. Very, very addictive.

When he finally gentled the kiss and released her mouth, he blew out a breath. "Wow."

"What was that for?" She rested her forehead against his shoulder. Her hands slid down his chest and grasped his forearms.

"Ack!" Bridget threw herself forward and Phoebe put up her arms just in time to catch her.

"Hi, sweetie," she said. "We didn't mean to ignore you." Her face was red and she didn't meet Wade's eyes as she jiggled the baby and blew kisses against her neck, making Bridget giggle.

"For Mrs. Bridley," he said.

"Hmm?" She raised her gaze to his, but the connection to her earlier question seemed forgotten.

"The kiss," he said patiently. "Your neighbor is delighted that I'm home from Afghanistan. I didn't think we should disappoint her."

Phoebe's forehead wrinkled. "Oh." It was slightly gratifying to see that his kiss had scrambled her circuits so thoroughly. It was nice to know he wasn't the only one who felt that way.

He reached around her and held the screen door open, ushering her into the kitchen. "Interesting that she thinks you have a husband."

"I never told her that." Phoebe sounded startled.

"I guess she assumed. She's an interesting woman." He gave the adjective special emphasis, and Phoebe finally smiled.

"She's unique."

"Good word for it. How was your day?"

"My—? Oh, fine. How did you two get along?"

"Famously," he assured her. "I managed to change a couple of diapers and get more food into her than on her, and she took both her naps. So I'd say we were successful."

"Good." She looked genuinely pleased. "No emergency calls to Angie, hmm?"

"Nope. Not a one." He took the baby as she got down two glasses and filled them with ice and sweet tea. She cut a slice of lemon, which she squeezed into his, then stirred with a long spoon. As she slid one across the table to where he'd taken a seat, he said, "You remembered."

She stopped with her own glass halfway to her mouth. "Remembered what?"

He lifted his glass as if he were toasting her. "My tea. With lemon."

Her color had almost returned to normal from

their kiss on the porch, but it was back in an instant. "Just a lucky guess," she said.

Right. A warm feeling stole through him. She'd remembered.

She made spaghetti for dinner while he set the table and changed Bridget. It was just bizarre, Wade decided. To go from not even knowing how to find her to living with her in less than a week.

He had anticipated—hoped—that she would still be free and still have feelings for him when he finally tracked her down. And he'd thought about the rest of his life and he'd known he wanted it to include Phoebe. But he'd expected to court her, to date until she felt comfortable with him. So much for expectations, he thought, eyeing the cozy table, the baby in the high chair at one end, and the easy way Phoebe moved around him as if he'd always been there to get in the way.

He'd take this any day, although it certainly hadn't been anything he'd imagined in his wildest dreams.

While they ate, he told her about the other dad with the eight-month-old son he'd met at the park earlier, and she recounted her day. He set Bridget in her infant seat while he helped Phoebe clear the table, and then he said, "I'd like to invite my father to visit at Thanksgiving or Christmas. Do you have a preference?"

She was still looking at him and her eyes went wide. "Thanksgiving or Christmas?" she said faintly. "The holiday season is more than a month away."

He was puzzled. "Yeah. And…?"

"Exactly how long are you planning to stay in my house?" There was a note of what sounded like panic in her voice.

He looked at her closely, unsure he'd heard her right. "I don't have any plans to leave," he said evenly.

"But…but you can't just live with us forever! What if I wanted to—to get married or something?"

"To who?" He couldn't have kept the note of naked aggression out of his voice if he'd tried. He hadn't seen any signs of a man in Phoebe's life, but that didn't mean there wasn't one. "Is there somebody I should be worrying about?"

"No." As soon as the word popped out, she closed her mouth abruptly, as if she was aware that she'd just given him a major tactical advantage.

"Good." He stepped closer and she backed away, but the table was behind her and she couldn't go any farther. And he stepped forward again, until they were almost nose to nose. He reached for her wrists and captured them with his hands, then very slowly leaned forward until their bodies were pressed together from neck to knee. And just like the first time on the dance floor, he felt that little frisson of awareness, that feeling that this was right, click into place. "If you want to get married, that's fine. But the only man who's going to be putting a ring on your finger is me."

She gaped at him. Literally stood there with her mouth hanging open. "Marry…you?" Her voice was faint.

"Yeah." Dammit, she didn't have to act so repelled by the idea.

"No way."

Her instant refusal rattled him, but he wasn't about to let it show. "Why not? We share a child."

"That's not a reason to get married!"

"It is in my book," he said, struggling to keep his voice even. "You and I grew up in the same community, we have a lot of memories in common. We owe it to Bridget to give her a solid foundation." His eyes narrowed. "Don't you ever wish your childhood had been a little different?"

"I—no." She shook her head, avoiding his gaze, and he wished he knew what was going on behind those blue eyes.

"Why not?" he asked again. "Give me three good reasons why you won't marry me."

She was silent, looking aside with her head tilted down.

"You can't, can you?" He still held her hands and he slowly raised them, pulling them around his neck. She didn't embrace him but she didn't drop them when he released her hands and slid his arms around her, settling her more tightly against him. "We are good together, Phoeber," he said in a lower tone, "and you know it as well as I do. We know each other so well. We could make this work."

He put one hand beneath her chin and lifted her face to his, slowly setting his lips on hers. Her mouth was warm, her lips pliant as he kissed her, but slowly she began to respond, kissing him back with an ever-growing fervor that he remembered from the single time he'd made love to her. The response awakened the need for her that always lurked just beneath the surface, and he growled deep in his throat as he gathered her even more closely against him, pressing her head back against his shoulder as he sought the depths of her mouth.

She clung to him, giving him everything he demanded. Sliding one hand up her hip, he slipped it beneath the bottom of her sweater. The skin above the waistband of her skirt was warm and silky, and an even stronger surge of desire shook him.

"Marry me," he muttered against her mouth.

"This isn't fair," she said, pulling her mouth back far enough to get the words out.

He kissed the line of her jaw. "I don't care about fair. All I care about is making us a family."

Was it his imagination or did her body tense the slightest bit?

It was definitely not his imagination that she withdrew from the kiss slowly but surely, stepping back and straightening her sweater. "Give me time to think about it. This is the rest of my life we're talking about here." Her voice was quiet but he recognized that tone. When Phoebe dug in her heels about something, there was no budging her short of using dynamite. And he had the sneaking suspicion that might not even do it.

"It's the rest of all of our lives," he reminded her.

"I know." She sounded weary. "Let me think about it."

"When can I expect an answer?"

She spread her hands. "I don't know. We can talk again…when we come back from California. All right?"

He nodded grudgingly, not happy about it but unwilling to push further in case he really annoyed her and she decided she couldn't stand him for the rest of her life. "All right."

The following weekend, Wade made the travel arrangements for their California trip. The weekend after that, they left right after Phoebe took leave from school at lunch on Friday.

Bridget fussed for a bit early in the flight but, after a bottle and some cuddling, she settled down and went to sleep for a while. As Phoebe looked down at the beautiful baby girl in her arms, she was amused again by the determined little chin…oh, that was Wade all over.

Wade. Amusement faded as she thought of his marriage proposal, if it could even have been called that, and the fist squeezing her heart tightened painfully. He wanted to marry her to make a home for their child, and because they knew each other well enough to make it work. But he hadn't said anything about love.

Could she marry him, knowing that he didn't love her the way she wanted? Oh, he cared for her, she didn't doubt that. And he clearly desired her. But he'd *loved* and desired Melanie once, and she knew that her sister would always hold his heart. She, Phoebe, had never expected that she'd have any part of him, much less marry him and bear his children, so how could she complain?

As the jet began its landing descent, Phoebe hungrily gazed out the window. There was Mission Bay, the water sparkling in the sunlight, and the golf course of La Jolla. The university, the naval base, the zoo. The lighthouse, high atop a cliff.

The freeway heading north was packed with traffic all rushing to exit the city, all driving at typical breakneck speed California-style. She could hardly wait to be in the middle of it.

And before she knew it, they were. Wade had rented a car for the long weekend since he didn't have a car of his own. He'd never seen the need before, he'd told her. When he'd come home, he'd just driven one of his parents' vehicles.

As they entered the outskirts of their old neighborhood, Phoebe realized she was holding her breath.

It still looked much the same. Small yards shaded by flowering trees; tricycles, bikes and skateboards littering yards and driveways; brilliantly colored flowers fronting many of the carefully kept small homes.

You could see the ocean from the end of their block, she knew. And as Wade drove to the end of the dead-end street and turned around so that he could stop the car along the curb in front of his father's house, she craned her neck to look out over the steep cliff just beyond the barrier the city had placed there.

She couldn't see the beach, which had to be

reached by going down a steep, winding road from the top of the hill, but the vast expanse of the ocean lay before her. Today it was a deep, dark blue, with bouncing whitecaps tossing spray into the air in all directions. A wave of nostalgia hit her like a rough breaker, smashing over her, swamping her.

She'd missed that view so much. Who was she kidding? She wasn't an East Coast girl. She loved the wild, untamed Pacific. She wanted Bridget to grow up with memories of smooth, rounded cobblestones littering the beach, of water so cold it made your teeth chatter. She wanted to take her daughter to the pretty beach in Laguna Niguel where they had spent a day each year on a sort of family mini-vacation, to tell her stories about her grandmother and her Aunt Melanie….

But it was harder here, Phoebe thought, swallowing. Here where all the memories of her sister and her mother lurked, it was harder to ignore her grief and go on. That had been one of the main attractions about the job in New York. But now the past she'd run from had caught up with her, and because of her own stupidity, she owed it to Wade to stop running and let him get to know his daughter.

Phoebe turned her gaze to her old home, four doors down the street, wondering about the family who lived there now. Did they have a pet? Her mother's poodle, Boo-Boo, had dug holes all over their backyard until he'd gotten too old to do more than lie on the porch and yap at the neighborhood kids on their bikes.

Were there children? She couldn't tell from the outside. The garage door was down and there were no bikes or kid equipment littering the yard. And a tall hedge made it impossible to see into the backyard. Was the lemon tree her mother had planted still there?

"Hey." Wade's voice was quiet. "You okay?" He touched her back lightly.

"I'm okay." She squared her shoulders. "It's odd to come back here and not be able to go home, if you know what I mean."

He nodded. "I can imagine, even though I've never experienced it."

But in a way, he had. "How different is it without your mom?"

He shrugged. "Not so. Dad always did give her a hand with the housework and cooking, so it's not like he was helpless."

"But the dynamics change." Oh, did they ever. Some of the most miserable times of her life had been the weekends and college breaks she'd spent at home in the first year after her mother had passed away. It wasn't like it had once been before between Melanie and her. They'd each been grieving, but instead of drawing closer, their grief had isolated them and she'd found herself reluctant to visit as much. It was easier to stay on campus and immerse herself in her life there than it was to go home and enter the silent world of grief that she and Melanie had shared. Mel had stayed in their house, gone to a community college. She'd never really gotten away from the memories and Phoebe had sometimes wondered if Mel resented her for that. It had been Melanie's choice to keep living there, but had it kept her grief from lightening?

Phoebe grieved, too, but life had gone on and, somewhere along the way, she'd made the decision to do the same thing.

"I guess you know all about the way a family changes," he said quietly.

She nodded.

"When your mom died, things changed. But after Melanie died, your whole world was different, wasn't it?" The quiet sympathy in his voice was nearly her undoing.

She swallowed. "Yes. Losing Mom was hard. But losing Mel... Logically, I know that her death wasn't the catalyst for my life taking such an unexpected turn, but sometimes it seems as if one thing just led to the next."

A muscle jumped in his jaw and she realized he had clamped his teeth tightly together. "I guess it must." He sounded as if his words were being dragged from him and she glanced at him, wondering what on earth was wrong.

"Are you feeling well?" she asked as she unbuckled Bridget's car seat.

That appeared to startle him. "Yeah." He indicated the child still sleeping on her mother's shoulder. "Let's go in and introduce Sleeping Beauty here to her grandpa."

Phoebe's stomach was in knots as Wade guided her to the side porch door that the family always used. He opened the door and gestured for her to precede him. As he entered behind her, he called, "Hey, Dad. Where are you?"

"Hello." A deep rumbling voice much like Wade's came from the direction of the kitchen.

Wade stepped around her and headed down the hallway leading to the kitchen, and a moment later his father appeared. "Well, this is a surprise! I thought you were going to be on the East Coast for at least a month." The two men grabbed each other in a typically male, back-pounding hug.

Phoebe stood, rooted to the spot in horror. A *surprise?* Hadn't Wade told his father about Bridget yet?

"...someone here I want you to meet," Wade was saying as the men walked toward her.

Reston, Wade's father, did a double take when he saw her standing there. "Phoebe Merriman. I didn't know you were back in town, honey! It's great to see you—and who's this?" His tone was filled with delight. "I didn't even know you'd gotten married and here you're a mama."

An immediate silence fell, awkwardness hanging in the air like thick smoke.

"Aw, hell." Reston scrubbed a hand over his face. "Forget I just said that. Mothers don't have to be married these days, I know." He stumped on toward Phoebe, and she remembered that his uneven gait was the result of arthritis that forced him to favor one hip. When he reached her, he peered down at the sleeping child she had shifted to hold in the cradle of her arm. "Aren't you a beauty?" he asked, his tone tender as he brushed a finger along Bridget's cheek, catching one fiery curl on his fingertip. He chuckled. "Got that Merriman red hair, didn't she?"

Phoebe nodded, forced herself to smile. "When she was born, all the nurses laughed because it was sticking straight out all over her head."

Wade cleared his throat. "Ah, Dad? Can we sit down?"

Reston straightened and shot his son a wary look. "Okay. You bringing bad news?"

Wade shook his head. "No, I think you're going to like this news." He ushered Phoebe ahead of him into the living room and took a seat beside her on the couch. "There's no easy way to tell you this, so I might as well just say it. Phoebe and I...well, the baby's name is Bridget and I'm her father."

Seven

I'm her father.

Phoebe wondered if Wade's words sounded as shocking to his parent as they did to her. How long was it going to take before she accepted that Wade was really alive—and in her life for good, if he had his way?

Reston Donnelly's eyes widened and his mouth fell open. "Get out!"

"It's true." Wade smiled at his father's obvious astonishment. "You're a grandfather."

Reston's gaze flew back to Bridget. "That's—you're—she's my granddaughter?"

Wade nodded.

"Why…?" Reston cleared his throat. "Why didn't you tell me?"

"He didn't know," Phoebe said hastily. She couldn't bear the look of hurt on Reston's face. "I'm sorry I didn't tell you—"

"Phoebe thought I was dead." Wade cut off her attempt at apology. "She heard the first news after my unit got cut off, but she never got the correction when I was found."

Reston's head snapped up from his inspection of Bridget, his expression changing from hurt to horrified. "Oh, honey. If I'd known where to find you, I'd have let you know. No one knew where you'd gone after…"

"I know. I needed a fresh start."

Reston nodded. He looked back down at the child in Phoebe's arms. "I imagine you did." His gaze landed on his son. "How'd you find her?"

Wade uttered a short bark of laughter. "Hounded every person she'd ever known, hoping someone could tell me where she was. I finally got lucky with one of her high-school friends."

"Must have been the shock of your life when he showed up alive." Reston transferred his gaze back to Phoebe.

"You could say that." No way was she getting into that minefield. "Would you like to hold her?"

Reston nodded. "You bet." Phoebe's heart melted at the look in Wade's father's eyes. Dazed. Delighted. Tender.

Reston nodded. "Please." He settled back in his chair as Phoebe rose and approached, laying Bridget in his arms. He cradled her in one gnarled hand, gently brushing her cheek with the other. "Oh, you're a little beauty," he whispered. "Bridget. Bridget Donnelly. That's a good Irish name." He shook his head and the light reflected the sheen of tears in his eyes. "Your grandma surely would have loved you."

Phoebe's chest hurt as she fought not to sob. She didn't dare glance at Wade. She could imagine the wintry expression on his face without having to see it. But she didn't try to correct Reston's assumption about Bridget's last name. There would be time for that.

Bridget started to fuss and Wade said, "Here. Let me see if I can settle her." Phoebe did glance at him then, but he wasn't looking at her. He lifted the baby and held her against his shoulder; it was amazing how natural the gesture looked after such a short time. Bridget quieted immediately and Wade grinned. "She's turning into a daddy's girl."

Phoebe relaxed, one of those silly maternal things that happened when one's child was well-behaved. Before Bridget, she'd never understood how parents could be so uptight. A screaming session in the middle of Wal-Mart could change your perspective pretty quickly. She dug in her bag and handed Reston a photo album into which she had slid pictures of Bridget right after her birth and at various ages since. "I brought you some pictures."

Reston moved to the sofa and patted the seat beside him. His face was soft. "Sit down here and tell me about her."

"I'll join you." Wade's voice was quiet.

She glanced up at him, but he was looking at the album and wouldn't meet her gaze. She knew he'd looked through the photo albums she'd kept since Bridget's birth…but she'd never told him much about his daughter's early days, she realized.

Remorse shot through her for about the zillionth time, and she mimicked his father's motion, patting the cushion on the other side of her. "That would be nice. I haven't told you that Bridget was almost born in the middle of a wedding."

Wade froze. "What?"

She tugged on his arm and he sank down beside her, patting Bridget's back in a distracted manner.

Smiling, she opened the photo album. On the first page, she'd placed the only picture she had of herself during her pregnancy.

"This picture was taken the day Bridget was born. I went to the wedding of a coworker and the photographer snapped this shot before the service while I was standing at the guest book." She chuckled. "It's a good thing he got a picture of me then!"

"You went into labor at the wedding?" Wade was looking a little green around the edges.

"I was already in labor," she corrected. "But I was too dumb to realize it until about halfway through the ceremony. I just thought my back hurt from being on my feet so much the day before."

Reston guffawed. "Bet you'll never be that dumb again."

A silence followed his hoot of laughter. A *pregnant* silence, she thought, as she cast around for a response. Would she ever be pregnant again?

Wade wanted her to marry him…but she hadn't really let herself dwell on exactly what that would mean. Would he want other children?

An involuntary quiver deep in her belly made her shiver suddenly as her thoughts immediately turned to how those children would be created. Every nerve cell in her body homed in on Wade's large, warm body sitting so close to hers. Hastily, she shoved the photo album into Wade's hands and leaped to her feet. "I'd like to freshen up."

Sometimes it seems as if one thing just led to the next.

Wade could still hear the grief in Phoebe's voice as he lay in the single bed in his childhood room that night. That phrase had been haunting him.

God, but he felt like the lowest of the low. She hadn't said it, and he was pretty sure she hadn't even thought about how it had sounded. But he knew that her life would never have turned out the way it had if it wasn't for him.

If it wasn't for you getting her pregnant, you mean.

Well, yeah, that was what he'd meant. If he'd kept his hands off her, if he'd given her the comfort that she'd really needed instead of the sex she'd thought would make her forget the pain, if he'd been less of a self-absorbed jerk afterward…. If, if, if.

No point in going any farther down that road. It was what it was. He and Phoebe had a daughter together. And they owed it to Bridget to work out their issues and give her the happy, stable home she deserved.

Which was why he had to figure out a way to get Phoebe to marry him. She had seemed so resistant to the idea. Why?

He was sure it wasn't physical. God knew, they had enough chemistry between them to start a brush fire.

Unable to sleep, he rose and padded down the stairs in his bare feet. The little photo album Phoebe had given his father lay on the coffee table in the living room. The streetlight outside cast a few bars of light across the room and he idly picked up the scrapbook and flipped through it. Phoebe had spent more time earlier taking them through Bridget's young life. Rolling over, sitting up, first teeth. Stuff he would have laughed at if the married guys in his unit had talked about it.

"Wade?"

Startled, he nearly dropped the album and he juggled it for a moment until he had it in his hands again. Phoebe stood on the lowest step.

"What are you doing?"

Her hair was down. Even in the darkened room, he could tell it was long. Longer than it had been a year and a half ago. He hadn't realized it because, until now, she'd worn it scrambled up in a messy knot atop her head. It should have looked ridiculous but it was oddly charming. And even more so since he was pretty sure she hadn't tried for that effect. For Phoebe, it was expedient to shove her hair up out of the way.

If it had been Melanie, she'd probably have worked on it for an hour in front of a mirror to achieve a like effect. *Melanie.* Were they ever going to talk about her? Her memory hovered between them like a helium balloon tied to a kid's hand.

"Are you all right?" She was standing there with a concerned look on her face, clad in what resembled a men's-style button-down shirt, although from the way it caught her at mid-thigh and fit her curves, he was pretty sure it hadn't been designed for a man.

"I'm not sure," he said slowly.

Before he knew what she intended, she was down the steps and across the room, placing one small, cool hand on his brow. "Do you feel sick?"

He looked at her, standing so close to him in the shadows of the small living room, her eyes wide and worried. "No," he said. "I'm not sick."

Immediately she began to withdraw her hand but he caught it before she could move away. "Don't go."

She stilled, but didn't speak. Her gaze flew to his face again as he tugged on her hand, drawing her closer. He threaded one hand through her hair, cupping her cheek, and rubbed his thumb lightly over her lips. She swallowed. "Wade, I…" She stopped and shook her head. "I'm glad we came to visit your father."

He smiled, letting his hand drift from her face to play with the cool, silky strands of hair. "Me, too. Bridget's already got him wrapped around one of those little fingers. Thanks for letting him give her a bottle tonight."

"He never stopped talking to her the entire time. Did you notice that?"

He nodded. "He sounded pretty ridiculous."

"Like someone else I know."

"Hey! I do not sound ridiculous."

"You're right," she agreed. "Just infatuated. Totally, ridiculously infatuated."

"It would be impossible not to be," he agreed. "She's perfect."

"Well, almost, maybe," she conceded.

"She's a lot like her mother," he said. "Wrapping men around her little finger."

She snorted beneath her breath. "You know darn well I never wrapped a man around any part of me."

Silence fell between them as her retort registered.

Immediately, his thoughts turned to the cabin in the woods where he'd made love to her. She'd been wrapped around him then, her long, slim legs gripping his hips as he'd plunged into her with so little restraint he winced at the memory even as his body responded to it. "I'd have to disagree with that," he said, aware that his voice had roughened.

Phoebe moaned softly, dropping her head so that her hair fell forward to hide her expression. "Bad choice of words."

He put a finger beneath her chin. She might not be willing to talk about Melanie, but he'd be damned if he was going to let her ignore what was between them, too. "Not so bad. It reminds me of making love with you." He caressed her bottom lip with his thumb again. "Do you remember what it was like between us?"

She drew her breath in sharply and her body tensed. For a moment, he thought she wasn't going to answer him at all. But finally, she whispered, "I remember."

He was more pleased than the two small words warranted that she'd admitted it. Sliding his arms around her, he drew her close. "Let's make a new memory."

She didn't resist as he found her mouth with his. His pulse doubled its rate when he felt her small hands creep around his back. Her mouth was soft and yielding beneath his, her body equally so. Touching the closed line of her lips with his tongue, he gently traced the tender seam until she opened for him, then deepened the kiss as he gathered her closer.

He took her arms and pulled them up around his neck as he feasted on her mouth. She was so much shorter than he was that she had to stand practically on her toes, throwing her off balance and bringing her body to rest against his. Her soft belly pressed against him and his hardening shaft nestled into the cleft at her thighs, sending a surge of pleasure dancing up his spine.

Tearing his mouth from hers, he kissed a trail along the silken column of her neck, then nuzzled the collar of the nightshirt out of the way. She had only buttoned it as high as the one between her breasts, and he exposed a generous expanse of her pale flesh until the shirt drooped off one shoulder.

"Beautiful," he breathed against her skin. He brought up a hand and cupped one breast in his palm, lightly brushing his thumb across the nipple through the thin fabric of the shirt.

She made a small sound and her head fell back.

"The baby was fussing so I—" Reston stopped halfway down the stairs with Bridget in his arms. Even in the dim light, Wade could see his father's eyebrows rising.

Phoebe jerked upright with a startled sound, but when she tried to pull away, Wade refused to let her go. She buried her face in the front of his shirt as Wade met his father's speculative gaze over her head.

"You do know this is how you got the first one, right?"

Wade couldn't prevent the snort of laughter that escaped. "No, Dad," he said. "This is absolutely, positively *not* it."

It was Reston's turn to grin while Phoebe made a quiet moan of mortification. "So," he said. "You gettin' married?"

"Yes," said Wade.

"No," said Phoebe.

If his father's eyebrows had moved any higher they'd have merged with his hairline. "I see." He turned and started back up the stairs with the baby, who appeared to have gone back to sleep. But just before he disappeared, he stopped and looked back, and his shadowed eyes held a sober expression that contrasted sharply with the grin of a moment ago. "That would please your mother," he said quietly to Wade. Then he looked at Phoebe, who still hadn't moved. He shook his head and his shoulders slumped. "Sometimes I still can't believe she's not here. She'd be tickled down to her toes with that baby girl."

"Old manipulator," Wade said quietly when he was sure his father was out of earshot.

Phoebe lifted her head from Wade's chest, although she couldn't bring herself to meet his eyes. His father's final words echoed in her ears, awakening all the guilt and remorse she felt for keeping the news of Wade's child to herself.

Looking down the path her life was about to follow, it didn't take a fortune-teller to predict heartbreak. Then again, if she didn't marry him, that was a given.

She knew she was going to say yes, even before she opened her mouth. She'd rather live with Wade, knowing he didn't love her the way she craved, than live without him. She'd thought he was dead and gone forever and it had felt as if half of her had died, too. She was going to take him any way she could get him, regardless of the pain she knew lay in wait.

"All right," she said quietly.

"What?" Wade looked puzzled. He was still staring at the doorway where his father had been a moment ago.

"All right, I'll marry you."

That got his attention. Wade's gaze shot to hers again and his gray eyes focused on her with a blazing intensity that made her cringe inwardly. "My father catching us kissing made you change your mind?"

She shrugged. "I just—I know Bridget deserves a family. An intact family," she amended. He'd been right. A child *was* a good reason to get married. Every child deserved a set of parents.

And grandparents. I will never forgive myself for depriving her of knowing her paternal grandmother. If it was for a day, or a month, or even years and years, I should have thought about how they would feel.

Wade was looking down at her and his eyes still felt like two lasers examining her soul.

God, had she really just agreed to marry this man? This man whom she'd loved since she'd been a child on the playground? She had reasons, she reminded herself. Bridget needed a father; she deserved a stable childhood with two parents. Raising a family on a teacher's salary could be done, but it wouldn't be easy. With Wade's help, they'd be able to give their daughter the things Phoebe wanted for her: music or dance lessons, sports opportunities, all the myriad activities that children of the modern world pursued.

Phoebe, on the other hand, only needed one reason to marry Wade: love. She'd loved him for what seemed like forever. And then he'd died and she'd had to accept it, though it had felt as if her heart had been permanently shattered.

And then…then she'd found out he hadn't died at all.

Her stupid heart had bounced back a lot faster than her head. She was still having trouble believing that all this was real. But her heart was having no trouble at all loving Wade with even more intensity than she had when she was seventeen years old and he'd belonged to her sister.

"Good," Wade finally said, startling Phoebe out of whatever internal argument she was having with herself. The expressions fleeting across her face ranged from tenderness to the deepest sadness he'd ever seen. He wasn't sure he wanted to know what she was thinking about. "When?"

"I don't know!" She looked startled again. "Do we have to decide tonight?"

He nodded. "Yeah. Before you change your mind." He snapped his finger. "I know. We could stop in Vegas on the way home."

Phoebe's expression was horrified; he almost laughed out loud. "I am *not* getting married in a quickie wedding chapel in the gambling capital of the world! Besides, what would we do with Bridget?"

He shrugged. "Take her with us?"

"No," she said. "Absolutely, positively no way. We go back to New York and apply for a license like normal people, wait until we get it, and do this right. I have no intention of telling Bridget we got married in Las Vegas on the spur of the moment."

"Or our other children." He tried to make it sound innocent; he couldn't resist teasing her.

"Our other—" She stopped and narrowed her eyes. "You said that just to rattle me," she accused.

He grinned. "Did it work?"

A wry smile lifted the corners of her mouth. "I guess it did."

He was still embracing her, still deeply aware of the pounding of his pulse, of her soft curves and the way her hips cradled him. Holding her gaze, he put both hands on her hips and pulled her more firmly against him. Then he shifted his hips slightly, pressing himself so snugly against her that he nearly groaned aloud. "I want you," he said quietly.

She closed her eyes. "Not here." Her voice was so soft he could barely hear her.

"No." He pressed a short, hard kiss to her full pink lips. "Not here. But soon."

Eight

They were off the plane in New York and heading away from the airport. Bridget had just fallen asleep in her car seat when Wade said, "Thank you for letting me bring Bridget out to meet Dad. He adored her."

He glanced over to see Phoebe smiling a little uncertainly. "You don't have to thank me." The smile faded. "I should have gotten in touch with you as soon as I found out I was pregnant."

Unspoken between them was the knowledge that his mother had never known she had a grandchild on the way, or a granddaughter.

"You should have," he agreed.

Even from the driver's side, not looking right at her, he could tell that Phoebe's body went stiff. The temperature in the car dropped about ten degrees. If he'd been looking to pick a fight, he'd have been satisfied with the first volley. But…

"But I understand why you didn't. And maybe it wouldn't have mattered," he said, and with the words, the hard knot of anger that had hidden deep inside him finally uncoiled. "My mother's body was giving out. After she had the first stroke, I learned a lot more about strokes, what causes them, what kind of progress stroke patients make, what therapies are used…. It's probably a blessing for both her and my dad that she didn't live for years with minimal function."

"How can you say that? Don't you think your dad would rather have had her alive in any condition—"

"I'm sure he thinks he would have. But while I was recuperating I saw a lot of victims of head injury and soldiers who'd had strokes after other catastrophic injuries. And I know my mother never would have wanted to live like that." He paused. "There's no dignity in some kinds of living. I wouldn't have liked that for either of them."

She nodded and her silky hair slid over the back

of his hand. It felt like cool silk and his one-track mind instantly shot ahead to the night looming before them. The night when they would put Bridget to bed and then it would just be the two of them. Alone.

The next few hours crawled by. They arrived back at Phoebe's house and unpacked the car, then had a late dinner. They'd lost three hours on the trip east but it was still only eight o'clock when Bridget went down for the night.

Wade followed Phoebe into the room as she laid the baby in her crib, and they looked down at her together.

"She's incredible," he said softly.

Phoebe smiled. "She is, isn't she?"

He put his arm around her shoulders and led her from the room. Phoebe tugged the door nearly shut as they entered the hallway. When she turned back to him, she met his eyes with a wry smile and blew out a breath. "I'm nervous," she said with a laugh.

He smiled. "You don't have to be." He took her hand and led her into the bedroom and across to the big bed in which she slept. Setting his hands on her shoulders, he drew her to him and slid his arms around her, simply holding her, absorbing the amazing sensation of having Phoebe in his arms.

She slipped her arms around his waist and snuggled close.

It was a sweet, sweet moment. Wade felt his heart swell with emotion. *I love you.*

He nearly said it aloud. Might have, except that he was a coward. Plain and simple, a coward.

The night they'd danced, he thought Phoebe had indicated she could care for him. But was it long-term? Sure, she'd made love with him—after her sister's funeral when no one in their right mind could say her judgment was sound. And she'd clearly been overwhelmed to see him again after she'd thought he was dead. But he was the father of her child. And they'd been friends since their own childhood. She didn't have to love him to be thrilled that he was alive.

She got so quiet every time Melanie's name came up that he could barely stand it. Did she blame him? God knew, she wouldn't be wrong. He should never have let Mel leave alone that night.

So he didn't speak aloud. Her very silence suggested that her heart wasn't entirely in this relationship and that made him nervous as hell. She might never forgive him for Melanie's death but there was no way he was going to let her shove him out of her life. He loved her, even if he could never tell her.

Tonight, he would show her.

He stopped beside the bed and took her into his arms. After a moment, she lifted her face to him and his heart leaped as he lowered his mouth to hers. Whatever else was between them, there was no arguing with the chemistry they created together. He kissed her for a long, long time, using his lips and tongue to show her how he felt, simply made love to her mouth until they both were breathing hard and his blood was pounding through his veins.

When he lifted the hem of her T-shirt, she raised her arms and let him pull it over her head. She shook her head as he tossed the shirt aside and her hair fell around her shoulders, emphasizing the lacy white bra she wore.

"You're beautiful." He reached around her and dispensed with the bra, and wanted to howl at the moon when the full, firm mounds of her breasts, capped by rosy nipples, were revealed. He cupped them in his hands and smoothed his thumbs over the taut tips as she lifted her hands to the buttons of his shirt.

She managed to get about half the buttons undone before she threw her head back with a half laugh and said, "I can't concentrate."

He smiled, lowering his head to the slope of her breast and tasting the tender flesh. "Can I help?"

He quickly tore the shirt open and shrugged it off, then unfastened his pants as well and pushed them off along with his boxers. Turning his attention to her pants, he unzipped them and put his thumbs at the sides, pushing until she, too, had kicked the last of her clothing away.

Then he urged her onto the mattress.

As he followed her down, he said, "Do you have any idea how many times I dreamed about this?" He cupped her breast again, pulling her close with one arm beneath her head. "You kept me warm on a lot of damn cold nights halfway around the world."

To his shock, her eyes filled with tears. "I was so mad at you for leaving," she said. "For not coming to say goodbye. And then—and then—"

And then she'd thought he was dead. Gone forever. He read the anguish in her eyes.

"Shh," he said. "I'm here, and I'm never leaving again." He smoothed a hand down over the silky skin of her belly as he bent his head and took one nipple into his mouth. Suckling strongly, his own body pulsed in response as her back arched off the bed and her hands threaded through his hair to hold him to her.

He eased his weight over her, settling himself into the heated cove between her thighs, feeling the damp curls and the soft, soft flesh below. He couldn't wait.

Slowly, he pushed into her, groaning at the tight, slick feel of her body clasping his. Too tight, he realized belatedly.

"Relax, baby, you're okay." He stopped moving and held every muscle still, though his body was screaming at him to move. Guilt ate at him. He should have been thinking of her, and instead all he'd been able to do was think about how badly he wanted to be inside her. It wasn't even completely sexual, but something more, instinct urging him to stamp every inch of her with his scent and feel, to make her his again in the most basic way there was.

"I'm sorry," she whispered, squirming with discomfort. "I had a couple of stitches after Bridget was born and—"

"Shh," he said, kissing away a tear that trailed from the corner of her eye. "It'll be okay. We're in no hurry here."

She was taking deep, fast breaths, her breasts heaving as she fought to cooperate, and he knew he needed to help her. He didn't want her first time after Bridget's birth to be something she just wanted to forget.

He lifted himself a little away from her and stroked one hand between them, down her belly to the spot where they were joined. His fingers found the tiny, tender button hidden in her curls. Lightly, hoping that she would enjoy his touch, he rubbed a finger over her. And nearly had a heart attack when her body jolted involuntarily beneath his, driving him even deeper into her tight sheath.

She sucked in a sharp breath and he said, "Did you like that?"

He felt, more than saw, her nod in the darkness, so he did it again, starting a small circular pattern that massaged the little nubbin gently. Her hips began to move beneath his and he felt her muscles quiver. His own muscles were trembling with the effort it took to hold still when everything within him was urging him to thrust forward, but still he resisted. Her hips were moving steadily now, creating a delicious rhythm in time with his circling finger and he locked his jaw, holding on to his control by the slimmest of threads as her motions drew him in and out, in and out.

"Oh, yeah," he said through clenched teeth, "Oh, baby, I'm sorry—I can't—I can't—"

Wait was what he'd meant to say, but he never got the chance. Without warning, she arched beneath him and he felt an incredible sensation as she came in heavy waves of completion, her inner muscles squeezing his aching flesh over and over again. Control fell away and he shoved his hips forward, then withdrew and hammered into her again.

She was still shaking and jerking beneath him as he felt his body gather, gather, gather—and then release in a hot, drenching burst of pleasure that went on and on and on until both of them lay spent, gasping for breath.

His head was on the pillow beside hers and he smiled as she turned her head and pressed her lips briefly to his.

The sweetness of the gesture humbled him. How had he left this woman without telling her that he intended to return and make her his forever? He'd been so wrapped up worrying about what he'd done to her when she was grieving and vulnerable, so determined to give her space to think, that he'd nearly lost his opportunity forever.

What if she'd met and married someone after she'd thought he'd been killed? The idea didn't bear thinking about.

Instead, he focused on the one thing that had been nagging at him since their discussion over the weekend. "So when do you want to get married?" he asked.

He felt her smile against his throat. "Sounds like you already have a time in mind."

"Yeah." He snorted. "Yesterday. How long will it take to get a license here in New York, anyway?"

"I have no idea what the law is here," she said. "Since you'll be home this week, why don't you find out? I assume that once we have a license we can just go to the courthouse."

"All right. Is that what you want?" he asked. "A civil ceremony?"

She shrugged and the motion sent a pleasurable chain reaction rippling through his system. "I don't need a big church wedding, if that's what you're asking. It would seem sacrilegious, given that we already have a child." She stopped, then said, "Unless you think that would be important to your dad. Will you invite him?"

He was warmed by the concern she showed for his father's feelings. "I'll invite him, but I doubt Dad is about to get on a plane. Not even for that. He's not going to care if we get married here."

"All right." She nodded, as if that were settled. "You find out what we need to do and we'll set a date."

He nodded. "Leave it to me." Then he moved his hips experimentally and grinned when her body clenched around him. "Hmm, wonder what we can do until then?"

She laughed as she drew his head down to hers.

And as he began to kiss her again, he thought of an idea for a unique wedding gift that he knew would mean a great deal to her. It was time to lay some ghosts to rest.

But he could pursue that tomorrow. Right now, he had better things to do.

A week passed, then two. They decided to get married in the first week of December, a simple ceremony at the county courthouse, and Phoebe planned ahead to take a personal day.

One evening in the beginning of November, he said, "I applied for a job in the private sector today. The thought of being stuck behind a desk working for the Department of the Army, having to move every couple of years, doesn't appeal to me."

She looked up from the papers she was grading. "What kind of work is it?"

He lifted a glossy dark folder that he'd been reading and passed it to her. "Private security."

"As in being a bodyguard?" She tried not to let her dismay show. Wouldn't a bodyguard need to live with or near his employer? Possibly travel with the individual, as well?

"Not exactly." He smiled. "I heard about this company from a friend of mine who got out of the service and went to work for them. This firm performs a number of different specialized services. They are called in when kidnappings occur, they're quietly hired for operations that the government wants done without any fanfare, they set up protective services for people and property. Last year they provided security for a huge gem exhibit at the Met."

"What's it called and where is it?"

"Protective Services, Inc." He hesitated. "The main company is located in northern Virginia, but they're planning on starting up at least one branch operation. The first one will be in L.A."

"So we'd move back out there?"

He nodded. "If you wouldn't mind."

"No." She smiled. "I wouldn't mind." Then she said, "Do you know what type of work they'd want to hire you for?"

"Actually, I'm hoping to run the whole branch," he said. "That's the position they need and if nothing else, being an army officer equipped me for organization." Then he grinned again. "The Long Gray Line is everywhere."

She stared at him. "What?"

"The Long Gray Line," he repeated. "The U.S. Military Academy grads are called that because of the uniforms we wore as cadets. Graduates of West Point have networking contacts all over the world.

A retired soldier who works for PSI graduated a few years ahead of me. One of Walker's buddies talked to a friend of mine who knew I might be job hunting and word got back to them."

"That's amazing. You didn't even go looking for this job, did you?"

"Not exactly. But I had already decided to take medical retirement so it might work out well. And I think I'd enjoy the challenge." He made a wry face. "I'd be bored to death doing the same old thing over and over every day."

"That's one reason I enjoy teaching," she said. "There's always something to challenge me. A child with a special need, a new approach to try, even parent meetings are rarely boring."

"I bet you're a good teacher," he said.

"I try to be. Teaching the next generation is one of the most important jobs there is, I believe." Then she gestured at the piles of paperwork in front of her. "And speaking of jobs, I'd better get back to work on these spelling tests."

"Ahh. Teacher talk." His smile flashed. "It turns me on."

Phoebe's hand paused, as she lifted her gaze to his. "Teacher talk turns you on?"

He rose from the easy chair and began to walk toward her. "Yeah. Wanna see?"

"Wade!" She made a token effort to scoot away as he grabbed her and pulled her against his body. "I've got to finish grading these papers. It won't take me long."

He paused. "How long?"

"Not long!" She twisted her arm so that she could see the face of her watch. "Ten minutes or so."

"Ten minutes? Sorry, can't wait that long."

"You're impossible," she said as he lowered his head and set his mouth on hers, then pulled her up against his body.

"Impossible to deter," he muttered against her skin, kissing his way along her jaw and sucking her earlobe into his mouth, swirling his tongue around it.

She felt her knees buckle beneath the sheer delight that being in his arms always brought. Wrapping her arms around his neck, she let her head fall back as her muscles went lax. Wade took immediate advantage of the exposed slender length of her neck, sliding his mouth down the warm, silken column, nuzzling aside the scooped top of the knit shirt to nip at her collarbone. Phoebe murmured with pleasure, her body humming, response blooming inside her.

He bent and slid his arms beneath her knees, sweeping her into his arms and carrying her up the stairs. She clutched at his neck as he took the steps two at a time. "I'm too heavy for this. You'll hurt yourself. Put me down."

He laughed aloud. "Do you know how many pounds I used to carry up the side of a mountain? Trust me, honey, you're not too heavy." He paused at the top for a deep kiss, sweeping his tongue into her mouth and enticing her into exploring him as well. "Besides," he said when he lifted his head, "when I was packing a load up a mountain, I didn't have this kind of incentive waiting for me at the top."

It took him only a moment to cover the steps to her bedroom, only a moment more to cross the room and set her beside the bed. Although she had steadfastly refused to allow herself to think of him during waking hours, she had dreamed of Wade over and over, even after she'd believed he was dead. But none of the dreams had ever come close to the heady reality of being in his arms. Even now, she wasn't sure it was real sometimes.

He pulled her shirt over her head as she set her small hands to work unbuttoning his, then unhooked her bra. She paused so that he could slide it off her shoulder and toss it aside, and then, as he cupped her breasts and began to lightly rub his thumbs across the rosy nipples, her hands slowed and fell away.

He tore his gaze from the sight of the plump,

beautiful mounds in his hands to look into her eyes. Heat and passion filled his gaze, and to her delight, she felt his body shudder in anticipation against her. Reluctantly, he took his hands from her and stripped off his jeans and briefs, then tugged her slacks and panties down and off in one smooth, efficient motion. He reached around her and peeled the bedcovers back before urging her down onto the cool cotton sheets.

Taking her hand, he guided it down between them to his aching length. "Help me."

He jumped when her small hand closed around him. Savoring the silken feeling of his body, so taut and hard, she tightened her grip the way she knew he liked and stroked him once, twice and yet again. His hips lifted and thrust against her and he growled. "Tease."

She lightly bit his shoulder. "Tell me you don't like it and I'll stop."

He sounded as if he were having trouble dragging air into his lungs. "Like that's ever going to—oh, baby, yeah."

As she positioned him at the throbbing entrance to her body, she lifted her hips. He was hot and solid and she cried out as he surged forward, embedding himself deeply within her. Her hands clenched on his buttocks, urging him to move, and within moments they established a fast, frantic rhythm that built a blazing fire within her. His body hammered against her, creating an ever-rising tension that stretched tighter and tighter until finally it snapped. As her body bucked and writhed in his arms, and then he was hoarsely calling her name as his body stiffened and froze in a shattering climax that left him shaking and gasping for breath.

When she could breathe again, think again, she stretched up and pressed a kiss to his shoulder. "Wow."

He snorted and chuckled. "Yeah. Wow." He rolled to one side and pulled her into his arms and she relaxed against him, enjoying the cuddling. "I think we've mastered that."

"You do? As an educator, I can tell you that research shows that even when a skill has been mastered, a certain amount of practice is necessary to reinforce the concept."

"Is that so?" He stroked a hand gently down over her hip and lightly squeezed her bottom. "In that case, I suppose we'll just have to keep practicing until we're sure we've got it right."

Now it was her turn to laugh. "Could take a while."

"It could," he agreed.

Nine

Wade had a job interview on Friday with the company out of Virginia, the specialized security firm that was setting up a new branch. He'd met the personnel director already, and today's interview, he told Phoebe, was with the owner of the company.

"He's going to love you." She picked up her coffee cup as he rose to put his dishes in the dishwasher. They'd gotten into a pleasant weekday routine in which they had breakfast together before she left. He usually had some kind of start on dinner before she arrived home, which meant she got her work done faster if she'd brought any home to grade, which meant that right after Bridget went to bed, she and Wade could go to bed, also.

Or at least go to the bedroom, she amended.

Every night he made love to her, stoking the blaze between them into a raging inferno of need. She awoke in his arms in the morning to a wild sense of unreality.

She'd had more than a year to accustom herself to the idea that Wade would not be a part of her life, and during half of that time she'd believed that he was dead. Sometimes it was difficult to believe that she really could be so happy. Although *happy* was a pale imitation of the feelings that rioted through her when she came through the door in the evening to see him there waiting for her, holding their daughter in the crook of one muscular arm.

When he pulled her to him and kissed her senseless, she was able to silence the one niggling voice in her head that reminded her that Wade might desire her…but he didn't love her.

"Don't worry about Bridget," she said. "Angie is watching her all day."

Wade nodded. "I could be back by lunch if this doesn't fly. If it does…it'll be late when I get home."

She rose on tiptoe to kiss him as he straightened his uniform, liking the way he'd said *home*. As if they truly were a family already. "Good luck."

She watched as he climbed into the rental car he still had, and waved as he drove off. "I love you," she murmured.

Would she ever be able to say it aloud? He seemed happy, and he clearly was thrilled with fatherhood. And when he touched her…well, they had no problems in that department. She smiled to herself as warmth radiated through her. But sometimes she caught him staring into space with a faraway expression on his face and she wondered what he was thinking about.

She was afraid she knew. And she was afraid to ask.

Melanie. Oh, she remembered everything that had happened the night of the reunion, the way he'd looked at her as if she were some new treasure he'd discovered—but that had been one single night. And even then, when he'd realized how upset Melanie had been, he'd been quick to pursue her.

To reassure her that there was nothing between Phoebe and him?

She would never know. Just as she would never know how much he still thought of her sister, how often his heart ached with loss.

Phoebe's insecurities, those feelings that had dominated her interactions with her sister most of her life, reared up and grabbed her attention every once in a while, reminding her that Wade had belonged to Melanie.

Never to her.

True, Wade seemed content now. But was it the familiarity of their friendship? His new father-hood? Guilt at leaving her pregnant and alone? She feared it might be all three.

But he's with me now. He couldn't make love to me like that if he didn't care for me at least a little. Could he? Stop being a pessimist.

The school day dragged. She wondered how Wade's interview went. She checked her mobile phone for messages several times during the day, but he hadn't called. Although she hadn't expected him to, she worried that things hadn't gone well.

He probably wouldn't call her if the interview had not been successful. For all the years that she'd known him, Wade had been an intensely private man about his deepest feelings; she suspected that if he didn't want to talk, prying any information out of him would be next to impossible.

It wasn't until she saw the familiar outline of her little home that her spirits rose. Bridget was in there, with Angie. The sight of her daughter, the feel of that little body snuggled into her arms, was always balm to her sad moments.

Angie was sitting cross-legged on the couch, watching an afternoon soap opera, when Phoebe came through the door. "She was great today," Angie informed her. "I laid her down for her afternoon nap about two so she shouldn't get up again until at least four. I put the paper and the mail on the table."

"Thank you so much," Phoebe said. "I really appreciate you coming on short notice."

"Not a problem." Angie gathered her things. "Wish me luck on my psych test."

"Luck." Phoebe winked and smiled at her as Angie left. She set down her bag of paperwork from the day and slipped out of her shoes, then headed for the kitchen to get a drink.

As she sipped her tea, she glanced through the mail Angie had laid on the kitchen table. She set aside two bills and the grocery store flyer that had coupons in it, tossed three offers for credit cards in the trash, and laid out two envelopes of what looked like personal missives for immediate attention.

The first was a thank-you from a fellow teacher for whom she and her coworkers had thrown a bridal shower. The second bore an unfamiliar return address in California. Curious now, she slit the envelope and extracted a single sheet of paper.

Dear Mr. Merriman,

Mothers Against Drunk Driving (MADD) thanks you for your generous donation in memory of your loved one, Melanie Merriman. May we express our deepest condolences on your loss. Melanie sounds as if she was indeed a special young woman.

With your donation…

Bewildered, Phoebe picked up the envelope and looked more closely at the address. The sender had gotten Wade's name wrong on the envelope: it read Wade Merriman and she hadn't even noticed that it wasn't for her. Additionally, a change of address label had been slapped over the original and she realized it had been forwarded from his father's home in California.

She reread the letter—and suddenly it began to make sense, horrible sense, and the small, fragile bubble of hope she'd allowed herself to feel burst.

Wade had made a donation in Melanie's memory—*in his loved one's memory*—to a charitable organization known nationally for its education programs targeting drinking and driving. His *loved one*. Phoebe registered the hit to her heart as desolation spread through her and tears stung her eyes.

It wasn't that she begrudged the money, or the

thought. A part of her treasured the realization that her sister's name had been so honored. But now there was no way she could pretend that their marriage would be anything more than a convenience.

Now she knew for sure that there was no way Wade was ever going to love her because he was still in love with her sister. She sank down in a chair at the table and reread the letter twice more. Then she realized that if the letter hadn't been forwarded, she never would have known about the donation.

A sob escaped without warning. She clapped a hand over her mouth, but the truth confronting her wouldn't be denied and her efforts to resist the tears were futile. She had known Wade didn't love her. She shouldn't be so upset by this.

But she was. Not just upset, but devastated.

How could she marry him? Her heart wasn't going to be able to take that kind of beating day after day. She'd been kidding herself, believing that she could love him enough to make a marriage work. Even for the sake of her sweet baby girl sleeping upstairs, she couldn't do it.

At that thought, another sob welled up and tears began to stream down her face. Giving in to her misery, she laid her head down on her arms and cried.

Wade let himself into the house, wondering where Phoebe was. The baby monitor on the end table was silent, so she wasn't in Bridget's room. Could she be napping? Doubtful. He had yet to see her sleep during the day. Maybe she had taken Bridget out in the yard.

He crossed the living room and headed into the kitchen—and stopped short as he caught sight of her. She was slumped in a chair with her arms on the table, her head buried. Fear gripped him. "Phoebe! Sweetheart, what's the matter?" He rushed forward. Was she ill? Dear God, had something happened to Bridget? Panic nearly stopped his heart. "God, what's wrong? Is it Bridget?"

He knelt beside her chair and put an arm around her shoulders to hug her to him—and she exploded out of the chair halfway across the kitchen.

"Don't," she said between sobs. "Just—don't." She fumbled in a drawer for a tissue then turned away, her shoulders shaking with misery. "Bridget's fine."

A huge wave of relief swamped him momentarily, only to rush back as he realized she hadn't told him anything about herself. "Then what is it? Are you…" He could barely bear to utter the word. "Sick?"

She whipped back around at that, immediately grasping what he was asking. Her mother had gotten sick and died; so had his. "Oh, no, Wade. There's nothing wrong with me."

Except that there was. Her eyes were swollen from crying, her nose pink. She blotted her eyes and blew her nose while he stood. "Then…what?" he finally managed to ask.

She tried to smile, but her lips trembled and she quickly abandoned the effort. "I can't marry you."

What? "Why?" It was the most obvious question and he was too confused to think of a better one.

She sighed. "I just can't. It wouldn't be fair."

Fair to whom? "What the hell are you talking about?" Heat rose. He knew his tone was too rough, too angry, but— "Dammit, you scared me half to death! I thought something happened to Bridget or you. And now you tell me you won't marry me but you won't tell me why?"

A brittle silence followed the furious torrent of words, but she didn't speak, merely stood there with her eyes averted. And in her stance he read determination. He knew Phoebe and he knew that posture.

But what—? It hit him then. Stunned, he sank into the chair she'd bolted from. "It's because of Melanie, isn't it?"

She sucked in a sharp breath and nodded, and he saw a tear trickle down her cheek.

"Lord God above," he said quietly. Silence

reigned again as he absorbed the information. He'd wondered—no, he'd feared—for more than a year, that she blamed him for Melanie's death. It had kept him from contacting her after the first time they'd made love, and it had cost him the first months of his child's life.

When he'd finally decided to try to talk to her about it, she had been gone. And after he'd found her, after he'd learned about Bridget, his guilt had taken a backseat while he had adjusted to father-hood and pretended that everything was fine and that Phoebe would love him and that they'd spend the rest of their lives together.

He scrubbed his hands over his face and looked down at the table, unable to stand seeing the pity and regret he knew he would see in her eyes.

A letter lay on the table and his name caught his eye. His first name, anyway. As he scanned it, he realized what it was. The foundation to which he'd made the donation in memory of Melanie had sent a thank-you note.

"I opened it by accident." Phoebe's tone was flat.

"I thought it would be a meaningful wedding gift."

"A *wedding gift?*"

"I'm sorry," he said. "I know there's nothing I can say to ever make it up to you—"

"You don't have to—"

"—and if it helps any, I will never forgive myself for letting Melanie die. If I'd been quicker, I'd have caught her. I've relived that night a thousand times and I know why you blame me." He halted for a moment. "I blame myself, so why shouldn't I expect you to?"

"Wade—"

"Don't." His shoulders slumped. "Just tell me what you want me to do now. Do you want me to leave?" His voice broke. "I will. I hope that you'll let me see Bridget sometimes, but I won't push—"

"Wade!"

At the volume and pitch of her voice, he finally stopped talking abruptly for the first time since she'd shoved away from his embrace.

Looking at the anguished set of his features, hearing the pain in his voice, she suddenly realized what he was thinking. It had nothing to do with lost love. *He was blaming himself for Melanie's death!* A tidal wave of shock, confusion and compassion crashed over her head and she forgot about her own pain.

"Wade," she said. He didn't look at her and she said it again, crossing to the table and touching his arm. "Wade, look at me."

Slowly, he lifted his gaze to hers and she was astounded by the pleading look in his eyes.

"I don't blame you," she whispered. She knelt on the floor beside his chair. "I've never blamed you. Melanie was impulsive. She had an ornery streak a mile wide. Her heart was that big, too, most of the time. She had been *drinking*. Neither one of us is responsible for what happened that night." She paused and put a hand to his face. "I don't blame you," she said again, urgently, as the look on his face eased fractionally.

"Then why?" He swallowed. "Why won't you marry me? God, Phoebe, I know I was a slow learner, but I realized that night at the dance that you were what had been missing from my life." He averted his eyes. "I took advantage of you after the funeral. I have no excuse, except that I had finally figured out that I loved you and I couldn't have walked away from you then any more than I could have stopped breathing."

He stopped speaking again then, and the only sound in the room was his harsh breathing and the hitching breaths she still took in the aftermath of her storm of tears.

Phoebe was frozen, his words hammering at her brain but not making sense. At least, not making sense in her current framework of reality.

"Phoebe?"

She sank down onto her heels and he looked alarmed. "I'm sorry. I shouldn't have—"

"You love me?"

He stopped. Searched her eyes, his own incredulous. "You didn't know?" He snorted. "I thought the whole damned world could see it."

"I didn't know," she confirmed. "I thought—believed that you still…"

"Melanie?"

She nodded. "When I saw the letter, I thought you'd done it because you still missed her, and that it was an accident that it came to this address."

"Oh, sweetheart, no." He put his hands beneath her elbows and stood, lifting her to her feet. "It was supposed to make you *happy*. I wanted to do something special to commemorate our marriage." He paused, looking down at her and she could see him choosing his words with care. "My feelings for your sister were only a crush. Infatuation. Mel and I weren't well suited. You surely could see that. We were over long before that reunion and I never regretted it."

As their eyes met again, she saw the beginnings of hope creeping into his expression. "You love me?" she said again. Stupid, she knew, but she wasn't quite sure she'd really heard it the first time.

His taut expression eased and the hope blossomed into a look that warmed her heart. "I love you," he said. "I've loved you since the night you asked me to dance and I realized I'd been chasing the wrong sister for a long time."

Her eyes filled with tears. "I love you, too," she said. "Oh, Wade, so much…" She smiled tremulously. "Pinch me. I must be dreaming."

"No way," he said. "Either the pinch or the dreaming. This is real, sweetheart. As real as that little girl sleeping upstairs." He gathered her against his body and pressed his forehead against hers. "Marry me, please, Phoebe?"

She tried to nod. "Yes. I would love to be your wife."

"Mother of my children," he prompted.

"Children? As in more than our one?" She slid her arms up around his neck and toyed with the collar of his shirt.

"Definitely more. Bridget would be spoiled stinking rotten if she was an only." He paused. "When did you realize…?"

"That I loved you?" She laughed. "At the risk of inflating your ego to an unforgivable level, I'll tell you. I can't remember when I didn't love you. I worshipped you when I was eight, nine, ten. I idolized you at eleven and twelve. By thirteen I was hopelessly infatuated. It tore me to pieces when you dated Mel."

"I never knew." His tone was wondering. "How could I not have known?"

"I wasn't exactly the most outgoing kid," she reminded him.

"Yeah, but you were always comfortable with me. You were—in love with me," he said ruefully. His expression changed. "God, I could really have blown it, couldn't I?"

She shrugged. "Doubt it."

Within ten minutes, he had her flat on her back in the big bed in her room. *Their* room, she amended silently. Soon she'd be giving herself and everything she had into his care.

Her attention abruptly veered back to the present as one warm, hairy leg pressed between her own legs and Wade's weight pressed her into the bed. She wriggled beneath him and he growled. "Wait."

"For what?" she teased, slipping her hands between them and rubbing his small, flat nipples into hard points.

"Tell me," he demanded, holding himself above her on his forearms, "that you felt it, too, that night we danced. Tell me it wasn't just me."

She slipped her hands down his back and he shuddered when he felt them moving lower, trying to pull him closer. Drawing back, he pushed slowly into the welcoming heat of her body, already soft and slick.

She murmured a sound of pleasure as she shifted her hips to accommodate him. "It wasn't just you." Then he lowered his head and claimed her mouth and she lost track of anything she'd intended to say as he began to move against her.

A short while later, she lay cuddled against his side. Wade was on his back, his arm around her idly caressing the ball of her shoulder, as another thought struck her. "Holy cow. I forgot all about your interview. How did it go?"

His hand stilled for a moment, then resumed its hypnotic rhythm. "Great!" She tilted her head back to see his face and he grinned at her. "I was offered the job."

"And you said yes." It was rhetorical and she was shocked when he shook his head in the negative.

"I said maybe," he said. His expression sobered, a sheepish quality creeping across his face. "I might have fibbed to you a little bit."

"Fibbed?" She was flabbergasted. "You made up the job?"

"No, no," he said hastily. "The job is real, and it's mine if I want it. But it's not in New York. In fact, it's not even on the East Coast."

"Where—? It's in California!" Could she get any more surprised? "Isn't it?"

"Southern California," he specified. "We'd have to move to San Diego if—"

"Yes!" She nearly shouted it in a totally un-Phoebe-like burst of enthusiasm as she pounded on his chest with her free hand. "You said yes, didn't you? We're going back?"

"I said it depended on my wife." He caught her and held her with ease as she flung herself atop him and wound her arms about his neck. "We wouldn't be in Carlsbad," he warned her. "I'd probably need to live somewhere closer to Mission Bay."

"Call them and tell them you'll take it!" She wriggled out of his arms and snatched up the portable telephone, thrusting the handset at him.

Wade laughed. "All right, all right. I'll do it in a few minutes." He paused, setting aside the phone and drawing her back into his arms. "Are you sure? I mean, I know you wanted to stay here and get tenure, and I can keep looking for a job around here if you'd rather not leave."

She detected the slightest trace of diffidence in his tone and her heart melted all over again. "You'd really do that for me?"

"For us," he qualified. "Wherever we decide to

live, I want you to be completely happy with the decision."

She sighed, sliding her hands into his hair and drawing his head down to hers. "Silly man. Don't you know I'd be happy anywhere with you?" She kissed him tenderly. "All I need is you, and our family. Going back to California would be wonderful, but all I really want is to spend the rest of my life with you."

And as he drew her back down to the bed, she realized the dream she'd had for so many years had truly become a reality. "I love you," she murmured.

"And I love you." He kissed her, then slid his hands down her body. "But I have to confess, that's not the *only* thing I want to do with you."

She laughed, too happy for words. Wade, the child they'd made together in love, and a future that looked as rosy as Bridget's cheeks. She thought of Melanie, and for the first time a true sense of peace filtered into Phoebe's heart. She had a hunch that wherever she was, Mel was doing a happy angel dance for her. And charming every male angel within sight.

* * * * *

THE HEART OF A MERCENARY

BY
LORETH ANNE WHITE

Loreth Anne White was born and raised in southern Africa, but now lives in Whistler, a ski resort in the moody British Columbia Coast Mountain range. It's a place of vast, wild and often dangerous mountains, larger-than-life characters, epic adventure and romance — the perfect place to escape reality. It's no wonder it was here she was inspired to abandon a sixteen-year career as a journalist, features writer and editor to escape into the world of romance fiction.

When she's not writing, you will fine her long-distance running, skiing on the trails, and generally trying to avoid the bears. She calls this work, because it's when some of the best ideas come. Loreth loves to hear from readers. Visit her website at www.lorethannewhite.com.

As always, to Susan Litman.
Without her I wouldn't be here.

To Marlin, who keeps me focused on the
importance of story in our world.

To the rest of my family for too many
reasons to mention.

And to Maretta and Toni, for just being there.

Prologue

18:27 Alpha. Republic of the Congo.
Sunday, September 21

The doctor's head sagged sideways. His eyes glazed into a fixed stare behind his protective goggles, and blood dribbled slowly down from the corner of his mouth, soaking into the white surgical mask bunched beneath his chin.

Sarah Burdett wriggled out of the coffin-size hole in the floor and scrambled frantically over the packed red dirt to where the doctor lay slumped against the leg of his autopsy bench.

She grabbed his shoulders. "Dr. Regnaud!" she whispered, her breath hot and damp under her own mask, sweat trickling down between her breasts. She tried to move him, to get a sense of his injuries, but as she did, his body flopped back onto the dirt and she caught sight of the dark crimson stain blossoming out over the fabric of his lab coat. Her breath caught sharply in her throat.

With shaking fingers she ripped off the clumsy plastic bags that covered the surgical gloves on her hands. There were no neoprene or rubber gloves in the makeshift clinic, no proper bio-safety gear. They'd had to make do with what they had. "Doctor…" She felt his wrist through her latex gloves. Nothing.

She yanked at his mask, searching for the carotid arteries at his neck, praying to find the faint beat of a pulse under her gloved fingertips. There was none.

Her heart plummeted. Dr. Guy Regnaud, a brilliant, kind, generous, warm-hearted man…was dead.

She was alone.

The soldiers had killed everyone. They'd stormed the compound, slain the nurses, the two nuns, the priest, even the patients. And they'd taken the seven autopsied bodies before dousing the palm-thatched roofs in petroleum and torching the mission compound.

Sarah lifted the doctor's goggles up onto his head with trembling hands, and looked into the fixed stare of his blue eyes. Even in death they seemed to drill into hers, driving home the urgency of the mission he'd handed her just seconds before the men had stormed the medical hut and shot him dead.

"Whatever happens, Sarah, get these samples to the CDC," Dr. Regnaud had whispered as he'd shoved her and a sealed bio-hazard container into a hole in the floor of the baked-mud hut. *"And trust no one. This is the Congo. Everyone has a price."* He'd concealed her tomb with a plank and a reed mat, while outside, gunfire peppered the compound and gut-wrenching screams sliced the air. Then the soldiers had burst in….

Tears welled in her eyes. Dr. Regnaud had saved her life, and it had cost him his own. The trembling in her hands intensified, shuddering uncontrollably through her entire body. Her protective goggles misted with tears and body heat. She fisted her hands against the fear. If she lost control now, she'd be as good as dead.

As she tried to focus, she slowly became aware of thick smoke billowing from the thatched roofs of the adjoining buildings. The air was growing black and bitter as the choking haze filled the clearing and hung low in the thick equatorial heat. Flames crackled louder, closer, brighter, engulfing the compound. The sound was so close…. With a dull jolt of panic she realized the roof of the hut she was in was also on fire. But she couldn't move. She felt dazed. Time stretched, slowed, warped. She couldn't begin to comprehend what was happening. Why had soldiers with assault rifles stormed out of the jungle in hazmat suits? Why had they taken the autopsied bodies?

"This is big, Sarah. Nothing science has seen before…" She latched on to Dr. Regnaud's words. For some reason, she alone had been spared death. She had to hold on to that. She had a duty now. She had to somehow get those biological samples to the Centers for Disease Control in Atlanta. She would not—*could not*—let the doctor down.

She made a quick sign of the cross over Dr. Regnaud's body, gently closed his eyes and then scrambled on her hands and knees toward the radio on the desk near the door.

She had no idea how to use it. How could she have been so stupid, so naive not to learn how to do this simple thing? She tried to tell herself she would've learned in a few more days. But the villagers had begun to arrive with symptoms of the horrific disease, and chaos had erupted. She hadn't had the luxury of time to even begin to understand this bizarre jungle environment, let alone figure out how to use the darn radio.

She fiddled with the dials and buttons, trying to recall what she'd seen Dr. Regnaud doing. Static crackled. Her pulse leaped. Her heart hammered.

"Mayday! Mayday!" Sarah yelled into the transceiver. Did people even say that anymore? Was it only for ships at sea? Or planes? Or old movies? *"Mayday! Help! Help! 9-1-1—"* Oh God, she was panicking again. This was Africa. They didn't know about 9-1-1 here. She cleared her throat, wiped the sweat from her forehead with the back of her sleeve, tried to get hold of herself. The smoke was scorching her nasal passages even through her mask. "This…this is Sarah Burdett. Emergency. Can anybody hear me? I'm a nurse from Ishonga clinic…northeast of Ouesso near the Oyambo River. Unidentified deadly virus…we've been attacked. Soldiers—"

A chunk of burning thatch crashed through the roof and exploded onto the floor in a shower of orange sparks. Acrid smoke instantly engulfed the room. Panic gripped her. *"Help me! Please, oh God, someone help me!"* The fire leaped to a stack of papers and crackled through a wicker basket. She dropped the handset, leaving it dangling by a wire from the desk. She had to get out or she'd be as dead as the rest of them.

Trying to stay beneath the pall of suffocating smoke, Sarah groped her way to an overturned metal cabinet. She'd seen a flashlight in there. She wildly fingered the dirt floor, searching the scattered contents of the drawers. She found the flashlight, stuffed it deep into a pocket under her plastic apron. She found another drawer, groped around inside, felt the doctor's handgun, jammed it into her other pocket. The soldiers had ransacked the room, but hadn't taken a thing, not even the gun. Whatever they'd been looking for, they hadn't found.

They had to be searching for the tissue samples in the bio-hazard container.

She crawled across the dirt floor, reached into the hole,

grasped the handle of the aluminum canister and yanked it free. Clutching her deadly package, Sarah stumbled blindly through the hut, out the door.

She froze in her tracks.

Blackened skeletons of charred wood and the shocking smell of burning human flesh seared into her brain. The wooden roof of the tiny clinic church burned fiercely, shooting a shower of orange stars into the night sky. She swayed on her feet as her vision blurred.

Move, Sarah. Do this for them. You owe them this much.

Gripping the container, she forced one foot in front of the other, woodenly making her way toward the periphery of the clearing, toward the living, breathing, inhospitable jungle. Her sneakers were still encased in plastic bags tied at her ankles, her hair still tucked into a cotton head covering, her protective apron still smeared with the doctor's blood.

She was only vaguely aware that her path was lit by burning huts, that night had fallen, fast and complete, around six o'clock, as it did every day so near the equator.

Twelve hours of blackness loomed ahead of her. And with it came sheer, sickening terror.

She was truly alone.

Chapter 1

Hunter McBride floated silently through the thick air, the nylon chute above him a dark blot against the star-spattered heavens.

As he descended, the sounds of the rain forest swelled to a soft chorus below him. He could hear the shrill chirp of crickets, the hollow drumming of chimps hitting buttress roots of trees as they hunted in the predawn. Moist heat and the rich scent of fecund growth wafted up on soft currents of air as the jungle itself seemed to exhale, alive and hungry and waiting below.

His nostrils flared sharply at the familiar scent of primordial life. Somewhere down there was the American nurse, Sarah Burdett.

And a deadly pathogen.

His job was clear. Find the nurse, dead or alive. Locate the pathogen and get it back to the Force du Sable base on São Diogo Island off the coast of Angola, where a level 4 biosafety lab was being set up to identify it. And he had to do it quickly, because the clock was ticking down on a global threat of almost incomprehensible proportions. Failure at any stage of this mission would trigger a series of events that could topple the U.S. government, bring death to millions and end democracy as the world knew it.

The Force du Sable—a highly secretive and deadly efficient private military company that Hunter had helped found—was all that stood between the status quo and a grave new world order. And they had until midnight on October 13—just twenty-one days from now—to complete what, until they'd intercepted the nurse's distress call, had appeared to be a mission impossible.

He double-checked his GPS coordinates and guided his chute toward the Ishonga clinic clearing, skimming over spiked raffia palms and towering Bombax giants that punched up through the forest canopy. The FDS knew the pathogen was being tested somewhere in central Africa, but they hadn't been able to pinpoint where. The nurse's Mayday had changed that. Now they had a location, and possibly even a witness—*if* the nurse was still alive.

Hunter landed with a soft thud on the packed dirt along the outskirts of the compound. He adjusted his night vision gear and quickly gathered his chute. He removed his combat pack, extracted a respirator, positioned it carefully over his nose and mouth and checked the hose connections. From the intel they'd received, the pathogen was not likely airborne, but they weren't sure. They knew only that it was one hundred percent fatal.

He checked his watch and pulled neoprene gloves over his hands. Almost immediately the extra gear peaked his core temperature, and perspiration dampened his torso. The humidity in this region didn't allow a body to cool itself. But Hunter knew how to handle the heat. Guerrilla warfare in tropical climates was his area of expertise.

He made his way toward the charred, skeletal ruins of the clinic buildings, where wisps of smoke still trailed up from hot spots. Burned corpses were scattered across the hardened earth between gutted buildings, the bodies twisted into shapes made all the more grotesque by the eerie gray-green monotones of his night scopes.

Hunter hunkered down next to one corpse, then another. He noted with detached interest that the bodies were untouched by machetes. These people had been shot and then burned—*not* the usual practice of local rebels. The victims had been massacred by someone else, for some reason other than civil war or tribal conflict.

He worked his way methodically through the compound, looking for signs of life, for clues, for the nurse. He found the burned-out radio in what appeared to be an operating room, and stilled. This must have been where she'd sent out her Mayday call. The FDS had traced her immediately to the Aid Africa organization, which had provided her electronic file instantly. Sarah Burdett, 28, divorced, a pediatric nurse from Seattle, had been the lone American stationed at Aid Africa's Ishonga clinic. She'd signed on with the nongovernmental organization only three months ago and had arrived in the Congo exactly two weeks ago. She was a complete neophyte in some of the most hostile terrain known to man.

The digitized image of Sarah Burdett suddenly sifted into Hunter's brain, and for a second all he could see were her soft brown eyes gazing down from the LCD screen in the situation room. Warm eyes. Innocent eyes. His jaw tightened.

That woman was *not* equipped to deal with whatever had happened here.

He quickly scanned the rest of the room. Broken vials and medical equipment were scattered everywhere. A metal cabinet had been toppled and the door of a generator-operated fridge hung on its hinges. Hunter noticed a hole had been dug in the dirt floor, a plank and a bunched-up rug pushed to the side. Had she hidden in there while her colleagues were massacred within earshot? Where was she now?

Hunter found more bodies in what must have been a hospital ward, judging by the wire beds and smoldering mattresses. The bastards had even killed the patients.

He crouched down and studied the victims. They were not likely to be harboring the disease. If the pathogen had indeed found its way into the general population and to this clinic, the soldiers would have gone to great lengths to remove the infected bodies. They'd have wanted to leave no trace of the pathogen's existence. He suspected that was the reason behind this attack.

He needed to find the nurse. She alone held answers that could help save the U.S. president and his nation.

Hunter picked his way to the outer buildings of the compound. In all, the fire had been swift and superficial, fueled by an accelerant, probably petroleum. Parts of one building on the east end had barely even burned. It looked like a storage shed.

He made his way over to the structure, pushed aside a fallen rafter, and poked at the blackened edges of a packing crate with the barrel of his AK-47. The charred container fell open in a cloud of soot that cleared to reveal tins of baby formula.

Hunter stared at the cans. The cherubic face of an infant on the labels smiled happily back at him in ghostly green night-vision hues. His throat tightened. He shut his eyes, and for a brief instant lost the rhythm of breathing through his respirator. It shocked him instantly. His eyes flashed open and he abruptly turned his back on the tins, on the smiling babies.

Keep your cool, buddy. Stay focused. Locate the critical personality. Extract the package. He'd done it a hundred times. It should be no different now.

So why had soft brown eyes and an infant's face suddenly rattled him? He drew a breath in slowly, willing his body to calm. He didn't want to think about why. He didn't want to recall the unborn child in his dark past. He didn't want to think about what the woman he'd once loved with all his heart had done. He had no intention of going anywhere near those ancient memories. They belonged to another man, the man he used to be. He checked his watch again. He needed to keep moving. The sun would rise in less than three hours.

He quickly broadened his search to the perimeter of the compound, and almost immediately spotted something small and white lying on the ground along the edge of the thick jungle fringe. He crouched down, lifted it with the muzzle of his gun. It was a surgical mask. A pair of protective goggles and bloody latex gloves lay next to it.

He studied the ground carefully. He could make out faint scuff marks in the packed earth, small footprints strangely blurred along the edges, as if the shoes were covered with something. His eyes followed the odd trail. They led to a break in the vegetation up ahead, a path.

Hunter skirted along the forest fringe, following the tracks to the path entrance. He dropped to his haunches. Someone else had been here. Several sets of heavy military boot prints virtually obliterated the smaller sets of fuzzy ones. He studied the new tracks, the crushed vegetation, and he saw something else in the dirt. He lifted it carefully with his fingers, sniffed. A hand-rolled cigarette.

He looked up.

If these smaller prints belonged to Sarah Burdett, she was being followed by at least three men. And they weren't far behind her.

04:58 Alpha. Congo.
Monday, September 22

She was drenched in perspiration. Her heart hammered so hard she could barely breathe. She couldn't go on. She had to rest, hide somewhere.

Sarah groped blindly at the dank soil as she crawled through the foliage, and felt something hard and smooth under her fingers. Roots. Using them to feel her way toward the base of a monstrous Bombax tree, she maneuvered herself into a sitting position and pressed her back deep into a crevice formed by the giant buttress roots. She dragged the biohazard container close to her feet and tried to remain still, but she was still shaking uncontrollably.

She'd been moving as fast as she possibly could for what seemed like hours, stumbling wildly down a crude forest path, guided only by the tiny halo of her flashlight. She'd heard men coming after her, yelling. And then she'd tripped and fallen onto damp ground and lost the flashlight. She'd crawled off the path, into heavy primary jungle where there seemed to be less undergrowth to hamper her movements. She'd kept going, blindly fumbling through the darkness, dragging the heavy container behind her, stopping only to listen for the soldiers. They must have heard her distress call and come back for her. She had no doubt they would kill her if they found her.

All around her she could hear sounds of terrifying, unidentified things, but the shouts of the soldiers seemed to have faded. She must have lost them by leaving the main path.

Her breathing began to slow a little, but with the momentary respite came a sinking sense of utter despair.

How in heavens was she even supposed to get out of this jungle, let alone get this container all the way to Atlanta?

Perhaps she could get it to a U.S. embassy. But the American embassy in Brazzaville was closed because of violence in the capital, the staff operating out of the embassy in Kinshasa for safety reasons. Even if she managed to get as far south as Brazzaville, she'd still have to take a ferry over the Congo River to Kinshasa in the neighboring Democratic Republic of the Congo. And even if the unreliable ferry service was running, she still didn't have the Brazzaville exit permits she'd need to get out of the country, *or* a visa for entry into Congo-Kinshasa…or the money she'd need for bribes to get the necessary travel papers.

She didn't even have a passport now.

The U.S. State Department warnings began to play through her head. *Travel to these regions is not recommended…. Night travel outside of towns and cities should be avoided….* She looked up into the impenetrable night that surrounded her. Who was she kidding? She couldn't even begin to think of getting through this *jungle.* She didn't know a damn thing about surviving in it. She had no compass. No map. *Nothing.* She'd been flown into this darkest heart of Africa by chopper and dumped into a patch of dense equatorial jungle barely known to Western man. It was an area still steeped in Marxist dogma, tribal sorcery and civil violence.

What *had* she been thinking even coming here? She didn't know anything about Africa, or aid work. She was a pediatric nurse who lived in civilized Seattle, a misty and *cool* city with paved streets, electricity and water you didn't have to boil before drinking. A city where leaves were turning gold and days were getting short and crisp. She should be there now. She should be shopping in a mall, wearing lipstick and a coat, buying something nice for dinner…and eating chocolate. Tears welled in her eyes.

Don't delude yourself, Sarah. You know exactly why you came here.

She'd come to escape that old life. She was trying to piece herself together after a bitter and humiliating public divorce. She was trying to hide from the echoes of an emotional nightmare she'd embarrassingly endured for years at the hands of her ex, trying to come to terms with the reality that she'd never have what she'd always wanted—children of her own, a loving husband, a big family, a white picket fence…the whole shebang. Her dreams had been shattered and she'd gotten lost somewhere back in that old world. So she'd run away, to Africa, to find some *real* purpose in her life, to validate herself as a worthwhile human being. To do some good for people who actually needed her…

Sarah blinked back hot tears. Now she was more alone, more blind, more lost than ever—not just emotionally, but physically. Coming to the Congo had been the boldest move she'd ever made, and it had turned out to be a terrible mistake. She'd never find her way back now, not unless God dropped some angel from the sky….

A soft sound jerked her back to her senses.

Sarah held her breath.

Then she heard it again, a quiet crack of twigs, barely distinguishable from the other noises. Her heart leaped straight back up into her throat and hammered hard. She peered into the solid blackness, trying to identify the source, but she couldn't see a thing. And she couldn't run.

She was trapped.

She pressed her back deeper into the roots of the Bombax

and slid her hand into her pocket. Quietly, carefully, she drew out the gun. She grasped the handle with both hands, found the trigger, curled her finger around it and aimed blindly into the darkness with shaking hands, praying she wouldn't have to use it. She'd never fired a gun before.

She stayed like that for what seemed like forever. Sweat trickled over her body as she listened for the noise. She'd never been more petrified in her life. The perspiration that soaked her skin began to cool, and she started to shiver violently. Something crawled slowly up her neck—some kind of caterpillar. She could feel hundreds of little hairy legs. She gritted her teeth, tried desperately to hold still as the worm inched up toward her hairline. But suddenly it stung like all hell. Sarah stifled a scream and flicked it off with her hand.

The movement cost her. Something rustled sharply in the leaves to her right. She swung the gun toward the source of the sound.

Then she heard it again.

She scrunched her eyes tight and squeezed the trigger. Sound cracked her eardrums and shrieks ripped through the jungle canopy as monkeys high in the trees scattered. Sarah screamed in reflex.

A huge hand grabbed her wrists, so tightly that she dropped the gun. She opened her mouth to scream again, but another hand clamped down hard over her jaw. She choked in fright. She felt her eyes bulge in terror, but she was blind in the blackness. All she could do was feel him. And her attacker was definitely male. He was down on the ground beside her, leaning his body into hers, his weight forcing her painfully against the roots. She could taste the saltiness of his palm pressed against her lips, feel the power and strength in his limbs. He was huge, solid like iron. And she was one dead woman. She was certain of it.

"You could kill someone with that gun," he whispered, his voice low and warm in her ear.

Her heart kicked into her throat. He wasn't one of the soldiers. They'd been yelling in French and Lingala. This man spoke to her in English.

She felt his hot breath against her ear again. "Shh, it's okay, I'm not going to hurt you."

She whimpered slightly.

He waited, his hand still pressed firmly over her mouth. "You gonna be quiet?" he murmured, his lips so close to her ear she could feel them brush against her lobe.

She nodded.

He slowly removed his hand from her mouth, grasped her chin between powerful fingers and turned her face toward his. But she could see nothing. She could only sense the size of him, feel his breath on her lips.

"Sarah Burdett?"

He knew her name! She choked back a hysterical sob. A maelstrom of emotions swamped her exhausted brain. Somehow, in this alien place, it mattered incredibly that someone knew her name.

"My name is Hunter McBride," he said softly. "I'm here to take you home, Sarah." He grasped her hands in his and coaxed her gently to her feet. She wobbled as she tried to stand.

"Can you move? Are you hurt?"

She didn't know. She'd been running on autopilot. She hadn't even begun to think about the pain in her body. Her neck was burning like fire. Her face was cut. Her back, near her left shoulder blade, ached deeply. Her knees and shins stung. Every nerve ending in her body was raw.

"Sarah, can you hear me? Are you hurt anywhere?"

She could detect a soft Irish brogue in his hushed words. *Irish.* Like her grandmother. And thinking of her gran made her think of home, of Seattle, of cool mist and rain, of comfort and the ocean and music....

Her knees sagged under her.

05:07 Alpha. Venturion Tower, Manhattan.
Monday, September 22

He checked his watch. Just after eleven on Sunday night. The sun would be rising in the Congo in precisely one hour. He pushed his chair away from his desk and stalked over to windows that yawned up from the polished mahogany floor. Hands behind his back, he stared out over the glittering skyline of his city, its lights like diamonds scattered over velvet. He liked to think of it as his. He'd been born here in New York City, grown up here. He'd conceived and constructed his global empire from here. It was from here that he and his fraternity had helped shape senators, congressmen, presidents and kings...and topple them.

He smiled ruefully. Usually the view contented him. But he was edgy tonight, unusually so. What they were putting into action now went way beyond the realm of the usual. It was bold. Unprecedented. And it had been decades in the making.

Only President John Elliot stood in their way now. The man's resilience had surprised them all and had necessitated a dramatic change in plans.

And there was another glitch. A small one, true, but he didn't tolerate glitches, no matter the size. Somehow the pathogen had infected villagers near Ouesso. Villagers who were *not* part of the trials, who were not supposed to be part of the warning sent to President Elliot. Villagers who'd ended up dying at the Ishonga clinic—a clinic that just *happened* to house Guy Regnaud, one of the world's most renowned epidemiologists.

Of all the damn luck.

He shoved his hands deep into the pockets of his crisply tailored pants. He'd ordered the local militia on his payroll to immediately eliminate every damn living thing at that clinic and to remove all evidence of the infected corpses and the disease. But he'd just gotten word that a nurse had managed to get out a distress call before escaping. Now she was missing. So were the samples that Dr. Regnaud had taken from the autopsied patients.

He told himself it was nothing. If the militia didn't kill her, the jungle would. And even if by some bizarre twist of fate she got out of that godforsaken place, it would take days, weeks, months even, before anyone in the U.S. even began to realize the implications of what she'd seen, or what was in that bio-hazard container, if at all. And by then it would be too late.

She was harmless, he told himself. Nothing would stop them now.

Nothing could.

Chapter 2

05:10 Alpha. Congo.
Monday, September 22

Hunter grasped Sarah's shoulders and steadied her on her feet, surprised at how slight—how right—she felt in his hands. He looked into her face. She was clearly terrified, her eyes huge and vulnerable. His chest tightened. She looked even younger than she had in the digital photo he'd seen. "Sarah, how badly are you hurt? Can you move?"

Her eyes flickered as she searched the dark for his face. "I…I think so."

He began a quick assessment of her condition. Her face was cut and bleeding just below her left cheekbone. A torn piece of fabric covered part of her hair; the rest escaped in a wild tangle of curls. She wore a ripped plastic apron over a long-sleeved blouse and a skirt. The apron was smeared with blood. She had thin cotton pants under her skirt. They were shredded, bloodied and muddy at her knees and shins. Ripped plastic bags covered her runners. It looked as if she'd been wearing at least two bags over each shoe. That explained the odd footprints he'd found.

Hunter recalled the surgical mask, goggles and gloves he'd seen lying at the edge of the clearing. Sarah Burdett had been wearing makeshift biohazard clothing. She'd obviously adapted whatever had been available at the compound. She must have been working with the infected patients before the attack.

An odd spasm shuddered down his spine. This young nurse and her colleagues had been working to save lives when those lives had been brutally taken. She was a healer. And he knew too well how the sight of pointless death cut to the quick of a soul born to heal.

Hunter steeled his jaw. Sarah Burdett had been through hell and back tonight, and by some absurd twist of fate she'd survived. But she was far from out of the woods, and his job was not to coddle her. Now that he'd found her alive, his job was to extricate her, and more importantly, extricate the pathogen he suspected was in the biohazard container at her feet.

"Sarah," he whispered against her ear, the contact sending a frisson over his skin, "can you tell me what's in the container?"

Her eyes flicked wildly around as if looking for escape.

His heart kicked against his ribs. "Tell me *exactly* what's in there."

"T-tissue, fluid, brain samples…from…" Her voice wavered and she began to tremble again.

He steadied her shoulders firmly. "Focus, Sarah. *Who* are the tissue samples from?"

"From seven villagers near Ouesso. They…they presented at the clinic with symptoms we didn't recognize. It…it, oh, God…"

She took a deep breath. "They all died. It was horrible, so violent. They began to attack themselves, us, anything that moved."

Hunter's pulse kicked up another notch. "Where are the bodies now?"

"They took them. Just the autopsied ones." A dry sob racked her petite frame. "They killed, burned everyone else—the patients, nurses, priest, even…Doc…Dr. Regnaud. He…he saved my life."

Hunter's grip tightened on her shoulders. "*Who* took the bodies?"

"Soldiers. They had automatic rifles…and were wearing hazmat suits."

Hunter clenched his jaw. This was exactly what they'd been looking for! This woman had just shaved days off their mission. He had to get her and the samples to a clearing where he could get decent satellite reception and where they could bring in a helicopter. He could patch up her injuries while they waited for evacuation. She could get a thorough exam at the FDS clinic on São Diogo.

"Sarah, we need to move—"

She jerked away from him suddenly. "Who *are* you?"

"Later. Right now we move, fast."

She backed away, shaking her head, clutching the canister tightly against her body.

Frustration nipped at him. "Sarah, there were at least three men tracking you before you left the path. I've taken care of them, but their bodies will be found by daybreak, and that's in exactly one hour. There'll—"

Her eyes went wide. "You *killed* them?"

Frustration snapped harder at Hunter. He did not have time for this. "I did what was necessary to keep you alive, Sarah. And there'll be more coming after them. Now if you want to live, you'd better move. Come—" He reached for the handle of the biohazard container.

"*No!*" she shrieked, yanking it away from him. "That's mine! I've got to get it to the CDC!"

Monkeys screeched and scattered high in the canopy above them. A dead giveaway.

"Damn it, Sarah!" Hunter hissed, seizing her upper arm. He dug his fingers hard into her flesh, jerked her body up against his and leaned close to her frightened face. He dropped his tone to a low growl. "Keep your voice down unless you want to die. Got it?"

She went dead still in his arms.

Guilt stabbed his chest. He softened his tone slightly. "I know you've been through hell, and I know you're not thinking straight, but you've *got* to trust me. Your life depends on it. Am I getting through to you?"

She clenched her jaw, said nothing.

Exasperation peaked in him. "Look, we have to get that container to a level 4 lab and get the contents identified ASAP. *That* is why I'm here and that is why you're going to do *exactly* what I say."

He moved his mouth so close to her ear he could feel the soft fuzz of her lobe against his bottom lip, and again a tinge of awareness caught him by surprise. "And that means no questions, no second-guessing, or you'll get us *both* killed. Do you understand me?"

She choked as if she was going to throw up. Hunter's heart twisted sharply in his chest. But he swallowed the discomfort. This was the only way to get through to her, to get her out alive. "Tell me you understand me, Sarah. I want to hear you say it."

Her eyes pooled with moisture but her jaw remained tight. "Yes," she said softly through clenched teeth. "Yes, I understand."

"Good." He prised the container from her fingers as he spoke. "Now here's the deal. I have night vision gear, you don't. I can see, you can't. I need you to hook your hand into my belt webbing here...." He grabbed her hand, guided it to his back, tucked her fingers into his belt. "I'll lead. I'll be your eyes. You just hang on and try to keep up. We move till daybreak, then we take cover and wait for the helevac."

He began to edge forward, but she resisted immediately. "Where are we going?"

He drew a breath in slowly, straining for patience. "The Shilongwe River, where we can get the chopper in."

"I...I was going to the Oyambo River," she protested. "I was going to—to the village there, to get help."

"So was your tail," he snapped. "You ready now?"

She made a faint little sound he took as an affirmative. "Stay directly behind me. Don't want to connect you with a back-swing if I need to use the machete to clear a path, understand?"

He took her silence as acquiescence, and he started to move. She stumbled instantly, dragging down hard on his belt, but righted herself just as quickly. Hunter moved slowly at first, picking the easiest route across small gullies, around ferns and raised roots on the forest floor. Sarah managed to find an awkward if staggering gait behind him, and he took it as a sign to increase the pace. They moved like that for the better part of half an hour before the earth turned boggy and began to suck and drag at their feet.

He felt Sarah begin to falter again, and then she stumbled, her hand slipping free of his belt. Hunter reached behind him, snatched her wrist and caught her. He tucked her hand back into his belt—and this time registered how slender and soft her fingers were, how fine-boned her wrist. It felt...*like Kathleen's hand.*

The thought exploded like shrapnel through Hunter, so sharp he stumbled.

He stopped, caught his breath, and killed the memory instantly. But the fact it had even entered his head rocked him to the core.

He blew out a long, slow breath as he tried to focus. He thought he'd totally terminated the memories. The past. The blackness. Himself. But now…now the murdered memories were sifting up like haunting mists from a decaying swamp, the dread rising inside him, making him feel things again. What in hell was wrong with him?

Hunter gritted his teeth. There was no freaking way he was going to start seeing ghosts in this forest. Not after so many years. Not after coming this far. This hadn't happened to him on any other mission. So why this one?

Deliver the package and move on. Another job. Another day.

He picked up the pace, knowing he was going too fast for her, yet unable to slow himself down.

Sarah could barely keep her balance as her rescuer suddenly upped the pace, and she was so out of breath she could hardly speak, let alone find some kind of logical order to the fragmented images and questions slamming through her brain. But she had to ask. "Why…are they after my container?"

"Later. Save your breath." His words were clipped.

"Who…will send a helicopter?"

"Friends. Keep moving."

His dismissive tone frustrated her. And she couldn't keep up at this pace. But she was terrified of protesting, of letting go, of irritating him to a point that he'd take her container and just leave her in the jungle to die. She had no idea who he was or who he worked for, and she didn't trust him any more than those murderous soldiers back at the compound. But right now he was her only salvation, her lifeline through the dark. She *had* to hang on.

The forest undergrowth grew thicker. Sarah could literally sense the tangle of vegetation knitting itself around her, creeping ominously closer. She stumbled again and again. Thorns and twigs and leaves tore at her clothes, scraped her skin. Tears of sheer exhaustion began to stream down her face. "Could…could you slow…down a little? I—"

"Keep moving!"

Her toe hooked under a knot of vines, and this time she wasn't able to brace herself. Her hand wrenched free from his belt and she went down hard and fast. Her chest slammed into the ground and air crunched from her lungs in a violent whoosh. Sparks of pain radiated through her torso, and for a terrifying instant, she couldn't breathe, or even move.

She felt him drop instantly to her side, felt his hands on her, easing her up into a sitting position. She gasped wildly for breath, but her lungs wouldn't open up.

"Easy, easy, Sarah. You're winded. Don't panic, just relax." His voice was calm, strong, quiet. He gathered her to his chest and gently rubbed her back as she struggled to breathe, until her lungs could take in air again, until the acute panic began to ebb and she realized she was going to be okay.

She expected him to release her then, but he didn't. He fell silent and continued to hold her against his body, a brooding, encompassing presence in the dark. She could feel the rough hair on his forearms and the hair at the base of his neck where his shirt was open. She could smell his masculine scent amid the rich layers of jungle smells. And she could sense him studying her. It made her feel naked, yet in a strange way, she felt a sense of refuge in his arms, a basic human comfort.

He placed a callused palm against her cheek, a confident, tangible strength transferring through his touch, as if the man was magically infusing her with the calm to do what she needed to do. "Are you okay?"

There was something about his voice, something in his touch

that made her want to believe she was. "Yes," she whispered. "Yes, I—I think I'm okay."

But the tears trailing furiously down her face must have betrayed her. He brushed them away with his thumb. The gesture made her heart twist and her tears flowed all the harder. Absurdly, she just wanted to stay in his arms. She wanted to bury her face against his chest, drink in his masculine scent, fold herself into his embrace.

"You've made it farther than most people could, Sarah," he whispered against her cheek. "You're strong, and you're going to be just fine as long as you hang in here with me for another twenty minutes or so. It'll be light by then. We should be in the clearing, alongside the Shilongwe. And once we're there, we can get you cleaned and patched up. Here…"

She felt something being pushed up against her lips—the mouth of a canteen. He cupped his hand around the back of her head and tilted the canteen toward her. Water trickled over her lips and down her chin and neck. Sarah gulped at it, but he pulled it away before she'd had enough. She groped in the dark for more.

"Not so fast," he said softly. "Need to save some for later. Ready now?"

She wiped her wrist over her mouth and nodded, feeling strangely refueled by his touch, by the fact that he actually seemed to care. As much as he terrified her, Sarah needed this man on a very basic human level.

He helped her to her feet. "The going will get a bit rougher from here, but not for long. Stay right behind me, clear of the machete." He took her hand and once again guided it around his back, hooked it carefully into his belt.

She heard the sickening sound of a blade being unsheathed, then the first two rapacious strokes as metal met vegetation. He began to move forward again, pulling her along, more slowly now. She edged after him, feet tentatively testing ground before transferring weight.

Gradually, gray shapes and shadows began to emerge from the cloak of pure blackness as dawn broke somewhere beyond the forest canopy. Fresh energy surged through Sarah. She'd made it through the night! She was going to live to see another day.

But almost instantly her flare of excitement was quashed as the indistinct shadows morphed into monstrous, prehistoric-looking trunks, knotted vines curling up them, nests of vegetation growing in the forks of their branches. Tangled lianas looped down from the canopy, some of them as thick as her wrist, some with inch-long thorns. Stems and leaves and vines all mixed so chaotically in the eerie dawn light that she couldn't tell where one plant ended and another began, what was growing up or what was growing down. There was absolutely no sense of order. And all around her, heat and sound began to swell. Birds, monkeys, other unidentifiable creatures, all rising to a riotous, raucous cacophony that tore at her ragged nerves. Sarah's heart began to pound even harder.

Being blind to what was around her had been better than actually seeing it all. Seeing made her predicament too stark, too real. This wasn't some horrendous dream from which she could waken. She was stepping out of the blackness into a living nightmare.

And as more light began to filter down through the canopy, the man in front of her took an even more formidable form than she'd imagined in the dark. He was well over six feet tall, with an unruly mess of pitch-black hair. He was wearing a combat vest, camouflage gear and black army boots. He had a military pack on his back and an assault rifle slung across his shoulders. It was the same kind of gun she'd seen both soldiers and rebels carrying since she'd arrived in the Congo. Yet despite his military gear, she could see no official markings on his clothing. Whoever he was, she'd bet her life he did not belong to any conventional army. And judging by the hypnotic swipe of his machete, the way he never lost the rhythm or power of his stroke, she'd also bet that he'd done this kind of thing many, many times before.

It made her hunger for a look at the face that went with the body, with the voice, with the powerful tenderness in his touch—the contradiction that was this man.

Then, so suddenly it shocked her, they broke out of the forest into a clearing. Sarah jerked to a stop, instantly blinded by light. She scrunched her eyes tight against the white pain, feeling as disoriented as a mole that had just been spat out of moist, black ground.

"Your eyes got accustomed to the dark," he said. "Give them time to adjust."

She stilled.

This time there was no harsh whisper or growl from his lips. The man had the languid and mellifluous bass tones of a late-night Irish DJ. Sarah became even more desperate to see him. She lifted both hands to shield her brow and angled her head, squinted one eye open. Then the other.

Her heart stumbled. She blinked once, twice.

And could only stare.

Chapter 3

Black camouflage paint covered his face, making the whites of his eyes leap out in contrast. He was studying her with those eyes in a relaxed, almost lazy fashion. His mouth, sensually sculpted, was absolutely devoid of expression as he appraised her.

A predator, that's what he was, acutely aware of everything going on around him. She didn't doubt for an instant that he could strike to kill in the blink of an eye.

Sarah swallowed the odd mix of awe, fear and admiration rising in her throat. She felt suddenly more powerless in front of this elemental male than she had in the deep jungle night.

He raised his machete and sheathed it slowly behind his

back, his eyes never breaking contact with hers. She had a sense she was being weighed, judged.

He reached for the canteen hanging at his hip, twisted off the cap, held the water bottle out to her, and smiled. The sudden whiteness of his teeth against the camouflage paint was predacious.

Sarah cringed instinctively toward the protection of the jungle foliage. A flock of birds scattered from the reeds along the river and fluttered squawking into the sky, exposing the red underside of their fanned tails. The surreal flurry of color in her peripheral vision, the sudden brightness of daylight after twelve hours of blackness, was overwhelming her senses. She stared at the water bottle in his huge, tanned hand, aware of her thirst, yet unable to move.

"You okay?"

Her eyes lifted slowly, met his. *"Who are you?"*

He smiled again, more gently this time, and the sunlight caught his eyes. A distant part of her brain noted the color of them, an unusual blue, so dark it was almost indigo.

"Here…" He pushed the canteen toward her. "Have some water. You look like you need it."

She moved to take the canteen from his hands, but as she did, she caught sight of the huge hunting knife tucked into a leather casing strapped around his massive thigh. There was dried blood on the hilt, and on his pants. Lots. She froze, thinking of the three men who'd been following her…. Her eyes shot back up to his.

"They would have killed you, Sarah," he said softly. "If I hadn't taken their lives, they would have taken yours."

She shook her head, not wanting to think about what this man had done with that knife. For her. She didn't want to be responsible for death…for anyone's death. She believed in life, in protecting it at all cost. That's what had driven her to be a nurse, a caregiver. Hugging herself, she backed toward the wall of vegetation they'd just come through, as if it might offer refuge from stark reality. But Sarah knew it held only darkness and danger. There was no going back. She had no choice. She had to go forward. *With him.*

He took a step toward her, placed his hand against her neck. Sarah caught her breath. She could feel a latent power almost vibrating through him.

He curled his fingers around the back of her neck, placed his thumb under her jawbone, and tilted her face, forcing her to look back up into his eyes. She had no doubt he could snap her neck in an instant, yet his touch had a solid warmth that seemed to flow right into her, that somehow went beyond protective into the realm of darkly seductive. A shiver rippled through her body at the conflicting sensations generated by the contact.

"Sarah," he murmured. "I'm on your side. I'm going to get you home."

Home?

A hiccup jerked painfully in her chest as she tried to choke down a sob. Wasn't that why she'd come running to Africa? Because her idea of home had been utterly demolished by Josh, the cold, powerful man she'd once thought she'd loved with all her heart? Her ex-husband had crushed her world. He'd taken everything from her.

She had no home.

"Trust me, Sarah." Hunter gazed into her eyes. "If anyone can get you out of here, I will. I promise you that."

She wanted to tell him it was not possible. No one could get her home. Not in a way that mattered.

He pushed the canteen into her hands. "Now here, drink."

He wrapped her fingers around the bottle. "You need to stay hydrated. Take what you need—we'll be out of here soon. In the meantime, I'm going to head out into that clearing over there—" he pointed to a patch of grass that grew luminescent green and tall in the sunlight "—where I can get a decent satellite signal. I'm going to call for our helevac and then we can get you cleaned up while we wait for the chopper, okay?"

She nodded numbly.

He turned and made his way into the clearing—with her biohazard container. The long grass parted around his sleek, powerful form, his hair glinting blue-black in the sun.

"Trust me, Sarah."

Could she? She sank onto the trunk of a massive fallen tree and drank deeply from the water bottle as she studied him in the distance. He crouched down among the tall grass and took what looked like a stubby phone out of his combat vest, pulling a thick antenna out the top.

"Trust no one. This is the Congo. Everyone has a price." What was this man's price? What on earth had she gotten mixed up in? Her brain didn't want to think. Couldn't. She was too tired to even formulate the questions.

She set the canteen down on the log beside her and clasped her hand tightly around the small gold crucifix that nestled at the hollow of her throat, seeking comfort in the familiar shape. Her grandmother had given her the small cross for her fourteenth birthday, her first birthday after her mother died, and Sarah had worn it ever since. It grounded her, reminded her of the good things she'd had in life. Sarah clutched the keepsake, closed her eyes and lifted her face to the sun.

Then she heard Hunter's voice in the clearing. He was speaking in fluent French. Her eyes flared open. The soldiers who had attacked the compound had been yelling in French.

She listened more closely. The inflection and resonant intonation of his words were no different from the haunting sound of the locals. Her chest tightened. Was he allied to the soldiers who'd attacked the compound? She hadn't been able to see anything of them other than their black hazmat suits. Had he come after her because he'd known she had the pathogen? Was this all just a ploy to get her container? But then why hadn't he killed her back in jungle?

"Trust no one."

He signed off, pocketed his phone, looked sharply up in her direction. Something had changed in him. She could see it in his posture. Her mouth went dry.

He stood in a fluid movement, a gleaming panther rising out of the grass. And in that same liquid motion, he adjusted the sling of his assault rifle, swinging the weapon from his back to hang ready at his side. He picked up her biohazard container and stalked through the long grass toward her, until the shadow of his huge frame blotted out the sun that had warmed her face.

"Chopper will be here within the hour." His voice was gruff and there was a new razor-sharp glare in his eyes. He seemed somehow less human, and the change frightened her.

She shrank back. "Will you *please* tell me who you are, who you were talking to out there?"

He didn't answer. He grasped her arm, lifted her brusquely to her feet and moved her closer to the jungle fringe, his eyes scanning the far edges of the clearing as he moved.

"What is it?" she asked nervously.

"Stay close to the forest cover. We need to move down to those flat rocks at the river's edge, under that tree. We can clean and patch you up there while we wait for the helo."

Hunter escorted Sarah down to the water, every sense alert.

He scanned the far bank of the wide, sluggish river for the slightest signs of movement as they went. Jacques Sauvage at the FDS base had just informed him there'd been a coup in Brazzaville early this morning. Insurgents had stormed the president's residence before dawn. President Samwetwe was now missing, and all borders were shutting down. Sporadic fighting had already spread as far north as the Shilongwe. That meant rebels could be anywhere at this very minute. And it meant that he and Sarah were suddenly fair game from all sides of this war. They were running from not only the militia who had razed the Ishonga compound, but also from unidentified rebel cadres as well. They had to get out of the Congo, fast. The whole place was set to blow.

He sat Sarah down on a slab of rock near the brown waters of the Shilongwe and squinted toward the sky. The chopper would come in from the north, from Cameroon. There was a wide sandbank about twenty yards into the shallows. It would land there. If his guys made it into Congo airspace undetected, they should be here in about forty-five minutes.

That was already cutting it too close.

He turned his attention back to Sarah. She was watching him intently. Tears, dirt and blood streaked her cheeks, and her eyes were huge with fear. *Of him.* She didn't trust him. Who in hell could blame her? What horror had those big brown eyes seen?

Hunter felt an odd little spasm in his chest. He recognized it for what it was: anger. Protective anger. Anger at the people who'd done this to her. Because this woman was *not* equipped to handle the situation. She did not deserve this. How she'd managed to get this far was beyond him.

Then he saw what she was nervously fingering at the hollow of her throat—a small crucifix on a delicate gold chain. His jaw tightened and he stared at her fingers. In this merciless jungle, where you had to take life in order to live, where dark spirits and primal forces ruled, she was seeking the comfort and protection of her civilized God.

The sight forced him right up against the acid memories of his past. And for a fleeting moment his mind was touched by a sense of déjà vu, the distant sensation of icy mist trailing over his face on the night he'd fled Belfast—the night the police had come to arrest him for allegedly killing his fiancée. He shook off the poisonous memory. Why was he even thinking about this garbage? It was ancient history.

But he couldn't tear his eyes away from her hand...from her. She looked so out of place against the backdrop of tangled primordial forest. She didn't belong in this dog-eat-dog world. Her God wasn't going to protect her from this jungle. What on earth made Hunter think *he* could? Something swelled so sharply in his heart it hurt.

He clenched his teeth. He didn't want to feel these things, these protective urges. Not again. Not now. Not ever. That was not who Hunter McBride was anymore. That man had been dead and buried for fifteen long and bitter years.

"Are you going to tell me who you are now?"

For a nanosecond he wasn't sure who the hell he *was* anymore. He mentally shook himself and crouched down in front of her. "My name is Hunter McBride. I—"

"Are you one of them?"

"Them?"

"The militia. The soldiers who attacked the clinic were carrying the same weapon as you, were speaking the same language."

"Sarah, there's a reason everyone out here carries an AK. You can jam it with mud, water, whatever, and it'll still shoot straight without blowing up in your face. And the French…" He shifted slightly on his haunches, the sun hot on his back. "It's one of the country's official languages. My colleagues and I speak it, along with just about everyone else in this region."

"But you're not with the French—or Belgian—armed forces." It was an accusation, not a question. "Who *are* you with?"

Hunter's lips twitched. He hadn't expected the Spanish Inquisition. In spite of what she'd just been through, this woman still had spunk. "You're right, I'm not with the Belgian or French military, but I *am* French—"

"You sound Irish." She made it seem as though she almost wished he *were* Irish. And absurdly, it made a part of him want to say that he was. It made a part of him want to explain. He bit back the urge.

"I'm a citizen of France," he said bluntly. And then he cursed himself for saying it at all. It was none of her damn business where he came from, what passport he carried and why. And it wasn't his job to tell her. His job was to get her—and the pathogen—out. That was all.

"Look, I'm just going to give it to you straight. That canister contains a bioweapon that will be released over the three biggest cities in the United States in exactly twenty-one days. That's New York, Chicago and Los Angeles."

He could tell from the skeptical look in her eyes that she didn't believe him.

"We've been looking for that pathogen, Sarah. We knew it was being tested somewhere in central Africa, that unethical clinical trials were being conducted on innocent villagers, probably under the guise of a vaccine program. But we didn't know exactly where until we intercepted your call. It seems that those clinical trials went sideways and villagers outside the control groups were infected. They found their way to your clinic and died there. The soldiers were sent to cover it up."

She shook her head. "This can't be true. I…I don't believe you. I *can't*."

He shrugged. It wasn't his job to make her believe. He just had to make her cooperate.

Despair clouded her gaze. "Who…who would *do* such a thing?"

"We don't know. Yet. But our intelligence tells us there *is* an antidote. Once we identify this disease, we can begin to think about locating that antidote. That in turn could lead us to whoever is behind this, but we don't have much time."

She shook her head again, her eyes looking strangely distant. "Our patients died within days. Within twenty-four hours they all showed signs of advanced dementia. Then they lost coordination, reason, and became psychotic." She paused, her features growing tight. "They lashed out at anyone who tried to help them, scratching, biting like wild animals. Even at themselves, tearing their own flesh. It…was terrifying. We had to restrain them or I'm sure they would have killed us." Her eyes flashed up to his, desperation in them.

"What happened then, Sarah?" he asked, a little more gently.

"A painful and messy death. Lots of hemorrhaging. It was something Dr. Regnaud had never seen or heard of before in his life. And he is…was…a world-renowned epidemiological specialist, you know."

Hunter nodded. "I know. And this *is* the disease we've been looking for, Sarah." The FDS had seen film footage of the effects, footage sent to President Buchanan as a warning. He jerked his chin toward the canister. "That's a cryogenic container. How long have we got?"

"Dr. Regnaud preserved the samples with enough liquid

nitrogen to last maybe two weeks. He'd planned to fly the canister out on the next chopper." She looked at the biohazard container, then at him. "Hunter, if this gets released in the U.S.—"

"We can't let that happen, Sarah. We must do everything in our power to stop this, and you can help us."

A frown furrowed her dirt-smudged brow. "Us?"

"My team, the Force du Sable. We're a private military company based on the island of São Diogo off the northwest coast of Angola. We contract out to various countries and organizations. This time it's the president of the United States."

"You're *mercenaries?*"

"Right."

"I see." Her jaw tightened ever so slightly and a hint of disapproval shifted into her eyes. For some reason the change in her expression really bothered him. He opened his mouth to speak, to defend himself, his profession. Then he shut it abruptly. He didn't have to justify himself to this woman. To anyone. He didn't even know why the hell he even felt compelled to do so.

"I promised to get the container to the CDC in Atlanta." A note of defiance now laced her voice. "I *have* to get it to Atlanta."

"Can't use the CDC. Can't use anyone or any organization within the United States—they've all been compromised. It could trigger the biological attack. We have to use an outside source. There's a level 4 lab being set up at the FDS base on São Diogo. We're taking it there."

"I don't understand. Why would going to the CDC trigger the attack?"

Hunter pushed out a soft breath of frustration. In spite of the need for secrecy, he had to tell her what he could. She'd be more likely to cooperate if she understood the scope of this thing.

"The threat comes from a group *within* the U.S. An inordinately powerful cabal we believe is comprised mostly of Americans, some with very significant connections to the country's power structure. Until we know who they really are, we can't be sure who is connected to whom or what. If they are tipped off, if they get even a hint of the fact we now have their pathogen and are attempting to identify it, they will launch the attack immediately, and *that* is why we can't risk using the CDC."

Her eyes flickered. "I…I just can't imagine why Americans would kill their own people. What do they want?"

"We don't know," he lied.

"What about the soldiers who attacked the compound? How do they fit in?"

"Hired by the Cabal."

She narrowed her eyes. "You're a mercenary. I know men like you, Hunter. You work for whoever has the cash. How do I know you aren't working for this group, just like those soldiers back at the compound? Why should I trust *you?*"

"Because you don't have a choice, do you?" He leaned forward. "And there's one thing you'd better believe. If I *did* work for the Cabal, you'd have been dead hours ago."

Alarm flared in her eyes.

Guilt spiked in Hunter. The woman was in shock. She was doing her best to think straight, to protect herself, and here he was, taking offense. What in hell was wrong with him? It wasn't her fault mercs had a bad rep. And she was right—she had zero reason to trust him. But he didn't need her trust, just her cooperation. Yet an absurd part of him *wanted* her trust, wanted her approval.

He hadn't felt that in a long, long time. And it made him angry. With himself, and indirectly, inexplicably, with her.

He gritted his teeth, focused on reining in his emotion. He needed to keep his mind clear if he wanted to get her out of the

Congo alive. And that meant he had to get her wounds cleaned and patched up as soon as possible, because infection in this climate was a very real—and very deadly—risk.

He cleared his throat. "Come on. You need to rinse that dirt off in the river so I can get a good look at your cuts and sterilize them." He touched his fingers to the gash on her cheek. "And this here needs a butterfly suture or two."

She sat rock-still as he touched her face, her eyes wary, and in them he could read the beginnings of distaste, for *him,* for what he was.

And suddenly it cut him. It rankled beyond all reason. He'd just saved her life. She had no right to judge him like this. She didn't know a damn thing about him.

Hunter got to his feet. "Look, Sarah," he said coolly. "I don't need your trust. I don't need you to like me. All *you* need to know is that because of what I am, I have the goods to get you and that container out of this jungle. And yes, I'm getting paid to do it. I intend to get the job done."

"I'm…just a job," she said quietly.

"You got that right." And that's exactly how he was going to think of her from now on. No more dead memories. No more sappy feelings. He was going to get her into that chopper, deliver her safely to São Diogo. Mission over.

The others could take it from there.

She looked down at her hands in her lap and began to fiddle with her fingers. "Men like you really *can't* care, can you? It's always about the bottom line."

His brows shot up. What the hell? Men like *him?* What was with this woman? Did she have any idea what she was doing to him? How she was making him care? About her, about what she thought of him? Jesus, she was even making him think about Kathleen.

Caring for a woman once had cost him everything just short of his life. He refused to take that risk again.

"You know jack about me, Sarah." He grabbed her arm, pulled her to her feet. He ignored the righteous flash of indignation in her eyes as he marshaled her down to the water's edge.

"Now get into that river. Get yourself cleaned up and then take your shirt off."

Chapter 4

06:53 Alpha. Shilongwe River.
Monday, September 22

Sarah spun round as he released her arm. "What did you say?"

"I said take your shirt off." He turned his back and made his way over to the rock. Slipping off his pack, he crouched down and set his rifle at his side. He extracted a first aid pouch from his pack, rolled it open and began laying out equipment on the flat, iron-red stone. The sun glinted off his glossy blue-black hair.

"My…shirt?" she asked, suddenly deeply uneasy.

"The wound on your back is bleeding." He didn't look at her as he spoke.

Sarah lifted her hand over her shoulder and fingered the spot where her back throbbed. With surprise she felt tacky wetness, torn fabric…and a deep gash. When her hand came away, there was fresh blood on her fingers. She'd thought what she was feeling was deep muscular pain. She hadn't realized she'd been wounded.

"And your knees. Need to see those, too. Roll up your pants, rinse the muck off, then get back over here." He still wouldn't look at her as he spoke. He'd written her off in some fundamental way.

Sarah turned from him and stared at the ominous, swirling currents of the Shilongwe. She couldn't see below the surface. She couldn't even begin to imagine what parasites, protists or primitive bacteria lurked beneath the milky, rust-colored waters. The Congo was full of unidentified microscopic killers. And macroscopic ones. She shuddered, turned back to look at Hunter McBride—a killer of another kind.

"The water…it's brown. It's—"

"As hygienic as you're gonna get." He tore open a sealed packet of suture strips, attention focused on his task. "The color's mostly from minerals in the soil."

But when she didn't respond, didn't move, he glanced up. Sarah swallowed. His eyes had gone cold and his blackened features were hard, almost brutal. The change was unsettling. It was as if the man inside was suddenly gone.

Had *she* done that to him? Had she actually managed to offend this powerful mercenary and somehow shut him down? For an instant, Sarah wondered what really made him tick. But just as quickly she pushed her curiosity aside. Why should she care about Hunter McBride? Sure, he'd saved her life, but this was his job. She meant nothing more to him than that. He'd said so himself. Besides, she abhorred what he did for a living. It went against every fiber of her being.

His hard eyes held hers and a muscle pulsed softly under the black paint at the base of his jaw. The sun beat down on her head and she felt her face begin to flush under his scrutiny, but she wasn't able to look away, break the intensity of his stare.

He shrugged suddenly. "Hey, stay dirty if you want." He turned his attention back to his task. "Get infected, maybe die. Or clean up and live. You're a nurse, Burdett, you know the odds out here. Your choice."

The use of her last name, the sudden bluntness of his words, winded her. There was absolutely no hint of feeling in his deep, gravelly voice, no nuance of the compassion she'd detected earlier. His sudden offhandedness hurt, much more than it should. Sarah hadn't realized just how much she'd needed a sense of connection to another human being in this foreign, hostile and very frightening environment.

She clutched her arms tightly over her stomach and a cold loneliness began to leach through her chest. It was a feeling she knew too well; the same dead sensation had filled her when she'd seen the tabloid photos of Josh and his heavily pregnant mistress under the big black headline that blared Twins. It was the same hollow ache that had swamped her when she'd learned she would never be able to bear children. It was the same sick feeling that had gripped her when Josh had told her she was a fool for not realizing their marriage had been over for years.

Sarah hugged herself tighter. Josh had been right on that count. She *was* a fool for not having recognized the coldhearted psychopath lurking behind her husband's charming smile. She was a fool for allowing him to abuse her emotionally for so long, for allowing him to make her feel like a barren failure of a woman.

Men like Josh didn't know how to care.

Tears pricked her eyes at the sudden unbidden and overwhelming memories. Sarah turned to face the river. She hated herself for what she'd allowed Josh to do to her. She hated *him*. And she detested his Machiavellian drive. He was a mercenary. Like Hunter. Sure, Josh didn't look like Tarzan here, and he didn't carry guns and knives. He wasn't paid to kill—not in a physical way. But he destroyed lives nevertheless. And like Hunter, he did it for cash. Josh was a mergers and acquisitions giant. His jungle was concrete and his weapons were stocks, bonds, coercion, fast cars and pretty women. And one of those pretty women was now carrying his babies—a famous model-of-the-moment who was attracting tabloid attention and dragging Sarah's pain into the public eye.

Sarah furiously blinked back her emotions. She was *not* going to let Josh haunt her so many miles away. She would never allow a man to make her feel like that again. She steeled her jaw, ripped off her bloodied apron, bent down and yanked her torn cotton pants up over her shins. She scooped up the reddish-brown water and splashed it over her legs, wincing as she tried to wipe away the memories along with the dirt.

She didn't know why she'd let Hunter's bluntness get to her. Maybe it was the incredible tenderness she'd glimpsed briefly in his eyes, felt in his touch…and the way she'd reacted to it. Another wave of emotion threatened. She cupped the warm river water in her hands and splashed it angrily over her face, gasping from the pain that radiated from her cheek. Whatever she'd glimpsed in Hunter, it was gone now. And she wasn't going to let it affect her. She'd come to Africa to kill that emotionally abused and needy part of herself. She'd come here to grow strong, to play a vital role as a human being, a woman.

She froze as the reality of her situation slammed home. She glanced at the bloody apron bunched up at her side. Lord, she was damn lucky even to be alive, to have been given a second chance. Her stomach churned as images of the carnage at the clinic hit her again. She stared numbly at the mesmerizing, slowly swirling water, but couldn't make the pictures in her mind go away. They churned in her head like the curling current of the river, making her dizzy, sick.

What was taking her so damn long? Hunter glanced up from his first aid kit and stilled. She'd stopped undressing. She was just standing there like a zombie, brown water lapping at her shoes, her pants rolled up under her skirt, her arms clutched tight to her waist. Then he realized she was trembling like a bloody leaf.

He reached for his rifle, slung it over his shoulder and pushed himself to his feet. He took a step forward, then held back. No. He'd shut down, shut her out, and he was going to make damn sure he kept it that way.

Deal with it, Burdett.

But she didn't deal with it. Instead, she turned slowly to face him. Hesitatingly, lifting her eyes to meet his. She looked absolutely haunted, lost. Crushed. Even the bright, feverish fear that had lit her eyes was gone. She'd been completely, emotionally demolished in the space of a few minutes. The muscles in his neck bunched tight.

Guilt and compassion tangled in his brain, making his mind thick. Hunter shook off the sensation. He was determined to feel zip. She was a package. He'd get her delivered. That was it.

She took a step toward him. "Hunter…"

He held his ground, said nothing.

"Hunter, I—I'm sorry, I… My buttons…" She held her hands out apologetically. "I can't seem to make my fingers work. I…I can't stop the shaking. Could you please help me with my blouse?"

He blinked sharply. She wanted *him* to undress her? His mouth went bone-dry.

"Could you help me?"

"Ah…sure." They were just buttons, right? How many times

in his life had he undone a woman's blouse? Too many to count. So why in hell was he actually *afraid* to touch her again? This was beyond ridiculous.

She stepped closer and his heart began to thud. He adjusted the sling of his rifle, swallowed hard and lifted his hand, moving it up to the valley between her breasts. He gripped one teeny, round button with his fingers before he realized he'd need his other hand, too. He swore softly to himself—you'd think he'd be able to undo the buttons of a blouse without thinking this hard. He slipped the pearly button out of the fabric, moved his hands down to the next one, purposefully avoiding her eyes, trying to keep a laser focus on this simple task.

Then the back of his hand brushed against the soft, warm swell of her breast, and his control was shot. Heat speared his belly and began to stab with each beat of his heart. Hunter moistened his lips, forced himself to concentrate. He moved his hands to the next button, barely able to breathe. "There." He blew out the breath he'd been holding, and looked into her eyes.

Was he imagining what he saw there? A flare of need? A yearning? A connection that went beyond the physical…words that needed to be spoken, but couldn't be? His heart beat even faster. But she averted her eyes and turned away abruptly.

He used the momentary privacy to swipe the back of his hand hard across his mouth. Sweet heavens this woman had a crazy effect on him, not just mentally, but physically. He hadn't seen *that* one coming.

With her back to him, Sarah hesitated, then slowly slipped her long-sleeved blouse off her shoulders, exposing a thin white cotton camisole with a hint of lace around the edges. Hunter was transfixed. He couldn't have looked away if he'd tried.

He noted the ragged slash in the fabric, the fresh blood. A vengeful fire began to smolder deep within him. The wound wasn't that bad, but it looked rudely invasive against the virginal white of her cotton top. He fingered the hard lines of his weapon, seeking mental clarity in the familiar shape. *Cool. Stay cool.*

She lifted the camisole up over her head, the movement lengthening the long muscles that cradled her spine. She wasn't wearing a bra. He swore softly to himself as perspiration pricked under the paint on his face and dampened his back. It was getting damn hot out here. Watching Sarah undress wasn't making things any cooler. But he'd be damned if he could look away. He swiped his wrist over his forehead and moistened his lips, forcing himself to concentrate clinically on the gash across her left shoulder blade.

It wasn't deep, but needed to be cleaned and sterilized. And it required several surgical strips to pull the edges together. He tried to clear his throat. "Here, sit on this rock so I can work on you from behind."

She acquiesced in silence. Hunter crouched down behind her, shifted his gun to his side and took a tube of disinfectant gel from his kit. He rubbed it over his hands before moistening a gauze pad with a ten percent solution of Povidone iodine. He touched the disinfectant-soaked pad to her skin.

Her body jerked in reflex.

He hesitated. He knew it stung like all hell. He wanted to tell her to take it easy, to relax. He wanted to talk her through it. But he couldn't. He needed to think of her as a job. Anything else was dangerous. Besides, she was a nurse; she knew what was coming. He touched the pad to her skin again and wiped the wound clean. He could see no debris in it, but to be safe, he irrigated the cut thoroughly with a strong stream of the same antiseptic solution from a syringe. Sarah gasped, but still he said nothing. In silence he applied antibiotic ointment, then forced the edges of the now-clean gash together, holding them down

tightly with three suture strips. He made sure her skin was dry
and then covered the whole thing with a transparent, waterproof
bandage, sealing the wound completely. This was necessary in
wilderness environments, especially tropical ones. In places
like this, even a small nick could end up killing a person.

"Done," he said.

She reached for her torn camisole, and as she stretched out
her arm, Hunter caught sight of the smooth, full roundness of
her breast, the profile of a dusky pink nipple. An involuntary
spasm rippled through him.

He looked sharply away. But it was too late. Desire was
already swelling and surging inside him. He bit it back,
clenched his jaw. He checked his watch, the riverbank, the
dense wall of foliage, the sky...*anything* not to look at that
sweet ridge of spine down the center of her back as she slipped
the camisole over her head. He had to keep his cool. He still
had to clean the cut on her cheek. He had to touch her again.

She turned to face him. Hunter avoided her eyes, motioned
for her to sit back down on the rock. He knelt in front of her,
poured antiseptic solution onto a dressing and began to wipe
the dirt from the cut on her cheekbone. She shivered and closed
her eyes as the burn of the solution met her skin. His body responded instantly to her movement. Again, he fought off the
unwelcome sexual longing.

He carefully picked a few embedded bits of dirt out of the
cut with forceps, conscious of her breath on the back of his hand
as he worked. Then he used the syringe to flush the cut. She
winced, but still he said nothing. He applied the antibiotic and
then sealed the edges with two suture strips.

"There you go. Wasn't as bad as it looked."

Her eyes fluttered open and Hunter's heart tripped. Up this
close he could see tiny flecks of gold in the chocolate-brown,

and he could see that her lashes were honey-brown on the tips. She truly was beautiful, in a very natural and pure way. A golden angel.

Jesus, he was losing it.

He ran his wrist over his forehead again, then silently cursed. The movement had transferred greasepaint onto his hands. He'd have to disinfect them again because he still had to tend to her knees and her arms.

He clubbed his errant thoughts aside, rubbed more sterilizing solution over his hands and began to work on cleaning and disinfecting the smaller scrapes and cuts on her knees and arms. She sat motionless, watching his every move.

He finally rocked back on his heels and looked up into her face. "There, that'll keep you going for a while."

She gave him a brave smile. "Thank you, Hunter."

He couldn't help but smile back. Without thinking, he reached up with both hands and removed the ripped blue-and-white cotton cloth from her hair. Tangled mahogany curls tumbled down around her face and fell to her shoulders, the sunlight bringing out burnished auburn highlights. For an instant, he could do nothing but stare. Sarah Burdett might look as soft and gentle as a broken angel, but inside this woman was a surprising core of iron-willed strength. He'd seen it.

She'd lived through a brutal massacre, escaped her attackers. She'd taken hold of that biohazard container and fled into the dark jungle with every intention of somehow getting her lethal cargo all the way to Atlanta. It was an impossible task. How in hell had she planned on doing that?

And to top it all, in spite of her fatigue, after all she'd been through, after *he* had saved her life, she still had the moral fortitude to question his profession and subtly show her disapproval. It made Hunter want to know more about what drove this woman, what really fired her from the inside, what had *really* brought her to Africa.

But he wasn't about to ask.

The less he knew about Sarah Burdett, the better. Because in a couple of hours they'd be on São Diogo Island and she'd be out of his hands. He turned abruptly away from her and began to pack up his first aid kit.

"You'd make a good doctor, you know?"

He didn't look up.

"You have a healing touch. I've worked with enough medical professionals to know."

He clenched his jaw, flipped the kit closed and reached for his gun. He shoved himself to his feet and stared up into the haze of viscous heat that hung over the river. The chopper would be here any second, and not a moment too soon.

Sarah frowned. Something was eating this man big time, something that had wired him with low flash points. She studied his rough profile as he scanned the sky, and a small ping of regret bounced through her heart at the thought that she'd never find out what it was. It was in her nature to want to help, to make people feel better…. But as fleetingly as it had come, the notion was gone. What she really wanted more than anything was to get out of this place and to get Dr. Regnaud's container to safety. It was the one thing that had kept her going through the night. And it was holding her together now. Barely.

She watched Hunter scanning the sky, then the wide ribbon of brown water, then the grassy clearing behind them, his eyes moving gradually toward the thick wall of vegetation at the far end. He tensed. Sarah's heart skipped a beat. She peered into the haze above the trees, trying to see what had alerted him, but couldn't make out a thing. Nerves skittered through her stomach. She stood, came to his side. "What is it?" she whispered.

He lifted the muzzle of his gun, pointed to a spot just above the canopy. "Smoke. Over there."

Sarah shielded her brow and squinted into the distance. "Where?"

Then all of a sudden she could see it. A faint wisp of white separated from the haze and curled up out of the trees. It grew dark and acrid as she watched. Then it began to billow and boil into the sky, black and furious—just like the smoke at the clinic compound had.

"Oh my God," she whispered.

"It's a village along the Oyambo." Hunter studied the smoke with narrowed eyes, not a hint of emotion on his face. "They're looking for you."

Her heart dropped like a cold stone. "But…but why are they burning the village? If they didn't find me, why would they *do* such a thing?"

He said nothing.

She clenched her fists in frustration and glared at Hunter. *"Why?"* she demanded. She needed an answer, needed to understand.

His features remained implacable. "They'll backtrack now. They'll pick up our trail before long."

Horror swamped her. This could *not* be happening. She couldn't take any more. No more. Not another second in this awful place.

Hunter turned his back on the smoke and scanned the trees along the opposite bank of the Shilongwe. "Sarah?"

She couldn't answer, couldn't talk. Couldn't think. All she could do was stare at the billowing black smoke and think about what had happened at Ishonga.

"Sarah—" he grabbed her arm "—listen to me! *Focus.* The helo will come from there, see? From the north. Look."

She moved her head woodenly. He was pointing his gun upriver.

"When it does, we have to move fast. And I mean *fast.* Do *everything* I say. No questions. Got it?"

She stared at his blackened face. It was totally expressionless, showing no glimpse of compassion for what was happening in that village along the Oyambo. The man was inhuman.

Resentment pooled in her stomach. She wanted to get away from him, from this place. Far away.

"Do you understand me, Sarah?"

She forced herself to nod numbly.

"Good. Now see that sandbank, just beyond the shallows?" He pointed into the river. "That's where our guys will land. As soon as the chopper approaches, we wade out there. You hang on to me. Got it?"

Before she could answer, Sarah heard the distinct and distant chop of helicopter blades, the sound expanding and contracting through levels of humidity along the river. Her heart began to jackhammer. The machine materialized, silver in the shimmering, white-hot sky. It banked and flew in low along the course of the brown river. The sound grew louder. Deafening. Water rippled and flattened out in concentric circles as it closed in. Trees bowed. Leaves flew and birds scattered.

She felt Hunter's hand grip hers. Her heart tripped in a panicky lurch of fear and relief. In a couple of hours she'd be out of this hellish place, away from this man and everything he represented.

The helicopter hovered over the sandbank, and she could see the pilot inside giving a thumbs-up. Hunter yanked her forward. "Head down," he yelled over the roar of the lethal rotor blades as he pulled her into the river.

Warm water filled her shoes instantly and thick silt sucked

at her feet. He drew her in deeper. Faster. The brown water was now above her waist. It was deeper than she'd thought. She could feel the current dragging at her clothes. The downdraft from the chopper plastered her hair onto her head and whipped the ends sharply against her cheeks. Tears streamed from her eyes as she squinted into the force of the wind. Hunter dragged her in even deeper. She hung to him for dear life. They were almost there. Then she heard a crack.

Hunter froze. So did she.

Then another sharp crack split the air.

Gunshots.

Terror sliced through her heart. "Someone's shooting at us!" she screamed, the vortex of wind and sound sucking up her words and flinging them out over the water.

A bullet pinged against the chopper, then another. Everything blurred into slow motion. Sarah registered the pilot making signals to Hunter. He gestured back. The chopper lifted, veered sharply up to the left and climbed high over the treetops.

Sarah stared in dismay as the metal beast, her only hope of rescue, her lifeline, disappeared, becoming a silver speck in the shimmering heat of the Congo sky.

A bullet slammed into the river right next to her, shooting a jet of water into her face. She opened her mouth to scream, but before any sound came out, Hunter's hand hit her hard on the back of her head, knocking her facedown into river. She spluttered, choking in a mouthful of water that tasted like sand. She tried to wriggle free, to gasp for air, but Hunter yanked her under. She held her breath. She couldn't see. He drew her down deeper, and suddenly she could no longer touch the bottom. Water swirled around her, tangling her skirt up around her hips, her hair over her face. She was running out of breath. She tried desperately to fight Hunter's death grip, to reach the surface.

But she couldn't. He held on, keeping her under. Her lungs were going to burst. *He was drowning her! She was going to drown!* She felt herself being pulled sideways as the current merged with another and doubled in strength. Then it tripled, sucking her into a cold deep channel, dragging her to the bottom.

And everything went black.

Chapter 5

07:42 Alpha. São Diogo Island.
Monday, September 22

"We lost McBride's signal there, 'bout thirty klicks south of the Cameroon border." December Ngomo pointed at one of the LCD screens mounted along the wall, his heavily-accented voice reverberating through the FDS situation room.

Jacques Sauvage moved closer to the screen. He narrowed his eyes, studied the terrain in silence, his concentration pulling at the scar that sliced down the left side of his face. "That where the pilot saw them go under?"

"*Yebo*," Ngomo said in his native Zulu.

Rafiq Zayed looked up from the report in his hands. "Any chance he lost coverage when he went back into dense bush?"

"Negative," said Ngomo. "The signal was lost right there, in the Shilongwe River."

Sauvage cursed under his breath. The satellite phone that emitted McBride's GPS signal may have been damaged.

Or worse.

They all knew Hunter had a backup radio, but breaking radio silence now would be suicide. It would broadcast their location to anyone who had the equipment to tune in. They had no way of knowing now whether their man had taken a bullet and gone down.

Sauvage turned to Zayed. "You have the chopper on standby in Cameroon?"

Zayed nodded, his liquid eyes intense under hooked brows. "But sending it in now would be a death mission. Airspace has completely shut down in the north. Whole place is set to blow, and anyone with half a brain is getting the hell out."

Sauvage checked his watch. "Then we wait." Time was not a luxury they could afford, but they had little alternative now. "If McBride is okay, he'll head north, to the border." He turned his back on the screen and engaged the eyes of first Zayed, and then Ngomo. The corner of his mouth curled slowly into his characteristically crooked smile. "It was looking too smooth, *non?* Trust Irish to take the tough way out." Sauvage used their affectionate tag for McBride. But apart from his Irish accent, the men knew nothing about Hunter's past. McBride, Sauvage, Zayed and Ngomo *never* talked about the past. Not in a way that mattered. It was an unspoken pact among these men. It went to the heart of the bond between them.

All they knew was that Hunter had arrived at the gates of the Légion Étrangère—the French Foreign Legion—fifteen years ago with a thick Irish brogue and a look of murder in his strangely colored eyes. That look had eventually left him.

Mostly. But the brogue had stayed, only softening, becoming veiled after years of his speaking only French.

These disparate men had understood each other back then, as they did now. For hidden reasons of their own, each had been driven to the gates of Fort de Nogent in Paris, desperate to seek asylum with the notorious "Legion of the Damned," where a man could bury his past in order to fight for France. If he survived his contract, he could come out with a new identity and a French passport. A shot at a new life.

They'd all earned their second chance by coming close to death in the name of a country that was not their own, fighting with a crack army of foreigners, the biggest and most legitimate mercenary force in the world. They'd served in places like Bosnia, Rwanda, Zaire, Chad, central Africa, Lebanon, Somalia, the Gulf. They'd developed the Legion mind-set, where soldiers of many nations and many pasts had to set aside differences and stand by each other and die for a foreign nation. The resulting bond that had formed between the men was formidable, sealed with discipline, trust, solidarity and respect for tradition.

It was this mind-set, this philosophy, that McBride, Sauvage, Zayed and Ngomo took with them when they left the Legion to form the Force du Sable, an efficient, lean, private military company that over the last ten years had developed a reputation for having trained some of the most skilled and dangerous soldiers on earth—fearless warrior monks who now served as a model for future rapid-action units in a modern world of limited-intensity conflict and terrorism.

Zayed's eyes flashed back to the LCD screen and he gave a soft snort. "Tough way out? That terrain between the Shilongwe and the Cameroonian border is some of the most hostile known to man. Plus he's got the nurse with him."

"McBride's come out of worse," Ngomo said simply, and turned back to his computer, his massive hands dwarfing the keyboard.

08:03 Alpha. Shilongwe River.
Monday, September 22

As the river widened and the current slowed, the drop in velocity and Sarah's limp weight began to drag Hunter down. Wet clothing didn't help. At least the sealed biohazard container was buoyant, as was his waterproof pack. With the container in one hand and his other arm hooked across Sarah's chest, he gave slow, powerful scissor kicks, swimming diagonally across the current, using it instead of fighting it.

As he moved downriver, he scanned the wall of tangled vegetation that crowded the banks for any signs of movement, but saw none. The forest was dense along this stretch. There was likely no one about for miles.

Hunter soon found what he was looking for—a break in the vegetation. He aimed for a gentle slope of white beach about a hundred yards downstream. At least they were moving in the direction of the Cameroonian border.

He neared the bank, sought footing in the silt, dragged Sarah up out of the water and laid her down on the sand. He immediately checked the seal on the biohazard canister. To his relief, it was secure. His rifle and machete were also still strapped across his back. He shrugged off his pack, glanced around. The place was deserted. They'd be safe for a while.

He turned his attention to Sarah, and his heart stalled. There was froth around her mouth and nose, and her skin was going blue. He dropped to his knees, felt for a pulse.

There was none.

Guilt rammed into his heart. He hadn't realized she was this far gone. He'd been too worried about being shot at, too worried about losing the pathogen. He quickly opened her mouth, clearing away foam, checking for any foreign material. He placed one hand on her forehead, tilted her chin back with the other, opening her airway. He pinched her nostrils shut, sucked in a deep breath of air and put his mouth over hers.

He blew a slow and steady stream of breath into her, his eyes fixed on her chest, watching for a sign that air was getting into her lungs.

He waited two seconds, saw her chest rise and sink as the air expelled from her lungs. He sucked in another deep breath and once again positioned his lips over hers, keeping his eyes trained on her chest as he blew. He saw it rise again. He quickly located her breastbone and began chest compressions, alternating compressions with breaths, again and again.

Hunter's whole body ached. He was wet with river water and sweat, being steamed alive under the equatorial sun. His vision began to swim, and the guilt in his heart was nearly overwhelming. He'd thought of the biohazard container first. He'd thought of the mission, of the millions of people who would die if he didn't get the pathogen out of the jungle. But perhaps, just maybe, if he'd tended to Sarah a second earlier... Hot anger swirled through the cold guilt in his chest. He'd be damned if he was going to let her die!

He gritted his teeth. He'd gotten her this far. Now he was going to take her *and* the pathogen all the way.

He sucked in another deep breath of air and forced it steadily it into her lungs, mechanically pumping her heart.

And then suddenly, he felt the small flutter of a pulse. Hunter's heart stumbled, kicked hard against his ribs. Her limbs spasmed and her stomach began to heave. He quickly flipped

Sarah onto her side and she retched violently, expelling river water and lumps of foam.

Relief, thick and sweet, surged through his veins. He held her as she heaved. Color was returning to her skin, oxygen getting into her blood.

Hunter's eyes burned hot with gratitude. His jaw went tight with the sense of triumph over death, and he lifted his face to the sky. And for an instant he almost found himself yelling thanks to a God he no longer believed in.

When he looked at her face again, she was watching him, her eyes dark hollows in a pale void. He wiped her mouth with the edge of his wet shirt and tried to smile. "You made it."

She said nothing, just stared at him.

He sniffed back the strange cocktail of emotions burning in him, and lifted a wet ribbon of hair from her brow. "I'm going to move you up the beach to some shade, okay?"

She closed her eyes, nodded.

She felt like a wet rag doll in his arms as he carried her up the small strip of sand. He laid her down in the shade of a palm, but as he tried to step away, she grabbed at the fabric of his shirt, balling it in white-knuckled fists, her eyes wide like an animal snared in headlights. She was terrified he was going to abandon her. She saw him as her lifeline.

If only she knew.

"Hey, it's okay, I'm not going to leave you," he said, lowering himself onto the sand beside her, knowing that if it really came down to it, he couldn't keep his word. He lifted her head, rested it on his lap, tried to stroke some of the sand from her damp hair, and while he did, racked his brain for some comforting reassurances he could whisper to her.

But nothing came to him. He felt totally useless. He could satisfy a woman physically, knew what places to touch, how to drive her to such dizzying sensual delirium that she would scream out for release. But emotionally? This was uncharted territory for Hunter McBride. He had no idea how to simply make a woman feel safe. Christ, he'd barely managed to keep her alive.

The tang of remorse stung his tongue. He told himself he'd done the right thing, he'd kept his priorities straight. And if it truly came down to the wire, if he was literally forced to choose between Sarah Burdett or the pathogen, he'd *have* to go with the latter. There was no option. That was his job. Black-and-white. Pure and simple. Because if they didn't get this lethal bug into a lab and find an antidote, millions would die three weeks from now—people just as innocent and unprepared as Sarah Burdett.

One life to save millions. Law enforcement agencies the world over dealt with equations like that on a daily basis and made the same decisions.

So why did he feel like crap?

Sarah stirred on his lap, moaned softly, the soft weight of her breast rubbing against the inside of his forearm. Heat speared through his belly.

Hunter angrily swallowed the sensation. Jesus, this was not the time. He looked away from the transparent fabric of her camisole, away from the dark outline of her nipple under the wet cloth, and forced himself to breathe. To plan. To think clear, hard, cold logistics.

He wasn't going to be able to move Sarah for a while. She was going to need rest. And then she'd need food, water. They'd be safe here for a few hours, but they would have to get going by nightfall at least. He needed to contact the FDS base.

Hunter reached for the front-left compartment of his flak jacket. His fingers met fabric, and his heart skipped a beat.

The flap had come undone.

He thrust his hand into the pocket. Empty. He cursed under his breath. His satellite phone, their one and only secure link to the outside world, was gone. He must have lost it in the Shilongwe. How could the flap have come loose? Had he even secured it? He cursed aloud in French. If he'd been totally focused on the job this would never have happened.

Now he was stuck with Sarah in the middle of bloody nowhere, with no contact with the outside world, just the two of them in a war-torn country set to blow. And over their heads hung the threat of a biological attack, and responsibility for the lives of millions of Americans who would die if he failed to make it out alive, and soon. It didn't get much better than this.

He swore again. Wasn't much he could do about it now apart from waiting until she was up to moving again. They were going to have to make it out on foot. No question about that. He and Sarah were going to have to physically hack their way to the Cameroonian border, and because of her, the going would be slow. Real slow. Time he didn't have. Time the president of the United States and his people didn't have.

Hunter squinted into the sky, checked the angle of the sun. He figured they couldn't be more than thirty miles from Cameroon, if they went along the river. But that wasn't an option. The route they'd have to take would work out a lot longer than thirty miles, and a lot tougher than following the course of the river.

He looked down at Sarah. She was asleep now, breathing easily. He'd need to get her out of those cotton pants so they could dry. Things had a nasty way of rotting against your body out here. But there was no freaking way he was going to try undressing her again. She could do that herself when he woke her up again in a few minutes. In the meantime, he had his own gear to dry out.

He rolled out from under her, stood up, then hesitated. Her wet sneakers *would* have to come off now. Drying her shoes and socks out before nightfall was a priority. Fungus, bacteria and rotting skin were some of the biggest hazards in the jungle, and she was going to need her feet if she wanted to live. He figured he could handle her shoes without coming undone.

He crouched down, untied her wet laces and removed her sodden sneakers, along with the wet tennis socks she was wearing. He paused, looking at her feet. They were narrow, with beautiful arches. Her skin was pale, and her toenails were painted the white-pink of spring blossoms. Nail polish in the jungle? A smile sneaked across Hunter's lips and tenderness blossomed softly through his chest.

He wrung the water from her socks and spread them out on a rock in the sun to dry. He stared down at them and shook his head. They had a pale yellow trim and little yellow pompoms on the back. Pompoms in the jungle? Maybe they'd come in handy as fish lure when they got hungry.

He shrugged out of his combat vest and shirt and draped them over the rock next to her socks. Then he squatted on the hot sand and began to toss stuff out of his pack, checking to see if anything was wet. He kept his rifle at his side and a constant eye on the river and jungle border.

Sarah squinted into the harsh daylight, the movement pulling at the bandage on her cheek. She touched it, confused. Where was she? Images sifted into her mind—the helicopter, her lifeline disappearing into the shimmering sky…the shooting. Water. *The container!* She jerked upright. Where was Hunter?

He was a few yards from her, sitting on a rock by the water, cleaning his gun. He was naked from the waist up, a darkly tanned and potent figure against the white glare of the sand. Sun glinted on his black hair, and his body gleamed with perspiration and humidity.

He stilled, looked up suddenly and smiled. "Hello."

Sarah's jaw dropped. The black face paint was gone, and what was left was magnificent. Not beautiful. Magnificent in a gut-slamming, powerful male kind of way. How he was looking at her, how the light caught his eyes, clean took her breath away.

She closed her eyes. Maybe when she opened them again, life would seem more real. But he was still there when she flicked them open. She was still on the banks of some brown river in the heart of the Congo, with one of the most dangerous-looking males she'd ever seen in her life. Panic licked through her. She struggled to get up, but the world spun and she sank back.

"Hey, take it easy," he said, pushing himself to his feet in a fluid movement. Holding the barrel of his rifle in one hand, he stalked over the shimmering-hot sand. The dark hair that covered his pecs glistened with moisture and gathered into a sexy whorl that trailed down the center of his rock-hard belly and disappeared into the belt of his camouflage pants. Sarah just stared. Her brain wasn't working right. Everything looked surreal.

He crouched beside her, rummaged in his pack and handed her a foil pack of army-style rations and a canteen of water. She noted with relief that the biohazard canister sat alongside the pack, right next to her in the shade.

"Get some fuel into your system," he said. "And then we can get you out of those pants."

"I beg your pardon?"

A twinkle of amusement flickered through his eyes. "We need to make sure your clothes are dry, Sarah. We move at nightfall. As soon as the sun sets, we're off."

"What?" Alarm flared in her. "At night? Why? Where are we going?" She sat up stiffly. "Where *are* we, Hunter?"

"Still on the Shilongwe. We washed a couple of miles north. We need to try and make it to the Cameroonian border now."

"Cameroon! How?"

"We walk."

"You have *got* to be kidding!" But even as she spoke, she could see by the look in his eyes that he was dead serious. Tongues of panic licked through her. She could *not* go through another night in the jungle. "Why…why can't you just call your people and get them to fly another helicopter in like you did before?" She looked around frantically. "It could land here…couldn't it?"

Hunter cocked a brow. "My people? The ones who get *paid* to do this sort of thing?"

"Yes, them." Being rescued seemed a pretty good option right now, by mercenaries or not. But judging by the expression on his face, that was not going to happen anytime soon. A cold dread seeped into her chest. "You…you're not going to call them, are you?"

"No."

"Why not?"

"Lost the phone in the river."

"Oh my God. So we're…"

"Yes, Sarah. We're on our own."

She looked up at the sky. It would be dark in a few hours; the sudden cloak of pure blackness dropped at precisely 6:07 local time. Panic edged into her throat. She couldn't do this again. It had taken everything just to survive the night before.

He was watching her intently, appraising her on some fundamental level, deciding if she had the mettle to make it to Cameroon. The fact sobered her. It reminded her of why they were here, of what was in the biohazard container, of Dr. Regnaud. She swallowed, tried to find her voice. "How…how long will it take?"

"Maybe three days, if we're lucky."

Three days! And this morning she'd believed she'd be out of the Congo within the hour.

"It would be quicker if we went down the Shilongwe, but we can't risk that. There are settlements, people along the riverbanks. We can't chance being seen. We can't trust anyone right now, Sarah."

"Why not?" She wasn't sure she even wanted to know the answer.

"There was a coup in Brazzaville this morning. The entire country is in a state of civil war and we're foreigners, Sarah. We're sitting ducks. We're anyone's enemy."

She stared at him. "You mean the people shooting at us from across the river had nothing to do with the soldiers who attacked the clinic?"

"Probably not."

"Then where are the soldiers?"

"Probably tracking us."

She shuddered, clutched her arms over her knees. "And you really think going through the forest will be safer than along the river?"

"Tougher, and slower. But yeah, it'll be safer, and the sooner we manage to reach the Blacklands, the better."

"Blacklands?"

"The dense jungle swamp of the interior. Locals believe the area is cursed. No one ventures in there apart from Pygmy tribes and wild animals. It's unlikely anyone will follow us in there."

"Cursed? You *are* toying with me…right?"

He smiled. "It's a local superstition born out of an Ebola outbreak several years ago. Villagers who'd been hunting in the swamp region brought the disease out with them. Anyone who came in contact with them got sick, started dying. As is the custom, the village elders consulted with their sorcerer, who told them the area had been cursed by evil spirits and that anyone who ventured into the region should be banished from the tribe, or killed. This helped control the spread of Ebola, and the belief in the curse became entrenched in local culture. No one ever goes in there now. Superstition in this place is supremely powerful, and it's not a force to be ignored. Out here, it's the law of life, and there's a reason for it. It preserves life."

"Well, I'm not going in there, either," she said. "I'd rather take my chances along the river."

He snorted softly. "You have less chance of stumbling over the Ebola virus in the Blacklands, Sarah, than you have of running into hostile militia along the Shilongwe."

"It's…it's not just Ebola. It's…" She glanced at the forest fringe. "There has *got* to be another way, Hunter. Please understand…I just can't do it. I can't spend another night stumbling blind through the jungle."

He studied her at length, his eyes growing cool. He looked suddenly distant, dangerous again. It made her nervous.

"I…I mean it," she said, her voice wobbling. "I just don't have it left in me. I—I can't."

The muscle at his jaw began to pulse softly. She could see he was thinking, trying to figure out what to do with her. And she didn't like how it made her feel a liability.

"Sarah," he said finally, "I can't force you to do it." He rose to his feet. "Stay here on the Shilongwe if you want. I'll take the pathogen, make better time without you. It's your choice." His eyes bored down into hers. *"It has to be."* He turned, strode down the beach, seated himself on the rock and resumed cleaning his gun in silence.

Her jaw dropped. He wouldn't leave her alone, would he? Could he really be so coldhearted?

She couldn't be sure. She didn't know Hunter McBride at all. She had no idea what he might be capable of. A mad terror began to nip at her brain, skewing her logic. Josh would do it. He'd leave her here. Sarah had learned the hard way just how cruel a man could be. She'd seen Josh walk out on six years of marriage without blinking an eye, and then send in his lawyer to pick the rest of her bones clean. Tears pricked at her eyes.

"You…you really don't care, do you?" she called out to him.

He lifted his dark head, studied her in silence. "No, Sarah, I don't." He turned his attention back to his weapon.

She jerked herself to her feet, swayed under a wave of dizziness, grabbed at a tree branch to steady herself. "Damn you and all men like you, Hunter McBride!" She yelled at him out of hurt and frustration and the sheer fear of going back into the nightmarish jungle. *Damn Josh*. This was his fault. She'd never have come here if it hadn't been for him.

Hunter ignored her, continued cleaning his gun.

She wanted to scream. She felt utterly powerless. She spun around and began to march blindly down the beach, barely noticing the burning heat of the sand under her bare feet, barely registering the wall of foliage next to her. Tears pooled in her eyes. She had no idea where she was going, she just had to move, do something. And above all, she didn't want him to see her crying, didn't want to give the brute the satisfaction of having pushed her over the edge.

"Stop!" His voice barked through the air.

Hesitation rippled through her, but she continued stumbling

along the small strip of sand. She had no intention of listening to him, of jumping at his each and every command.

"Now, Sarah! Stop!"

This time she did stop. This time she could not ignore the urgent bite in his voice. She started to turn around, but as she did, her breath congealed in her throat.

Everything moved into slow, sick motion. She saw him raise his arm, saw him flick the machete. She heard it whopping through the air, saw the blur of motion as it whipped toward her face….

Chapter 6

The machete sunk into the trunk of a tree with a dull *thuck* and quivered from the impact. The head of a snake fell to her feet, followed by a writhing, brown body. Sarah screamed.

"Don't move!" Hunter growled as he strode over the sand. He jabbed at the snake's head with a stick and the decapitated head bit down viciously on the wood. "Survival instinct lives longer than the snake," he said, tossing the head and stick into the bush. He stalked over to the tree, yanked his machete out of the trunk, used the blade to lift the snake's limp body. He held it up for her to see. "Black mamba. Gets its name from the color of its mouth," he said. "Shy bugger, but incredibly fast and very lethal if disturbed."

He tossed the snake's body into the forest, turned, pointed his machete at her face. "Next time, listen. If you're interested in living, that is." He stepped closer, his eyes drilling into hers. "I'm giving you the choice, Sarah. You have to *want* to live." He pointed his blade to the green abyss behind him. "You have to choose to tackle that jungle with me, or you won't survive." He watched her face, allowing his words to sink in. "It's that simple."

He turned abruptly, strode back down the beach.

Sarah sank to the sand in a heap. She was at his mercy. Completely. She was dependent on this brute of a man for every aspect of her existence. She felt sick. She reached for the comfort of her cross at her throat…and felt nothing.

Her heart stopped.

She fingered her neck wildly, searching for the delicate gold chain.

It wasn't there.

The little crucifix she'd worn every single day since she was fourteen years old was gone. It must've been ripped from her throat in the river.

Her brain went numb. She clutched her naked neck with both hands. The Congo had stolen her last link to civilization, the last vestige that helped her define her notion of self, of who she was as a human being in this primitive environment, of where she'd come from.

And now this man had stripped her to her very core.

Hunter glanced at the sky. It would be dark within fifteen minutes. Working mechanically, he started packing his gear.

Sarah was sitting in the lengthening shadows at the edge of the beach, silent, watching the river. She had barely moved since he'd told her to get out of the sun and to eat and drink something. She'd obeyed like a zombie. At least she *had* eaten.

And she'd rested. But she hadn't uttered a word. And the blank look in her eyes bothered him.

He tried to shut out thoughts of her as he worked. But as he scooped his stiff, dry shirt off the rock, he caught sight of the pair of white socks with their little yellow pompoms. His heart gave an odd spasm. He felt terrible. No matter how he tried to shut himself down, he hated the way he'd handled her. But the truth was, he didn't have a clue how to deal with this woman. Or how to cope with the things she was making him feel.

But Hunter did know one thing. He wanted to bring Sarah Burdett out alive. And for them to succeed, it was absolutely imperative that she obey his orders. And it was essential that she *wanted* to succeed. Because the journey was going to physically challenge every molecule in her body and test the limits of her mind. Without willpower at this point, she quite simply wasn't going to make it. And if his actions and his words had belied his intent, if they'd spooked her and made her think, so much the better.

Hunter cinched his backpack closed. Gear packed, he scooped up her socks along with her cotton pants. He strode along the beach, held her clothes out to her.

She lifted her eyes slowly. The bruised look in them almost choked him but he said nothing. Neither did she. She just took her clothes, and that's when he noticed the delicate gold cross that had nestled in the hollow of her throat was missing. He crouched down beside her. "Sarah," he said gently. "Where's your crucifix?"

She swallowed and blinked a little too fast. But other than that, she showed no emotion. "Lost it in the river, I guess." Her voice was flat.

Hunter's chest tightened. He'd seen what that little gold symbol had meant to her. And he knew the power of symbols, especially in a place like this. In losing her icon, she'd lost a basic belief in herself. He reached for her hand, covered it with his own. "I'm sorry."

Her eyes cut sharply to his. "Why? What's it to you, anyway?"

"I understand," he said simply.

Her brown eyes probed his. "How could a man like you possibly understand?"

Her question forced him momentarily to seek an answer within himself. It pushed him, once again, toward the slippery murk of his past, but he pulled himself back. It would serve no purpose. The answer, his reason for understanding, was not going to help her. She'd lost a trinket that had linked her to her psyche, to who she was as a person, and with it she'd lost her motivation to survive. He knew the signs well. And in this state, she wouldn't last another day.

What Sarah needed most was a vivid mental picture of herself making it out of the Congo. She had to *believe* she would. She needed faith in herself. And he alone had to give that to her.

He looked away, studied the river, trying to come up with something. It was tougher than he'd thought. He turned back to her. "When you get home, Sarah, what's the first thing you're going to do?"

Her eyes widened. Good, he'd elicited some kind of emotion, even if it was surprise. It bolstered him. He flashed her the warmest smile he could muster and settled back onto the sand beside her, his hand still covering hers. "Think about it, Sarah. Picture it."

She stared blankly at him.

"I hear Seattle has great coffee," he offered. "Personally, I could do with an espresso. But I wouldn't mind trying one of those—what do they call those things—lattes?"

Anger sparked in her eyes. "Don't patronize me, McBride. How the hell do you know I'm from Seattle, anyway?"

He blinked. "Jeez, Sarah, I'm not trying to patronize. And

I've seen your Aid Africa file. They gave it to us after we'd intercepted your distress call."

Her eyes flickered sharply. "So you know everything about me?"

"Hardly everything."

She pulled her hand out from under his and looked away.

He raked his fingers through his hair. "Okay, you want it straight?"

"Darn right I do. It's not like you've tried to coddle me or anything. And it's not like I have anything left to lose now."

He winced. "Ouch. You don't play fair."

"And you do?"

He studied her carefully. This woman wasn't just lost. Something elemental had shifted in her. There was a new rawness, a hint of lost innocence. "Look, Sarah, whatever I've done up until now has been purely in the interests of your physical survival. And I'm sorry if I hurt you. I truly am. I'm sorry you've lost your crucifix. I think I know what it meant to you—"

She opened her mouth to protest.

He held up his hand. "Hear me out. All I'm trying to do right now is to give you a goal to hang on to, something that'll pull you through emotionally. You can handle the physical side of this, I don't doubt that, but not without the right mind-set."

Her mouth opened slightly. She stared at him, a range of emotions pulling at her features. At least he'd knocked her out of the zombie state. It was a start.

"It's plain old survival psychology," he explained. "When people are lost in the wilderness, I mean truly lost with zero hope of rescue, more often than not it's the thought of home, the memory of a loved one, their children, something like that that pulls them through. People who have survived against ridiculous odds often say they did it *for* someone. For someone

waiting back home. *Home,* Sarah." He purposefully emphasized the word. "I want you think about Seattle, about home."

Her jaw tensed. She looked away from him and stared at the
river. "I'm not going back to Seattle. It's not my home anymore."

"Why not?"

She shook her head, still not looking at him. "A man like you
wouldn't understand."

A man like him? There, she'd said it again. What man "like
him" had hurt this woman, wrecked her notions of home?
Hunter wanted to touch her. He picked up a twig instead,
cracked it between his fingers. "Why don't you try me, Sarah?"

She spun back to face him, her eyes luminous. "It's none of
your damn business, McBride." She grabbed her socks, started
to ram her feet into them. "If you want me to voice a reason to
get out of this…" She swiped angrily at a tear that escaped and
looked him straight in the eye. "It won't be for *you.* Or for me.
It'll be for Dr. Regnaud. A man with integrity. A self-sacrificing
healer. A man you could *never* match, McBride. And it'll be for
all the staff at the Ishonga clinic. Warm and generous people.
People who *care.*" She lifted her chin, but couldn't hide the
husky catch of emotion in her voice. "And in spite of what *you*
think, I don't want the disease in that canister—" she pointed to
the biohazard container "—to hurt anyone else like I saw it hurt
the patients at the clinic." She grabbed her runners, shook them
out viciously, checking for scorpions. She yanked her shoes
over those ridiculous socks and pushed herself to her feet.

She stood over him, legs braced, the sinking sun lighting her
from behind, showing the curvy outline of her hips and the lean
lines of her legs through the thin cotton of her skirt. The orange
glow of the sinking Congo sun spun a halo of burnished fire
around curls that had dried into a wild and springy mass. In
spite of the situation, in spite of what she was saying, all Hunter

could think at this instant was that she looked unbelievably attractive. And the fire now flashing in her eyes and in her voice lit his soul.

Sarah Burdett had come back to life—and so had his body.

"Believe it or not, McBride, I actually *do* want to stop this thing you told me about."

Part of him wanted to smile. But he controlled the impulse, leery of making her feel patronized. Because that was the furthest thing from his mind. This woman had just earned his respect. Some people, when you knocked them down, just got up tougher than before. He was beginning to see she was one of them. And it forced him to realize he may have been wrong.

Maybe, despite her naiveté, Sarah Burdett *did* have the goods to take on this jungle.

He got to his feet, came close to her, hooked a knuckle under her jaw, tilted her face so that the setting sun caught the gold flecks in her eyes. "Touché, Sarah," he said softly. "You're more woman than meets the eye, do you know that?"

She shivered slightly but didn't back away, didn't break eye contact. Her physical reaction to his touch, to him, sparked a shot of unwanted heat into his belly. And this time Hunter didn't pull away, either. He kept his fingers against her skin, enjoying the softness, the closeness of the contact.

For a second, they just stood like that, embraced by the warm orange light of the sinking sun, separated momentarily from their environment, aware only of each other. It was as if an invisible and tenuous bond was being spun around them, a new level of unspoken understanding.

Sarah's lips parted slightly as she looked up at him, and Hunter could see a sensual awareness darkening her eyes. A thrill rippled through him and he wanted to pull her into him, feel her curves against him. He wanted to press his mouth over those warm, soft lips—lips he'd breathed life into only hours ago. But it would be flat-out wrong. This woman was vulnerable. She was also completely dependent on him. And if she was at all attracted to him physically, there was a good chance it was desire born out of the wrong kind of need. He pulled away slightly and a sudden look of nervousness skittered over her features.

"I…I'm not dumb enough to think I don't need you right now, McBride," she said softly, her voice layered with a husky thickness that made his stomach swoop. Just the thought of her needing him on *any* level was making him too hot, too hard.

"I'm dependent on you for every aspect of my existence. I know that. I haven't got a clue how to get myself out of here. But it doesn't mean I have to like it…and it doesn't mean you have to be an ass about it."

He raised a brow.

"And it doesn't mean you have to try and prove it to me at every opportunity."

A grin tugged at his lips. Look who was giving it straight now.

"But…" Her eyes flicked away for an instant. "Do we *really* have to go back into the forest tonight? Can't we wait until morning?" She glanced at the wall of jungle, then at the biohazard container sitting under the palm tree. "We'd move faster in daylight, wouldn't we? And maybe your people will come looking for us. If we stay out here on the beach, on the river, they'll have a better chance of finding us. They'll see us." A pleading hopefulness lit her eyes. Hope he had to crush.

He sucked in a deep breath. "Sarah, no one is coming. Forget about being rescued. The FDS is not going risk flying a search party around Congo airspace now. They don't even know if we're alive. All they do know is that *if* we're okay, we'll head for the border. And they'll be ready and waiting for us there, in Cameroon." He allowed his hand to drop from her face and trace down the column of her neck and along the smooth, taut skin of her arm. He encircled her wrist and pulled her gently closer, his body acting separate from his mind.

"We're on our own. We have to do this ourselves, you and me. There is no other way out."

She swallowed, her eyes still searching his, as if looking for a lie.

The sun was now a deep blood-orange and dipping behind the trees. The clock was ticking. Time was running out on them, on President Elliot, on the American people. Hunter cupped her cheek. "We *have* to go. Now."

She stared at him in silence for a long while. "Okay," she said softly. "Let's go, then. Let's get that canister to a lab." She paused. "I owe it to some very good people."

And in that instant Hunter felt a stab of something a whole lot different from lust, and with it a primal male urge swelled in him, an urge to protect a woman he was beginning to care about. There was just no way he could think of Sarah as a package anymore. And that, more than anything, unnerved him.

Because it could end up costing them both.

21:00 Alpha. Congo jungle.
Monday, September 22

Hunter adjusted his night-vision gear and swiped away the perspiration on his forehead. They'd been moving uphill along a narrow ridge for the last two hours. There was a sharp drop to the left, and it was hot, hard and careful work. Sarah was panting heavily behind him. She'd lost her footing twice in the last fifteen minutes, taking her shockingly close to the cliff edge. She was tiring and she needed a break.

Hunter stopped at the top of the ridge. He had a good vantage point from here. In the distance, the Shilongwe snaked between walls of dense vegetation, the water a gleaming silver ribbon under a narrow sliver of moon. And beyond it, the forest canopy mushroomed as far as his eye could see, spiked occasionally with raffia palms and multitiered emergent giants. The ground up here was dry and rocky. It was a good place to give her some rest.

"We'll stop here awhile," he said softly, as he took her wrist and guided her down to the ground.

"Thank God," she whispered.

Hunter sat beside her and handed her water. She took it, drank, handed the canteen back and moved right up against him. He smiled into the dark. Whether her contact was driven by fear or affection, it didn't matter. It just felt damn good to have her so close. Hesitatingly, he wrapped his arm around her. She snuggled even closer, and something achingly sweet and hot blossomed through his chest.

Hunter closed his eyes and sucked in air. Not since Kathleen had he felt this sensation. How could he not have realized he'd been missing this over the last fifteen years? How could he have been so empty as to not even know how hollow he'd become?

He sat quietly, content in the moment, enjoying the sensation of Sarah's body folded into his. He listened to her soft exhalations as she slept, and he watched the shimmering, twisting snake of a river far below.

Then something caught his eye. He tensed, stared hard at the river.

Coming round a distant bend in the Shilongwe was a boat, moving slowly, silently, flowing with the current, engines turned off, a searchlight panning the beaches as it moved.

Every muscle in his body snapped tight. He watched as the boat came closer. He could make out six men, soldiers with berets and guns. His gut twisted. The soldiers must have traced them to the banks of the Shilongwe, heard reports of the aborted rescue attempt, and come downriver after them. They probably didn't know if he and Sarah were alive or dead. But that could change as soon as their searchlight hit the beach they'd left at nightfall.

Hunter had done his best to erase their tracks in the sand with palm fronds. And because it was night, there was a chance the soldiers might miss the signs. But he wasn't going to bet on it. And he sure as hell wasn't going to tell Sarah. This would be more than she could handle right now. Her newfound resolve was still too fragile. She was still too exhausted. Knowing the militia were on their tail could break her completely. He had to find a way to keep her moving—*fast*—until they reached the Eikona River and crossed into the Blacklands, where there was a chance they wouldn't be pursued.

He nudged her awake. "Sarah," he whispered. "We need to move."

"Already?"

"Right now."

23:59. Venturion Tower penthouse, Manhattan.
Monday, September 22

Low autumn clouds swallowed the lights of the Manhattan skyline, and a sharp wind flicked rain against the glass. He paced the length of his windows, conscious of his reflection against the dark panes.

His point man in the Congo, Andries Du Toit, had told him their militia had picked up the nurse's tracks. That was the good news. The bad news was that someone was helping her run.

He cursed softly, swiveled on his heels, paced back along the length of the windows. Someone else had to know the importance of what was in that biohazard container; someone who had access to a helicopter, a bigger network. A real uneasiness bit into his usual steely calm.

He needed the woman alive. They had to make her talk. He had to find out who else knew about the pathogen, who was helping her. Because if whoever was with her was even remotely connected to the U.S. president, he had no choice but to launch the attack immediately. He checked the green glow of his watch. It was almost six in the evening, almost Tuesday in the Congo. He needed to meet with the others as soon as possible.

The phone rang, startling him. He jumped and grabbed the receiver. "Yes?" he barked.

"Dad? You okay?"

"Olivia, darling." Warmth flooded through him as he greeted his daughter. "I'm fine, just…planning my day tomorrow."

She hesitated. "You sure you're all right?"

He smiled broadly. "Of course I am. Just a small business glitch. I'll have it sorted out by morning."

Chapter 7

The day dawned to the high-pitched shrieks of African grays and a troop of gray-cheeked mangabeys proclaiming their territory with wild staccato barks and obscene deep chuckles.

Sarah winced at the monkeys' discordant sounds. They scraped against nerves already raw from stress and exhaustion. She'd been on her feet for almost a full twelve hours now, stumbling blindly behind Hunter with invisible things tearing at her clothes and skin. The night had taken a severe toll on both her mind and her body, and as a nurse, she knew she'd pushed herself to her limit. She was about to collapse physically, and snap psychologically.

And once again, with daybreak came oppressive heat and

humidity. Perspiration oozed a steady trail between her breasts and down her belly, plastering her camisole to her skin. Plus Hunter had made her wear her long-sleeved shirt overtop. She stumbled to a stop, wiped the back of her sleeve over her wet forehead. "Hunter," she said. "I need a rest."

"Not now." He didn't break his stride.

"I mean it!" she called after him.

He halted in his tracks. For a second he stood stock-still, as if trying to control his irritation before facing her. Then he turned around slowly, his face glistening with moisture and his eyes sparking with what she could only imagine was frustration. "You have got to keep moving, Sarah."

"No." She refused to budge. "I need rest. I know my limits."

Impatience flickered over his face. It made her feel like a tiresome piece of baggage. And that made her want to lash out at him.

He took a step toward her. "Sarah." His voice was low, firm. "We'll rest when we get into the Blacklands."

"Right." She slapped at a bug biting her neck. "The cursed land, the land that time forgot, where no one will find us." She bent over, rested her hands on her knees, trying to catch her breath. "Could I at least have some water?"

"Not until we find another source."

She knew he was right. She'd drunk most of his water while they'd waited for their rescue chopper, thinking they'd be out of the Congo soon. But she was dehydrated and was going to collapse soon if she didn't get some liquid into her system.

He must have seen the desperation in her face because his voice softened ever so slightly. "Sarah, I know this is tough, but we should reach Eikona Falls within the hour, and that means drinking water. And once we cross the Eikona, we'll be heading into some very dense primary stuff. It'll be darker, just a little cooler, and we can risk making a fire, which means dry clothes." He smiled slightly in encouragement.

She stared at the curve of his mouth, and the exhausted and rebellious part of her brain wondered if his smile was false, if it was just a pretense at camaraderie designed to fuel her hope. Because just a second ago she'd seen the raw impatience in his features. He was doing a damn fine job of hiding it now, behind that smile.

Josh used to play that game.

"Come, let's go." Hunter turned, slashed at a liana thick as a python.

But she could not go on. The muscles in her legs were ready to give out. She desperately needed to lie down. Even the dank carpet of slippery, rotting leaves and lurid-colored fungi was beginning to look appealing.

But Hunter kept moving forward, away from her, the thick curtain of foliage swallowing him as she watched. Panic licked at her stomach. "Damn it, McBride, stop!" She yelled after him. *"Please!"*

Hunter jerked around. "You have *got* to keep moving, Sarah."

"Just a few minutes? How can a few minutes hurt?" She slapped at another bug and began to peel her long-sleeved shirt off. She was desperate to get cool, to feel air on her arms.

"Don't do that," he warned.

She paused midmotion and glared at him. If she heard one more brusque command come out of Hunter McBride's mouth she was going to scream. *Don't do this. Don't do that. Do this. Do that.* It was all she'd heard through the black night as he'd dragged her at a breakneck pace through the forest. "Why not?" she snapped. "I'm dying of heatstroke here, in case you hadn't noticed." She swatted at a cloud of irritating black insects hanging around her face.

A look of strained patience tightened his features. "Better than being chewed to mincemeat by bugs." He fished into one of the many pockets in his flak jacket, handed her a small bottle of repellent. "They go for the wettest parts of your body—armpits, groin. They want the salt. Best you keep that shirt on, keep covered."

"It's sopping wet," she protested, and hated herself the minute the words came out of her mouth. But she'd completely lost the ability to be cooperative.

A muscle pulsed dangerously along his jawline. "Put the bug juice on, Sarah."

She smeared the insect repellent over the exposed areas of her skin, the chemical fumes nauseating to her empty and already queasy stomach. She handed the bottle back to him and watched as he carefully secured the flap over the repellent. Sarah wasn't able to stop what came out of her mouth next. "I wish you'd lost the damn bug juice instead of the phone. At least we could've gotten help."

His hand stilled. His brows lowered and a quiet, dark thunder crept over his features. He took a step toward her.

Sarah cringed, instinctively backing up against the trunk of a tree. Oh God, had she pushed one of his buttons again? She'd called his skill, *him,* into question. And he didn't like it. Not one bit. When was she going to learn to keep her stupid mouth shut?

"Sarah," he said ominously. "We're on the same team, and don't you forget it. I want to get you *and* this canister out." He clapped his huge hand over the biohazard container he'd secured to his belt with a piece of cord. *Her* container.

"I'm…I'm just stating the obvious. If we had the phone—"

"Did you not hear me? The phone would make no difference. No one is going to fly into Congo airspace. Not unless they want to die. Do you want that, Sarah? Do you want to make people die?"

She bit her lip. This man did not play fair. And she was a fool for pushing him. She'd seen he had low flash points, and she had no idea what could—or would—make him snap. She didn't want to find out. She did not want to be on the wrong side of Hunter McBride in a dangerous mood.

He came even closer, his breath mingling with hers in the moist jungle air. And for an insane moment she thought he was going to kiss her. She thought he was going to force his mouth down hard over hers and savage her right there on the jungle floor.

The thought both terrified and excited her. A mad part of her even wanted, needed him to. She needed to physically tap into his strength even while she was lashing out at him, pushing him away. Maybe this was what Stockholm syndrome was all about. Maybe she had developed an unnatural and deep attraction to her intoxicatingly powerful captor for fear of the alternative—certain death.

His mouth came even closer, his lips almost brushing over hers. Her breathing faltered and her world telescoped in on itself. She closed her eyes.

He traced her jaw very gently with his fingers. "And maybe, Sarah, just maybe, the phone is gone *because* of you."

She flashed her eyes open. "What? Oh, I get it. You lost it because you were too busy looking after me, is that it? I'm a pain in your butt. You think I'm holding you up—"

"You *are* holding me up," he said simply.

Anger bubbled up through the strange mix of sensations swimming through her. She glared into his eyes. "Well, let me tell *you* something, Hunter McBride. Without me you wouldn't have your precious pathogen all boxed and ready to go. You'd still be running around looking for it somewhere in central Africa."

He didn't move a muscle; not even a flicker ran through his strangely colored eyes. His mouth, his body were still just as close.

Sarah's knees started to wobble, but she forced herself to meet his smoldering intensity head-on. "Think about *that,* McBride. Count the days I've saved *you,* and you'll see that dragging me along is a pretty damn small price to pay. So I'd really appreciate it if you'd cut me some slack and let me rest for a damn minute."

Light glimmered in his eyes and a smile tugged at his lips. "Now *there's* the spirit I want to see."

Her jaw dropped. Oh, she saw what he was doing! He was finding hot buttons to make her angry, to feed her energy, anything to kick her in the mental butt and keep her moving through the damn jungle. He was manipulating her emotionally.

Her heart went stone-cold.

That's exactly what Josh used to do. He'd toy with her emotions to get her to react the way he wanted her to. And it had taken her years of psychological and emotional manipulation before she'd even recognized it for the abuse it was, before she'd seen how Josh had been twisting her mind to first blind her to his affairs, and then to make her accept them, as if she were somehow to blame, as if it was *her* fault that her husband needed to look elsewhere for sex. And the fact that she was unable to bear children had played right into his manipulative hands. He'd used it to make her feel worthless as a woman.

Sarah suddenly felt embarrassed. She covered her face with her hands. In her exhausted, dehydrated state she was confusing things, coupling old pathological reactions with the present. She was allowing Josh to get to her even now, a continent and an ocean away. She was seeing him in Hunter McBride. That wasn't fair. But she was too tired. Too tired to think, to stand… She sagged back against the tree and allowed herself to slide down to the spongy ground.

Hunter crouched down beside her. "Sarah?"

For an instant she thought he was going to touch her, and she braced herself. But he didn't. Her heart swooped even lower with hurt, rejection. When was Josh going to stop haunting her? She burrowed her face into her arms.

"Sarah?"

She gritted her teeth, refused to look at him.

"Sarah, *look at me.*"

"I know what you're doing, McBride," she mumbled into her arms. "You *wanted* to make me angry." A dry sob shuddered through her body. "You're doing what Josh used to do to me."

"Josh?" Hunter's brain spun. The Aid Africa file had indicated she was recently divorced. "Is he your ex?"

"Just forget about it!" she muttered.

Hunter frowned. What had her ex-husband done to her to make her feel like this so many thousands of miles away?

But he didn't have time to ask, to coddle. Not if he wanted to save her life. Those soldiers couldn't be far behind. He placed his hand on her shoulder. "Sarah, honey, listen to me, I'm just trying to help get you moving. I want to get you out of here, alive—"

She jerked her head up, brown eyes glistening. "Don't you *honey* me. I'm just a job. You said so yourself. That's it, so quit messing with my head."

"Sarah, that's not—"

"Not what? Tell me it's not true. Tell me you weren't manipulating me."

"Jesus." He dragged his hand through his damp hair. He was at a complete loss for words. "Of course I'm trying to give you motivation. Your mind is the most important survival tool you've got out here. But you're misinterpreting things. You're fatigued." He grasped both her shoulders, forced her to look up into his eyes. "Listen, Sarah, the militia picked up our tracks last night. Six men are coming after us, and you can bet your life they're moving much faster than we are right now."

Her eyes widened in shock. "How…how do you know?"

"I saw them on the river last night, and there's a good chance they picked up our tracks on the beach."

Her eyes flicked wildly around. "Why didn't you tell me?"

"Because you can't afford to panic, like you're doing now. It drains physical resources. You use too many calories, need too much water, can't focus, you make mistakes. Panic is a deadly emotion out here." He paused. "This is not about mind games, Sarah. This is not about you or me or your ex. This is about pure survival."

She stared at him, visibly trying to tamp down her fear. She was struggling both emotionally and physically—and it ate at him. But he *had* to get her moving. He reached for her arm, helped her up.

She hesitated, then looked deep into his eyes. "Tell me one thing, Hunter," she said, very, very softly. "If you are forced to choose between me and that container, which will you pick?"

"Sarah, that's not fair, and you know it."

"Tell me."

His mouth tightened with bitterness. He would have no alternative but to choose the container. That was his job. Those were his orders. "Sarah, you're tired—"

"See? I'm right." She shoved her damp tangle of curls off her forehead. "At least I know where I stand, what I'm worth in this game."

"Sarah…" He reached for her.

She jerked away from him, held up both hands. "Please don't touch me. Don't mess with my head anymore."

His jaw clenched. There was no time for this. And even if there was, there was zip he could do about it. She was twisting everything, making him feel about as lost and confused as a water buffalo in New York City. "Fine," he said. "Whatever. You win, now let's go." He turned and swung viciously at a liana with his machete, dislodging a bunch of epiphytic orchids as he did so. His boots stomped over them as he pushed his way into the forest.

Sarah stared at the crushed blooms in his wake. Oh God, what had she just done? Because of her obsession with her past, with Josh, with her own failures, she'd pushed away the one man who *could* give her the strength to get through this.

She put her fingers to her temples, trying to gather herself. She'd made the mistake of thinking she could put her past behind her by just packing up her life and getting on a plane. But instead, she'd dragged her baggage all the way over the ocean to Africa, into the very heart of the Congo. And it was chasing her down right now, just like those soldiers coming after her.

Sarah could see now that no amount of running was going to help distance her from the effects of Josh's emotional abuse, her past mistakes. They were going to haunt her right into the Blacklands and beyond, unless she found a way to tackle her own ghosts.

Hunter was right. It had to be *her* choice. She had to want to survive. She had to find a way to do this. She had to look into herself, figure out how to sever the past and move forward with only the good memories, not the bad ones. She needed to envision a future for herself, just as he'd said back on the beach—a future beyond the jungle, beyond Josh. She had to try and picture it. Trouble was, she couldn't.

"Sarah!"

She forced her exhausted limbs to move. "Coming…coming." She stepped around the bruised petals and followed him deeper into the jungle.

* * *

They broke through the tangle of foliage so suddenly Sarah thought they were going to pitch straight over the cliff and tumble down into it. She groped instinctively for a branch—anything to help hold her back from the hungry, churning maw below.

The Eikona River.

The ground literally fell away at her toes, where a rocky chasm yawned. Tens of feet below, to her right, a torrent of white water raged through a tight gorge and boiled angrily out the other side, rising in violent waves several feet high that fell back on themselves with a booming sound. The explosive action sent a plume of white mist right up the cliff face on which they stood. It formed tiny droplets on her eyelashes that flashed with rainbows of color when she blinked.

To her left, about five hundred yards downriver, the raging froth calmed and settled into a startling glasslike sheen of emerald-green, broken only by rocks that sliced through the surface.

The water then disappeared into space, under another cloud of white mist churned up by what sounded like a thundering waterfall.

The sight was so awesome, so spectacular, that if she wasn't so exhausted and sore, and her brain so numb, Sarah knew she'd find it heavenly. But right now she had a sick feeling that this was going to be just one more terrifying obstacle she'd have to overcome.

Her eyes cut to Hunter. He was surveying the cliffs as if looking for a way across. *Please, God, no! Don't tell me we have to cross this.*

"That's the Blacklands on the other side," he said. "Once we get across, we'll be safer. And closer to Cameroon—maybe only two days from the border if we keep moving."

Sarah gulped. "How do we cross *that?*"

"See that ledge down there?"

The blood drained from her face as she saw where he was pointing—to a rocky outcrop that hung above the point where the river narrowed into an angry, frothing mass and licked at a monstrous fallen log balanced precariously across the gorge.

"We need to work our way down there, to where that old Bombax has fallen over the gorge. We can use it as a bridge. I'll go first, test it, draw a rope across, secure it, and then you can edge over, using the rope for support."

Her mouth went bone-dry. She didn't think she could do it. But she wasn't going to whine. Not now. Never again. She'd come to Africa to prove she could be strong once more. And she was going to. Exhaustion and fear had almost gotten the better of her, but she wasn't going to let it happen again. She was going tackle her fears head-on—even if it killed her. Because what did she have left? She reached for her crucifix before remembering that even that wasn't there. Then she heard something else, a pulsing sound rising faintly over the hollow boom and thunder of the Eikona River.

It was a thudding so vague and strangely omnipresent she thought at first it might be the beat of her own heart or the blood in her ears. But it swelled around her, grew louder, faster, rising to a panicked rhythm that seemed to grip her heart and make it race along with the sound.

Her eyes flashed nervously to Hunter's. "What's that?"

"War drums."

She listened, trying to identify the direction of the noise. Was she imagining it, or was one set of beats being answered by others? The drumming seemed to be coming from all around her, from everywhere, emanating from the booming river, echoing through the core of every tree. It was the heartbeat of the very Congo itself.

Goose bumps crawled over her skin. She could feel the primeval beat right through her core, talking to the rhythm of her pulse.

"Sarah…" A cool edginess sparked in Hunter's eyes. "We need to get into the Blacklands now. Those drums—the dissention is everywhere."

She looked at him, then the river. The sound of the drums swelled, echoed. She shivered. "You're sure we won't…won't be followed?"

"Not by anyone local." He unslung his pack, removed a length of bound black rope. Talons of fear ripped through Sarah's heart as she stared at the rope. He meant it. She had to cross the Eikona. Her resolve wavered.

She glanced in desperation at the jungle, then back at the river, then at him. He was unraveling the rope. "I'm going to fashion a crude harness to help you down to that ledge," he said as he worked. "You go down first, I'll belay you from above. Once you get to the ledge, wait and I'll follow." He looked up. "Got it?"

She stared at him, unable to move.

He reached out, cupped her face. "Sarah, it's not a tough climb. You can do this." His eyes drilled into hers.

"I know," she whispered. "I know." This was her test. This was where she made her ultimate choice. If she lost her willpower now, she would die. She knew that. And she wanted to live, even if she couldn't yet picture a life for herself beyond this jungle.

Hunter studied her face for a moment, then nodded as if in approval. "Hold out your arms for me."

She did, and he looped the rope under them and around her back. She watched as he knotted the rope carefully above her breastbone.

"Ready?"

She slid her eyes up to meet his. This man was the most solid thing in her world right now. "Yes," she said quietly. "Yes, I'm ready." *In more ways than one.*

Hunter could see that something profound had changed in Sarah. The jungle hadn't broken her yet. She'd tapped into some well of inner strength, and she was doing her damnedest to hold on to that. It made him ridiculously proud of her.

He helped her edge over the first rocky outcrop, and began to feed the rope out gradually as she worked her way down to the ledge, bits of rock and sand kicking out from under her feet as she moved. She slipped suddenly, and the rope jerked taut. Hunter's heart stalled. But she found her footing again, dislodging a small shower of stones as she did. They tumbled down to the river and she turned her head to watch them go.

Don't look at the water, Sarah.

But she stared at the raging torrent below, unable to get going again. His throat went tight. "You're doing great, Sarah," he yelled over the roar of water. "Keep going. You can do it." He willed her to get moving.

Relief washed through his chest as she began once again to inch her way down. She finally found her footing on the ledge, and looked up.

Hunter blew out the breath he'd been holding, gave a thumbs-up and quickly climbed down after her. He reached the ledge and couldn't help what he did next. He yanked her into his arms and held her tightly, too tightly, for just a moment. He told himself it was to feed her resolve, but deep down he knew it was more. *He* needed to hold her. In more ways than one. And that meant he was in serious trouble. "You did great, sweetheart," he whispered into her hair. "Just one more leg and we're over."

She said nothing, just nodded, but he could see that her face was porcelain with fear.

He quickly untied the harness and secured his polypropylene rope to a solid piece of rock jutting from the cliff face. He looped the other end around himself, then glanced up at the jungle fringe along the top of the cliff. Still no sign of the militia. The quicker he and Sarah got over the river and into deep cover on the other side, the better.

"Okay, Sarah, hang ten here. I'm going to draw the rope across the log, secure it at the other end and come back for you. Got it?"

She nodded. Her lips had gone thin and white and she was trembling. He had to move fast, before she lost it.

He edged out onto the thick log and his boot slipped almost immediately. He caught himself, hesitated. The wood was rotting under the constant spume of mist, and covered with a slick layer of black detritus. He steadied himself, bounced lightly, testing his weight. The fallen log was solid enough to hold them both and seemed securely planted against the opposite rock face. He edged sideways along it, feeding the rope out as he went, testing resistance with small bounces. The awkward cylindrical shape of the biohazard container tied to his belt threw his balance off. The thing weighed maybe eighteen pounds, and he had to concentrate on compensating.

River mist saturated his hair and droplets began to drip into his eyes. The rope was also wet now. But Hunter made it to the narrow ledge on the opposite side, and again looked up at the rock face. It wasn't that steep on this end. It would be a fairly easy scramble up into the forest cover. He just had to get Sarah across. He drew the rope taut and secured it to the trunk of a sapling that grew out the rock face. Grasping the rope, he made his way quickly back over the log to Sarah.

He held his hand out to her. "Your turn."

She stared at his hand, unable to move.

"Sarah, you *want* to survive. Make it happen."

She clasped his fingers, a little too tightly, a little too desperately. Worry pinged through him. He told himself he had to exude calm. He had to show that he had confidence in her. He guided her hand toward the rope as she edged her feet onto the log.

"It's slippery, but solid. Just work your way along slowly. Hold the rope with both hands, but don't lean into it. Don't think about the water. Don't even look at it."

She let go of his hand and grabbed the rope, immediately putting too much of her weight into it, and swaying out over the water. Hunter's heart kicked. He jerked the rope back so that her weight was once again centered over the log, almost losing his own balance in the process. The biohazard container lurched around his thigh, threatening to topple him.

"Easy, Sarah. Easy does it. Keep your weight over your feet. Just use the rope as a guide."

She swallowed hard and began to shuffle sideways, making little moaning noises as she went. He moved slowly alongside her, muttering words of encouragement, ready to grab her if she slipped.

They were completely drenched now, Sarah's hair plastered to her face and her knuckles white on the rope. Her movements grew jerky as she neared the center of the gorge. Hunter could literally see her losing her nerve. She made it to the middle, where the boom of the water was loudest, echoing between the rock walls of the canyon. Waves licked up toward the log. She faltered, then froze. "Just a few more steps and you're more than halfway," he yelled over the roar.

She glanced nervously at the opposite bank, subconsciously leaning toward it as she did. The motion shot her left foot out from under her, and she went down onto log with a scream, just managing to hold onto the rope with one hand. The movement knocked Hunter off balance. He flailed backward and the canister swung wildly out behind him. He grabbed for the rope, catching himself, but his added weight jerked it from Sarah's hand. She screamed as she clutched at a small bit of branch, just managing to halt her slide off the log and into the river. Her feet dangled precariously over the churning white water as she stared, wild-eyed, up at Hunter.

He dropped flat onto the log. "Sarah! Give me your hand!"

But she couldn't seem to make herself let go of the small, rotting branch she was hanging on to for dear life. He could literally see it tearing loose. It was going to go at any second.

He lunged for her, grabbing her arm just as the branch gave way. The canister swung out over the water, threatening to pull him over, too.

Hunter hung on to Sarah desperately as she swung over the gorge. He could feel his grip on the log slipping as the black detritus began to slough off. Her arm was also slick with river mist, and he could feel he was losing his grip there, too, gravity and her weight conspiring to fight him, the river hungry and waiting below.

She began to slide from his grasp, and the waves licked at her shoes. She flailed wildly with her free hand, trying to grasp the canister hanging almost within her reach. She grabbed it just as her arm slid free of Hunter's hold.

The fresh weight on his belt yanked him sideways around the log. Hunter swore as he dug his fingers into the rotting wood, knowing that if he lost his grip, they would both go down.

He clung with all his might, but the thin cord on his belt gave, snapping free with a jerk.

His heart lurched. He scrambled up onto the log, and the last thing he saw was Sarah's hair churning like brown streamers in the white water before the foam swallowed her completely.

Then he saw her head pop up downriver, the canister lolling

in the waves beside her—both heading inexorably toward the smooth, glassy sheen of water racing toward the falls.

He could never reach both before one went over.

He faced the choice. Sarah or the canister.

Her life, or the lives of millions?

Hunter plunged feetfirst into the roiling maw.

Chapter 8

Sarah thrashed against the roiling current, but the powerful Eikona sucked her under, whirling her along.

She forced her eyes open, trying to figure out which way was up and which was down, but all she could see was a milky-green blur. She was running out of breath, and she didn't even know which way to push for the surface! Terror squeezed her lungs. She knew she was being hurtled toward the falls, could already feel the change in the water… *She was going over.* But just as the knowledge slammed into her, she felt something grab at her.

Hunter!

Hope kicked at her heart. She began to fight harder against the current, struggling to find the surface. She felt the iron strength in his arms as he pulled her toward him, hooked his arm around her chest and dragged her up through the water until they popped to the surface like corks. She gasped for air as he towed her diagonally across the ribbed sheen of water that surged toward the falls, and into the calm of an eddy. He hauled her roughly up a slope of rock, dumped his pack with a thud beside her. His gun and machete clattered down beside it. "Use them if you need them!" he yelled over the roar of the falls.

And he was gone, back into the river, cutting across the glassy, swollen surface with smooth, powerful strokes. Sarah's heart stalled as she saw him heading for the biohazard container bobbing dangerously close to the brink of the falls.

It was impossible. He'd never reach it in time. She watched in numb horror as Hunter was swept sideways faster than he could close the distance between himself and the canister.

She saw him near the container, grab it. Her heart jerked against her ribs. He turned, began to swim toward her. But he was moving backward even faster. She caught her breath.

He wasn't going to make it!

Sarah leaped to her feet, pressed her hands over her mouth as everything began to unfold in sickening slow motion.

Hunter was pulled to the edge of the falls, and for a second he seemed to hang there, poised in the mist on the knife edge of the swollen, glassy river. Then the Eikona sucked him over and he disappeared into the steaming sky.

"No!" she screamed. "Oh, God, no! Hunter!" She spun around, hysterical. She didn't know what to do! Then she spotted his pack, his gun, his machete. He'd left all his equipment. *He'd known all along he wasn't going to make it.* She was on her own. He'd left her all the tools he could for her to try to survive without him.

For a second sheer terror paralyzed her. She wouldn't believe it. She could *not* believe he was gone. He was invincible. He was her lifeline. She choked with emotion. No, he wasn't invincible. Hunter McBride was only human in spite of everything she'd learned and thought about him. He'd saved *her* first. Her life *had* meant more to him than his mission.

Tears streamed from her eyes. Oh God, she had to find him! She pressed her hands to her temples, trying to think. She'd need his pack if she found him. She'd need the first aid gear, food, whatever else he had in it. She grabbed it, hefted it up to her back, but it swung violently, throwing her off balance. Her wet runners slithered out from under her on the slick surface. She crashed down onto the rock, landing hard on her hip. But she barely registered the explosive spark of pain. She scrambled back onto her feet, repositioned the pack on her back. It felt incredibly heavy in her weakened state. Bowing under the weight of Hunter's gear, she grabbed his assault rifle and machete, slung them over her shoulders.

How in heaven had he carried all this stuff, and hacked through the bush at the same time? How could he have possibly looked so relaxed under all this hot and cumbersome gear? Sarah clenched her jaw against the strain, staggered awkwardly over the rocks in her sodden runners. She reached the muddy bank, grabbed a fistful of coarse grass, dragged herself up off the rock slab. On hands and knees she clambered up the steep slope toward what looked like a narrow path along the ridge.

Breath rasping in her throat, fear slamming her heart into her ribs, she reached the path. She bent over to catch her breath, saw animal tracks in the red soil. She lifted her eyes. It was a narrow game path leading toward the falls, where it disappeared alongside the booming curtain of water. She suspected the trail led all the way down to a big calm watering hole at the bottom of the falls. She'd seen something just like this on a nature program.

Sarah staggered along the path, fatigue and panic making her sway wildly under the weight of Hunter's pack and gun and machete. Her hair was plastered to her face, her wet clothes chafed her skin and her feet skidded and squelched in her drenched shoes. But she was blind to it. All she wanted was to get down that path and find Hunter.

But the jungle fought her every step of the way. She tried to run, making it to the edge of the falls before the weight of the pack swung her sideways and she skidded on vegetation slick from the heavy, constant mist churned up by the thunderous falls. Sarah landed hard on her butt and began to slide downhill alongside the crashing curtain of water. She held the gun tight at her side, worried it would go off as she tried to control her hectic tumble down the steep path. She hit a rock, lurched head over heels, came to a dead stop. Blood thudded loudly against her eardrums.

She had to focus. What had Hunter said? Panic could kill you. She forced herself to breathe, and peered nervously through the mist and rainbows.

She could see something down below. A dark, limp shape lay at the edge of a tranquil, turquoise-green pool at the base of the falls. She froze. The shape was unmistakably human. It was him, had to be, lying facedown in the mud, sprawled out, unmoving. Her heart stalled. A part of her didn't want to believe it was Hunter. She willed him to move, to show some sign of life. But he didn't.

"Oh God, Hunter," she whispered. "Please be alive. Please be alive. Please be alive…." She repeated the words over and over like a mantra as she scrambled down the path to the rim of slippery, rust-colored mud.

She stopped at the bottom, afraid to go up to the water's edge, petrified of what she might find. She began to shake violently, and tears made her blind.

She swiped them brutally out of her eyes. *Control yourself, Sarah. He needs you now.*

God, she hoped he *did* need her, that she would find some sign of life in her invincible mercenary, the hardened man who had touched her so tenderly, helped give her willpower. The man who—she choked on a sob—the man who had chosen *her* life over everything he'd been trained to do.

She began to squelch toward his limp form, swallowing her trepidation and forcing herself into clinical mode as she got closer.

He was lying on his stomach, his right arm twisted at a strange angle, his fist still clutched around the handle of the bio-hazard container. One side of his face was in the mud. His eyes were closed and his skin was gray. Sarah's heart plummeted. She'd seen that look before.

She knelt at his side, her heart beating light and fast. "Hunter?" she whispered as she touched his face. His skin was ice-cold. "Hunter!" She grabbed his shoulders and shook him. She could not, would not, lose someone else to this jungle. Not him, not Hunter. He had to be alive. "Hunter!"

She felt him move. Her heart pounded against her ribs. "Hunter?"

He lifted his head slightly out of the mud and his eyelids fluttered open. He stared at her, slowly registering his surroundings. Then he grimaced. "Hello, angel."

A wave of emotion surged through Sarah, so strong it stole her breath and ability to form words. Hot tears of relief filled her eyes. She smiled and placed her hand against his muddy cheek. "Thank God, oh thank God you're alive."

He closed his eyes briefly and his body shuddered.

"How…how badly are you hurt?"

He tried to lift his head again, groaned, let it fall back into the mud. She winced and a new set of fears crept into her heart.

He tried to move again. "Help…help me up, Sarah." He ground out the words through clenched teeth. "I need to get up there…by the trees. Less mud there." He maneuvered himself onto his good elbow, his eyes bright with pain. "And we…must…stay…near cover." He swallowed a bark of pain as he tried to sit up.

"Maybe…maybe you shouldn't move. Maybe you should lie still until—"

His eyes cut to hers. "Until what? The ambulance comes?"

It hit her then, the implications of being hurt in the wilderness. There was zero hope of help, no civilized system to come to their aid. They had only themselves, two humans against a deadly jungle where only the fittest survived. And now the balance of power between her and Hunter had shifted squarely onto her shoulders. *He needed her.* And she had the skills to help him. She could no longer be a victim in any way. It was up to her now.

The realization shot a jolt of determined fire through her body. She couldn't afford raw fear now. She had to focus and fight—for him.

She sucked in a steadying breath. "Hunter, before I help you move, you have to tell me exactly where you hurt, so that I—"

He was feeling his left shoulder with his good hand. "Anterior dislocation of the sternoclavicular joint."

Surprise rippled through her. "What?"

"My left shoulder—" he groaned as he forced himself onto his knees "—it's dislocated."

"How do you know?"

"I know. I can feel it."

She stared at him, momentarily stunned. "It…I mean, it could be broken, or—"

"No." He staggered to his feet, gasped as pain punched through him. "I…felt it go…when I tried to keep hold of the container as I went under at the base of the falls."

"You're sure?"

"Of course I'm sure! The muscles are already going into spasm. You've got to help me reduce it immediately, Sarah." His eyes pierced hers. "I need my arm. We *both* do if we want to get out of here."

He was right on that count. And if his diagnosis was correct, the top of his left humerus had been forced forward out of the shoulder socket. The longer it stayed that way, the less likely it was they'd manage to get it back into place without surgery. And that was impossible. If left untreated, he'd be seriously disabled and in constant and debilitating pain.

He started to stumble through the mud, holding his injured arm steady with his good hand. "Bring the container," he called back to her as he made his way up to the trees.

Sarah grabbed the handle of the biohazard canister and got to her feet. She squished through the mud after him, the gear on her back weighing her down.

He sagged under a tree where the red laterite was packed hard. She removed the rifle and machete slings, shrugged out of his pack and dumped it on the ground. He gave her a grin twisted with pain. "You *are* an angel. You brought all the gear."

A wedge of pride jammed into her. She smiled. "Yeah, I did."

His eyes trailed over her. "You got a bit messed up, though."

She glanced down at her clothing and a crazy giggle rippled through her. She looked like an urchin out of a Dickens novel. "Guess I was in a bit of a hurry."

He nodded, and his tacit approval warmed her. She felt suddenly as if he respected her, as if they were part of a team now. And she couldn't begin to articulate what that meant to her.

He slid his hunting knife out of the sheath on his thigh, held it out to her. "Here."

She stared at it. That knife had killed her pursuers.

"Take it, Sarah. Cut my sleeve off."

She swallowed her mix of feelings and clasped her fingers around the hilt, felt its weight in her hand. She needed this knife to help heal him now. This was her present reality. And in some strange way, in taking hold of that knife, she felt as if she'd just become part of this strange system, this living organism of a jungle that was probably the most competitive natural arena on earth.

She lifted the fabric of his camouflage shirt away from his shoulder, poked a hole through it with the hooked tip of the blade and jerked her hand back. The blade sliced neatly through the strong material. She pulled the sleeve loose and maneuvered it carefully down over his injured arm.

She recognized the profile of a dislocated shoulder instantly. The next thing that struck her was that his muscles were rock-hard and in serious spasm.

She placed her hands on his shoulder. His skin was hot. She fingered along his joint, locating the position of the bones. "You're right," she said. "I can feel the medial end of the clavicle here—" she moved her hand over his skin "—and the head of the humerus here. It's an anterior dislocation."

He said nothing, just watched her intently.

She checked the pulse at his wrist and compared it with the strength of the pulse at his elbow. She let out a silent sigh of relief. The major blood vessels that passed through the shoulder area were undamaged. "Pulse is fine." She pinched the back of his hand. "You feel that?"

"Yeah, I felt a nibble."

She smiled. His muscles were so tense and his skin so taut it was impossible to grab enough flesh between her fingers to give a real bite. But the fact he'd felt it at all showed his nerves were in working order. She pinched his rock-hard deltoid muscle, just below his shoulder on the top of his arm. "And that?"

He nodded. "That, too."

Relief surged through her. His axillary nerve, one of the most vulnerable in this sort of injury, was undamaged. This was looking to be a straightforward dislocation. All she had to do now was manipulate the joint back into place without damaging any nerves in the process. That was easier said than done. His muscle tone, strength and size were phenomenal, while she was slight in stature and in a weakened state. She was no match for his body. His muscles were going to fight her every step of the way.

She rocked back on her heels, pushed her wet hair off her forehead. How in heavens was she going to do this?

He was watching her, reading her mind. "You have to fix it, Sarah."

"I…I know. It's just—"

"Do it, Sarah. *Now*. We don't have time to waste. The longer we leave it the more my muscles are going to fight you."

She began to remove her shoe. "Lie back."

Hunter lowered himself slowly down onto the packed earth. The pain in his left shoulder was excruciating, and his muscles had tightened to fight against the injury. This was going to take time—time they could ill afford. They needed to get well into the cover of the jungle before the soldiers arrived and sighted them from the opposite bank of the river.

Sarah positioned her butt in the dirt at his side, one shoe off. "Ready?"

Hunter stared at the little yellow pompom on her wet sock, and in spite of his pain, he felt a smile in his heart. This woman was something else. "Yeah, I'm ready."

She positioned her socked foot in his armpit, wrapped both

her hands around his wrist and leaned back, exerting pressure with her foot as she began to pull his arm.

His nerves screeched in pain and his muscles contracted in resistance. But she kept the pressure steady, consistent, fighting his body. He knew Sarah had been running on empty before her plunge into the river, and she had to be even more drained now. But she kept at it, color beginning to rise in her cheeks.

He felt his muscles begin to give, and a groan of pain escaped him. Shock flared in her eyes and he felt her release the pressure slightly. "No." He ground out the word. "Keep…pulling." This could take upward of twenty minutes, the way his muscles were protesting.

Perspiration began to bead on her brow and glow on her face. Her limbs started to tremble with the effort. "This…this isn't working, Hunter," she gasped.

"Pull, damn it!"

She gritted her teeth, scrunched her eyes tight, held the pressure. Hunter used every ounce of mental strength to force relaxation into his spasming muscles. And finally he felt them begin to release. "Hold…hold it now!"

Sweat poured down her brow and she steadied the pressure. He could feel the muscles in her leg quivering with the sustained tension. But she was good. Damn good. A pro. He could feel her twist his arm, maneuver his bone ever so slightly, timing herself, releasing movement when she could sense give. She eased, waited. Eased. Waited again. Then suddenly he felt the telltale bump as his shoulder jerked back into place. The intensity of pain subsided almost immediately.

Hunter released a huge breath of air, and his body went limp. He laughed out loud in sheer relief, couldn't help himself. "God, you really are an angel, you know that?"

She kept her eyes closed. She just sat there, hunched over,

her face streaked with mud, her hair a wet tangle, one shoe on, one shoe off, her wet sock with the pompom now streaked with bloodred dirt. And in that instant, Hunter had never seen anything more endearing, more appealing, than this woman.

He pushed himself to a sitting position. "Sarah?"

She still didn't open her eyes. Tears began to leak out from under her lashes and drip silently down her cheeks, tracking crooked trails through the dirt. A sensation washed through his body, a feeling for her so deep and so explosive he couldn't begin to articulate what it was. He'd done the right thing going after her. He knew it in his heart. He would never have been able to live with himself otherwise.

She opened her eyes and looked right into him, into his soul. "Thank you," she whispered. "Thank you for coming after me." She leaned forward, cupped her hands around his face and brushed her lips softly over his. "I didn't believe in you. I'm so sorry."

He closed his eyes, shuddered. How could a simple touch be so sweet, words so achingly painful? It was as if she'd just ripped a yawning chasm of need right through the very center of his heart, an empty void so deep and vast that he knew he was going to spend the rest of his life trying to fill it. *Damn this woman.* The rawness, the explosive clout of the unexpected emotion was almost too powerful.

"Hunter?"

He couldn't talk to her. Not now. He had to get control of himself. He climbed to his feet and reached for his gun. They needed to fill the canteens and get into jungle cover ASAP.

"Hunter—"

"My knife, hand me my knife," he barked. He knew his words were clipped, but he couldn't stop himself, couldn't handle his feelings.

Her mouth dropped open slightly. Confusion knitted her brow. She reached for the hunting knife at her side, handed it to him. "What about your arm? We should splint it. I should check the pulse again to see that we didn't—"

"Later. We move now!" he snapped. He turned his back on her, angrily blinking back the hot burn in his eyes. Christ, he hadn't shed a tear in fifteen goddamn years. He wasn't about to go soft now.

Chapter 9

Sarah's triumph in having helped Hunter—a man she'd viewed as invincible—had fired her with a fierce new determination to survive. It also gave her a deep sense of her own value, something she'd been lacking for a long, long time. The old Sarah, the person she'd been before Josh, was finally poking through, and in her heart she was feeling strength again. But the nurse in her was still worried about the mercenary.

She watched Hunter carefully as he led the way along the narrow, rutted game path. The going was relatively easy here, the ground drier, the trees tall and covered with white lichen. But the two of them had been walking for almost four hours since he'd gone over Eikona Falls, and she could see he was beginning to weaken. He'd given her the biohazard container so that he could keep his left arm immobile, but he insisted on carrying the rest of his gear himself. She wished he'd allowed her to splint his arm. If he fell, it could pop out again.

"Hunter," she called to him.

He stopped, turned around. The strained tightness of his features, the bright sheen in his dark eyes startled her. She hoped he didn't have some internal damage he wasn't telling her about.

"Could we take a rest?" This time she wasn't asking for herself, she was asking for him. She knew he wasn't going to stop because *he* was tired.

"Not yet." He began to turn back.

"Hunter! I insist."

He glanced over his shoulder, cocked an eyebrow.

"I need to splint that arm, and I need to check your pulse again. The nerves could've been pinched when the bone went back into the socket."

A grin twitched along one corner of his mouth. "That the nurse I hear talking?"

"Damn right. You have *got* to take a break. You said we'd be safe here in the Blacklands, once we got into the trees."

He studied her.

"Well? Are we safe now?" She angled her head. "Or were you lying just to mess with my mind again?" And with a little spark of surprise, she realized she'd just joked about something that up until this second had been dead serious to her.

That smile tugged at his mouth again. "Another hour," he said. "Then we rest."

She scowled at him and put her hands on her hips.

His grin broadened. "I promise."

"Okay, but I'm going to hold you to that promise, soldier."

* * *

The day grew hotter as they moved deeper into the Blacklands, and her clothes, still damp from the river, chafed against her skin. The sound of a bird—*tok tok-boo, tok-tok-boo*—seemed to follow them constantly.

"What *is* that?"

"Red-crested cuckoo. Each bird calls to the one in the next territory as we move."

It made her feel creepy, as if they were being watched, their progress being telegraphed from one cuckoo camp to another in some kind of jungle code. A chill of foreboding crept over her skin. She hoped Hunter was right when he said no one would follow them into this place.

They broke into a clearing and were hit with such a fierce wave of sunlight and heat that it stole her breath. A narrow corridor of grassland stretched out in front of them, perhaps half a mile long, bounded by thick shrubs and low forest. Golden grasses swayed gently in the hot breeze. She could see blue sky, huge cotton candy clouds scudding across it, driven by an invisible wind high up in the stratosphere.

Sarah stepped forward into the grass, and a cloud of butterflies the size of small birds fluttered up into the air. They were scarlet and yellow, some spotted and dashed with streaks and whorls of iridescent blue. Others were speckled with orange and brown, like autumn leaves that had come alive and taken flight. Sarah gasped. "It's…it's so beautiful," she whispered. "I never expected to see anything like this in the middle of the jungle."

"Edaphic savannah," said Hunter. "Little natural savannahs entirely enclosed by forests, pockets of grassland on soil too run-down to support even the smallest trees." He scanned the area with narrowed eyes as he spoke. "Usually you find them along sandy riverbeds that dry out when the stream changes course. Almost nothing is known about them…." He glanced at her. "What you're seeing is damn rare. This ecosystem is unique to this region of the Congo basin, and it's protected because few people dare venture in here."

She moved her hand slowly through the cloud of dancing butterflies. "A slice of pure Eden," she whispered to herself. "Cursed by the spirits or protected by the gods, it's a matter of perspective."

Hunter looked at her, a mix of interest and surprise crossing his features. "Exactly."

"We can rest here," she said. And it wasn't a question.

He consulted his watch.

She glowered at him. "You promised, Hunter. We can dry our clothes here, and I *must* splint your arm."

"Anyone ever tell you that you're bossy?"

"Anyone ever told you that you're insufferably pigheaded?"

He smiled again and the sunlight caught his eyes. Something cracked in her heart. She hadn't seen him smile like that. Genuine, gentle almost. It was as if he'd let his guard slip momentarily, and she was seeing the true man inside, the man behind the mercenary.

She reached for his pack. "Here, let me help you off-load this." He didn't argue, which vaguely surprised—and concerned—her. He turned around, allowing her to help him shrug out of his gear without putting pressure on his shoulder joint.

"You really should've let me carry more stuff."

"I'm fine." He crouched down, untied the roll of canvas and nylon that was secured at the bottom of his pack. "Hammock," he said as he flicked the roll with his good arm, sending it unraveling, the ropes flying. "Doubles as a decent ground cover." He handed her a corner and she helped him spread it near the roots of a tree at the edge of the clearing. The shade here was dappled, the sunlight not too harsh.

"Give me your shirt." She held out her hand. "I'll hang it in the sun."

He arched a brow, studied her. "This how you treated the kids in your ward?"

"Kids were more cooperative."

He shrugged out of his flak jacket and undid his shirt buttons with one hand. "What made you become a pediatric nurse anyway, Sarah?"

"How'd you know I was a pediatric nurse?"

"It was in your file."

Reality intruded and with it a twinge of unease. She nodded. "I see. Well, I love children, always have." She lifted her eyes, met his.

He studied her carefully as he shrugged out of his one-sleeved shirt. "Something tells me you're a sucker for the vulnerable, Sarah." He handed her his damp gear. "You're a born nurturer. It's your strength."

"And weakness," she muttered as she took his clothes. She hesitated, looking at his pants.

A grin ghosted his lips. "I keep the pants. For now." He sank down onto the hammock, leaned back heavily against the tree trunk and closed his eyes with a sigh.

Sarah removed her own long-sleeved blouse and the thin cotton pants from under her skirt. She ventured out into the long gold grass and draped their clothes over a scrubby bush in direct sunlight. She was surprised to feel how dry his high-tech gear felt compared to her stuff. The heat burned down on the top of her head, her shoulders and the bare skin on her arms as she made her way back to him and the shade. She sat on the tarp next to him and removed her socks and shoes. She wiggled her toes in the warm air and sighed. "Feels good," she said. "What about you, your boots?"

"I'm good. Jungle gear. Breathable."

She frowned. He wasn't relaxed enough to take his shoes off. He was still on guard. A niggle of unease skittered through her. She shrugged it off, pulled the first aid kit to her side, extracted a roll of bandages. "Okay, soldier, sit up and get that arm into position."

He did, his eyes locking on to hers. Up close they were the color of an evening sky slipping into velvet night. His breath was warm against her face, his scent masculine. Her heart skipped a beat, then kicked into a fast, light pace. She was suddenly very conscious of being so close to his naked chest, the dark hair that covered his powerful pecs, the glorious way it nestled between ridges of honed muscle and disappeared into the belt of his pants. Warmth unfurled low in her belly. She felt a little giddy.

She told herself it was fatigue, dehydration, lack of food, oppressive heat. Or maybe it was just the dizzying, life-affirming thrill of having once again cheated death.

Whatever it was, she hadn't expected to feel wild sexual attraction out here in the jungle. She swallowed against the dryness in her mouth, looked away from his eyes and began to wrap the bandage around him. She noticed her hands were trembling slightly as she worked, and it had nothing to do with fear.

"There. That'll help keep it still." She blew out the breath she hadn't realized she'd been holding, and made the mistake of looking back up into his eyes.

They smoldered with a dangerous, dark electricity, and the air seemed to suddenly pulse with the heat of it. Sarah couldn't speak. The mutual attraction was undeniable. And for a dizzying instant she felt as if they were poised on the knife edge of a torrent, just like he'd hung for a second at the brink of Eikona Falls. She feared what would happen if they were plunged into the depths of what swirled between them. In truth, she was flat-out terrified of feeling anything like this for a man as powerful as Hunter. She'd made that mistake before.

And it had cost her everything.

"Thank you," he said, his voice low and husky.

She jerked her mind back, swallowed once more. Then pinched his deltoid muscle. Hard.

"Hey, I felt that."

"Good," she said, and pinched him again, harder, this time on the back of his hand.

"That, too. I'm beginning to think I wouldn't want to get into a heavy tussle with you over taking my medicine."

She shook off the sensuous image that leaped into her mind, cleared her throat and checked his pulse at his wrist, and then at his elbow. "Looks like you'll live another day."

He studied her, a wickedly playful light beginning to twinkle in his eyes. "So, nurse, just how am I going to get my shirt back on?"

"What?"

He jerked his chin toward the bandage she'd used to carefully strap his arm to his chest.

She clapped her hand to her head and sank back against the tree, the heat of embarrassment warming her cheeks. "I wasn't thinking."

"Where did you say you went to nursing school?"

She began to laugh. It felt damn good. It released all the pent-up tension, the sexual heat.

He touched her jaw. She stilled instantly. He traced her profile lightly with his fingertips. "Do you have any idea how gorgeous you are when you laugh like that?"

She bit her lip, suddenly nervous. He'd put his attraction into words. It made it too real, something to be dealt with. She was afraid, not ready. And yet she was. She wanted him to touch her—wanted it with such a sudden deep and desperate need it overwhelmed her.

It was as if he read her mind. He smiled, a genuine, warm, caring smile, and dropped his hand from her face, reached for his pack, fished in an outside pocket, took something out. "Here." He held it toward her. "Reward for saving my ass back there."

She gaped. "Oh. My. God. *Chocolate!*"

"Want some?"

"Are you kidding?" She lunged for it.

He jerked it just out of her reach, wiggled the chocolate bar in temptation. "What's it worth to you?"

"Saving your butt again."

"That'll do." He handed it to her.

She tore it open. "Oh, my God, I can't believe you have chocolate. Hunter…I think I love you."

He stilled.

Oops. What had she just said? She looked slowly up into his eyes.

His face was dark. Unreadable. "You mean that?"

Her heart began to palpitate, her palms grow moist. "I… I—" Lord, what was it she felt for him?

His face cracked into a grin. "I'm kidding. You gonna share that? I want at least a third."

She moistened her lips and broke the soft chocolate bar in two, thankful for the task. She handed him half and popped a squishy square into her mouth.

She closed her eyes, leaned back against the trunk and let it melt over her tongue. It tasted like heaven. "Mmm, this is so good. It's the best chocolate ever." She opened her eyes as sugar surged through her depleted system. "You know, the night I escaped the clinic, I was hunched up in the roots of that Bombax tree, in pitch darkness, petrified, not knowing what on earth to do next, and you know what I was thinking?"

"What?"

She broke off another square. "I was thinking about buying chocolate, in a mall. I was thinking the stores in Seattle would be getting in Halloween stuff by now. Can you believe that? I was staring death in the face, and all I could do was think about candy."

"The mind seeks comfort in strange ways." He looked away from her over the gently swaying gold savannah grass, and his eyes grew distant. "Sometimes you have no control." He snapped back from wherever his thoughts had taken him. "And now? What're you thinking now?"

She stopped munching. "Now?"

"Yeah, now."

"I…I'm just happy to be alive right now. I'm not really thinking about anything," she lied. She could feel her face flush as she said it. She was a pathetic liar. But there was no way she was going to go near telling him what she was really thinking, about how damn attractive she found him, about how the way his hair disappeared into the belt of his pants made her want to melt from the inside out.

"You're not thinking about home now?"

"I told you, I don't have a home anymore." She forced a smile and held up her last piece of chocolate. "Besides, I have everything I need right here."

"Everything?" The muscle at his jaw pulsed softly.

She watched it, feeling her own pulse match his rhythm. She swallowed hard. He was doing the damnedest things to her body with a few words. She had to talk about something else, so she switched tables on him. "What're *you* thinking?"

"You don't want to know what I'm thinking, Sarah." His voice was husky as he said it.

Her cheeks went hot. She flicked her eyes away but something delicious tingled low in her stomach.

"Tell me about your ex," he said suddenly.

"What?"

"What happened? What did he do to you?"

She stared at him. Her marital failure was none of his business. Or maybe it was. Maybe she'd made it so by her ridiculous outburst back near the Eikona River.

He waited for her to answer. A bird called in the distant treetops, a long series of hoots, descending in scale and dying away to a single pitiful *hoo*. It was an eerie, lonely cry. A shiver chased over her hot skin. Maybe she needed to tell him, to share. Maybe she had to get this off her chest. Perhaps it would give her some sense of closure.

She sucked in a breath. "Josh left me for another woman." There, she'd said it. So why did it make her feel as if she'd just stripped off her clothes in front of Hunter and bared her body and soul? She waited, nervous, for his judgment, and at the same time hated herself for feeling this way. *This* was what Josh had done to her. His leaving her should *not* be a reflection on her worth as a woman. She shouldn't feel that she would be somehow judged lacking by his actions.

She knew all of that, but just couldn't shed it. That sense of failure, of inferiority had become a part of who she was. And not being able to bear children hadn't helped. Josh had used that against her, too. He'd abused her caring nature, used her every weakness to undermine her. And he'd done it so insidiously, and over so many years, that she'd finally integrated a sense of worthlessness.

It had become a part of her psyche. *This* was what she had

to shake. This was what she had to find a way to face down. She just wasn't sure how. But she had a sense she'd begun. Finally. And it was this jungle and Hunter that were, in a perverse way, showing her she really did have the courage and strength inside to do it.

He was studying her intently. She glanced self-consciously down at the chocolate wrapper in her hand, fiddled with the foil edges.

"Why did he leave you?" he asked, the words so simple.

"It's…it's complicated."

"Try me."

She looked up into Hunter's eyes. How could she tell him the real reason? How could she tell this *übermale* that she was pathetic enough to have allowed this to happen to her? It was humiliating. It made her furious with herself.

He hooked a knuckle under her jaw, made her look at him. "Sarah, talk to me."

"It…it was my fault. I should've walked out on him when he first started having affairs."

"Why didn't you?"

"You have to know Josh to understand. He's…he's powerful. He had a way of controlling my emotions. He…made me feel…inadequate."

Flint hardened Hunter's eyes. "Did he hurt you?"

She tensed at the overt aggression in his tone. "No, not in the way you think. Not physically. Just emotionally." She steeled herself. "Josh was…*is* a sociopath. He's charismatic, incredibly charming when he wants to be, but he's completely manipulative, ruthless in getting exactly what he wants out of a person." She hesitated. "Now that I have some distance, I can see that he'd been abusing, manipulating me emotionally for years. I should've seen it coming. I should never have allowed it to get as far as it did."

The muscles in Hunter's neck went stiff. She could almost feel the anger begin to vibrate off him. She had a sudden vision of Josh squaring off with Hunter, and there was no doubt in her mind who would win. Hunter McBride was a better man than her ex in every possible way.

"Why did you marry him, Sarah?"

Her chest went tight. Her eyes began to moisten. She didn't want to think about Josh. She wanted to forget the past. "Hunter…I—I don't really want to talk about it. I want to forget. I *came* here to forget."

He leaned forward. "But you can't forget, can you, Sarah? It's followed you. You can't even talk about it without feeling shame. I can see it in your eyes."

She bit her lip, fiddled with the wrapper in her lap. "I know. You're right." She lifted her eyes to his. "How did a soldier become so deep?"

"By making his own mistakes." He covered her fidgeting hand with his. "So why did you marry him?"

She sucked in another breath. "I told you, he can be a real charmer. We met soon after I got my first job at the children's hospital. He'd just been transferred to Seattle and was in line for a big promotion." She looked at the chocolate wrapper in her hand. "He's a mergers and acquisitions giant. He literally swallows people and businesses for a living without blinking an eye, and I didn't even see it, how mercenary he was, even back then. I totally fell for him. I loved him with all my heart, but now that I look back, I see that he probably never did love me. I simply fitted his needs at the time. Having a young, obedient trophy wife was just the kind of image he needed to cinch his big promotion. He got it, and he never looked back, just kept right on climbing. That…that was six years ago." She hesitated. "Now he doesn't need me anymore. He's moved on to a beautiful younger woman with a famous name—a model who's carrying his twins. It's gotten him into the papers, the tabloids…just what he wanted." Sarah paused, stared at the gold grass waving in the warm wind. "It's really quite shocking to realize you've wasted so much of your life on someone who never once gave a damn. Men like him can't care."

"Ah, I see. You were comparing him to me."

She whipped her eyes to his. "It's not true, Hunter. You're *not* the same. Josh would never have saved me over that canister. He would have let me die. *You didn't.*" She looked right into his eyes. "I am so sorry I judged you. I…I've been burned, and that makes me…careful. I just don't trust myself to make good judgments anymore."

He sat silent, his eyes glimmering, a powerful current pulsing through him—one she couldn't identify.

"What gave you the courage to finally leave him?"

She liked the way he said that. It implied he believed she'd found some inner strength. But she hadn't. "Josh left *me*, Hunter. He walked out the door the night I confronted him about his latest affair. He wasn't even bothering to be discreet about it anymore."

"His affair with the model?"

Sarah angrily sniffed back her emotion. "Yes. And you know how I found out about it? My friends didn't tell me. They were embarrassed for me. They didn't want to hurt me. But nothing could have hurt or humiliated me more than standing in that checkout line at the grocery store and seeing my husband's face staring at me from the magazine racks—my husband with his arms around another woman, a very pregnant woman."

Bitter tears blurred her vision. Sarah scrunched the chocolate wrapper into a tight little ball in the palm of her hand. "I actually put my sunglasses on before I got to the register. What a fool. I mean, who was I kidding?" She gave a light, nervous laugh. "I bought the magazine and went straight to the store bathroom. I locked myself in and read about my husband and his lover and the babies they were having. I sat there until the store manager banged on the door. I…I went straight home, waited for Josh. I sat in a chair, watching the front door, numb, just waiting. He came in after 2:00 a.m., and when I confronted him, he looked at me as if I was a pathetic stray animal. And— and he told me I was an idiot for not having seen that our marriage was over long ago." She stared at the balled chocolate wrapper in her hand. "My husband just turned and walked out that door, and I never saw him again. He sent his lawyer instead. I…I was such a fool, Hunter."

He grabbed her jaw, jerked her face to his. "Don't you *ever* say that." The ferocity in his voice startled her.

"It's *not* your fault, Sarah."

She wanted to thank him for saying that. She wanted to lean into him, to fold herself into his arms, to feel the radiating warmth of his solid chest, but she held back.

"That man is a sick bastard who took advantage of your most generous quality, Sarah. People like him prey on people like you." A raw anger glittered in Hunter's eyes. "Any man, Sarah, *any* man who walks out on a woman like you knows zip about life."

That did it. She couldn't hold it in anymore. Tears erupted and spilled in a curtain down her face. He gathered her to his chest and held her firmly against him and she sobbed, until his bandage was wet with her tears.

"Let it out," he said softly, stroking her hair. "Let it go, Sarah. Let it *all* go."

She felt herself begin to relax. But just as she did, every muscle in his body stiffened.

She shot her eyes up to his.

They'd gone ice-cold, dangerous. His face had completely changed. He'd become the fearsome man she'd first seen back at the Shilongwe.

Her heart began to pound. "What is it?"

He lifted a finger to his lips. "Put your shoes on," he whispered. "We've got company coming."

"What?"

He shifted his eyes to the trees at their right. "From over there. Listen, the cuckoo."

She heard it, *tok tok-boo, tok-tok-boo, tok tok-boo, tok-tok-boo,* the same sound that had followed them all the way from the Eikona River. Someone was coming. Someone had crossed the river into the Blacklands. Fear rose in her throat.

"I thought you said we'd be safe here," she whispered.

He pushed his AK-47 into her hands. "Take this."

Shock flared in her chest. "Why? Where…where are you going?"

"Just take it. I'll surprise them from the back," he whispered. "Make as if you're going to fetch the clothes. Get away from the trees here, out into the open. Keep the AK slung over your shoulder, ready at your side. If you see anyone, use it."

Her body went icy. "I…I can't. I've never used a rifle."

"Here's the trigger. All you have to do is aim and pull it. And Sarah…" he paused, looked deep into her eyes "…shoot to kill."

"I…I *can't.*"

"If you don't, they'll kill you first." He touched her face, then vanished like a ghost into the forest behind her.

Her mouth went dry. Her heart jackhammered against her ribs. And she heard it again.

Tok tok-boo, tok-tok-boo…

Chapter 10

Sweat dampened Sarah's torso as she edged away from the protective cover of the jungle and out into the clearing, toward their clothes drying over a bush. The heat of the sun was violent on her head; her palms were moist.

She kept her back to the clothes and faced the wall of green foliage, squinting against the white-hot glare, searching for a sign of movement, anything that might show her where the men were.

A twig exploded with a crack. She gasped, jerked around to the source of the sound, waited. Nothing moved. Blood thudded in her ears. She tightened her grip on the gun, curling her finger around the trigger. She tried to swallow. She stared at the shades of green in the forest fringe, trying to separate one dark shape from another. Another crack and a rustle sounded, to her right this time. She spun to face it. Oh God, how many were there? She was surrounded. She was a sitting duck in the clearing. Where was Hunter?

She heard another sound to her left. She swallowed her scream and spun around just as a massive soldier materialized at the edge of the trees.

Her heart stopped.

How long had he been standing there? How long had he been watching her from mere yards away? Her breath congealed in her throat. She couldn't move. Time warped in the heat, and sound slowed to the consistency of glue. Mesmerized, Sarah stared at the man's face.

His skin was glistening ebony, his cheekbones impossibly high. He wore a maroon beret cocked at an angle over his shining brow. But it was his eyes that held her. The whites of the soldier's eyes were almost yellow against his dark skin. And they were looking straight at her.

He moved slightly, and she noticed his sleeves were rolled up high against gleaming black biceps. He wore a red armband. His hands were massive. They held a rifle, just like the one in her own hands, and it was aimed right at her. Sarah stared at the muzzle of his gun. Why couldn't she make herself move? Why was everything happening so slowly? Why hadn't he killed her?

He took a step toward her. Sound coalesced into a dull, ringing buzz in her ears, and her vision narrowed to a tunnel of blurred color until all she could see was the end of the rifle aimed at her. Where was Hunter?

"Shoot to kill, Sarah...or they will kill you first." But she couldn't make herself move.

Then a noise, a strange sound, like one animal attacking

another, caused the man to jerk his head and his gun to his left. He raised his rifle, aimed at the source of the sound.

The sudden movement snapped Sarah back to life. Hunter! Oh God, the man was going to shoot Hunter! Sarah didn't think. She pointed the assault rifle out from waist level, closed her eyes and squeezed the trigger.

It all happened at once, in strangely slow time. Her gun exploded, kicking back into her stomach. She hadn't anticipated the thrust. She stumbled backward, tripped and flailed wildly. As she fell, she could see the soldier spin to face her. Sitting on her butt in the grass, she raised the gun again, squinted, aimed at his chest, fired. She heard a simultaneous crack as he shot at her. She heard, felt, a hot blur against her ear as the bullet whizzed past her head and shattered the bark of a tree behind her.

For a second everything stood dead still. She could feel the burning heat of the sun on her face, could smell the grass, like warm hay from the stables she'd worked at the summer she was fifteen. She could smell the acrid residue from the gun in her lap, feel the heat from the barrel against her skin. She could feel sharp bits of scrub cutting into her bare legs. Tiny insects darted in a soft cloud about her face, and grasshoppers clicked. Her heart banged against her eardrums.

Slowly, she pushed herself to a kneeling position so she could see over the grass.

The man's yellow eyes were wide. They looked right at her. He was holding his stomach, just below the diaphragm, and he was sinking slowly to his knees as blood oozed thick and shiny through his fingers.

Sarah couldn't breathe. Had she killed the man? She couldn't make herself look away from his eyes. They pleaded with her as he fought for life. Then he slumped forward into the long grass with a soft thud. She wobbled onto her feet, gun hanging in her hand. All she could see was the rounded hillock of his back, covered in drab olive camouflage, sticking up out of the long grass.

Her stomach heaved. Dizziness spiraled. She felt a heavy touch on her shoulder, and screamed. A flock of birds scattered, squawking, from trees across the clearing.

"Sarah, Sarah, it's okay, it's me."

She spun around, looked up into his eyes. Cold, hard eyes. His hunting knife was in his hand, blood on the blade.

"Looks like there were only two. I took care of the other one."

She began to shake.

"It's okay, hey, you're going to be okay." He touched her hair. "You did good."

She jerked out from under his touch, threw the gun to the ground, faced him squarely. "I thought you said they wouldn't follow us here! You said we'd be safe! You said—"

He tried to take her into his arms.

She backed away, shaking her head.

"Sarah, we *will* be safe. There were at least six men on the river that night, six men following us to the Eikona. It looks like these were the only two who dared to cross the river into the Blacklands. These were the only two who had the courage to defy the superstition. They're not locals. They're probably from the south. We should be okay from here."

"I don't believe you! I don't believe anything you say! What if they send more from the south?"

"We'll be gone by then."

"You're…you're lying!" She spun around, began to stumble through the grass to the man she'd shot. Hunter grabbed her arm, held her back. She fought against his hold. "He's injured. I shot him…I—I need to help him…."

"Leave him, Sarah."

"I can't…. I hurt him!"

"Sarah, he was going to shoot me. *You saved me.*"

"Let me go!"

"Sarah," Hunter growled. "He was going to shoot me and then kill you."

"He wasn't!" Tears flooded her eyes. "He *didn't* shoot me. He had the chance, but he *didn't.*" Hysteria began to cloud her brain, spin her logic dizzyingly out of control.

"Sarah, if he didn't kill you right away, he was going to do it later. Believe me. And it would've been far worse than anything you might imagine. If they wanted you alive, it was for a reason—information. They would have made you give it to them, Sarah. Then you would have died. Painfully. Brutally."

She yanked free of his grip, shoved at his chest with both hands, pushing him away from her. She glared at him. He was a complete stranger to her. What on earth had made her think she had a connection to this man?

He tried to touch her again.

"Don't! Don't touch me. Ever!" She whirled around and waded through the sharp blades of waist-high grass toward the fallen soldier. She crouched down next to his limp form, felt his neck for a pulse. There was none. His skin was still warm.

Remorse choked her. She jerked up to her feet. She had to get away. From Hunter. From this place. She had to get away from what she'd just done, from herself…hide from the fact that she, Sarah Burdett, had just killed a man. She'd looked right into his eyes and shot him dead.

She stumbled toward the cover of the thick jungle.

Hunter let her go. She wouldn't get far without him. She'd come to her senses soon. But right now she needed time. Space. This was a woman born to heal. The need to nurture and sustain life ran through the very fiber of her being. And she'd been forced to kill a man.

His heart ached for her. He knew…he knew firsthand how much it cut a healer's soul to take a life. How he'd felt the first time.

He watched her move through the golden grass in her white camisole and cotton skirt, the sun on her hair burning like auburn fire. And for an odd moment she looked like one of those bright shampoo commercials where the world smells like apples and strawberries and lemons.

He chewed on his cheek as he watched her near the trees. Hell, not even time was going to help this woman forget this. Nothing would. He knew how hard these things were to bury. And he also knew that she would forever associate him with this horror in her mind. If she was having trouble ridding herself of the specter of her ex-husband, there was no hope of redemption for Hunter. Not now.

His heart felt heavy as he crouched down next to the man she'd shot and rolled him over onto his back. Hunter checked the man's pulse, then searched his pockets for some kind of ID. He'd found nothing on the guy he'd killed in the forest, but Hunter knew already that both men belonged to the People's Militia. The red armbands and maroon berets told him that. It was the same red armband they'd glimpsed in the digitally enhanced footage sent to warn President Elliot. It was the armband, along with the equatorial vegetation, that had clued them in to the general location of the pathogen. Sarah's Mayday had pinpointed it.

Hunter took the soldier's handgun and his knife. He found cigarettes in his breast pocket. American cigarettes. He flipped the pack over, read the surgeon general's warning. They'd been packaged for sale to a U.S. market, not an African one. Nothing new about that. Stuff was smuggled into the Congo for bribes on a daily basis. Hunter went through the other pockets, found nothing but a book of matches from a bar in Brazzaville. If that's where this man came from, it would explain his disregard for the Blacklands curse. Not that it had done him much good.

Hunter patted the pockets on the guy's thigh, felt something, took out a corticosteroid nasal spray, for allergies. He turned the cylindrical container over in his palm, read the logo on the label. It was manufactured by BioMed Pharmaceutical. He read the prescription stuck across the cap of the spray. The man's name was Manou Ndinga and his nasal steroid had been prescribed by a Dr. Andries Du Toit.

Hunter glanced up, keeping an eye on Sarah, who was pacing up and down along the jungle fringe. He chewed his inner cheek. BioMed was a major U.S. pharmaceutical company based in New Jersey. But to his knowledge, they hadn't been supplying any central African clinics. They didn't have any kind of contract that he knew about, unless they were working through a subsidiary to market to Africa. But then the steroid wouldn't be bearing the BioMed logo. Still, that didn't necessarily mean a thing. Medicines were in short supply in the Congo and were sold on the black market daily. Long transparent plastic sheets of brightly colored antibiotics alone were hawked on each ferry crossing between Brazzaville and Kinshasa.

But now he had names, and that was a start. Dr. Du Toit might be a nongovernmental organization doctor with some rural clinic, or he could be working more closely with the military, perhaps even a militia doctor on staff. Once Hunter made it back to the FDS base, December could check into Du Toit's background along with his link to BioMed and to Ndinga here.

Hunter slipped the nasal spray into his pocket. He tucked the knife into a sheath at his ankle and the gun into his flak jacket. He removed the soldier's satellite phone. It was new, sophisticated technology. Most of the Congo militia cadres he'd come across were ill-supplied and used mostly radios, not high-end equipment like this. This guy even had a high-tech, fold-up solar charging device to go with his phone. That meant whoever was supplying these men had access to cash—and was going to be looking for results.

A phone like this could be tracked. Hunter looked up. Whoever was paying these soldiers probably had a position on them right now. But it would take time for them to round up men from the south, men who knew jungle warfare and who would be prepared to defy the powerful local superstition of the Blacklands territory. Hunter removed the batteries, disabling any tracking device. He tossed the phone into the grass next to the slain man and made his way to Sarah.

She was pale as a ghost. Her fists were bunched at her side, and the muscles in her neck stood out in narrow cords. Her mouth was strained and her lips flat.

"You okay?" He could see she wasn't.

She glared at him.

He wasn't sure what to say, either. She'd need to decompress, he knew that much. They were going to have to debrief her properly when he got her to São Diogo. He fingered the nasal spray in his pocket. Now was probably not the time. Hell, there was never a right time in a game like this. He took the spray out, held the canister out in the palm of his hand so that she could get a good look at it. "Do you recognize this logo, Sarah?"

Her jaw tightened. She refused to even glance at his hand.

"Sarah, this is a corticosteroid supplied by a U.S. pharmaceutical company. To the best of my knowledge, they have no Congo business connections. I need to know if BioMed supplied your clinic with medications, equipment, vaccines, samples, anything you can tell me."

She slowly lowered her eyes to his hand and stared at the medicine. "Yes."

"You mean BioMed *did* supply the Ishonga clinic?"

"No. But yes, I've seen that triangle logo."

"In Seattle?"

"Ishonga." Her voice was toneless. She looked up at him. Those lovely brown eyes were empty, as if part of her had died with that soldier. Hunter felt oddly deserted. It was as if she'd left *him* on some elemental level.

"I saw it on one of the hazmat suits," she said. "I saw it when I was looking out the window…when they started shooting the nuns…before Dr. Regnaud hid me in a hole in the floor."

His heart kicked. "Why didn't you tell me this?"

"I…I hadn't realized I'd seen it." He could hear emotion creeping back into her voice as she began to relive her horror. Color was also seeping back into her cheeks. "I…I was in a panic at the time."

"Are you positive this is the same logo?"

She turned away from him, clutched her arms against her waist. "I can see it," she whispered. "If I close my eyes I can see it exactly like a picture. It's burned into my brain. All of it." Her voice caught. "I…I guess I just hadn't wanted to look at it…again. If I look, I can see…" Her voice wobbled, then faded. She squeezed her arms tighter around her waist, her knuckles going white as she tried to hold herself together.

A pang of remorse stabbed Hunter. He hated pushing her back into those memories. But he had to ask her for more. He had to make her look back and think about what else she might have seen or known that could possibly be relevant.

He cleared his throat. "And this doctor—" he read the prescription "—Dr. Andries Du Toit, you ever heard of him?"

She nodded. "Dr. Regnaud was asking all the patients

about him," she said. "One of the women who died of the disease had told him that Dr. Du Toit was heading up some medical program in the interior for the army. Her boyfriend was in the militia, and he'd apparently told her about it." Sarah turned slowly to face Hunter. "I didn't think too much about it. Everything was going so crazy with the patients coming in."

He thought for a moment, processing what she had just told him. "Sarah, if Du Toit was working on clinical trials for the pathogen, that woman's link to her boyfriend in the militia could've been how the disease got out of the control group. And Regnaud's questioning everyone is probably what tipped the Cabal off and got him—and everyone else at the clinic—killed."

He stepped closer to her, took her arm, tried to draw her nearer. She resisted, her eyes hostile. He dropped his hand, feeling helpless. "This is a huge breakthrough, Sarah." But even as he said it, he felt defeated.

"Sure." She turned her back on him.

Hunter stared at the rip in her camisole, at the bandage he'd placed over her cut. In spite of this new lead, his heart felt incredibly heavy. He had a weird need to share this little triumph with her, but she wasn't interested. She was preoccupied with the fact she'd killed a man, and that wasn't just going to go away. How was he ever going to make this right for her?

He rolled the medicine tightly between his palm and fingers. It was probably a good thing. He'd lost sight of his reason for being here when he'd plunged into the river to save her over the biohazard canister.

It was the wrong decision to have made for his mission, for his team. But he knew he'd do it again in a heartbeat. He just wasn't capable of doing otherwise. And *that* was his problem.

That's what he *did* regret.

She'd gotten in under his skin, and he'd lost his edge. She'd made him *care*. And a man who cared had something to lose.

He wasn't prepared to lose anything again. Not in that way. Ever. He tightened his fist around the spray container. Yeah, it was better this way. If she needed this distance right now, so did he.

And it would be in the interest of both of them to keep it this way.

He turned away from her in silence and began to pack his gear. The sling she'd strapped over his injured arm had come undone in his struggle with the soldier, and having his arm bound up like that in the first place had just about cost him that tussle. The only real risk in not having it splinted was the possibility of dislocating it again. And if that hadn't happened in hand-to-hand combat, it wasn't going to happen now.

Hell, the only reason he'd allowed her to bandage it at all was because he'd sensed she needed to do it. *That* was the kind of mistake you made when you cared.

The kind that could cost a life.

He hefted his pack onto his back and reached for the biohazard container. He had to get this new intel into the hands of his men ASAP, so that December could start digging into BioMed's pharmaceutical business—and into Dr. Andries Du Toit.

14:13 Alpha. Congo.
Tuesday, September 23

"We lost them east of the Eikona River." He paused, deeply uneasy over how this latest development was going to go down in Manhattan. They were already blaming him for the infected patients outside the trial group. Silence stretched, crackled over the distance. He cleared his throat, spoke again. "It looks like they're going to make a run for the Cameroonian border."

"How did you lose them?" The man's voice was dangerously calm. "You had a visual, you had coordinates. How can one woman possibly lead a trained army on a wild-goose chase through equatorial jungle?"

Tension whipped across Du Toit's chest. This didn't sit easy with him, either. The woman was definitely being helped by a professional, but he wasn't going to say that; it would only inflame things further.

"Even if they do make it out of the Blacklands, they'll be calling for backup at some point. If they so much as touch a radio frequency, we'll be ready. They will *not* make it out of the Congo alive."

Chapter 11

They traveled in increasingly oppressive silence, the biohaz-ard container clunking annoyingly, rhythmically against Hunter's thigh as they made their way deeper into the heart of the Blacklands. Heat pressed down on them and the air turned the consistency of pea soup. The ground became swamplike, the muck sucking at their feet. Each breath, each step, each swipe of the machete was becoming an increasingly laborious effort.

Hunter saw a set of giant leopard prints tracking through deep black mud. He looked up into the low branches, searching for signs that they were being stalked by the silent jungle predator. He couldn't see the creature, but that didn't mean it couldn't see them. He slapped at a tsetse fly that had stuck itself to his neck.

Damn. Insect repellent was useless against the bloody persistent creatures. The sluggish things were twice the size of a housefly and caused deadly forms of African sleeping sickness. He swatted another one on his arm, stopped and wiped the back of his wrist over his forehead. His body was drenched and the salt of exertion stung his lips. This was by far the worst terrain they had traveled through, and Sarah was not doing at all well.

He turned to look at her. Her skin was pale, her cheeks sunken. Flies and tiny bees buzzed around her. She was making zero effort to swat them away.

"You okay?"

She said nothing.

Worry tightened his chest. He took some twine from his pocket, crouched down and tied the cuffs of her pants around her ankles in an effort to keep the bugs out. Damn flies were biting right through his army pants, and her thin cotton was not a whole lot of protection.

He looked up at her. Still no response. He handed her some water and she drank in silence as he crouched again and checked his topo map and compass. She needed sleep. Food. He had to get her to higher terrain before nightfall, find somewhere to camp. This swamp was no place for humans.

He traced his finger along the contour lines of his map and breathed a hot sigh of relief. There was a chance they could make it out of swampland before dark. They could set up camp for the night, and if they got going by first light tomorrow, they could potentially make it to an abandoned rubber plantation on the banks of the Sangé and be out of the Blacklands and crossing into Cameroon by Thursday.

He got to his feet, pocketed his map. "Had enough water?"

She handed him the canteen.

His chest knotted. No amount of food, rest or water was

going to fix what he saw in her eyes. She'd been forced to go against absolutely everything that defined her, and she was dealing with it in a real bad way. He was going to have to do something about it or she wasn't going to make it out of here, but he had a sinking feeling that it would be no use trying to talk to her.

He was part of her problem.

21:03 Alpha. Blacklands.
Tuesday, September 23

Sarah watched as Hunter tossed another branch onto the fire and glowing sparks showered into the night.

She clutched both hands tight around his tin mug and sipped her tea. He'd made it strong and black, with lots of sugar to disguise the chemical taste of the water purifiers. The sweet, strong flavor reminded her of her grandmother's brew. Her gran believed tea was a remedy for the soul. She'd pushed a big mug of strong, sweet Irish breakfast blend into Sarah's hands the day her mom finally succumbed to her battle with cancer.

The fire cast a ring of flickering light around them, holding the encroaching blackness at bay. Smoke lay heavy in the air and burned her eyes, but it was keeping the bugs away and that suited her fine. She didn't have the energy to swat at them.

She watched Hunter over the rim of her mug as she sipped. He sat on a stump on the other side of the fire, keeping his distance.

She wanted to hate him, but couldn't. She wanted to talk, but couldn't. It was as if she'd been imprisoned inside her own body by the heinous thing she'd done.

He glanced up, caught her watching, but she couldn't even react. She'd gone physically numb, some neural connection severed in her brain to save her from her own mental anguish.

He picked up a stick, jabbed it angrily into the flames. His jaw was set. His skin glowed in the copper light, and a dark lock of hair hung over his brow. Sometime between the clearing and now, he'd cut off his other sleeve, matching the one she'd sliced off to reduce his dislocated shoulder. He'd probably done it for comfort. It accentuated his biceps, and in a distant part of her brain he looked beautiful, in a wild and dangerous way. The way you might think of a jaguar—an animal that killed to live.

She wasn't like him, could never be. She didn't understand how he could do what he did and live with himself. All she wanted was to get away from him, from this nightmare.

He jerked suddenly to his feet, stalked around the fire and sat on the log at her side. "Sarah, we *have* to deal with this."

She tightened her fingers around the mug, stared into the flames.

"I keep thinking I might be able to pull you through as long as you hold up physically, but…it won't work. You won't make it." He paused. "I want you to make it, Sarah."

She felt her pulse increase. But he was still at the other end of a tunnel, not quite reaching her. She knew he was trying. She just couldn't respond.

"What you did was the right thing. You need to understand that. You have to know what a vital role you're playing." He leaned forward, arms on his knees, the firelight catching his eyes. "So I'm going to tell you. And what I'm going to tell you is highly classified."

Interest flickered through her, but she stared intently at the flames. She didn't want to look into his eyes. They would suck her in again. She *wanted* to stay numb.

"This is not just about a biological attack, Sarah. It's far worse. If the Cabal—the group I mentioned to you—is successful in what they're ultimately planning, they will change the course of global politics, of history. If we don't stop them within the next—" he checked his watch "—nineteen days, twenty hours and fifty-seven minutes, democracy as we know it will be dead. And the world will be a very different place."

She turned her head, slowly lifted her eyes to his. "What do you mean?"

His shoulders relaxed almost imperceptibly, as if an invisible burden had been lightened just a little. He raised his hand to touch her, but took hold of another stick instead, used it to poke tentatively at the fire. "The Cabal plans to take control of the U.S. government by midnight October 13—exactly three weeks before the presidential election."

Sarah felt light-headed. She couldn't quite make sense of his words. "What do you mean, 'take control of the government'? Like a coup?"

"In a manner of speaking."

"Is…is that possible?"

"Yes. Very. It's been in the works for decades, and the Cabal is only days away from succeeding. All that stands between them now, Sarah, is you and me, and a few good men."

She lowered the tin mug to her lap. "I don't understand. How would they do this?"

"Like I told you, the Cabal is a clandestine group of inordinately powerful men. We don't yet know who they are or exactly what they control, but we do know their influence is vast, and it's global. Their goal is power, the ultimate power— control of the most influential government in the world."

"But *why?*"

He snorted softly. "Why does anyone want power or control?" He placcd his hand over her knee. "I'm sorry, Sarah, but when you were handed that biohazard container, you instantly became a pivotal pawn in a deadly global power game.

It's not fair, you don't deserve this. And I'm going to do what it takes to get you through it." He paused. "But I need you to stay strong. You have to understand that what you did back there in that clearing was the right thing."

She stared at him. "How," she said slowly, "how does the Cabal plan on overthrowing the U.S. government?"

He chewed on his cheek and studied the fire for a while. "President Elliot is dying. He's being slowly assassinated by an unidentified stealth disease that appears to be eating away at his brain—a biological bullet administered by his own Secret Service, just one of the organizations the Cabal has managed to infiltrate. It's a disease very similar to the one in that canister, except this one moves much, much more slowly."

She felt the blood rush from her head. She glanced at the canister. The orange-and-black biohazard symbol emblazoned on the side flickered in the firelight with a life and warning of its own. *A container of death.* "How...how long does the president have?"

"Months, maybe. But his mental faculties are expected to deteriorate sooner." Hunter's eyes pierced hers. "No one knows this, Sarah. Only his personal physician, the FDS, and now you. And it must stay secret. Elliot is trying to hold on to his health just long enough to secure a second term in the November 4 election. At the moment, there is no doubt he'll win. News of a terminal illness will scuttle that."

"But why is he even running if he knows he's going to die as soon as he takes office? It doesn't make sense."

"If he bows out now due to ill health, Vice President Grayson Forbes will become the next president of the United States. Elliot can't let that happen because Forbes is the Cabal's man."

Sarah's brain spun. "But if President Elliot dies *after* winning the election," she continued, "Michael J. Taylor becomes the next U.S. president, because Taylor is Elliot's new running mate."

"Exactly. The Elliot camp denied Forbes a place on the ticket. An unusual move, but not unprecedented, and a serious blow to a faction that has been trying to maneuver Forbes into the Oval Office for years."

"A Cabal faction? *Within* the party?"

Hunter nodded. "Grayson Forbes has been groomed by this Cabal faction for years, and they made their big move when they threw his hat into the ring in the lead-up to the last presidential election. Elliot, however, narrowly beat out their man for the presidential ticket at the party convention, and Elliot's camp picked Charles Landon over Forbes for a running mate— a real slap in the face to Forbes and his people. It cost them both the presidency *and* the vice presidency."

"But then why did Elliot make Forbes vice president when Landon died of cancer last year?"

Hunter jabbed at the flames with his stick and sparks spattered into the night. "Landon didn't die naturally, Sarah. He was assassinated."

A chill ran up her spine. "By the Cabal?"

"Yes. Elliot was then informed via his own bodyguards that he, too, had been inflicted with a biological bullet, but his death would be slower than Landon's. It would resemble a rapid form of Alzheimer's, leading first to dementia, and then death within six months—giving him just enough time to name Forbes as replacement vice president. If he failed to do so by the appointed date, they told him a deadly pathogen would be released over Los Angeles, New York and Chicago."

"Why didn't President Elliot tell everyone what was happening? Why didn't he get help?"

"The Cabal told him the virus would be released instantly

if he so much as even *thought* of engaging any of the traditional agencies available to him. The president became a virtual hostage in the White House, his every move, his every communication monitored by his own Secret Service. He was trapped by the very security system designed to protect him. The only man he knew he could trust for certain was his personal physician, Dr. Sebastian Ruger. He's been communicating with him in secret, in writing, in the White House medical suite."

Sarah blew out a stream of air. "So President Elliot did the Cabal's bidding and named Forbes vice president."

"Only in order to buy time to come up with a plan. The Cabal, however, expected him to become incapacitated and die shortly after the nomination, or at least well before the November election."

"But he didn't…he *hasn't.*"

Hunter smiled wryly. "He's a very determined man, Sarah. Whether he's still alive because of that, or because the biological bullet is not functioning exactly as anticipated, it's forced the Cabal's hand. If they lose this last little window of opportunity to get their man into power now, it will destroy decades of positioning. They won't get another opportunity like this. So they've issued the president an ultimatum—step down from power by midnight October 13, citing health reasons, or they will release the pathogen."

Sarah shivered in spite of the warmth. "I can't believe I'm even asking this, but why don't they just kill him before the election?"

"An overt assassination, especially days before the election, would spin the country and the global economy out of their control, and it would send the world on a witch hunt. That kind of economic disaster and scrutiny is something a bunch of imperialistic capitalists is *very* keen to avoid. They need this to look completely natural if they are to stay anonymously in control behind the scenes, and they can't afford to implicate Forbes in any way. He has to appear a strong and *rightful* leader. He has to be respected and trusted by the American people for them to be able to launch the next phase of their plan."

Sarah could barely begin to comprehend the scope of this, or the fact that she was slam-bang in the middle of it, playing a key role in an American nightmare in the middle of the Congo jungle. "I can't believe these men would actually kill millions of their own people to get into power."

"These guys make Machiavelli look like the fairy godmother. They'll do anything to justify their end, and they've shown us they have the biotechnology to do it—*and* the will to use it."

She fiddled with the handle of the tin cup. "What *is* the next phase, Hunter?"

He took the mug from her hands, tossed the dregs onto the fire with a sizzle. "Once the Cabal gets Forbes into power, they're going to want to keep him there. They're going to use their arsenal of high-tech bioweapons, like your pathogen there—" he jerked his chin to the container "—to launch a series of contained attacks in the U.S. The Forbes government will maintain the attacks are being perpetrated by terrorists or rogue nations, and he'll declare the country at war. Congress will in turn grant Forbes broad powers to manage the national economy and protect the interests of the nation. We suspect he'll declare martial law, call in the National Guard, curtail civil liberties and declare another election impossible for the foreseeable future."

Sarah stared at him. Who was Hunter, really? What had brought this powerful man to this point in his life, to this inter-section with her? What had made him a mercenary? There was something deeper in him, something gentle buried beneath his armor—a kindness. She'd felt it in his healing touch, seen it in his eyes. And she had a sudden burning need to know him. Totally.

"What about the election next month?" she asked, her eyes fixed on his.

He shook his head. "I don't think there will be one—not if this Cabal gets their way. We believe the continued well-timed 'attacks' will put the Forbes government in a position to 'retaliate' by launching preemptive military strikes against foreign states that allegedly harbor the so-called terrorists or philosophies. And in doing so, the Cabal will be covertly launching a new era of aggressive imperialism designed to feed the pockets of the major transnationals that we suspect are controlled by Cabal elite."

"Some of this is conjecture, isn't it?"

"Only some of it. And it's the president's conjecture, not ours. He believes that if Forbes gets into power he'll immediately start the slow process of appointing Cabal puppets into key judicial, military, intelligence and economic positions. The long-term goal will be to effect the kind of legislative and constitutional change that will enshrine Cabal power for decades to come." Hunter threw another log onto the fire. "And he'll start by naming a new vice president to replace himself."

Sarah watched the flames gobble at the fresh piece of wood, and the hunger to know Hunter more intimately burned deeper in her. She studied his stark profile in the flickering light. He might be a mercenary, he might kill people with his bare hands, he might exist in the shadows of civilization, but he helped people sleep at night—whole populations who would probably never find out what he'd done for them.

"Hunter," she said softly. "How did you—how did the FDS get involved in all this?"

"The president's physician, Dr. Ruger, was at a U.N. conference in Brussels two weeks ago. So was my colleague

Jacques Sauvage. Sauvage handles FDS operations and was at the conference to lobby for an international standardized code of conduct for private military companies. Ruger managed to get to him in the washroom. He used the opportunity to covertly enlist us on behalf of President Elliot." Hunter paused. "It's a close to impossible mission, Sarah. But we took the job. Someone had to."

"The president *personally* hired you guys?"

"Everything else has failed him, and we were the one opportunity that presented itself. Besides, he knows our work, our reputation. We've contracted to the States before through a covert arm of the CIA."

It dawned on her suddenly. "Hunter, even if we *do* find the antidote to the disease in that container, it's not going to stop them…is it?"

"No. It won't. But if we can identify the pathogen within the next two weeks and find an antidote, we could save many lives. But most importantly, we hope to find some kind of biological fingerprint in the pathogen that will lead us to the lab that created it, and in turn that could lead us to whoever is pulling the Cabal strings."

The fire was dwindling, the jungle night creeping closer. She rubbed her arms. "So this is why they want to kill me," she said softly.

"Sarah, they don't know that you know any of this. If they thought you did, and if they knew that I'd been engaged to try and help the president, they'd launch the attack immediately. You're just a loose end right now."

He placed his hand on her knee. "And that's another reason you *had* to shoot that man. If they'd captured and tortured you—and they would have tortured you—you'd have been forced to disclose your connection to the FDS and by extension, the president. They would have launched the attack. You saved millions of lives by taking that one."

She bit her lip, trying not to see the dead man's eyes in the yellow of the flames, trying to understand what she'd gotten herself into. "But they'd prefer to avoid launching the attack before Forbes got into power, wouldn't they?"

"Yes. However, they *will* risk it rather than lose their last shot at getting their man into the Oval Office." Hunter took her hand. It was warm, comforting. "You did the right thing, Sarah. And…and I'm proud of you."

Her heart kicked at his words. "I used to think that taking a life was *never* justified. Now…now I just don't know." She didn't know anything anymore. There was no more black-and-white, just shades of gray.

He didn't answer. And they sat in silence, watching the flames die. Something screeched in the forest and she moved a little closer to Hunter. He put his arm around her. "We should get in the hammock."

"How do you do it, Hunter? How do you do this kind of thing over and over again, and still live with yourself?"

He stared at the coals for a while. "I'm really not that different from you, Sarah. At heart I think you and I are pretty much motivated by the same thing."

"How so?"

"We both want to help people who can't help themselves. And in places like this, people like you—nurses and doctors— need people like me so that you can continue to do your jobs. Whether we like or not, we're two halves of an uneasy partnership."

He drew her closer. "Besides, who else is going to come to

the aid of a lone American nurse who calls 9-1-1 from the heart of the jungle?"

That made her smile. "I wasn't thinking."

He gave her a squeeze. "Come on, it's bedtime."

01:03 Alpha. Blacklands.
Wednesday, September 24

Hunter could feel every soft curve of Sarah's body against his as gravity forced them together in the center of the hammock. It was strong enough for two, but made for one, with a cover over the top and mosquito netting around the sides. He lay there, zipped into the tiny cocoon with her, breathing the same air as her, fingering his gun and listening to the sounds of the jungle and the bump of bugs against the fabric. He was almost afraid to breathe too deeply. Each inhalation seemed to push yet another part of his body against hers, and he didn't want her to know that the contact had made him as hard as a rock.

Sarah moaned softly in her sleep and stirred, the movement pushing her breasts against his chest. Heat spurted to his groin. It didn't help that he was already stiff and aching with need. Hunter closed his eyes. This was pure torture. So much for maintaining distance, he thought wryly. Because right at this minute he was being squeezed as close to this woman physically as he was emotionally. He wondered just what it would take to finally tip him completely over the edge of control.

The hours ticked by interminably as he listened to her breathe, his own rhythm falling in time with hers. As dawn crept into the sky, he began to wonder what it might be like to sleep with her every night, wake up next to her each morning. Make sweet, hot love…. He caught his breath sharply. Not because of the pulsing ache in his belly, but because he'd thought of tomorrows. With her. How in hell had that one sneaked up on him? Hunter McBride couldn't offer a woman like Sarah Burdett anything, let alone the promise of a new day. And that's why he couldn't touch her.

She moaned softly and moved again. Hunter groaned. This mission was testing him in ways he'd never dreamed possible.

Chapter 12

08:00 Alpha. Blacklands.
Wednesday, September 24

They'd been on the move for two hours when a rumbling roar resonated through the forest, so loud it froze every molecule in Sarah's body.

Hunter's hand shot up. "Don't move!" he growled.

A crash of breaking brush sounded to her left. Sarah's heart leaped to her throat. Hunter made a quick motion, as if he were patting a basketball. *"Down!"*

She dropped to the ground, heart crashing against her chest wall. He crouched next to her. "If he comes at us," Hunter said in a hushed voice, "don't look in his eyes. Look at the earth."

"If *what* comes?"

"Gorilla."

She stared very hard at the forest floor, trying to make her body still.

They waited. A small cloud of bugs flitted about her face, but she didn't dare flinch. Her muscles began to ache. But there was nothing, no more sound. The beast was somewhere just out sight, watching them, waiting. She could sense it.

Hunter reached for a bush, pulled down a thin branch and began to strip the fat, shiny leaves off with his hand, crushing them in his palm, making a crackling noise.

"Do it," he whispered. "Make as if you're grazing. The sounds are familiar to him. If he hasn't seen us yet, this *will* alert him, but at least we won't take him by surprise."

Sarah swallowed against the dryness in her mouth. She didn't dare look up from the ground. She groped for the bush, pulled at the leaves, scrunched them furiously in her fingers.

"Over there," Hunter whispered. "Look."

Sarah raised her eyes slowly. Just beyond the bushes, partially obscured by leaves and brush, was the biggest wild beast she had ever seen uncaged. He was a mass of muscle on all fours, facing away from them. A shock of silver hair coated his impossibly broad back. The gorilla slowly turned his leathery face toward them, and gazed right into her eyes. Sarah's heart clean stopped. Everything about the animal screamed danger, but beneath his thick domed brow, his round eyes were liquid brown, gentle, full of intelligent curiosity. Looking into the eyes of the silverback, she felt as if she were staring right into the living heart of the jungle, a place as old as time. Her heart pumped back to life at the strange primal connection. A sense of awe overcame her, and for a moment she forgot her fear.

But all of a sudden, the silverback lurched up onto his back legs, pounded his chest and barreled at them with a gut-rumbling roar. Sarah gasped, jumped back, falling onto her butt. The gorilla stopped just short of them, reared up and beat his chest again.

Hunter's hand clamped on her arm. "Don't move!" he murmured. "Stop looking into his eyes. He sees it as a challenge."

Sarah glared at her toes as hard as she could, heart palpitating, palms damp. She could barely breathe. Slowly, the big old male silverback turned, gave them a last glance over his massive shoulder and swaggered off into the forest. All she could hear as the sound of crunching undergrowth died down was the blood rushing in her ears.

She let out a soft and shaky whoosh of air.

"Are you all right?"

She turned to Hunter. "That's the most incredible thing I've ever seen in my entire life," she whispered. "Was he alone?"

Hunter's brows raised. An odd look crossed his face as he studied hers. "You're not afraid?"

She laughed. "Petrified."

His eyes narrowed slightly. "But in a different way."

It wasn't a question, it was an observation. And with a strange jolt, she realized he was right. Something had happened to her. She'd been pushed beyond panic, beyond blinding fear, and what was coursing through her blood now was raw survival instinct. It was empowering, not debilitating. It made her acutely aware of everything around her. Sarah realized with mild shock that she felt strangely centered and in control. She'd been stripped of everything and driven to rock bottom. She'd been forced to kill a man, and everything else paled in significance.

He nodded slightly, as if confirming to himself he was right. Then he smiled, a warm light twinkling in his eyes. "I think he was."

She jerked her mind back. "What?"

"Alone. Wait here, stay low."

Hunter edged forward, pushing leaves aside with his machete, creeping through the foliage like a wild animal himself. He paused, listened, waited. Moved forward again, waited. Then he flicked his hand up, calling her to his side.

She crept over to him. "Has he gone?"

"Looks like it." He placed his palm in the center of a wide and squashed-flat circle of leaves and twigs. "This was his nest."

"They make nests?"

"The old male does. He builds his nest on the ground. His family, wives, children—they build platforms to sleep on up in the trees. He protects them from below." Hunter glanced up, scanning branches up in the canopy. "I don't see any platforms up there. This old guy's probably too old for family, that part of his life over…" Hunter's voice faded as he squinted up into the trees, his hand resting on the flattened twigs.

Sarah studied his rugged profile. He seemed momentarily distant, as if he were seeing something beyond the branches, beyond the forest. As if he was trying to feel what the old gorilla might have been feeling.

"Did his troop just leave him?"

"He would've been challenged and beaten by a younger male for them to have done that. Survival of the fittest. The younger genes keep the troop strong." Hunter scanned the trees again as if searching for the proud old male.

A strange sense of sadness filled her heart. "Will he die, then…alone?"

Hunter's eyes cut to hers. "Yes. Alone." He stood abruptly, turned away from her and ran his fingers through the straggly leaves of a plant that grew almost as high as her shoulders. "This is what he was here for. See the red fruits at the base of the stems? That's wild ginger. Gorillas love it. Look." He pointed out fruits that had been peeled, sucked dry and cast aside. She hadn't noticed them. She hadn't even known to look.

"And what's that?" She pointed to broken clumps of dried, dark brown mud near the bases of several trees.

He raised a brow, studied her face, and a smile ghosted his lips. "Termite nests. Gorillas smash them open and eat the grubs. Good protein." With the muzzle of his AK he poked at a lost little grub wriggling on the ground. A wicked playfulness lit his eyes. "Hungry?"

She pulled a face. "Not *that* hungry."

He laughed, held out his hand and helped her to her feet, drawing her close to his chest as he did. Sarah stilled at the look in his eyes.

For a second, silence hung thick, and a hot current pulsed between them, an invisible but tangible connection. The light in his eyes faded, darkening to something more feral. Sarah swallowed. She found herself looking at his mouth, becoming conscious of her own. She wasn't afraid he might kiss her, she *wanted* him to. A hot thrill of anticipation zinged through her, and for a fleeting second she thought she might act, might just lean up to him and put her lips to his. Because she could see he wanted her.

But he looked abruptly away. "We should get moving."

Disappointment spread through her, but the residual hum of desire remained, making her cheeks warm as she followed him into the forest.

As they moved deeper into primary jungle the air grew cooler, richer, more full of oxygen, the scent somehow greener. Sarah felt as if they were working their way slowly back in time. The tree trunks here were massive in size and spaced farther apart, giving the area a cathedral-like quality. She stopped, looked up in wonder. Branches knitted in a dizzying architectural puzzle all the way up to a translucent dome of green that quivered high in a wind she couldn't feel down on the forest floor. These trees had to be hundreds upon hundreds of years old. How could she have been blind to all this incredible beauty around her?

She felt Hunter watching her. Cautiously, she lowered her eyes and met his. That elemental wariness was back in them, a dark, predatory hunger. Heat rippled through her. She blinked, a little self-conscious under the intensity of his gaze and her instant physical reaction to it. "This place...it's incredibly beautiful," she said, her voice husky.

"Yes." He didn't break his gaze. "Very beautiful."

Warmth flushed her face. She glanced away, cleared her throat. "It's...so natural, yet it reminds me of the architecture of an ancient cathedral I visited in Barcelona. There's a similar ethereal quality to the light, the space. I don't really know how to put it into words...it has a timeless, almost sacred feel." She looked up at him. "That cathedral was probably built around the time some of these trees started to grow."

"When were you in Spain?"

She tensed at the blunt delivery of his question. "Six years ago...for my honeymoon."

His eyes narrowed. He adjusted the rifle at his side. Was the mercenary actually showing possessiveness? Was he uncomfortable thinking about her and Josh together? A ridiculous warmth blossomed through her at the notion. It made her feel good...about *herself.*

And then she realized what had just happened. She'd thought about the beauty of that cathedral, not about Josh. Not the honeymoon. Not her failed marriage. Not all the dark feelings that always came when she remembered anything associated with her ex-husband.

Excitement bubbled in her heart and she couldn't contain it. "Hunter, this the first time I've been able to think back to a time I shared with Josh without actually thinking about *him*."

Hunter's expression didn't change. His eyes remained dark, watchful.

She didn't care. She blew out a breath she felt as if she'd been holding for years. She almost wanted to cry with spontaneous relief. "It's… I feel free." She laughed lightly, tears pricking her eyes. "Here I am, on the run in the jungle, being chased by—by militia, a group bent on dominating the world, poisonous bugs, snakes, gorillas and…and all I feel is *exhilarated,* free of my ex, can you believe it? How weird is that! Am I going totally insane?"

A smile crept along Hunter's mouth. A dimple deepened in one cheek and creases fanned out around his eyes. "Not *totally*."

She'd made the hard-ass soldier smile, really smile. She'd made him reveal a dimple she hadn't seen before. He was truly happy *for her*. Damn, it felt good. She grinned. His eyes sparkled in response, edging her over, and she did it. She gave a little spin, her arms held wide.

Hunter threw back his head and laughed—a laugh that vibrated right through her, filled her with happiness. She spun again, round and round under the trees, her arms out, her hair lifting around her. Monkeys cackled in response. She found it funny that even primates in the trees saw the humor in it all. She spun faster and the world spun with her, and then suddenly without her. The ground dipped one way, the branches the other in a kaleidoscopic blur of green and brown and yellow…. She teetered, tripped, flailed and fell. Hunter caught her, and her body slapped hard against his chest.

She held still, the world racing wildly around her, the sound of blood again rushing in her ears.

Then everything grew hushed, even the monkeys. It was as if the whole jungle was holding its breath. She slid her eyes slowly up to his, and swallowed. The mirth, all signs of happiness in his eyes, were gone, replaced instead by dark, blatant hunger and the raw stamp of arousal etched along the lines of his mouth.

She could feel the thud of his heart, hard and fast, against her breasts. She could smell his maleness, feel the dampness on his arms, his hair rough against her skin. Heat seeped into her belly. The world narrowed around her.

He clasped the back of her neck suddenly, threaded his fingers into her tangle of hair, tilted her head back and covered her mouth with his. Raw lust exploded instantly, buckling her knees. He caught her at the small of her back as she sagged, yanked her hard up against his torso and sank his tongue into her mouth. Sarah's vision swam. She opened her mouth to him, tasting his salt, feeling his teeth, his size, the rasp of his stubble against her cheek. His tongue slipped around hers, searched her mouth, forceful, rough, hungry. He slid his hand down to her butt, pulled her higher up into himself, and she felt the hardness in his groin press against her pelvis. Dizziness clouded her brain and she began to pulse with a hot ache, a desperate need to open herself to him.

Nothing in this world could have held him back. Nothing in this jungle could have made him stop. For some absurd reason, Sarah's joy, her newfound sense of freedom, made Hunter feel he suddenly had a right to do this. And the idea made him blind with hunger.

And now that his reins of control had snapped, his appetite was savage. He couldn't get enough. She moved invitingly against him, opening her mouth wider, challenging him, firing him with her own hunger. He grasped her breast, rasped his thumb over the thin fabric, found her nipple hard and tight. He groaned, moved his hand down over her stomach, cupped her between her legs. She slicked her tongue around his. She wanted him. Completely. And it made him wild with the need to consume her, totally, right now, right here, under the trees.

He began to draw her down to the ground, his body acting without his mind. But as he did, a flare of logic cut through the blinding curtain of his desire. He hesitated. This wasn't right. It had been wrong last night and it was still wrong, for all the same reasons. He pulled back, shocked at how his desire had blinded him, how it had completely consumed him like that.

Sarah felt stunned, as if something had been ripped right out of her. She opened her mouth to ask him what had happened to make him stop wanting her…but she couldn't. She couldn't face the rejection. Not from him. Not now. Hurt and confusion welled through her. She looked away. This was ridiculous. She was being way too emotional about everything. But she couldn't help it. Everything was coming out unfiltered. All her senses were heightened, everything coming straight from her gut and heart. *Dumb. Dumb. Dumb.* She was stupid for even acting on her impulses. She should know better. Hadn't she learned?

He placed his hand gently against her cheek, tilted her face, forcing her to look back into his eyes. "Sarah." His voice was hoarse, his lids thick, his breath heavy. "I…I'm sorry. I can't do this."

She nodded, tried to look away.

But he held her firm. "No, look at me, Sarah. I can't do this to you because…because—" He jerked away, turned his back on her, dragged both his hands through his dark mop of hair. He stood still for a minute, then turned again to face her. There was a strange light in his eyes, almost a vulnerability, and his mouth was twisted in a kind of pain, as if he was trying to hold a tidal wave of stuff inside.

It dawned on her slowly. This man hadn't rejected her. He was fighting with something inside himself. He was hurting. The notion tugged gently at the nurturer in her. She touched his arm. "Hunter, it's okay, really. I—"

"No, damn it!" He raked his hand viciously through his hair. "It's *not* okay." He sucked in a deep breath, forced it out. "You're special, Sarah, you're…too damn special for me. I can't do this to you. We…we're too different."

She shook her head, bemused. "You said we were the same at the core, Hunter."

"I lied, okay?"

She stared at him, speechless.

"Look, Sarah, I can't offer you anything. You were right, our lives are worlds apart. When we get out of here, I go on another mission. That's what I do. You…you need—"

She pressed her hand against his mouth. "Shut up," she said softly, gazing right into his eyes. "I said it's okay. And don't try to tell me what *I* need. I'm not asking for promises, Hunter. Right now I'm just figuring out how to be in the present. I'm only just getting rid of my past. The future is more than I can deal with right now." She paused. "You just do your job and get us out of here, okay?"

He covered her hand with his, pressed it hard against the stubble on his face and closed his eyes. He remained like that for a while, as if drinking her in, as if finding his center again.

When his eyes flashed open, the cold, controlled mercenary Hunter McBride was back. Sarah blinked. Had she even witnessed what she just thought she had? Had she actually seen through a chink in this man's hardened armor and glimpsed something inside—an old-school guy, a gentleman who wouldn't kiss her because he couldn't promise her tomorrow?

Something swelled so fast and sweetly sharp in her chest that in that instant, she thought she might just be in love with this man. He was everything she hadn't expected.

Hunter McBride was both a mercenary *and* a gentleman.

11:01 Alpha. Congo-Cameroon border.
Wednesday, September 24

Andries Du Toit studied the black clouds massing along the horizon. There was a thunderstorm brewing. The air had that thick, electrical feel about it. He turned his eyes to the red haze of dust being raised by his troops moving north along the Congolese side of the border, then turned his attention back to his map, smoothing it out over the hood of his Jeep.

"We should have this section of border covered by nightfall," he said. "If they try and make it out of the Blacklands, they'll have to cross somewhere between that point there on the Sangé and that point to the west." He jabbed his finger at the map. "They won't come around that way—that's razorback mountain terrain." He looked up at the militia leader in his employ. "Keep scanning all radio frequencies. The instant they try to make any kind of contact, we'll have them. They *do not* escape the Congo, *comprends*?"

"Oui, je comprend."

"Alert the rest of the People's Militia and the rebel cadres in this entire region, lead them to believe you have reliable intel that President Samwetwe is being smuggled into Cameroon sometime within the next seventy-two hours. Suggest they capture anything that moves. What we don't have covered, they will." Du Toit glanced at the clouds again.

"If we're lucky, they'll be found before they even get close to the border."

Chapter 13

The forest canopy thinned and the vegetation turned to thick brush. The sun baked down on Sarah's hair, her skin began to burn and her throat grew parched. They needed to find another water source soon. Hunter whacked at the leaves with his machete, his arms glistening with perspiration, his black hair damp over his brow. The muscles in Sarah's forearm began to cramp from toting the awkward, heavy biohazard container. She tried to mesmerize herself with Hunter's slashing motion, tried to ignore the burn in her thighs and calves, the deep ache in her shoulders.

He stopped suddenly, breathing hard. "See that?" He pointed his machete blade at a strange pattern of herringbone scars cut into the bark of a tall, skinny tree. Below the scars the trunk had begun to grow over a rusted metal cup.

"And that?" He pointed to another tree, same size, same pattern in the bark. Sarah began to notice more trees, all similar in size, spaced the same distance apart.

"Rubber trees." He wiped his wrist over his brow. "We're about ten klicks farther north than I figured."

"And this is good?"

He grinned. "This, Sarah, is an abandoned rubber plantation." He waved his machete over the scrub. "Sangé River should be only a few hundred yards in that direction." He took out his map, crouched down, spread it over his knee. "See, we're here. The plantation runs up this way, along the banks of the Sangé. The farmers used the river to ship their product north—" he looked up at her "—right into Cameroon."

Nerves bit at her. "Are we still in the Blacklands?"

"Just. The plantation lies along the edge of the Blacklands border." He turned his attention back to the map. "From our most recent intel, there should be a mission station there—" he jabbed his finger on a bend in the Sangé "—run by two Italian priests." He glanced up at her. "If we can secure a canoe from that mission, we can float into Cameroon tomorrow night under the cover of darkness."

Sarah swallowed. She had a sinking sense that her time with Hunter was almost over.

He folded his map, slipped it back into his flak jacket and got to his feet. "We can rest up in the plantation buildings tonight. We should find food there—whatever they used to grow should still be growing wild. Then we move out of the Blacklands at dawn." His eyes grew serious. "They'll be expecting us to cross somewhere in this region, Sarah. Travel will be different, dangerous. Once we get to the Italian mission, we'll lie low until dark." He glanced up at a ridge of clouds massing along the distant horizon. "And if that cloud continues to move in from the north, it'll be in our favor. The night will be pitch-black."

They broke through coarse brush and moved onto the wide banks of the Sangé River just after noon. The water flowed slowly, cascading in places from rock pool to rock pool. Two hippos waded on the water's edge, and a huge black-and-white bird with a down-curved beak flew with swooping movements over the surface. The water was such a welcome and life-affirming sight that Sarah slipped her hand into Hunter's without thinking. He gave her fingers a squeeze.

They rinsed off in the pools, filled the canteens and walked north along the riverbank in silence. Two fish eagles soared high above them on thermals of air. Sarah stopped to watch them, and couldn't help noticing the bank of ominous clouds encroaching from the north, black and swollen with rain. It made her tense on some gut level. Even the air around her felt charged.

Hunter must have sensed her growing apprehension because he smiled and pressed his index finger under her chin. "Hey, it's just a thunderstorm, and it's not going to arrive before nightfall. We can take shelter in the old plantation mansion."

But it wasn't the rain she was worried about. It was more a sense of time leaking through her fingers, of reality creeping closer, of unspecified danger waiting for them beyond the Blacklands. Some weird part of her was not quite ready to leave this cursed region, to cross into Cameroon, to say goodbye to Hunter. They hadn't been together that long but it had been intense, and it had the feel of forever. Emotion choked her throat as they resumed their trek along the shimmering white-hot sand. She told herself it was nothing. She was just tired.

He stopped suddenly, drew her to his side, pointed down-river. "Look, there it is."

A large double-story structure rose out of a riot of glossy green vegetation at the curve of the riverbank. As they neared, Sarah could see black and red mold growing across what must have once been a white facade. Cerise bougainvillea scrambled up the walls, snaked along the lintels of glassless windows and exploded in a mass of color over the rusting tin roof. A stone veranda ran along the front of the house, and vines with white flowers tangled around stone columns. Banana palms and papayas grew in a thick grove along one side of the crumbling mansion in what must have once been a fruit and vegetable garden. Nature was devouring what had likely been an exotic home for some large colonial French family.

"What happened?" she whispered in awe. "Where did the people go?"

"Most colonialists fled the region when the Marxists took over," said Hunter, studying the mansion. "But I reckon this plantation was abandoned during the last Ebola outbreak."

"You think they got the disease?"

"My guess is they could no longer get people to come and work this massive plantation once the sorcerers declared the area cursed. They had no choice but to leave." He took her hand. "Come, let's go check it out."

Hunter led her up crumbling stone stairs flanked with clay pots bursting with weeds and flowers gone wild. The heady scent was almost overwhelming in the heat. Sarah could also smell the hot tin of the rusting roof and the underlying musk of decay.

They stepped onto the floor of the veranda. It was scattered with leaves and twigs and dead flowers. A stone fireplace and large oven had been built into a wall at the far end. Whoever had lived here must have enjoyed outdoor cooking and entertaining. Sarah could almost imagine the family sitting out here on cane chairs, sipping cocktails, watching animals come to water in the Sangé as the sun dipped behind the trees. She could almost hear their distant voices speaking in French, the echoes of children laughing in the house.

Hunter dumped his pack, and she jumped, her mind jerking back to the present. He carefully pulled open the creaking double doors that hung on rusted hinges. Sarah peered into the gloomy interior.

Vines draped across the windows, blocking out sunlight. Her eyes adjusted slowly and she began to discern the shapes of a sofa, chairs, a table, odd bits of furniture covered in sheets and left behind. She stepped inside and cobweb curtains billowed in her wake. There was an overpowering smell of mold and rotting wood inside. A snake slithered through the leaves on the floor on the far side the room. Sarah jumped, her heart quickening.

"Looks better out on the veranda, huh?"

She nodded, almost overwhelmed by the sense that a family had once lived here, laughed here, cried here, made love here, had children here. And now the place was simply a husk permeated with a hollow sense of abandonment. It was, she realized with a jolt, that same hollowness that Josh had left in her when he'd walked out the door. She turned back to Hunter, suddenly needing to touch him, to feel his vitality, the security of his strength.

A frown creased his brow. He lifted a strand of hair from her cheek. "Hey, you okay?"

"Yeah." She smiled. "I'm fine."

His features relaxed. "How about you try and clean up the deck a bit, maybe gather some fruit—"

"Excuse me?"

He grinned. "—while I go catch us some fish. Equal division of labor, no chauvinism intended."

She laughed, suddenly grateful to be focusing on the present. "And just how are you going to catch fish?"

A wicked gleam lit his eyes. He slipped his hunting knife out of its holster, pointed the blade toward the river. "See that tree hanging over the bank there, the one with the yellow fruit?"

She squinted into the haze.

"The locals call it a fishing tree. The fish wait under it until one of those yellow fruits drops off then…bam—" He crouched down in a blur of movement and lopped the pompoms off the back of her socks with his blade before she even realized what he was doing.

"Hunter! *What the—*"

He stood up, held the grubby yellow pompoms out in the palm of his hand, his eyes laughing. "Perfect lures once I get my hook into them." He angled his head. "I knew you'd come in handy at some point, Burdett."

She scowled at him.

He winked, closed his fist around her pompoms. And in that moment she had a warm sense of being part of a couple, the two of them at ease and comfortable with each other. It was a nice feeling—one she hadn't had in more years than she could recall.

Night had fallen thick and fast. The storm clouds had moved in, swallowed the stars and the small sliver of moon. Darkness was now complete, save for the roaring fire Hunter had built in the fireplace on the veranda. He'd lit it after the sun had gone down so no one would see their smoke, and he'd raked glowing coals over to one side to slowly roast the fish he'd cleaned by the river.

They'd both washed in sweet water he'd managed to crank up from the old well on the property, and Sarah had swept the veranda with palm fronds. She'd laid out his hammock as a tarp and taken great pleasure in personally lopping off banana leaves with his machete to serve as plates for the fresh fruit and fish. She'd found fat candles in what was once the kitchen area of the mansion, and positioned them around the deck in a circle to ward off crawly things.

A velvet breeze stirred as the storm closed in, making the candlelight quiver, and lifting the fragrance of the tropical night into the air. The smell of flowers mingled with the comforting scents of wood smoke and the coming rain.

Sarah sighed, feeling utterly content. This was the most delicious meal she could ever remember, and although the night sounds of the jungle rose in a raucous crescendo across the river, she felt safe on the covered deck of the old house, with the fire and candles and Hunter and his gun at her side.

She'd enjoyed cutting down the fruit, in spite of the snake she'd disturbed, and the spiders. Wielding the machete to provide for their dinner had empowered her in a way that had surprised her. And she'd taken great pleasure in cleaning off the veranda, arranging the candles and the slices of fruit on the banana leaves and putting a flower in her hair.

It made her realize that while she'd come to this wild place to do good, to offer her help to others, to challenge herself in a new environment, she still really loved the simple pleasure of creating a beautiful home. It was a pleasure Josh had stolen from her, and it was the last thing she'd expected to rediscover in the heart of the cursed Congo jungle.

"Fit for kings," Hunter said as he leaned back on his elbow next to her, eyes on the fire. He was relaxed enough to have taken his boots off, and he was naked from the waist up. She studied his rugged profile, the hardened and scarred muscles of his torso, and smiled sadly. He was right when he'd said they were different, that they needed different things. While she was coming to the realization that what she really wanted, *needed,* was a home—a real home, full of love and warmth— Hunter McBride was just about the furthest thing from it. There was nothing mainstream about this man. He existed on the fringes of society, and she had a sense it was something no woman could take from him. This man could not be put in a container behind a picket fence. He *belonged* in untamed places like this.

He caught her watching. He smiled, reached up and touched the flower tucked behind her ear. "Nice."

She smiled back, caught his hand in her own before he could move it away from her face. "This is your injured arm, Hunter."

He grinned. "Yeah. And it's doing good, thanks to you."

She made a mock frown. "You never put that sling back on after you…fought with that soldier. You think I didn't notice?"

He moved a little closer to her. "So?"

"You were just humoring me back in the clearing when you let me bandage you up, weren't you? You wanted to give me a sense of purpose, a job."

"And you did it so well." A mischievous light danced in his eyes. "Even though there was zero chance I could get my shirt back on."

She jabbed at him. "You're awfully smug in your medical knowledge, you know. How does a soldier know so much?"

He looked away, the play of firelight and shadow hiding his expression. A fat drop of rain hit the tin roof. The breeze shifted, intensified. Leaves rustled.

"Rain's coming."

"You're changing the subject, Hunter. Where *did* you get your medical knowledge? What did you used to do before you joined the FDS?"

His features hardened. He stared at the flames for a while. "I served with the Légion Étrangère—French Foreign Legion."

Surprise flared in her. "The Legion? It still exists?" She'd heard about it. Her father, an armchair military buff, had loved to tell her old war stories, and among them were tales of the famous and exotic French Legionnaires—men's men in a landscape of hot deserts, dense jungles and fierce combat. He'd told his stories with such passion and excitement, she'd often wondered how much of it was really true, but the notion he might've been embellishing hadn't bothered her one bit. She suspected her dad had fancied himself as one of the Legionnaires in his dreams of adventure. And she'd happily lived the dream with him on cold winter nights by the fire.

He'd stopped telling the stories, though, after her mother had died. And Sarah had missed that connection with him more than he could ever have imagined. If he'd known just how much it had hurt her, how desperately cut off he'd made her feel on top of losing her mother, it would have broken his heart.

"The Legion still exists, but apart from military experts, I guess not many people know that it does. The force currently has about 8,500 professional soldiers and 350 officers ready for rapid-action deployment anywhere in the world at extremely short notice." Hunter still wouldn't look at her. He stared instead into the crucible of flames he'd built in the stone oven.

Intrigued, she drew her knees into her chest and leaned forward. "How long did you spend with the Legion?"

"I fulfilled my five year contract." He grunted softly. "If you want to leave any earlier than that, you have to desert. And then they come hunting for you. It's not pretty when they find you. And they *do* find you."

Sarah looked at the flames, as if she might see what he was seeing in them, see into his past. From what history she knew from her father, if the French Foreign Legion had forged Hunter's character, it explained an awful lot about him.

Her dad had told her that the Légion Étrangère was often referred to as the Legion of the Damned. It was an army comprised completely of foreigners—hard men who were usually running from something back home, men who had to set aside cultural differences and learn quickly to communicate in French. Men who were prepared to give up their pasts, their countries, their families and their homes in order to fight and die for a country that wasn't their own.

It dawned on her then that the whole French Foreign Legion was a mercenary army, and it had been modeled on generations of private armies in Europe that went before it. So why should what Hunter did for a living now be so unpalatable to much of the world? Sarah suddenly felt like a hypocrite. As a young child she'd relished the exotic tales of combat, but she'd grown into a woman who abhorred war. Was it because her dad's stories had seemed so foreign, so fictional, so far removed from her reality that they had existed in a separate part of her psyche? Maybe it was because the time spent with her father was so special she just refused to see anything negative about it.

She studied Hunter's profile, a clearer picture of him emerging in her mind. Her father had told her that when a man joined the Legion he could take nothing of his past with him, no clothes, no cash, no trinkets or photos. Everything was confiscated, even passports. A man literally had to check his past at the gates. And *if* he survived his contract, he earned the right to become a French citizen. He was given a new passport, and if he wanted, a new name and new identity documents. It was the perfect place to officially bury a troubled history.

"My dad used to tell me stories about the Legion," she said softly.

His eyes flashed to hers. "He did?"

"He told me that if a man wanted to hide from something terrible he'd done, he could join, and after he'd served his contract, *if* he survived it, he could—"

"Be rectified, get a new identity."

"Yes. He said criminals did it to avoid the law."

Hunter gave a dry laugh. "Criminals, refugees, revolutionaries, paupers, poets and princes—all welcomed into the French Foreign Legion since King Louis Phillipe established the force in 1831. Yeah, I've heard those stories, too." His eyes held hers. "That's the romantic version, Sarah. It's not quite like that now. Not *that* easy for a criminal to get in."

Was he mocking her? She studied his eyes. "Why did *you* join, Hunter?"

He shrugged. "Must've read the same stories your dad did, got the same romantic notions in my head. You know, the promise of exotic adventure in a man's world. Hot sun, victorious combat, cool desert nights, cheap wine—" he cocked a brow "—and of course, compliant females."

Warmth tingled over her skin at the thought of sex with Hunter.

He looked away. "Or maybe it *was* the promise of a cloak of official anonymity, the promise of a new life."

Sarah had an uncomfortable and growing sense that this was the truth. His accent was Irish, yet he'd told her he was a French citizen. He had to have been rectified. But why? What had driven him to do it? What dark past was Hunter McBride hiding from?

"Is your name really Hunter McBride?"

The fire popped and cracked. The wind rustled in the trees and fat leaves clacked together. A few more drops of rain plopped on the tin roof. He sat up suddenly, reached over, took both her hands in his.

"Yes. I wouldn't hide that from you. Not now."

What are you hiding then? "You're Irish," she said. "At least you were before you became French."

"That was another lifetime."

"And you don't want to tell me about it?"

A darkness sifted into his features. His jaw hardened and his eyes turned cold. That look of danger was back. She wasn't sure she wanted to know the truth about Hunter McBride. "It's okay," she said, backpedaling. "Maybe…maybe some other time."

"Yeah." He picked up a twig blown in by the wind and tossed it at the fire. "Maybe another time."

But there wouldn't be one. The notion of a future hung unarticulated between them. The wind whipped a little harder and the fire wavered. Drops of rain began to bomb steadily against the tin roof, and the banana palms swished against the walls.

Hunter stared into the coals. His heart was thudding hard. He'd allowed Sarah to push him right up to the very edge of his past, but he was incapable of going further, incapable of giving her the whole truth.

Yet he'd crossed a line with her—in more ways than one—and he knew in his gut there was no turning back. He just didn't know if he could go all the way. Or why he should. She'd be out of his life within seventy-two hours.

If they were lucky, by this time tomorrow they'd be in Cameroon. He'd use his radio to contact the FDS. It would be risky, but not as risky as using it in the Congo. The FDS had an agreement with the Cameroonian government, and FDS soldiers were free to operate in the area. He could have Sarah on an FDS chopper within an hour or two of crossing the border.

Hunter would then move on to the next phase of his mission, which was to help "kidnap" Dr. Jan Meyer from his research station in Gabon. The man was a world-renowned expert in infectious diseases and affiliated with the Prince Leopold Institute of Tropical Medicine in Belgium, Europe's answer to the CDC. If anyone could identify the pathogen it was he. The FDS knew Meyer would come to the São Diogo lab willingly, but in the interests of secrecy, they couldn't let him know about the pathogen until they had him sequestered. They would make it look as if he'd been taken hostage by rebels for cash, and they'd set up a fake negotiating system in an effort to stay under Cabal radar. The next major challenge would be to find an antidote in time.

Time.

Hunter stared at the hot orange embers as the fire began to die down and rain drummed on the roof. Everyone was running out of time. Even him, for God's sake. He'd be forty-three in a few weeks. Jesus, what was his life all about, really? How often did a woman like Sarah come a man's way?

And what fool would honestly let her go?

He jerked to his feet and threw another log onto the fire. The rain came down even harder, waves of sound hammering over the roof with each gust of wind. A loose sheet of tin began to bang somewhere, and wind began to moan eerily through the old structure.

Sarah was watching him in silence, those beautiful warm brown eyes liquid with the reflected light of the flames, searching his face for answers. He sat down beside her, unable to talk.

"Hunter." She touched him, fingers soft on the skin of his arm. "I didn't mean to pry." Her eyes glimmered. "I care about you. I…I just want you know that."

Wind tore suddenly at the banana palms and rattled the leaves. Thunder rumbled in the distance and lightning flashed. The rain came down in a solid silver curtain, and water began to drip through rusted nail holes in the roof.

Hunter stared at her hand, pale and smooth against his sun-darkened skin. His throat tightened. Emotion began to burn in his chest. When had he last felt a touch like that? When had anyone *cared* about him?

He lifted his eyes slowly and his gaze meshed with hers. The warmth, the tacit permission, the invitation he saw in her eyes engulfed him in a dizzying wave.

She got to her knees, leaned forward, her lips slightly parted, her lids low and sultry over her eyes. And Hunter's heart clean stopped. Thunder crashed. His heart kicked back at twice the pace. She placed her hand against his face and brought her mouth closer to his.

She was going to kiss him.

His mind raced, scrambling again for all the reasons he shouldn't do this. Then her lips touched his, brushed over them, soft as butterfly wings. His stomach swooped and his mind went blank. He closed his eyes, tried to hold himself still, but his muscles began to tremble.

She brushed her mouth over his again and then he felt the tip of her tongue, wet, soft as velvet, run over his lips. Hunter groaned as he grew hard and his groin started pulsing with each beat of his heart. He could think of nothing beyond losing himself deep inside this woman.

But just as he reached up to cup her head, to pull her mouth down harder on his, she drew away.

His eyes flared open.

She sat back on her heels and was watching his face. Arousal flushed her features, and he could see that her nipples were pressed hard against the soft fabric of her thin camisole. Another wave of delirious heat swooped through his belly. But he didn't dare make a move. Not this time. This had to be her decision and hers alone. She had to be sure.

Lightning cracked again and thunder followed almost immediately. The storm was right over them now. The rain hammered and the piece of tin banged louder, faster.

She moved her hands to the hem of her camisole, and with her eyes holding his, drew it slowly up over her belly, then her breasts, then lifted it over her head.

Hunter's mouth went bone-dry.

She sat in front of him, naked from the waist up, breasts aroused, her burnished tangle of curls brushing her shoulders.

He shook his head mentally, thinking for a fleeting moment he was dreaming. But he wasn't.

She stood up, wriggled her skirt down over her hips, taking her panties with it. She stood absolutely naked in front of him, the firelight flickering gold over her creamy pale skin.

She wanted him, all right. He tried to swallow, couldn't. He stared at the dark delta between her thighs, and the hot, pulsing ache in his groin screamed for release. He lifted his eyes slowly, trailing them up from the insides of her thighs to her belly button, up slowly to her breasts. She was beautiful and there was nothing shy about her. Those facts sparked something dark and savage in him. He clenched his teeth. He wanted to haul her to the ground, plunge himself into her…but he didn't want to make it happen too fast. He wanted her to take him where *she* wanted. He had a sense she needed it that way. She needed to be in control. And a part of him found intense delirious pleasure in the notion.

She knelt down slowly, bringing her mouth close to his ear as she reached for his belt. Her hair fell across his chest as she whispered, "I want to see you naked, Hunter McBride."

His mind swooned. He moved his head around to kiss her, but she pressed her fingers to his mouth, holding him back. "Naked first," she murmured.

Hunter closed his eyes as she undid his belt buckle. This woman just didn't stop surprising him. How could a man have ever let her go? How could *he* let her go? He felt himself swell into her soft hands as she freed him from his zipper. He groaned with pleasure as she clasped her hand around him and began to caress him. He watched her face as she stroked him to an unbearable pitch. She smiled, her lids heavy, and began to tug his pants down over his hips. He lifted his body to help her.

Thunder crashed again and sheet lightning illuminated the sky. The world flickered like old movie. She sat back on her heels and ran her eyes brazenly over his body.

He leaned forward to grab her, to pull her down onto him. But she restrained him with the palm of her hand against his chest, slowly straddling his legs. The idea of her thighs parting over him nearly drove him wild. His heart began to palpitate and his vision swam. He placed his hands on her hips, ran them up along the contours of her waist to the swell of her breasts. He cupped them, squeezed, grazed his thumbs over her nipples. They grew even tighter. She lifted her chin, tilting her head back, and moaned softly. Her motion had the effect of opening her legs wider, slanting her pelvis toward him.

He slid his hands back down along her waist, down the outside of her thighs and then slipped one hand around her buttocks and moved the other to the inside. The skin here was unbelievably smooth and soft. With the hand on her behind, he tilted her pelvis even more, and cupped his other palm over her hair, his fingers seeking the soft folds within. He found them, slipped his fingers up inside her. She was wet, slick, hot. She moaned again, sinking some of her weight down onto him, and her eyelids fluttered in pleasure.

For a second Hunter couldn't breathe. And in the next second he couldn't hold on any longer. In a swift movement born of years of hand-to-hand combat, he had her flat on her back and was kneeling over her. With one hand he pinned her wrists to the floor up over her head, with the other he traced the line of her breasts. Shock—and desire—flared in her eyes.

He grinned. "My turn, Sarah."

Chapter 14

The savage look in his eyes shot a thrill through her. He had her hands trapped above her head, her body exposed, at his mercy. He knelt over her, phenomenal in his nakedness, pure male power and potent arousal. The wind gusted, blowing a fine mist of moisture over her hot skin. Sarah shivered.

He leaned down, caught the lobe of her ear between his teeth and whispered words in French she couldn't understand—and didn't need to. The seduction was rich enough in the way he said them. Waves of scarlet pleasure wheeled through her brain. He traced his mouth down the column of her neck, over her breast and down her stomach, tasting, teasing, flicking with his tongue as he moved along the length of her body. He reached her thighs and she felt his hands part her, then she felt his tongue. Hot. Wct. Her world narrowed to just the sensation. His tongue flickered, traced the part of her that throbbed with each pulse of blood through her body, then suddenly thrust hard and deep. She cried out in delicious shock. His tongue moved inside her and she arched her back, aching for release. But just as she thought she was going to explode, he withdrew.

She gave a crazy sob of relief, desperately eager to hang on to the painful pleasure of her need, not ready to let go yet.

He knelt between her thighs and used his knees to push her legs open wide, impossibly wide. He leaned over her, covering her body with his, and she felt the hot, smooth, rounded tip of him enter her. He watched her face as he slowly, rhythmically, dipped just the tip of himself into her, not once breaking visual contact. Sarah tilted her pelvis up in desperation, opening wider to him, aching for all of him. He smiled, dark and feral, and then plunged deep into her with a hard, guttural groan.

She gasped. He was incredibly hot. He moved inside her fast, hard, faster, the slippery heat of his friction against swollen nerve ends almost unbearable. Her eyelids fluttered. Crimson waves spiraled through her brain. She could control nothing that was happening in her body. He rocked his pelvis hard against hers, thrusting deeper each time. Her nerves screamed for release, and suddenly her muscles exploded around him. She dug her nails into his back and swallowed a cry as contractions shook her.

Her release pushed him to the edge. He took her jaw, made her look at him, and with a final hard thrust, he shuddered into her.

Sarah lay naked, enfolded in his arms, the tropical air soft on her skin. Rain still fell in a curtain around the veranda and clattered on the tin roof. The fire crackled as it died down to embers.

She could not have imagined anything like this in her life. She'd left a cold and dreary Seattle with a dead heart, and she'd come to the Congo to liberate herself. And she had, in just a few weeks—but she'd also stumbled into an adventure and met a man beyond her wildest dreams.

She closed her eyes, sighed softly. Whatever happened now didn't really matter, she told herself. She'd finally lived. She'd be okay. But she knew she was lying. She just didn't want to entertain the thought of never seeing him again.

She tried to force it from her mind. She told herself it wasn't worth worrying about a future when they might never make it to Cameroon alive. This might be all there was going to be for her, and at least she'd have found herself and found pleasure on the night before she died. She curled against him and drifted into a deep, contented sleep.

Hunter lay awake, holding her, feeling the softness of her bare skin against his, listening to the steady drum of rain on the tin roof, drinking in the musky scent of her sex. He felt himself stir again with a soft, pulsing need. He could have her all over again right now. Just the thought made him harder.

She shifted against him, her head nuzzling into the crook of his armpit, her messy curls tickling his face. He tangled his fingers through them, playing with the light spring in them as they curved around his hand. She began to make soft little snores and he smiled into the dark. Who would have thought a sound like that could make him feel so complete? Who'd have thought that lying naked with an American nurse in the ruins of a colonial French mansion, on an abandoned rubber plantation in the heart of equatorial Africa—with a lethal bioweapon at their side—could feel so absolutely right, so natural, so normal? A soft laugh escaped him. It sure beat a regular date.

A gust of wind swished the banana leaves against the building. The rain was dying down, the scent of wet soil was rich and the air felt cool. He reached for his shirt, pulled it over Sarah's shoulders, careful not to wake her. She needed her sleep. Tomorrow was going to be rough. The militia would be watching, waiting for them to try and make a run for the border.

He closed his eyes and said a silent prayer that he'd manage to get her through alive—and shock speared through him.

His eyes flashed open and he stared up at the rusted roof. Wow. A prayer? Hunter McBride hadn't treaded there in fifteen years.

The rain stopped shortly before dawn, and the whole jungle rustled with the sound of fat drops on thick leaves. As light seeped into the sky, he watched rainwater leak down through a rusty hole in the tin. He hadn't been able to sleep all night. This place, he thought as he stared at the roof, was like a symbol of the husk that was himself. Once solid, once full of love and the promise of life, but now in a cursed no-man's land, abandoned, empty, getting a little older, crustier, meaner each day, crumbling one piece at a time while the world passed him by.

Sarah stirred in his arms, her breast a soft warm weight against his chest. He stroked her hair. She filled this space. With her candles and beauty and nurturing warmth, she'd managed to create a sense of home in the middle of nowhere. She filled *him,* made him feel alive. She made him want to live. Really live. She made him want more than what he had right now.

He closed his eyes. Right now he was free. He had nothing to lose. And that's the way he'd wanted it since the day he'd lost everything. That's why he'd joined the French Foreign Legion. Falling for Sarah meant losing that freedom. It meant he once again *had* something to lose. And a man with something to lose had fear. It was not something he needed in his line of work. Part of his success as a warrior lay in his complete lack of fear, his willingness to take risks daily that could cost him his life.

She stirred again and her eyelids fluttered open. "Hey."

He stroked her cheek. "Hey to you, too."

A sleepy smile crept over her lips.

No. He was wrong. He wasn't free right now. That was forty-eight hours ago. He'd already crossed the line. He already had everything to lose. He just didn't know what in hell to do about it now.

Sarah propped herself up on her elbow, her breasts brushing against him, her hair wild and lustrous over her bare shoulders, her eyes sexy with sleep.

She traced his lips with her fingers. "Why are you smiling?" Her warm brown eyes were full of soft light. What would it be like to wake up to that beautiful face every morning? To lose himself in her each night, to make babies, to give her the children he knew she'd love? Could he make it happen? Did he want to?

Hesitation flickered through those eyes. "Hunter? Come on, tell me what you're thinking. What's making you smile like that?"

He filled his lungs. What the hell, why not just say what was on his mind this very second? It wouldn't kill him, would it? *Push yourself, you jackass. What have you got to lose? Nothing you haven't lost before.*

"I was thinking about you. And I was thinking about this house, about what it must have been like, full of life, laughter and…you know, children. I was thinking about how much you love kids." He rolled over, dragged his knuckle softly across her cheek. "I was thinking what a wonderful mother you'd make."

Her smiled faded. Hunter wavered. He had a sudden sinking feeling he was heading down a one-way street about to meet an oncoming bus he couldn't see.

"And?" she asked.

He noted in some part of his brain that his pulse rate had just increased. "And…and I was thinking what fun we could have making those babies." There, he'd hung his heart right out for the first time in fifteen years.

Her body tensed and something shuttered instantly in her eyes. She sat up, stared down at him, didn't say a word.

A pang of uneasiness speared through him. The wind stirred,

leaves clattered against each other. A cry echoed in the jungle. He knew it; he should never have spoken his mind. He didn't know how to do this stuff anymore. He should have stuck to what he knew best. "Sarah, what's the matter?"

She looked away. Something was wrong. Very wrong. He sat up. "Sarah—"

She grabbed for her shirt, shoved her arms into the sleeves and fumbled with the buttons. He noticed her hands were trembling.

"Sarah, talk to me."

She spun around, glared at him. "You're messing with me."

"Oh, sweetheart, I had no intention…" He reached for her, but she moved out from under his touch.

"You…you said we were different."

He frowned. He wasn't sure what he'd said. Different. The same. It didn't the hell matter to him anymore. "Where are you going with this, Sarah?"

"You—you said…" Her eyes glimmered. "You said you would go on to the next job. And now you're thinking of children…of…" A tear leaked out of the corner of one eye and trailed down her cheek.

He blinked. His mind reeled. He was confused as all hell. Here he was thinking *maybe* they could take a shot at a future. Just maybe he could make some changes, try to figure it out so that he could be with her…and she didn't want it. What was this? A one-night stand? Was *that* what she wanted? To prove something to herself? To validate herself as a woman, or something? Did she have *any* idea what she meant to him?

He dragged both his hands through his hair. This had been a mistake. A big mistake. He'd known in his gut it was the wrong move.

"Look, Sarah, you asked what I was thinking, so I told you." He got up, pulled his pants on. He was angry, no, *furious,* at himself. Afraid. Hurt by her odd rejection, the notion that she might really have meant it when she'd said that she didn't want anything from him, that she wanted to try and exist only in the now. He didn't want to believe that. It was out of character. There was something else going on here, and he'd be damned if he could see what it was. He cinched his belt tight, stared down at her. "I was thinking about how much I want to be with you. You wanted things from me straight, well, that's about as bloody well straight as it gets." He grabbed his shirt.

Her bottom lip began to wobble. Tears ran down her face, but the look in her eyes was angry. "Why have *you* never had kids, Hunter? Why didn't *you* get married and do it? Why don't you want to tell me about Ireland? *What the hell are you hiding from?*" She was shaking now.

He stared right into her eyes. "I *did* want to get married, Sarah," he said slowly, quietly, the cold mist of that memory circling his heart. "I was engaged. Things went wrong."

Uncertainty flickered across her features. "And...and you wanted kids?"

"I did, very much."

"And now?"

He felt a little ill. "Sarah, kids don't have anything to do with this—"

"And now?" she insisted.

Tension tightened the muscles around his throat. "I just told you I was dreaming about kids. I just spilled my guts, for chrissakes." The sun burst over the forest canopy, exploding yellow light onto the veranda.

"What happened in Ireland, Hunter? Why won't you tell me about it?"

He cursed softly. Ten seconds ago he would have. He'd finally been ready to go there. Now? He just couldn't do it. He'd read her wrong. He'd read *himself* wrong. He was better off the way he was. Past buried. Dead. Gone. Forever.

He tightened his jaw. "Ancient history, Sarah. It would serve no purpose now. Get yourself together while I scrounge up some breakfast. We leave ASAP."

He turned, stalked off the veranda, took two crumbling stairs at a time, his brain spinning sickeningly. He stopped for a second at the bottom of the steps and caught his breath. What in hell had just happened back there? He swore again. This was his fault. He should never have slept with her. He was all too aware of the uncharacteristic things people did under stress. Sleeping with him had probably been one of them, something she was already regretting.

Whatever was going on in Sarah's head, she was going to need time after this mission to decompress. There was no point in pushing her now. And he'd be better off focusing on getting out alive, and then just letting this whole thing go. Who had he been trying to kid, anyway? He'd been absent from mainstream life for way too long to even begin to think he could give Sarah what she needed.

He steeled himself.

He had a job. *Focus.* They'd be out of the Blacklands within two hours. Then he couldn't afford to think about another goddamn thing until he'd gotten her and the biohazard container over that border and into Cameroon.

His mind firmly back in the zone, Hunter stomped off into the bush to find breakfast.

Sarah stood at a broken window and watched Hunter stalk into the jungle. The dripping vegetation and haunting river mist seemed to swallow him whole. She looked up at the sky. It was clear above the shroud of fog, but in the distance, to the north over Cameroon, strange dust-orange clouds were mushrooming again. She shivered in spite of the steamy morning warmth and clutched her arms around herself. She was afraid. Afraid because she was falling for him. And her fear had pushed him away. She wasn't a fool. Sarah knew even as the stupid words had come out of her mouth that her subconscious was trying to sabotage her. Because deep down she knew it could never work. She'd already been through it all in her mind. You just didn't change a man like Hunter McBride. You couldn't take the mercenary out of a man. And she couldn't change who she was for him, either.

But that hadn't stopped her wanting him, and it didn't stop her wanting him now. God, she wished she'd never seen that look in his eyes when he'd told her his thoughts. It made her want his children in such a deep, primal way it hurt. She tried to tell herself it was the jungle, it was everything she'd been through, it was the fact she'd been stripped down to her raw emotional core.

Sarah shoved her hair back from her eyes with both hands and tried to force some logic into her brain. She still really knew nothing about Hunter's past, about why he'd joined the Legion, about what he was running from. And it was better that way. She needed a home in her future. A man on the run didn't.

She bent down, began to roll up the hammock. A scorpion scattered over the stone and disappeared into the cracks.

09:32 Alpha. Congo.
Thursday, September 25

Hunter's eyes had gone hard. Even his face seemed carved from granite. He was once again the fearsome and implacable man she'd first seen back on the banks of the Shilongwe River. It was as if the Hunter she'd come to know in the Blacklands had never existed.

He was leading her along a narrow path. The red dirt under her feet was packed hard and this alone was unnerving. It meant the path was well-traveled, and it meant they could encounter someone at any time.

He spun round suddenly, grabbed her arm and yanked her down into the thick bush along the trail. The movement was so harsh and quick she opened her mouth to cry out in surprise. He clamped his hand hard over her lips before she could, muffling her shock. His eyes bored into hers, fierce with warning. He waited for her to calm down before he removed his hand, then he lifted his finger to his lips and pointed into the trees. She saw and heard nothing at first. Then she caught snatches of voices growing louder, more distinct. Several men speaking Lingala were coming their way. She could hear the boots now, thudding along the trail of packed dirt, coming closer.

Sarah turned to look at Hunter. He glared at her, his eyes telling her not to move a muscle. She saw the hunting knife ready in his hands.

The sounds grew closer. A man spoke loudly and others laughed in response. They rounded the bend in the trail and came into view. Her heart began to palpitate as she recognized the uniform of the man she'd killed. There were seven, no, eight militia soldiers with maroon berets and red armbands marching right toward them.

They came so close she could smell them, and a panicked part of her brain wondered if they could smell her, too. She held herself motionless as the dust-covered boots thudded inches from Hunter's and her hiding spot. She could see them clearly, high black webbing around the ankles. Sarah could barely breathe. Then she saw the blood on one man's boots and gasped softly. The soldier stopped suddenly, listened. Hunter tensed instantly, moved the knife forward.

The soldier slowly scanned the trees behind him. Then he turned his attention to the bushes along the trail. He was so close Sarah could see the beads of perspiration on his brow under his beret, and she could see there was blood on his machete. Her heart went stone-cold. His eyes moved gradually toward them. One of his comrades called back to him. He paused, seeming to look right at her. Then he turned and answered loudly in Lingala. One of the men up ahead laughed and yelled something. The soldier chuckled quietly in response, turned on his heels and began to follow the others down the path.

Sarah started to shake. Oh God, she couldn't go through all this again. Hunter placed a hand on her shoulder. "Be strong," he whispered. "And Sarah, do *everything* I say and we may stand a chance of getting out of here."

She nodded. She'd heard it all before, back on the Shilongwe. She suddenly wanted to get as far away from him as she possibly could, and from everything he represented.

"You ready?"

She nodded fiercely. She was more ready, more determined to get out of this place than he could begin to imagine.

The trail wound back down to the banks of the Sangé. The river here was wide and sluggish, the sandbanks a deep ochre color. The heavy morning mist had burned off and the air was oppressively still. As they moved along the water, they heard drums, soft at first, then growing louder, beating faster until they matched the rhythm of Sarah's pounding heart. The sound echoed along the river and pulsated in the thick, hot air.

Sarah glanced at Hunter. There was no sign of emotion on his face, but she knew now the drums were not good. She recognized the unique rhythm of the beat from the Eikona River, the drumming that had sounded after the clinic and the village were burned, after news of the coup in the south. No matter how Sarah tried to calm herself, her heart kept beating harder, trying to match the rhythm of the drums. It made her body break out in a drenching sweat and it fed her fear.

When they reached a wide bend, Hunter motioned for her to move off the path and crouch down in the bushes. He left her like that while he crept along the bank, staying just under cover of the trees, his rifle ready in his hands. She had no idea what he was looking for, or what might have alerted him. He disappeared around the bend for what seemed like forever. Then all of sudden he was back, working his way along the bank. He made a motion for her to join him.

She edged over the sand. "What're the drums about?"

"Trouble." He pointed above the trees in the direction he'd just come. Faint wisps of black smoke snaked into the air and birds circled. Big birds. *Vultures.* Her chest constricted. Her eyes shot to Hunter.

"The Italian mission has been attacked."

No. She shook her head. No. She started to back toward the trees, tripped, stumbled. He shot his hand out, grabbed her wrist, his fingers curling around it like a metal cuff. "We have to go there, to see if they left a boat we can use."

"Hunter," she whispered, "please, I…I can't. I can't see anything like that again. Ever. Please." She tugged against his hold. "I beg of you."

His eyes remained fiercely cool, his grip firm. She glanced back at the jungle, a part of her wishing she could go back in there, go back in time, back to the Blacklands, just hide forever at the mansion on the white banks of the Sangé in lands protected by ghosts with the man she thought she'd met in there.

"Sarah." His voice was as hard as his hold on her wrist. "It's the *only* way."

12:13 Alpha. Italian Mission.
Thursday, September 25

Hunter wouldn't allow her to enter the riverside compound. He'd left her hiding among a cluster of straight-stemmed palms while he crept into the clearing to see if there was a canoe he could salvage.

Sarah crouched near the base of a palm and watched a snake slide through the leaves across the path from her. She didn't move. She didn't even feel any fear. In a part of her brain, she marveled at how much the snake's skin resembled the decaying leaves it moved through, at how the little cluster of tiny horns on its nose looked like bits of twig. Before she'd come to the Congo she'd gone to several Aid Africa briefings in Washington. Among other things, they'd shown the recruits pictures of the snakes, insects and plants that would kill people very quickly. She couldn't remember them all, so many things could kill humans in this area. The only reason she knew that she was looking at a Gaboon viper now was because of the funny rhinoceros cluster on its snout. *Their fangs deliver fifteen drops of venom a shot. Four drops will kill you....*

Funny the things one recalled. She'd never have noticed the viper if she hadn't been sitting stock-still. Concentrating on the lethal reptile took her mind off thinking about what had happened at the Italian mission. The soldiers they'd seen along the path earlier that morning had come from this direction. The blood on the man's shoe must have been shed at this mission.... She looked up, staring hard at the little weaver birds darting between woven nests that hung from the scruffy green-and-brown palm fronds. She focused on the nests to keep her mind from the vultures. She thought they looked like straw Christmas baubles, the way they hung in the trees. She tried to count how many weeks it was to Christmas, wondering where she would be—

Hunter suddenly materialized in front of her, making her catch her breath. The man moved as quietly as a snake when he wanted to.

She looked up into his eyes, trying to see what he might have seen. But his face was absolutely expressionless. "There are canoes," he said. "We can't wait until dark. We must take one now, try and get a ways down the river, find a place we can hole up until nightfall."

She began to rise to her feet. He stopped her, placing his palm on her shoulder. He crouched down to eye level and took her hands in his. "Sarah," he said quietly. "We have to go through the compound to get to where the canoes are beached."

She swallowed, nodded.

His eyes lanced hers. "I don't want you to look. I want you to focus on following me. Just move fast and keep looking at me."

Her heart began to pound. "Have...have they been killed?" she whispered.

"Yes."

"All of them?"

"Yes."

"Even the priests?"

He nodded.

Her stomach turned over and she stared at her toes.

"Come." He took her arm, pulling her to her feet. "We have to move quickly."

Sarah concentrated on the backs of Hunter's boots as he led her through the center of the mission compound. But she could smell the sickly sweet scent of spilled blood, the acrid scent of burned thatch. Sweat dampened her skin. In her head, she could see Dr. Regnaud's glazed eyes behind his goggles, could hear screams of the nuns back at the Ishonga clinic, could hear the moans. The moans seemed real…too real…. She faltered, suddenly unable to move, unable to discern memory from reality. She watched Hunter's boots moving away from her. Then she heard it again, a moan. Her heart skipped a beat. *It was real!* She glanced up. "Hunter! Stop!"

He halted, spun round.

"Someone…someone's hurt. I can hear them."

He took two strides toward her, grabbed her arm, digging his fingers into her skin. "Come," he growled.

"No!" She tried to yank free of his hold. "Listen."

She heard the low moan again. The sound was coming from the trees behind the wattle-and-daub hut to her left. Sarah turned to look, and bile heaved to her throat as the carnage around her filtered into her vision. Several bodies were scattered around the clearing. Massacred with machetes. She clamped her hand over her mouth.

Hunter flung his arm around her, protecting her from the sight with his body. He lowered his face to hers. "Sarah, just keep moving. Don't look."

She jerked free and ducked out of his hold. *"Someone's still alive."*

"Sarah—"

She spun and stumbled over the dirt, making her way around the hut with its partially burned thatch roof, trying not to absorb too much. But she was compelled to find the source of the sound.

She found it in the shade of a kapok tree.

A young woman lay sprawled on the red ground. Blood covered the side of her head and face, and her belly was round and swollen under her T-shirt. Her eyes were open and she stared right at Sarah and moaned softly.

"Oh my God!" Sarah rushed forward, dropped to her

knees at the woman's side. "Hunter...come quick, help me. She's pregnant!"

His hand gripped her shoulder hard. Her eyes shot up to his. "We've got to do something!"

"Sarah, we have to *leave. Now.* There's nothing we can do for her."

"How can you say that! How do you know?" Sarah turned to the woman, felt for a pulse at her neck. It was very weak and rapid. Her skin was cold to the touch, and Sarah's fingers came away covered in blood. She quickly lifted the woman's T-shirt and palpated her swollen belly. She felt a movement under her hands. Her heart stopped, then started racing. "Oh, God, the baby's alive." Sarah felt the woman's belly again. She could tell by the height of the woman's expanded uterus that the fetus was probably at thirty-eight weeks' gestation. "I—I think it's term," she whispered.

She glanced at the woman's face. Her eyes were rolling back, her lids fluttering. She was losing consciousness. Sarah felt quickly for her pulse again. It was thready, barely there. *They were losing her.*

Sarah felt utterly helpless and bewildered. She'd know how to help in a hospital situation. But out here? She reached up, grabbed the fabric of Hunter's army pants. "The baby—we've got to do something!"

He crouched down, looked into her eyes. "Sarah," he said softly, urgently. "You *can* help. You can help by staying alive yourself, by getting this pathogen out so that it can be identified. You can help by saving the lives of millions upon millions of innocent people. People just as innocent as this woman and her unborn child here."

She stared at him, speechless. How could he ignore this pregnant woman?

"Think of it as triage, Sarah. You have to help those with the most chance of survival first. Sometimes the decisions are tough."

"No." She shook her head, jerked away. "I can't. I can't leave this woman and her baby to die alone with the vultures circling up there. *I just can't.* I have to at least make them comfortable." She glared at him. "And don't try to make me leave. You made me shoot a man. Don't make me do this, too."

His eyes narrowed. He clenched his teeth and a muscle in his neck began to jump fast. He glanced at his watch and cursed viciously under his breath. Then he shrugged out of his pack, dropped to his knees beside her, felt for the woman's pulse, began to palpate her stomach.

Sarah's mouth dropped open. He moved like a professional.

He turned the woman's head to the side, exposing a thick, gelatinous puddle of blood and a clean machete gash that sliced right through her skull into gray brain tissue. Sarah's stomach bottomed out. Hunter was right. There was no hope for her. How she'd held on this far was incredible. She had to be doing it for her child.

Hunter glanced at Sarah. "She's going into cardiac arrest. We've got five minutes."

"What?"

"To save the fetus. Pass me my pack. Quick." He unbuttoned his shirt as he spoke, shrugged out of it.

Sarah stared at him.

Hunter reached over her, grabbed the pack himself, extracted the first aid pouch, rolled it open, began to snap on a pair of latex gloves. He hesitated for a millisecond, then closed his fingers around the scalpel. "Get the flashlight out, Sarah. Position it at the side of my head, shine it on her stomach as I work."

Her brain felt sluggish. She realized they were in the shade. He'd need light. How did he know what he was doing? She fumbled in the pack, her mind racing. She flicked the light on.

"Use one hand for the torch, Sarah. Take those gauze pads in the kit with your other hand, use them as laparotomy sponges, pack off the fluids as I work. I don't have clamps, I'll need to move fast. Use my shirt for the baby. You're going to have to be ready to do neonatal resuscitation if necessary, while I look for equipment in the huts. Mission should have antibiotics, blankets, formula, especially if they were caring for a young woman like this. They'd have been ready...." He lifted the scalpel as he spoke, performing a neat midline abdominal incision that would allow fast access to the uterus.

Sarah's chest clenched. Her mind reeled. By God, this man knew *exactly* what he was doing. He was a professional. There was no doubt in her mind.

Hunter McBride was a surgeon.

Chapter 15

She was small and coffee-brown with black hair, and she was the most exquisite and perfect little thing Sarah had ever laid eyes on. She hadn't been breathing when Hunter took her out, but Sarah had managed to resuscitate her while he went through the partially burned-out huts and found blankets, bottled water, antibiotics, disposable diapers and prepared formula.

They'd cleaned her tiny body, and Hunter had clamped and sterilized her umbilical cord and administered preventative antibiotics. The baby girl was an excellent weight—Sarah judged her to actually be on the higher end of the normal spectrum. Her mother had obviously received excellent care and nutrition at the mission, and all of this gave the child one hell of a fighting chance.

Sarah knew from experience that a healthy newborn of good weight could survive up to a week without any care as long as there was no umbilical stump infection, which could lead to systemic infection or tetanus within a couple of days. Plus they were more than lucky to have found formula. The gods had been looking out for this little girl, she thought as she stroked the infant's silky head.

Hunter had explained to her as he'd loaded the canoe that the missionaries would've been prepared for the young mother to leave the baby with them and return to her village once she'd given birth. If she was here to have her child, it was likely because she'd become pregnant through an act of violence and rape. It was all too common in this region, and in some tribes, a baby conceived in that manner was considered dirty and unwanted. It would have been discarded as soon as it was born. This young woman would have come to the Italian mission in a brave and desperate act to save her child. And she would likely have left it with the priests to be put up for adoption.

Sarah lifted her camisole and cuddled the newborn against her naked skin, a soft flannel blanket wrapped over the little back. This skin-to-skin contact was called kangaroo care, and it increased an infant's chances of survival tenfold. It also helped the child bond with the mother. She'd seen it done at the children's hospital when police had brought in a newborn found abandoned in a bus shelter. Sarah had taken a special interest in the care of that baby, helped nurse it back to health, and had been utterly heartbroken to see it leave.

"See?" she whispered as she stroked her hand over the soft spot on the newborn's skull. "Everything happens for a reason, little sweetheart. You've got a better chance with me and Hunter here than most kiddies born out in the jungle, you know."

The baby stirred slightly and made little suckling noises. Emotion welled sharply in Sarah's chest, and a soft, maternal warmth shot through her blood. What she was experiencing was indescribable, overwhelming. It made her feel as though she could take on the world, do *anything* to protect this innocent little life.

She looked up at Hunter. He sat in the stern of the canoe, facing her, still naked from the waist up, his chest muscles rippling under tanned skin as he maneuvered their craft into a dark and narrow tributary of the Sangé River. His face was still completely devoid of emotion. Not once during the entire operation had he showed any sign that he was feeling a thing. But she knew he had to have been. She'd glimpsed enough to know that whatever armor this man had managed to erect around himself, whatever iron-willed control he exerted over his emotions, there *was* someone under it all who cared deeply enough to have done the things she'd seen him do over the last few days. She wanted to talk to him, to ask him. But she sensed now was not the time.

Drums continued to thrum in the distance, echoing in faint waves of sound as his paddle dipped and splashed softly in the deep, black water. Trees began to crowd in, branches hanging low over the narrow waterway, muffling sound. Water hyacinths and orchids grew in thick reed beds along the shore. A fish plopped, startling Sarah, and she could see a monkey the size of a man standing in the fork of a tree, watching them. Nerves began to eat at her. She pressed the baby closer to her chest.

The canoe rocked gently as Hunter paddled. He scanned the encroaching bush constantly, his gun resting within instant reach of his fingers.

17:19 Alpha. Sangé River.
Thursday, September 25

They sat under trees on a slab of warm rock that jutted out into the small tributary. The cloud-filled sky turned a dirty orange as the sun began to sink toward the horizon. Hunter absently fingered his rifle, making sure it was at his side, ready. Cloud cover was good. It would mean complete blackness tonight and additional protection as they tried to cross the border into Cameroon. Rain, however, would not be good for the baby.

He turned to look at them. Sarah was trying to nurse the little infant with a bottle of prepared formula. She tapped the nipple against the baby's cheek, and her mouth instantly began to root around for it. She found the nipple and began to suckle, beetle-black eyes fixed intently on Sarah's face. His heart clenched tight, so tight it almost choked him. Hunter blinked back the weird hot surge of emotion and looked out over the river.

It was deserted here on the banks of the tributary, but they'd heard gunfire earlier, to the north, and it concerned him. There was way too much activity in the region. Something wasn't right.

"Hunter?"

He flicked his eyes to her.

"You're a surgeon."

It wasn't a question, and her voice was completely neutral. He studied her carefully. There was no judgment in her eyes, either. Sarah and he had both come to a point that went beyond judgment, and there was no use pretending now. He didn't even want to anymore. She'd forced him to pick up that scalpel and do what he'd been trained to do. He couldn't even begin to articulate what saving that little infant had done to his soul. He'd been outed. After all these years, the old Hunter McBride was back. Sarah had forced him be to the man he used to be, and there was no putting that past back into the bottle now. He just didn't know what the hell he was going to do about it.

"I *was* a surgeon," he said quietly. "In another lifetime. In Belfast."

"What happened?"

He moistened his lips, reached over and stroked the baby's hair. "We should name her."

"What happened, Hunter? What made you walk away?"

He sucked air in through his nose, scanned the trees across the water. It would be dark within the hour. They would have to move soon. He still had a job to finish.

"Hunter?"

He exhaled heavily. "It was more than fifteen years ago. I'd completed my surgical internship at the Catholic hospital in Belfast and taken a position on staff." Just thinking about it was rough. Making the words come out of his mouth was worse. He flashed his eyes to hers. "Sarah, it was a long time ago, and we really should—"

"I need to know, Hunter." Her gaze tunneled into his. "And I think you need to talk."

He gave a soft huff, nodded slowly. She was right. He couldn't bury this all again, not now. "I was connected. I was engaged to the hospital board director's daughter. Her name was Kathleen." He glanced at Sarah. "You remind me of her…a little." He paused, fingered his assault rifle. "No, that's not true. You did jolt my memory when I first saw you. You made me think about her, about the past. But…you're different." He smiled at her. "*Very* different. In the best possible ways."

The baby made a little noise. She'd had enough milk. Sarah set the bottle down and moved the infant up to her shoulder to burp her, all the time looking into Hunter's eyes, watching him, waiting for him to continue.

He said nothing for a while. The orange in the sky began to go purple. "Colin O'Brian," he said suddenly. "That was Kathleen's father's name. Big, big Catholic figure in the Belfast community, tons of cash, and major political clout. He first took me under his wing when my dad and two brothers blew themselves up in a bombing on his account. I was twelve at the time."

"What?"

"That's just how it was, Sarah. The region was deeply divided along political and religious lines, and each faction looked after their kind. Everyone accepted it. When my brothers and dad died they were considered heroes, martyrs for their cause, and my mother was well looked after by the community until she passed away—and she died a proud widow. But as a kid, I had this whole internal rebellious attitude to the conflict, to the death. It just seemed pointless to me, and when I saw my family blown up I got mad as all hell. But there was no place in my community for a fatherless kid to stand up to centuries worth of hatred. Instead, I developed this desperate need to mend the people that were broken by the violence. I wanted to become a doctor." He looked into her eyes. "Not just an ordinary doctor, Sarah, but a surgeon, someone who could sew people back together again. It was *my* survival mechanism, *my* way of fighting back."

He chewed on his cheek, trying to navigate the old memories, consolidate them into words. "Because of what my father and brothers had done for him and his cause, Colin supported me after they died. And he supported my ambition. He funded me through medical school and it saved me from being recruited by his underground factions. And I did the man proud,

Sarah—" he snorted "—so proud that the old guy was delighted to give me Kathleen's hand in marriage when I asked him."

A strange light flitted through Sarah's eyes. "Did you love her?"

He nodded. "Yeah, I did."

"What happened to Kathleen?"

He blew air out softly, tasting the bitterness in his mouth. "She cheated on me. She got pregnant."

Shock flared through Sarah's eyes and emotion skittered over her features. She reached for his hand, covered it with her own. Her touch made his chest hurt. It made his eyes hot.

"Who was the father?" she whispered.

"Son of the opposition. Kathleen cheated not only on me, but on her whole family. She slept with the eldest son of the leader of the Protestant faction, and she tried to hide her affair and her pregnancy from the whole community for fear of the potential political fallout." He turned to look out over the black river. "People have gone to war over lesser things, you know?"

"I know."

He sat still for a while. The sky began to darken and a hot breeze rippled the water. Sarah didn't ask any more questions. She was giving him time to go at his own pace.

Hunter ran his tongue over his teeth. "Kathleen went and got herself an abortion. In secret. She developed septicemia, and by the time she was admitted to hospital, it was too damn late to save her."

"Is that why you left Ireland to join the Legion?"

"No. I left because they blamed me for killing her."

"What!"

He nodded, slightly bemused at how easy it actually was to say these things to Sarah. It had been a secret bottled inside him for so long, he thought he'd never be able to talk about it, let alone feel this strange catharsis in doing so.

"I was Catholic, remember. In Colin's eyes that meant *no one* slept with his daughter until she was married. He immediately assumed I was the one who'd knocked her up, and he went blind with rage. He figured I was also the one who'd tried to take care of it. He thought I killed his daughter, my own fiancée, and he came after me with all the cash and power and fury he could muster. It started with my suspension from the hospital, and then the police came knocking. I was done for. Professionally. Emotionally. My life in Ireland was over."

She moved closer to him, just close enough so that her body lightly touched his. "I'm so sorry, Hunter."

He reached over and stroked the baby's head. "I would have looked after the baby, you know? I would have accepted her child as my own. That's the irony of it, Sarah. As much as her infidelity killed me, I would have protected her. She didn't trust my integrity enough to tell me."

"Betrayed in love...and in death," Sarah whispered. She lifted her eyes to his, as if seeing him—really seeing him—for the first time. "What did you do?"

"I wanted to die." He laughed softly. "The only thing that saved me was a book from my childhood library."

"*Beau Geste*...about the Légion Étrangère."

Startled, he stared at her. "How did you know?"

"Smart guess." She smiled. "It was one of my dad's boyhood favorites. It's the one that sparked his interest in the Legion." She looked into his eyes. "He'd like you, you know?"

"Your dad—he still around?"

She nodded. "Not my mum, though. She died when I was fourteen. Cancer. My gran kind of stepped in and looked after us both. She was Irish, too. She came from this huge Catholic family, lots of kids, tons of stories. It sounded such fun, and being an only child myself, I…I always felt I was missing out on something." She smoothed the blanket over the baby. "Maybe that's why I always wanted to have children, to fill some subconscious hole in my psyche. Goodness knows, perhaps that's even the reason I ended up working in a pediatric ward." She smiled a little self-consciously. "To tell you the truth, I don't think I really realized that until now."

"Can I hold her?"

Surprise, then delight rippled through Sarah's eyes. She leaned forward, moving the baby away from her chest, and wrapped the flannel blanket carefully around the tiny body. She handed the crinkled bundle to him.

He brought the small, soft, sleeping newborn up against the skin of his chest and studied the wrinkled face. The baby made a snuffling noise and her little mouth puckered and began to suckle at an imaginary breast. The sensation punched something so savagely primal through Hunter that for an instant, he couldn't breathe. His eyes turned moist. How could such violent potency coexist with such tenderness in one overwhelming sensation? Was that what it felt like to be paternal, to be a father? Holding this little life in his hands made him feel like a god. It made him feel as if he could conquer the world, made him *want* to.

He swallowed. "Sarah," he said, gazing at the child's face as it slept in his arms. "This is probably a really dumb question, given everything you've told me about your marriage, but why didn't you and Josh have kids, back in the beginning when you thought you were still okay together?"

She was silent for a while. "I can't have children."

He studied her face. "Medical reasons?"

She bit her lip and nodded.

He nodded in turn, saying nothing. He recalled her outburst at the plantation. It made sense now. Him telling her that he was dreaming of children, *her* children, must have cut her to the quick. He could only begin to imagine what it must be like for a woman who loved children with all her heart not to be able to bear them, and how a man like Sarah's ex-husband might have used that to undermine her.

Hunter turned his attention back to the coffee-skinned bundle in his arms. Her lashes were dark and silky, like her hair. She was so beautiful. So innocent, so very helpless. An orphan of war. "I always liked the name Branna," he said softly.

A mix of tenderness and unease crossed Sarah's features. She hesitated. "What's going to happen to her? She has no future."

He slanted his eyes to hers. "We can give her a future, Sarah."

Surprise flitted through her. She searched his face, looking for something, an answer to some unspoken question. Gunfire sounded in the distance, but her gaze remained steady, her eyes holding his, as if she desperately needed to know something. "Why did you join the FDS when you quit the Legion, Hunter? Why didn't you go back to medicine? What made you want to keep fighting…killing people?"

He could see where she was going with this. She didn't believe a man like him could give *anyone* a future, let alone this child.

"I was good at war. I excelled in the Legion. It became what I knew. And by that stage I was comfortably numb. I was with men who never talked about the past, never asked questions. I never had to think. I never had to *feel*. And that suited me fine. It *made* me good at what I do. And I didn't join the FDS, I formed it. Ten years ago."

"Formed it?"

"With three other guys who served in the Legion with me— Jacques Sauvage, Rafiq Zayed and December Ngomo. As our five-year contracts drew to an end, we began to look ahead. We saw a market for a small but highly efficient private force of professional soldiers modeled on the Legion's paramilitary regiment. We got contracts and began to build our business. Our reputation grew, and so did the bank accounts. We were based out of South Africa at first, but a change of legislation there put our business on the wrong side of the local law, so we had to find another location. We eventually signed a deal with the government of São Diogo. The island economy was dying, and moving our base and our business there was an ideal economic solution for the small nation. Our soldiers and their families now support the local economy, and the islanders support us."

"Those men, the ones you formed the FDS with, have they been rectified?"

He gave a wry grin. "We don't talk about the past, Sarah. Ever. They're men I will die for, and they will do the same for me. That's good enough."

She studied him in silence. It was almost dark now, the clouds low and the air thick with hot electrical energy. Gunfire sounded again, somewhere to the north. Hunter handed the little bundle in his arms back to Sarah. "It's time."

21:29 Alpha. Cameroon border.
Thursday, September 25

The night was pitch-black and hot. All Sarah could see was the oily shine of the rippling river and the dark shapes of trees along the shoreline. Water slapped lightly on the hull. She had no idea how long they'd been drifting northward. She figured they must be getting close to the border by now, and she thanked the Lord that she'd managed to stop Branna from crying. She liked the name Hunter had mentioned—Branna—

and that's who the baby had become in Sarah's mind. She stroked her little head, drawing comfort from the contact. The baby was sleeping now. Sarah just hoped she kept on sleeping while they crossed into Cameroon.

Hunter had helped her bind Branna to her chest using the blanket in the way the natives did. She'd be able to move faster this way.

She felt Hunter's hand on her knee, then his breath in her ear. "We're almost at the border," he whispered. "Don't let her cry. Be ready to move when I tell you."

Sarah swallowed. Perspiration prickled along her brow, the baby against her chest making her even hotter. She wished she could see what Hunter was seeing through his night-vision gear. She heard the slight splash and swoosh of his paddle, and she felt the canoe turn. They began to move faster, picking up a stronger current.

She heard another slight swoosh of his paddle and the canoe veered to her right. She felt a bump, then the brush of leaves over her face. He touched her arm, indicating that she stay still while he dragged the canoe higher onto the shore. She heard the slosh of water as his boots moved through it, felt the canoe jerk up onto the beach. He took her arm, helped her out.

Relief spurted through her. If they were getting out of the canoe, they must have made it over the border without incident. *They were safe.*

All they had to do now was move farther inland and Hunter would radio his contact. For the first time in days, Sarah actually began to think they might make it out alive.

But he grabbed her arm suddenly, held her motionless. She blinked into the dark, seeing nothing. Then she heard voices drifting in snatches over the water. Her heart started to thud. Lights flickered in the distance, as if people were moving through the trees with flashlights. Sarah's mouth went dry. Branna stirred against her body. She placed her hand over the infant's head, willing her to be still, but she began to cry. The lights up ahead stilled, as if the searchers were listening. A wild terror clawed through Sarah. She placed her pinkie in Branna's mouth and the baby began to suck. The flickering lights moved on and the voices began to fade.

Hot relief swooped through her.

They waited for what seemed like hours until they were sure the men were gone. "Looks like Congo militia crossed the border into Cameroon," Hunter whispered against her ear. "And it looks like they're hunting us. They know we're in the area. We need to get farther inland. Fast." He clasped his hand around hers, drew her deeper into the trees. They moved along what seemed like a winding path. Sarah tried hard not to stumble, worried she'd hurt Branna if she fell. The path widened and the surface under her feet began to feel much harder and smoother. The darkness was less complete here and she realized it was because trees had been cleared to make a dirt road.

They followed the road in silence for what must have been at least an hour until they heard the distant sound of an engine.

Hunter pulled her off the road and down into an overgrown ditch. She saw headlights flickering through the trees. Sweat trickled down her ribs. Branna moved against her and made a little noise. She was waking up again. The headlights came closer, the engine noise growing to a loud, rattling rumble. It was a truck, an old one. It clattered past them and Sarah's mouth filled with the taste of dust and diesel. They waited until all was silent and until the red taillights disappeared into the darkness.

"There's a clearing up ahead, Sarah, on the other side of this road. The chopper can land there. I'm going to radio in now."

She heard Hunter fiddling with his gear. Then she heard the whine and crackle of static as he adjusted the frequency. The sound was oddly comforting, a link to the rest of the world. And even though she could barely see a thing in the velvet blackness of the equatorial night, her mental horizons were immediately expanded by the sense of connection. She heard him speaking low, very low. "Bongani, this is Jongilanga, over. Bongani—"

The set crackled and a voice answered, the volume dropping as he turned it down. "Roger, Jongilanga. Coordinates? Over."

She heard him give their GPS coordinates. "We have hostiles in area, what's your ETA? Over."

"Twenty. Clear."

Hunter swore softly. Then all was silent. Sarah swatted blindly at a cloud of insects she could feel hovering near her face. He took her arm, helped her rise, led her back up the road. They began to walk briskly. He then guided her down what appeared to be another path toward more trees.

"I want you to lie low in the woods here until you see the chopper. Don't move until it's right over the clearing, then you run for your life, okay? There will be light, you'll be able to see where you're going."

A cold feeling of unease began to leach through her. "Where will *you* be?"

He guided her into a crouching position in the trees. "Wait here," he whispered. He took her wrist and wrapped her fingers around the handle of the biohazard canister. "And take this."

Panic ripped through her. "Why? Where are you going?"

He cupped her face in his palms, turned it to face him. "If the militia crossed the border into Cameroon and are looking for us, they will pick up my radio signal, and you can bet your life they're already on their way. I'm going to leave you and Branna here, and I'm going to try and engage them farther down the road, give the chopper a clear path in and you time to get out."

A cold dread took complete hold of her. "No, Hunter," she whispered. "You can't! You'll be outnumbered. They'll kill you!"

"I'll be fine. The FDS would've alerted the Cameroonian troops to hostiles in the area. With luck they'll arrive in time to do the real dirty work, but I must leave, *now,* or they'll be within shooting range of the chopper."

She opened her mouth to protest, but he muffled her words with a hard kiss. Then he pulled away, held her face, studied her quietly in the dark. "Wait for me on São Diogo, Sarah," he whispered. "I need to talk to you. We…have some things we need to work out." He hesitated. "I love you."

And he was gone, a shadow melting into the night, just the lingering, salty taste of him on her lips. Tears burned her eyes. Her heart thudded against her ribs. *He loved her.* And the notion that she might never see him again speared through her gut. She cradled Branna, rocking back and forth on her heels, trying not to let wild panic and desperation blind her.

She forced herself to calm down, tried to conjure up Hunter's comforting, grounding bass voice, imagine his eyes. Home. *He* was her sense of home. He'd said he loved her.

She was going to get out of this. She was going to do this for him. For Branna. For a chance at a future. The notion filled her mind, and suddenly she was no longer alone with a newborn in the dark. A quiet determination filled Sarah, and she waited in silence, Branna making hot little snuffling noises against her chest.

Then she heard it, a distant chop in the air, growing louder. Her pulse tripped into high gear. She could see the lights coming over the trees from the north.

Then an explosion rocked the air and orange light flashed in the distance, to the south. She heard gunfire. Another explosion.

Hunter!

The helicopter materialized over the tops of the trees, a massive black blot in the sky. It banked sharply and hovered over the clearing, the whir of lethal blades drowning out the sound of gunfire. As it lowered, a searchlight flashed on, illuminating the ground with a halo of white light, instantly bringing her world into focus. Long grass flattened under the downdraft. One side of the chopper was open, a man waving at her from the doorway. Sarah grasped the handle of the canister, hunkered low over Branna and ran for her life.

Somewhere beyond the trees she could see the faint orange explosions cutting through the blackness, but the sound of the chopper overpowered everything. She stumbled, almost fell, caught herself, ran a little more carefully, the blades of grass lashing at her legs. She couldn't afford to fall. She'd hurt Branna. The violent downdraft forced a stream of tears from her eyes and whipped her hair around her head. She was vaguely aware that Branna was screaming under chin.

As she reached the door, a giant of a man, in military gear with a pack on his back, jumped out, ran toward her. He took the biohazard container with one hand, her arm with the other. He guided her to the hovering craft, and another man reached down, hauled her up into it. She barely found her feet before the craft lifted sharply and veered up into the air and over the trees, leaving the first man on the ground.

A dark-skinned man with hooked brows guided her down onto a hard bench and began to strap her in. She realized she was shaking violently and Branna was screaming bloody murder.

"What about Hunter?" she yelled over the roar of the engine as the helicopter rose higher in the sky and banked again.

The man said something, but she couldn't hear him above the deafening din of the blades. The door was still wide-open. She leaned forward, could see the black trees fading into the distance. Terror clawed at her heart.

"You've got to get Hunter!" Hot tears streamed down her face. "He's down there! You've got to help him!"

The man motioned with his hand for her to calm down. She couldn't. Hysteria was overwhelming her. She just could not think of leaving him down there in that place.

The man leaned over her and she realized he was putting earphones and a mouthpiece over her head. She heard his voice in the set. "Sarah, I want you to stay calm. My name is Rafiq Zayed, I'm with the FDS—"

"Where's Hunter?"

He raised his hand. "He'll be all right." He had a rich Arabic accent and his voice was deep, smooth, strangely calming. A sense of rationality began to diffuse through her and she began to pull her surroundings into focus. She was in a big, hollow military craft equipped with the bare minimum. Rafiq Zayed sat on the bench opposite her. He was leaning forward, studying her with intense, piercing dark eyes. His face was angular and his glossy black hair was tied back in a ponytail.

Rafiq. That was one of the names Hunter had mentioned, one of the men he trusted with his life. The knowledge took the brunt off her panic. She began to rock Branna, trying to get her to suckle on her pinkie. Hunter had all the baby milk in his pack. "What's going to happen to Hunter?" she asked, much more calmly, speaking into the mouthpiece.

"December Ngomo—the man who helped you into the helo—he is with Hunter. They will be going into Gabon tonight. They will be picking up a doctor at a research station who will help us identify the pathogen you brought with you."

The hatchet of panic struck right back into her heart. "What do you mean? Do you know what he's been through? And what about the militia that came across the border—the fighting down there?"

A smile pulled at Rafiq's lips. "McBride has Cameroonian army support, and he and Ngomo will have air support into Gabon. It's a simple mission." He reached forward, placed a hand on her knee. "Don't worry. He'll be fine."

Sarah stared at him, barely able to absorb what he was saying. Hunter had hardly slept in days. What kind of men were these? She turned to look out the gaping doorway. She could see ocean below them now, shimmering like beaten black metal in the pale light of the small moon. She could see the pale purple hint of dawn along an endless horizon. She swallowed, turned back to Rafiq. "My baby needs milk. She…she needs medical attention. She's an orphan, a newborn." A sob of emotion choked her. "We rescued her. Her name is Branna."

Rafiq nodded calmly, as if this kind of thing was done daily. "We'll have her in the clinic on São Diogo in under two hours. I'll radio ahead and we'll have a physician waiting for both of you."

Sarah sank back against the cold metal and stared down at the sea. She could feel the steady, powerful throb of the machine vibrating through her. They were out of the cloud, and stars spattered the sky. She could see strips of land below, islands. She felt Branna sucking on her finger, her teeny little hands groping. And Sarah knew she could never, ever live with a man like Hunter. She just couldn't be with a man who got up every morning to do a job like this.

Tears burned behind her eyes. *He couldn't even get on the damn helicopter with them.* He had another job to do. He'd said it would be so, and he'd already moved on. That's how it would always be for him. Whether he loved her or not. She closed her eyes against the emotion that swelled though her. She'd known it would be like this. She'd known this feeling would come. She just didn't think it would hurt this badly.

If there was one thing she could take away from all of this, it was Branna. Sarah would adopt her. She would give her a future. She would nurture and cherish this innocent little life that had been born out of violence and chaos.

And even though she couldn't be with him, she would always cherish the man who'd saved them both and taught her how to be strong again.

Chapter 16

"Yes?"

Andries du Toit cleared his throat nervously. "We got them."

Silence.

It made him uncomfortable. "They were both killed in a shootout on the Cameroonian side of the border. The nitrogen in the biohazard canister ignited in a mortar blast. The pathogen has been destroyed," he lied.

Silence stretched again. Then the man in New York spoke, his voice dead calm. "What about the Cameroonians? What do they think happened?"

Du Toit mopped the sweat off his brow with his handkerchief. "They think it was rebels. We've done cleanup operations, taken care of their bodies. There's no sign we were ever there."

"Thank you," the man said simply. And the line went dead.

Du Toit swiped his handkerchief across his forehead again, then stuffed it into his breast pocket. He took another swig of his whiskey. He could *not* let New York know that he'd failed, that the nurse had escaped. Besides, it would all be over before anyone found out, anyway. Still, he'd play it safe. Once he'd collected final payment, he'd disappear—just slip into the wild of Africa. He'd done it before. He would do it again.

The man in New York replaced the receiver on his secure phone and ran his tongue slowly over his teeth. It appeared the glitch had finally been sorted out, thank God. Things could now proceed normally, just as soon as he'd taken care of the last loose end. He pulled open his desk drawer, withdrew a cell phone, the one he used only to contact his "caretaker." He pressed a button. He had to wait only one ring.

"Yes?"

"Kill Du Toit."

17:15 Alpha. FDS base, São Diogo Island.
Friday, September 26

Sarah followed the sandy path through the dune scrub, making her way down to the beach. The clinic doctors had tried to give her medication to help her sleep through the day, but she'd refused to take it. Perhaps she should have. She felt both overtired and edgy, as if there was too much caffeine buzzing through her system. But there was no way she could think of numbing herself and going to sleep while Hunter was still out there somewhere.

And this was exactly why she could never be with a man who did what he did for a living. It would kill her—waiting for days and nights for him to come home from his next mission, wondering *if* he'd come home. Wondering what he'd done, who he'd killed, knowing he'd never talk about it.

She sat on the highest dune, pulled her knees in close to her chest and stared out over the Atlantic. God, she hoped he was all right. She felt sick not knowing. At least Branna was fine. The doctors had put her in an incubator, just to be sure. She'd been a little dehydrated, but otherwise she was in perfect health.

Sarah watched the waves rolling relentlessly to shore, white spindrift blowing in the wind. Hunter had told her to wait for him. She gave a soft laugh. What a joke. She couldn't leave this little island paradise if she tried, at least not until she'd been fully debriefed and this whole mission of theirs was over. Rafiq had made that politely, yet perfectly clear last night. He'd said he'd debrief her himself tomorrow, once she'd rested a little.

A silver speck over the horizon caught her attention. Sarah shielded her eyes and watched as it came closer, the sound of chopper blades eventually reaching her over the crunch of the waves along the white beach. *Hunter?*

Her heart began to thud against her chest. She got to her feet, watched the helicopter near the island. The chopper buzzed right over her and came in to land on the helipad just behind the ridge of dunes.

She couldn't help herself; she raced along the ridge toward the area, then stopped and squinted against stinging sand as the helicopter settled onto the packed earth.

The door opened. December, the soldier who'd helped her into the chopper in Cameroon, hopped out and assisted an older man behind him. The man was stooped slightly, like a question mark. He had a shock of white hair, glasses and a lab coat that flapped about his knees in the downdraft. He must be the doctor from Gabon, the one who'd come to analyze the samples in Dr. Regnaud's container.

Sarah took a step toward the helipad, then froze as she saw Hunter jump down. He was still in military gear and his face was once again streaked with black paint. Even from here he looked wild, dangerous. Sarah's mouth went instantly dry and her heart began to jackhammer. She wanted to go to him, to touch him. God, she loved that man…a man she could never have.

December escorted the doctor to a Jeep waiting on the far side of the helipad, but Hunter stopped. He turned slowly, looked at her. He must have known she was there, must have seen her from the air. He stood still, just watching her, the slowing rotor blades whipping his black hair about his head.

Sarah couldn't hold back; his power over her was too great. She ran across the sand to him. "You…you're okay," she said breathlessly as she reached him, her simple words belying the tornado of emotion churning through her heart.

He took one stride toward her, yanked her into his arms and pressed his mouth down hard over hers, claiming her, holding her tightly, stroking her hair as he kissed her roughly, his tongue meeting hers, searching, needing. Sarah melted into him, hot emotion burning her eyes, searing her body. He pulled back suddenly, gazed deep into her eyes. "I missed you, Sarah."

She glanced away, afraid of what was coming next, of what must be said.

He lifted her chin, forcing her to look at him. "Sarah?"

"Irish!" December yelled from the Jeep. The engine was running, the doctor waiting, the pathogen waiting for him.

Hunter glanced at December, then back at her, not easing his hold. But a look of worry had shifted into his eyes. "Sarah," he said, his voice low, urgent. "We have to talk. I have a plan—"

"A plan?"

"For how we can be together. I want us—"

Her heart lurched sickeningly. She had to say it. She couldn't allow him to think there was a future for them. "No, Hunter."

He went stock-still. The rotor blades stopped turning, leaving only the whisper of the breeze through the dune grass at their feet, the thump of waves on the shore and the purr of the vehicle waiting across the helipad.

"No?"

"I can't be with a man like you. There…there is no us."

Confusion rippled across his features. "Sarah, I love you. I want to be with you. I—"

She pressed her hand over his mouth. "Don't do this."

"Irish! Now!"

He flicked his eyes to the Jeep, torn between duty and her. Again. She'd forced him to make the choice once, at great cost. She never wanted to put him in that position again. It wasn't fair.

He gripped her face suddenly with both hands, his gaze ferocious. "Sarah, I *know* you care for me. I *know* you want me. I've seen it in your eyes. I've felt it in your body. Tell me you don't want me, Sarah!"

Her throat went tight. She couldn't talk.

Desperation flared in his eyes. His hands tightened against her face. "*Tell me!* I want to hear you say it."

Tears welled in her own eyes. "I…I love you, Hunter. I want you with all my heart—more than you'll ever know. And I can't thank you enough for what you've done for me…in ways you'll never understand. You saved me. But…" Emotion snared her voice. "It—we—won't work."

His lowered his face to hers. "You love me. I love you. Isn't that enough?"

She shook her head. "You'll kill me, Hunter. I won't be good for you—"

"Irish!" December barked. "They need you in the war room ASAP!"

His eyes, lit with a mad kind of fury, tunneled right into her soul. "Just wait for me, okay? Promise me you'll wait, so that we can talk."

"No," she said softly. "I don't want to wait, Hunter."

The Jeep horn sounded. Despair clouded the mercenary's eyes, then turned to white-hot anger. "You're lying."

The horn sounded again.

"Go, Hunter," she said. "They need you. Go do your thing."
Go save the world.

He spun on his heels and stalked over to the waiting vehicle.

Nausea churned her stomach, but tears, release, would not come. She was empty, a husk ready to blow in the wind. She wiped a smudge of black paint from her face as she watched him swing himself into the Jeep. He was one of the most incredible men she'd ever met. She loved him. And he loved her. He'd proved it in the most profound way. Yet she couldn't have him. She watched him go, a cloud of dust boiling behind the vehicle as it disappeared over the ridge.

15:00 Alpha. FDS Base, São Diogo.
Monday, September 29

Sarah pushed open the heavy door that led to the war room, and noticed immediately that Hunter wasn't there. A mix of relief and pain punched through her. It had been almost three days since she'd seen him disappear in the Jeep. He hadn't come looking for her, and she hadn't gone looking for him. He'd probably seen that she was right, that this was for the best. For both of them. So why did it hurt so much?

Sarah stepped into the room and the four men seated around

an oval table looked up instantly. The sense of presence and power they exuded was immediate and tangible. A prickle of awe ran over her skin.

The dark-haired man at the far end stood as she neared the table, his silver eyes appraising her with cool, calculated concentration. He was tall, well over six feet, his face all rugged angles. She noticed he had a scar that sliced from the corner of his left eye all the way down to the base of his jaw.

"Sarah, thank you for joining us." His voice was accented with French and something more guttural she couldn't quite place. "I am Jacques Sauvage. You know Rafiq Zayed here, and this is December Ngomo. I believe you've met briefly." He turned toward the white-haired man seated to his left. "And this is Dr. Jan Meyer." Sauvage held his hand out to her, palm up. "Please do take a seat."

Her eyes flicked around the table. There were two vacant seats. She chose the one closest to the door, eyeing the renowned Dr. Meyer. She'd heard about him. Every medical professional who worked in Africa had. He was an internationally renowned expert in rare tropical diseases, affiliated with the Prince Leopold Institute in Belgium, Europe's answer to the CDC.

"We've gone over Zayed's debriefing report on you," Sauvage said. "And we'd like you to join us for the first portion of this meeting just to see if there is any information you feel might be inconsistent with your experience. If anything new comes to mind, please speak up. *Ça va?*"

Sarah nodded, still trying to place his accent.

"Bien." Sauvage seated himself and Dr. Meyer stood. The man looked tired, his wrinkles etched deep behind his wire-rimmed glasses. He adjusted the collar of his lab coat and hit a key on a laptop. The bank of LCD screens on the wall behind him flickered to life with images of cells taken under an electron microscope. He peered over the rims of his glasses at them.

"Sauvage has asked me to keep this brief. We've been working on the Ishonga samples around the clock for three days now." His English was perfect but his accent was heavily Dutch. "Fortunately, the integrity of the biological material was maintained at cryogenic temperatures due to the nitrogen vapor canister used during shipping."

Shipping? Sarah felt a ridiculous laugh bubble somewhere deep in her gut. Was that what she'd been doing in the Congo this past week? Shipping biological material? He didn't know the half of it.

"If you look at these slides here—" Meyer pointed to one of the LCD screens "—you'll see that the brain tissue of the Ishonga samples is riddled with holes, like a sponge. This disease has been eating through the brains of these patients." He turned back to face them, eyes intense over the rims of his spectacles. "This is *not* a virus and it's *not* a bacteria, or any other conventional disease agent. This kind of pathology—" he gestured broadly to the images behind him "—is more consistent with what we see in brains that have been infected with transmissible spongiform encephalopathies, or TSEs—"

Sarah leaned forward. "You mean mad cow?" Everyone in the room turned to look at her.

The doctor shoved his glasses up his nose. "Correct—more commonly known as mad cow disease in cattle or Creutzfeldt-Jakob disease in humans. I believe the Ishonga patients were infected with a unique, new form of TSE."

"But this can't be," said Sarah, images of the infected villagers flooding her brain. "This disease moved like wildfire. The villagers went mad and died within days, hours. TSEs take *years* to manifest. And these patients were violent—*that* doesn't happen with TSEs."

The doctor nodded. "Yes. I agree. This is highly unusual, but nevertheless I believe it *is* a form of TSE. The violence in this case actually helps facilitate the spread of the disease through the transmission of blood and saliva." He paused, pursing his lips. "Only once have I heard of anything even remotely like this—in a very rare and elusive band of bonobo chimps that live in a remote reach of the Congo Blacklands."

Every muscle in Sarah's body tensed, and for a moment she forgot the powerful men sitting around the table. "You think the bonobo disease has spread to humans?"

"I think the causative agent has been *engineered* to spread to humans."

Rafiq cleared his throat. "But if it's not a virus and not a bacterium, what *is* the causative agent?" His *R*s rolled over his tongue, his voice resonant with hints of Arabic and French inflections.

"It is my opinion that the verdict is still out on what actually causes TSEs," said Meyer. "However, the most common current scientific thinking is that the agent is a prion—a defective protein that forces other proteins in the host's brain to degenerate, leading to progressive dementia, and finally death. My theory is that someone has figured out *exactly* what causes TSEs—prion or not—and they've discovered how to manipulate it genetically. They have thus been able to create a whole new family of TSEs as yet unknown to science." He paused, eyeing the men around the table, his expression grave. "And from the description of the symptoms you have provided me with, I believe President John Elliot has also been infected with one these hybrid TSEs—albeit one that moves much, much more slowly than the Ishonga sample."

Sauvage leaned forward. "But it's the Ishonga one they're threatening to release as a bioweapon. How do you suppose they will do it if it's transmitted via bodily fluids?"

Meyer shook his head. "I don't know yet. It *could* be made

airborne, I think. Or perhaps they'd use a food or water source. I really need more time—"

"We don't have time." The deep voice resonated through the room. Sarah's heart tripped. She spun around.

Hunter McBride stood in the doorway and he looked drop-dead gorgeous. He was clean shaven and he'd had his hair cut, accentuating his eyes. He wore a crisp white T-shirt and faded jeans that should be declared sinful. He stared straight at her, right into her, and for a moment everything in her body stood still. Then her stomach churned with a sick sensation. He looked happy. He'd been away from her and he was…*happy*. She turned, forced herself to stare at Dr. Meyer, to concentrate on what he was saying.

Hunter stepped up behind Sarah's chair, gave her shoulder a quick squeeze and then went to sit in the vacant chair in front of the window. Her chest cramped tight. Hot emotion seared her eyes, but she blinked it back. How could one touch do this to her? How could he feign casual affection like this? She had to fight not to look at him.

"I'm *fully* aware of the time constraints," Meyer said coolly, eyeing Hunter intently.

"No offense intended, Doctor," said Hunter. "Just stating a fact. We have exactly two weeks to D-day now and we're no closer to the antidote."

The doctor shoved his delinquent glasses back up his nose. "On the contrary. There is one lab rumored to be working with something like this, and one scientist in particular. Her name is Dr. Paige Sterling and she's with the Nexus Research and Development Corporation in Hamān."

Rafiq tensed visibly. He placed his hands flat on the tabletop, his black eyes flashing. "How do we know this?"

"A defector from Hamān. He was brought to see me at the Leopold Institute by the French secret service two years ago.

I do consulting for the intelligence community on certain biological warfare matters," explained Meyer. "And this defector used to work in the Nexus compound. He believed the Nexus group was involved in creating bioweapons, and the Secret Service wanted to know if I thought his information was credible. But the man had no proof, and getting into the country to obtain any kind of proof is close to impossible. As you well know, Hamān is closed to all travel and all foreigners. The European intelligence community did, however, put together a task force, including myself, that has kept a watch from a distance over the years. But so far nothing has hit the radar—until now."

"But how do you know the Nexus lab is working on TSEs specifically?" said Rafiq, pressing his hands even more firmly against the tabletop, as if trying to contain something.

"I was given a list of the scientists stationed there. One of them is Dr. Sterling, an American. Both her father and mother used to work with that rare group of bonobos in the Congo I mentioned. And it was her father, Dr. Richard Sterling, who first told me about this rare form of TSE in the bonobos." Meyer ran a weatherbeaten hand through his shock of white hair, leaving it standing on end. "Richard and his wife disappeared in the Congo Blacklands shortly after he'd spoken with me. No one ever saw them again. That was about seventeen years ago. Paige went on to graduate, and continued with her parents' research. She was eventually recruited by the Nexus group. I presume they selected her specifically because of her controversial and cutting-edge work with TSEs."

December stood. "I've done some electronic digging," he said, his deep voice reverberating around the room. "Nexus, through a convoluted system of shell and holding companies, is ultimately controlled by BioMed Pharmaceutical in the U.S.—"

Sarah sat upright. "BioMed—that was the logo…the one I saw on the hazmat suits of the soldiers that attacked the Ishonga compound!"

December nodded. "*Yebo*. And BioMed, through Dr. Andries Du Toit, also supplied the militia soldier with the corticosteroid nasal spray. Du Toit is an exiled military figure from South Africa's apartheid days. He appears to have been on BioMed's payroll for several years, allegedly marketing the company's product to the African sector." December paused, shuffling the papers on the table in front of him. He found what he was looking for. "And the company that funded Dr. Paige Sterling's postsecondary education—Science Reach International—is indirectly controlled by BioMed as well." He looked up. "Science Reach International is the same company that financed Paige's parents' Congo-based TSE research before they mysteriously disappeared."

"There's a definite thread there," said Sauvage. "We need to get into Hamān ASAP."

"Do you think you'll find an antidote in Hamān?" Sarah felt a little awkward even asking the question.

"I don't doubt it," said Hunter. "The Cabal needs to control whatever it has created to be effective in the long term. For that it needs an antidote. And all the arrows are pointing to Hamān."

Sarah made the mistake of looking into his eyes as he spoke. The room and everyone in it suddenly faded to a blur and sound turned to a buzz in her head. She couldn't break the gaze. Everything unspoken seemed to hang between them over the polished dark wood table.

"Thank you, Sarah." Sauvage's voice jerked her back. She looked up sharply. His eyes were cool. He made her feel like a kid who'd been caught out in class.

"That'll be all for now," he said. "We appreciate your help." He turned to December, lowered his voice. "Get that Hamānian defector's name and get him onto São Diogo by nightfall tomorrow. We need to know *everything* he knows about the country and the lab compound. And we need to see if we can get to Du Toit without alerting the Cabal."

This was it. She was being dismissed. It was all over…in more ways than one. With a strange sinking sensation in her heart, she stood, pushed her chair back. Hunter rose, too. Sarah moved quickly to the door. She couldn't face him now. She reached for the door handle, just as Hunter leaned across her, barring her way. She caught her breath, stared at the tile floor. She couldn't look up, couldn't let his eyes suck her in again. He was too powerful and she was feeling too weak.

"Sarah," he whispered against her cheek. "Meet me at the coffee shop down at the bay at seven this evening. Okay?"

She glared at the floor tile. No, it was *not* okay. Staying on this island was going to be sheer torture. Three days had gone by and he hadn't even come over to the clinic to see her. Did he have any idea how much she missed him? How much her body ached for his touch? She slid her eyes slowly up to meet his. And her heart stalled. She suddenly couldn't say no. She'd known he would suck her in. Perhaps the dark and defiant and illogical part of herself even wanted him to.

"Okay?" he insisted, his breath warm against her face.

She nodded in spite of herself.

"Irish!"

He ignored Sauvage. "See you at seven, then." He leaned down and brushed his lips against her ear before turning to join his colleagues.

Sarah shivered, yanked open the door and stepped quickly out of the room. The heavy door swung closed behind her with a thud, suddenly alienating her from what was going on inside. She was not welcome, not part of the group even though she'd played such a vital role. And why should she expect anything different? This was their job. Not hers. It served as a stark reminder of why she couldn't live like this—on the perimeter of Hunter McBride's existence. She needed to forge a future of her own. For her and Branna.

She fisted her hands with resolve and marched down the stone corridor, knowing in her heart she would not—*could not*—show up at that café.

18:30 Alpha. São Diogo clinic.
Monday, September 29

Hunter found her sitting in a chair by the window, watching their baby sleep in a white hospital cot. The setting sun was turning Sarah's hair copper and painting a soft gold glow over Branna's skin. He stood in the doorway and watched in silence for a moment, a voyeur savoring a vignette of Madonna and child. Purity and peace, he thought, fingering the pouch in his pocket—a picture of life and hope and future. *His* future.

He swallowed the hard knot of emotion in his throat and stepped into the room. Sarah glanced up and shock flared in her features. Hunter could immediately see in her eyes that she'd never had any intention of coming to meet him.

He'd feared as much.

That's why he'd come here first. To save himself the disappointment, to cut rejection off at the head, to not give her a chance to say no. And he'd come as soon as he could get away from the war room. He'd been planning this moment for the last three days, but now, looking into her eyes, he had a sinking feeling she had already slipped from his grasp.

He nervously fingered the soft pouch in his pocket again. He couldn't seem to think of the words he needed. Hell, even guerilla warfare didn't do this to him. He was actually afraid. And he knew why—he had something to lose now. If he hadn't lost it already.

He said nothing, mostly because he was worried he was going to say the wrong thing. He moved over to the crib, kissed baby Branna on the forehead, aware of Sarah watching his every move. Then he stood to his full height, squared his shoulders, sucked in his breath and turned slowly to face her. He held out his hand.

She stared at it.

"Come," he whispered, careful not to wake Branna.

Sarah hesitated.

He leaned forward, grasped her hand and coaxed her to her feet. She resisted, her brows lowering in confusion.

"You *have* to hear me out before you turn me down, Sarah," he whispered. "Will you come?"

Her eyes flicked nervously to Branna, then back to him. She nodded.

He led her outside, sat on a stone bench and drew her down beside him. Dry pink bougainvillea petals rustled in the evening breeze and the Atlantic in the distance looked like beaten copper under the setting sun.

Hunter felt awkward, unsure of where to start. He had a sense he was only going to have one shot at getting this right. But Sarah spoke first.

"Hunter, I've put in adoption papers for Branna."

This was already getting away from him. "You'll just have to redo them, then."

Possessive passion flashed in her eyes. "I want to give her a home, Hunter, a future. I want her to be my child."

Everything he'd dreamed of was unraveling right in front of him. "She's *ours,* Sarah. I want *my* name on those papers."

She faced him squarely, lifted her jaw. "Look, I understand you brought her into the world and that you—"

Lord, he was hopeless at talking. He'd already walked into a minefield of his own making. He groped in his pocket, pulled out the pouch, shoved it into her hands, cutting her off.

Her eyes flicked between the pouch and him. "What's this?"

"Don't talk. Enough talking. Just open it." His heart slammed hard against his ribs. *"Please."*

Sarah studied him for a moment. Then she looked down at the velvet pouch he'd pushed into her hands. Slowly she peeled back the midnight-blue fabric to reveal a small translucent, golden pebble. She rolled it slightly in her palm and it caught the bronze light of the setting sun. She knitted her brow. "What is it?"

"Diamond. I got it in Luanda. That's where I've been these past few days." He reached out, closed her hand tightly around the stone, not giving her the opportunity to hand it back. "I wanted you to decide on the cut. I…I want you to decide on the shape, Sarah." He paused. "Like I want you to decide on the shape of our future. I…" He swallowed hard, took the leap. "I want you to think about being my wife."

Sarah's stomach bottomed out. Her jaw dropped and her head began to buzz. Her mouth went completely dry, words defying her. She couldn't even begin to articulate the thoughts that raced through her brain. She could literally feel the heat of the raw stone trapped in her fist. A diamond in the rough—like him.

"I want you to marry me, Sarah," he said again, as if she hadn't heard the first time.

She opened her mouth to speak, but he placed his fingers over her lips. "Before you say anything, you need to know that I'm not going back into the field. I've already discussed it with the guys. No more fighting. I'm going to requalify as a surgeon—"

"You…you *can't.*"

"Why not?"

"You can't…just change. I mean…" She looked into his eyes. "Hunter, what I mean is that your job is who you *are*. You belong out there. I can't even begin to expect you to change who you are for me. I don't want that. You'd regret it in the long run, and if you're unhappy, I'd also end up regretting it, too. I can't let you to do this for me."

She tried to hand the diamond back to him, but he tightened his fist around hers, pressing the stone into her flesh. "It's not for you, Sarah. It's for *me,* for *us*—for me, you and Branna."

She studied his face, bewilderment swelling in her. "You…you're dead serious, aren't you?"

"Of course I am." He took her shoulders in his hands. "See, Sarah, I'm not changing, I'm just going back to who I was—who I really am. And you helped me get there. You forced me to face something in myself. You showed me there's something inside of myself that I just cannot hide from anymore. You made me pick up that scalpel again. You made me feel what it's like to save a life again."

His eyes glistened. "You showed me how to stop running, Sarah." His grip tightened on her shoulders. "Do you understand how dead serious I am about this? I'm forty-three years old next month. I want you. I want Branna. I want to be a family. I want to be a doctor again. I want *you* as my nurse, as my wife—by my side. And I want to eventually work here, at this clinic. I want to be here for the islanders, for the FDS troops." His mouth twisted with emotion. "Nothing in the world is going to change my mind, so please don't turn me down, because then I'm going to be lost as all hell—and a bloody danger in the field."

She couldn't talk. Tears streamed down her face.

He wiped them away with the rough pad of his thumb and snorted softly. "I just realized how that must sound. This is not only about me. I think I can offer you something, too. I can offer you a home. Love. Hell, I'd give you the world if I could."

Sarah stared into his eyes. Was this really possible? She'd gone into the heart of Africa, found the courage to stare death in the face, and she'd come out with the child she'd dreamed of having. A man who loved her. A sense of home.

"I love you, Hunter," she whispered.

He smiled with such relief that she could feel it in his limbs. "Well, at least that part is sorted out. Now will you have that diamond cut and set, and wear it while you think about when you'd like to get married?"

She laughed through her tears. Then cried, and laughed again. She opened her hand and looked at the pebble in her palm. Rough. Rare. Precious. She wiped her face, stilled, looked up at him. His face was all raw emotion—a rough sculpture of power and vulnerability. She closed her hand around the pebble. "You know something, McBride?" she said softly. "You're damn good at keeping your promises."

He raised a brow. "I am?"

She sniffed, wiped a tear from the end of her nose. "You made me a promise back on the Shilongwe. You promised that if anyone could get me home, you would."

He smiled. "And you told me you had no home."

She smiled back happily through her tears. "That didn't stop you from getting me there."

"No," he laughed. "I guess it didn't." Then his face turned serious. "Would that be a yes, then?"

Sarah kissed the man she loved. "That would definitely be a yes."

Epilogue

Sauvage set the bottle of brandy and two glasses on the table. "So, Irish is leaving the field."

Rafiq said nothing and the darkness hid his expression. But Sauvage didn't need to see his face. He could sense the brooding intensity in his colleague. He felt it in himself.

He sat in silence, staring at the twinkling lights of the island homes up on the hill, and he smiled wryly in the dark. So there was redemption for some. If Hunter had found it, where did it leave men like himself and Rafiq?

Out in the shadows, that's where. He knew nothing about Rafiq, but he did know redemption was not possible for a man like himself. Not with his past.

Sauvage poured himself a glass, set the bottle down carefully. "You okay with going into Hamān?"

Rafiq's eyes flashed in the dim light. "Yeah. Why?"

"You've been quiet."

Silence.

He sipped his drink, welcoming the warmth of its caress down his throat. "You're the only one for the job," he offered, unnecessarily perhaps. "You speak the local dialect. You look the part. We wouldn't be able to get anyone else into the country without raising suspicion." He paused, took another sip. "You're more than perfect."

"I know. I am from Hamān."

Sauvage stilled, held the brandy in his mouth for a moment. This was the first clue he'd ever had about Rafiq's past. He said nothing, the weight of the revelation somehow reverent. Finally he spoke. "Will this be a problem for the mission?"

Rafiq's eyes glittered in the moonlight.

"No. It will not."

* * * * *

STRAIGHT THROUGH THE HEART

BY
LYN STONE

Lyn Stone is a former artist who developed an avid interest in criminology while helping her husband for his degree. His subsequent career in counter-intelligence and contacts in the field provide a built-in source for research when writing suspense. Their long and happy marriage provides firsthand knowledge of happily-ever-afters.

Dear Reader,

The operatives who work behind the scenes, gathering and analyzing information and acting on it on behalf of our country, deserve much more praise than they get. We hear about their mistakes and failures but never do we learn much about the extent of their success. I would like to thank them here for their contributions to our security.

My fascination for the various agencies grew out of a close association with individuals involved in the intelligence community. I witnessed firsthand how their jobs, frequent travel and the secrecy required of them impacted on the agents and on their families. I saw the courage of spouses who wait and the ones who go out, the camaraderie between those who watch each other's backs in the field, and the personal and professional pride in a job well done even when they aren't allowed to discuss it.

Though the characters I write about in my *Special Ops* stories are strictly imaginary, they meet the same real-life problems, the hopes, disappointments and dreams that our friends in intelligence encounter. Life is lived on the edge. Love is precious, yet too easily lost by a shift in priorities. Trust in a partner, on the job or at home, is not only nice to have, it is crucial.

So, that said, I hope you enjoy this tale set in the Greek Islands where the incredible sun-kissed beauty of the surroundings contrasts with the dark side of terror that brings Eric and Dawn to paradise on their mission.

Here, have a little mystery and watch love ignite under pressure...

Lyn Stone

This book is dedicated to Karla and Dawn,
two mischief makers who inspired me
to write this one. Thanks for your
enthusiasm and support.

Prologue

Alexandria, Virginia

Amazing what a paper clip bent into the right configuration could do to a lock. More amazing still, the fact that there was a paper clip in such a paperless environment.

The desk drawer scraped as Dawn drew it out, the sound echoing in the darkness. She hissed in a breath and directed the beam of her penlight over a couple of unopened packages of snacks and onto the lone, small notepad in one corner.

With gloved fingers, she turned it over. There were three eight-digit passwords scribbled on the back. She committed them to memory.

She glanced at the computer, now dark and in rest mode. Did she dare take time to boot it up and see what she could get into? No, it was enough to know she could if she wanted to.

What would Daddy think now of his helpless little princess if he could see her in action? His incessant coddling had nearly ruined her for doing anything useful with her life. Maybe her size or the way she moved gave men the impression she needed looking after. God knows, they all tried. But her size and sinuous dexterity made her perfect for this kind of work.

Holding her breath, she gently pushed the drawer closed. It meshed with the front of the desk with only a slight squeak.

Suddenly, calm deserted her and her senses went on high alert. Her skin tingled, her breathing grew shallow and her heart rate increased. Something was not right. The urge to hurry kicked in, threatening her concentration.

She pressed a button on her wristwatch and the luminous numbers blinked on. It was nineteen minutes later than she had planned to wind this up. The outside guard patrol had thrown her off.

No matter. She had what she'd come for. Now was the time to climb back up on the desk, disappear into the vent, replace that panel and get the hell out.

Just as she secured the last screw in the vent's panel and switched off her penlight, the office door opened. The lights clicked on and she heard voices, one of which she recognized immediately.

Dawn froze, peering wide-eyed through the metal slots of the vent.

At first she felt only anger that Paul Bergen hadn't trusted her to do this. After all those instructions and careful coordinating, he had shown up to check on her? It was eight hours too soon for him to be presenting a vulnerability report, and this lab wouldn't be the place for that anyway.

Then she decided he must be working another angle,

another assailable point of entry. She remained silent and still, watching, waiting for the two men to leave the lab so she could make her escape.

Only when Bergen stabbed the technician did Dawn realize what was really going down.

Chapter 1

McLean, Virginia

"So, she's either the hero of the hour or she's facing a rap for treason." Eric Vinland pursed his lips and doodled a little hangman's rope on his notepad next to the woman's name. He was conditioning himself to make the call of guilty if it came to that.

Damn, but he hated it when a woman got herself involved in something like this. Maybe the feeling harkened back to his early training that included looking after the "weaker sex," seeing that none of them came to any harm. Feminists today would rip him apart if he ever admitted that out loud. They'd be right to do that, too. Eric knew from experience that women could be every bit as capable, but also as greedy, sadistic and treasonous as men. "Comes down to him or her," he reminded himself.

"By her own admission, she was there at the scene so that about sums it up," Jack Mercier, Eric's supervisor and the agent in charge of the investigation, agreed. "Let's go so you can determine if she was involved in the theft and establishing cover by killing Bergen, or if she's playing straight with us. You're a hell of a lot faster than a polygraph."

Eric scoffed. "You know as well as I do that she will have been trained to beat a lie detector."

Jack nodded. "Yes, but she won't be prepared for your powers of detection, will she? I wish you'd arrived sooner. Internet sources indicate those plans for the radar shield are already on the block and we need to find out who's doing the marketing. God help us if they decide to download the damned thing to a buyer. It'll be like freeware before we know it."

"Too valuable to risk that happening. The seller will want to deliver and collect in person on this one."

Eric understood the need for urgency. He regretted his delayed flight from Seattle, but it couldn't be helped. At least the investigation there had been successful even if it had run longer than expected.

He followed the boss out of the borrowed office at FBI headquarters, down the corridor to the interrogation room.

"You do the inquisition. I'll observe," Jack ordered. He ducked into the room adjacent to Interrogation that contained the viewing side of a one-way mirror.

When Eric entered the next door, his fellow agent, Holly Griffin, stood propped against the table, speaking to the suspect. "Okay, let's have it again. From the top, please."

Eric's quiet entrance raised no reaction in either woman. Holly kept her eyes on the woman, Agent Moon, who had hers shut.

He zoned in on the redhead seated on the far side of the

table in the uncomfortable metal folding chair. He could read most people's minds like the Sunday funnies, but not this kid's. Not yet, anyway.

Her exhaustion was evident. The incident had occurred around midnight, and it was nearly dawn now. Her defenses should be way down.

She had her arms folded beneath her ample breasts, hands clutching her elbows so tightly her knuckles turned white.

She gave a huge sigh as she rocked forward in her chair. "Not another word without a bathroom break. I *swear* I've told you everything I saw, all I know, all I suspect."

Eric saw no point in torture. He gave Holly a nod when she looked over at him, and she promptly escorted the subject out. Holly, Will and Jack had been questioning her for a couple of hours now. Several empty soft drink cans sat on the table close to where the subject had been sitting.

Holly was the lone female agent in their group and married to Will Griffin, another of their number. Sextant was a tight unit of six, all with particular specialties. Holly's was profiling, combined with an amazing talent for organizing and analyzing gathered data. Though she denied having any extrasensory abilities, she was exceptional at filling in the blanks and hearing the unspoken.

Her husband, Will, was often blessed with remote viewing and occasional empathetic episodes. Joe Corda was psychic to some degree, though still identifying and learning to control what he could do. Clay Senate experienced visions of future occurrences, often hard to interpret, but always interesting to explore. Jack Mercier held it all together and made every attempt to develop scenarios utilizing whatever they were able to provide, however nebulous that input seemed.

Eric's powers had proved the strongest and most reliable

so far. Telepathy was his thing, but he did have sporadic success in other areas.

His fellow agents were thorough, but he had the edge they needed to grasp everything in her pretty head, thoughts she would never speak aloud.

Since he could first remember, Eric had possessed that gift. He'd been hired for the elite Sextant team because of it. Made up of agents recruited from other government agencies, Sextant's mission was to subvert terrorist activities. His academic and professional credentials were very good, but he knew that his ability to read minds had been the kicker when it had come to his being chosen for Sextant. Sometimes he thought Mercier depended a little too heavily on that aspect of him. Eric tried hard not to resent that his other talents were underused.

"Anything yet?" Jack asked over the speaker.

Eric glanced at the mirror. "I'm in the room thirty seconds and you want a conclusion? I haven't even seen her eyes yet. Doesn't take telepathy to sense her exhaustion and frustration, though. Could be she's about to blow."

"Then ratchet up the pressure," Jack said calmly.

Eric nodded and sat down, resting his elbows on the tabletop, and waited, reviewing the little he knew about the subject thus far from her hastily retrieved files.

Special Agent Dawn Moon, five years with National Security Agency, age twenty-eight. Earned a degree at twenty-three, double major in criminal justice and psychology, a master's in the former, trilingual, but mathematically challenged. Eric smiled at the perfunctory, handwritten notation about that last subject.

No outstanding debts, he noted, so she must be able to balance her checkbook. She drove a three-year-old Mazda and lived alone in a modest apartment in one of the less-desirable sections of Alexandria. She had been on her own since age eighteen; her only living relatives were her father, who lived in Charleston, and a male cousin who taught at Galludet College in D.C.

Eric mentally added that she was really very pretty in a girl-next-door way. If the girl in question was into crawling around dirty attics and basements. No makeup. No nail polish. Strictly business, this one.

She was dressed all in black, right down to her sneakers, and looked bedraggled after her wild adventure. Her hair was a mess, the curly red strands tousled and dusty, straggling out of the black scrunchie that held only half of it on top of her head.

He could picture her yanking off a hood, not bothering to fix it. That indicated a low vanity score. High in self-confidence, though, from what he had observed. He liked that mix, and it was not one he saw very often.

The only motive for a woman like Agent Moon to get embroiled in a treasonous act like this would be greed. That just didn't fit.

She returned a few minutes later, entering ahead of Holly. Without being ordered, Dawn Moon resumed her seat and immediately locked gazes with him.

That's when Eric first saw her eyes. They were probably the most arresting he had ever seen. Dark, fathomless and exotic. She really had the most amazing eyes. And a powerfully indignant glare.

He finally looked away, punched on the recorder that Holly had been using and identified himself as the interrogator and Agent Dawn Elizabeth Moon as the subject. He added the date and time. Then he began the questions. "What happened on the night of June 15 in the R&D lab of Zelcon Technologies?"

"I was concealed in the air-conditioning vent and I saw Agent Bergen do it," she said in a clipped, determined voice, not frazzled as it had been before. She had collected herself pretty well and in short order.

"Recap for me. I'm new," Eric drawled, watching her sigh with resignation at having to repeat the entire incident yet again to yet another stranger.

"At Bergen's orders, I was to gain entry to the R&D lab, collect proof that I had been there and get out without being apprehended. I should have been off the property by the time he arrived, but I was delayed coming in."

"By what?"

"A complication in getting past the patrol outside. I had to wait for one to stop, smoke a cigarette and carry on a cell-phone conversation before he resumed his rounds."

"When did you first see Agent Bergen that night?" Eric asked.

"When I was replacing the last screw in the vent panel after I had completed my assignment, established the vulnerability in security that Zelcon had neglected to address since our official walk-through and study of the building plans evaluation six months ago."

"And did you participate in that evaluation?"

"Yes." She paused, then took a deep breath and continued, her patience growing thin with all the repetition. "Anyway, I heard voices and I could see through the vent. A minute after the two men entered the lab, Agent Ben Bergen stabbed the tech with a hypo, woke up the computer, plugged one of those little attaché gizmos into a USB port, copied some information, put the thing in his pocket and walked out." She firmed her lips as if holding in a curse.

Eric remained silent for a full ten seconds, attempting

to connect with what she was thinking. Her face gave away a lot, probably distracting him. Attracting him, too, oddly enough. Her face, figure and attitude combined to stir something in him he really didn't want stirred at the moment. Certainly not by a potential suspect. He had to see past all that, get beneath her surface.

When nothing came through on the mental front, he threw out more questions. "But you did nothing to prevent the theft of technology that could be critical to our nation's safety? Isn't that your job, Agent Moon, enforcing national security? That's what you were there to assess, right?"

She calmly placed her hands palms down on the table-top as if she meant to rise, but she didn't. Instead, she spoke calmly, deliberately and in a professional manner. "He had brought in at least one hypo containing an obvious knock-out drug or poison and might have had more, or maybe other weapons for all I knew. I remained concealed because I was unarmed."

Eric picked up sincerity, but he got that from her tone of voice and expression. Nothing from her mind. There were none of the telling mannerisms of a liar present. However, she would know what those were as well as he did. As agents, they would have had virtually the same training, probably by many of the same instructors.

"Why unarmed?" he asked. "You were issued a weapon."

She sighed. "As I have stated at least a dozen times, the vents are a tight squeeze. Inches count, and anything I felt was not needed, I left off. It's not as if I would have been shot if discovered. They would simply have held me until my reason for being there was verified. Please, will you tell me if that tech is dead?"

Eric continued watching her eyes, as open as he could get to receive visuals, feelings, words, anything from her.

He stood suddenly, fairly looming over her, blatantly attempting to intimidate. "What did you do then, inform your superior of what had just happened?"

"Paul Bergen *was* my superior!" She compressed her lips again and shook her head, then ran a hand through her hair, snagging out the scrunchie and tossing it aside. "To answer your question, no, I did not inform anyone at that time. I scrambled out of there as quickly and soundlessly as possible and followed Bergen."

"In your car? You do have communication equipment in your vehicle, do you not?"

"Yes. But I didn't call it in to the duty agent then. What could I have said that would be believed? I needed to find out more. Why Agent Bergen copied what he did and where he was going with it. I saw him deliver it and accept a briefcase. Then the man he delivered it to abruptly shot him two times in the chest, once in the head and took the case back. Then he left in a dark-colored Dodge. I got a partial on the tag."

"Where did this take place?" Eric asked.

"In the parking lot of an apartment complex just outside McLean. I checked to see if Bergen was still alive. He wasn't. Then I immediately phoned our director and waited there as he ordered me to do."

"Could you identify the man who shot Agent Bergen?"

"Yes. He was just under six feet tall, light skin, dark hair, mustache, square jaw. Approximately 180 pounds, late thirties or early forties. No distinguishing characteristics, but I would definitely recognize him if I saw him again. He walked beneath a streetlight as he reached his vehicle. I was less than eight feet away, hidden in the bushes."

"But you didn't try to stop him or follow him?"

She rolled her eyes. "He had a nine-millimeter in his

hand with only three rounds fired. I had a penlight. I'm good, but not *that* good."

Eric concentrated as heavily as possible on her thoughts. That was his primary function in this instance. Maybe he was trying too hard. He couldn't get a thing from her.

She was mad as hell with him and everyone who kept badgering her. Why did they keep harassing her when they should be busy finding that guy who had the disk? It was easy enough to gather all that from her without a brain tap. It was written all over her face.

Suddenly she furiously slammed her fist on the table. "*Do* something about it, will you! Find out what Bergen copied and recover it! Can't you people understand this is crucial?"

"We do." Eric straightened and glanced at the mirror Jack stood behind. "Do *you* know what information was copied?"

"No! How would I know? But it was on a secure computer in a lab that's kept locked. I can't think it was merely a grocery list."

He ignored the sarcasm. "And you're certain you could identify the man?"

"Absolutely." She glared at Eric. "I'd know him anywhere."

Eric looked down at her and smiled. "Thank you, Agent Moon. We will be wanting your help with that. And please don't worry, we are on this, using all the resources we've got."

Her expressive mouth dropped open and her dark eyes widened to the max. His sudden switch to civility apparently shocked her.

He still couldn't read her. Some people were like that, but he was usually able to get around it given a little time and the right circumstances. He wasn't worried.

"Excuse me for a minute," he said, acknowledging both her and Holly with the request. With that he left the room and joined Jack in the next one.

The minute the door closed, Jack asked, "Well?"

"For what it's worth, I believe she's telling the truth, but I have to admit, she's not a good subject. You know as well as I do there are some heads I can't crack. She could be one. Whether that's by chance or her own design is anybody's guess at this point. However, *all* of her physical and verbal responses indicate she's innocent and being perfectly honest. I'd bet on it."

Jack nodded. "I agree. She was the one who made the call even if she was a little tardy about it. Of course, she could be covering her ass by giving us Bergen's. He's dead and can't defend himself."

"But you don't think that's the case," Eric said. "Neither do I. I'd stake my reputation that her story's legit, even if she is a closed book, mindwise."

"It's early yet to be that definite, given that you can't read her thoughts. We can't afford to be wrong about this. Could you try a little remote viewing? See if you can pick up anything on this guy?"

"If I had something he'd touched, it might work, but as it stands, your guess about what's going on is as good as mine." Eric glanced through the mirror at Dawn Moon. "I believe her."

Jack held his silence for a minute. "Okay, I'm releasing her. Let's put her to work with you. She can positively ID the man. I will be Control on this op. Holly, Will and Joe will assist in the internal investigation here at the Bureau. Clay will assist you and Moon. Money was probably Bergen's motive for selling out. The buyers' incentives will be varied. You will be one of them."

"Terrorists will be lined up," Eric said with a sigh. "Al-Qaeda right up front."

"We'll have to work on that assumption. That shield would be perfect for concealing activity in desert training camps. You'll go in as Al-Dayal," Jack said. It wasn't a question. He glanced through the mirrored window into the interrogation room, where Dawn Moon waited impatiently for what would happen next. "Wherever this leads, you'll take her with you."

Eric didn't want to work with Agent Moon, not on this. "I'm best alone on jobs like this, Jack. If I go into it as a potential buyer, that means some high-wire walking with no net. If you insist on my having backup, I'll take Clay. At least he has a working knowledge of Arabic."

Clay Senate was the guy to have at your back, a quiet mountain of bronze muscle with keen intelligence to match his physical strength. His marksmanship skills were legendary, and, even without a weapon, he was lethal. It always amazed Eric how a man of Clay's size and appearance could blend into any environment and go virtually unnoticed until he decided to strike.

Mercier countered the argument, if not the suggestion. "Don't worry, Clay will be involved. A money man like Al-Dayal naturally would have a bodyguard and Clay will fit the bill, but I want Moon with you, too."

"Consider, Jack. If this goes where I think it will, a woman wouldn't be any good to us where meetings are concerned. She'll have to stay secluded in the damn hotel."

"Then you can use a micro-cam and feed her faces to look at. I want her with you. Maybe this shooter is only a thug working on behalf of some organized group, but I have a strong feeling this job is a one-man show. I want that man."

Well, that settled that. One did not argue with Jack's

strong feelings. Also, the agent in charge had the final say. Eric followed Jack's gaze, watching the woman work to control her nerves. "Will you be clearing this mission with her director?"

"Not necessary. For all intents and purposes, Moon's ours until we are satisfied she's given us all she knows, so that won't be an issue. And it could be that Bergen's not the only one in his outfit who was involved in this. Let's keep the whole thing close to the vest until we see how it plays out. You can manage Moon, can't you?"

When you can't read her thoughts. Eric understood the unspoken addition to Jack's question. "Sure. Her face is an open book, even if her mind isn't. If I see any indication that she's a liability, I'll notify you and you can have her yanked."

Mercier nodded. "Fine. I'll call John Q. and have appropriate passports and identification readied since you can't go in as Americans. You might try teaching her a few words of Arabic."

"No, that won't be enough. I guess I could pass her off as my wife. Say she's…Andorran or something. Yeah, that would work since that country is located between France and Spain and she's fluent in those two languages, according to her record."

Fifteen minutes later, Eric returned to the interrogation room where Jack and Holly waited with Agent Moon. She was reviewing photos of possible suspects on Holly's laptop and apparently having no luck.

He entered and approached the table. "I think Bergen sent you on the security gig because he intended you to take the fall for this."

"Why didn't he just steal it and be done with it?" Dawn demanded. "He was perfectly capable. Why set up such an elaborate scheme and involve me?"

Eric explained, "If you look at it from his perspective, it's not a bad plan to get what he wanted and deflect any suspicion from himself. He was too large to crawl through the vents, the one vulnerable point of entry. Obviously you two discussed this hole in security for his report after you did the scheduled daytime analysis with the escort, so you knew exactly how to get inside. That much was detailed in his write-up, very carefully."

"I did get inside. That was the plan. *His* plan."

Eric continued as if she hadn't spoken. "If he had lived, he could have reported that you decided to take advantage of it without sanction, went in at midnight and copied the info. Caught in the act by the tech, you eliminated him and went out the way you came in. You knew the tech's body would be found, the theft discovered, so you disappeared. He would have seen that you did."

"Unless that technician's still alive and corroborates my story, you know I can't prove it didn't go down exactly like that," Moon admitted. "But it didn't."

She remained still as death, her eyes like brown lasers.

Eric agreed that it hadn't. "Bergen entered with the tech's cooperation, unwilling or otherwise. The tech punched in his codes and provided iris and print identification. Bergen would have known how to circumvent the surveillance cameras. No one shows up on those as entering by normal means, even the tech."

"The tech is dead," she said in a small voice.

"Yes. And the surveillance tapes are copies of one night last week when the place was deserted. Bergen was a busy guy."

"So you *do* believe me," she said, exhaling with relief.

"Enough to arrange for your help in the mission. We need to catch the shooter and grab that information before it hits the wrong hands. For the duration of this investigation, you'll be my partner. We're going after this guy, Agent Moon, wherever that takes us."

"Any objections to following through on this?" Mercier stated it like a challenge to her, implying that if she refused, they might suspect that she was in on the theft with Bergen, an accessory to treason and murder.

She'd see it as a test. Eric sensed her hesitation and didn't blame her for it.

He almost hated Mercier for leaving her with that fear, for using it to gain her compliance and take away her choice. This would be a damned dangerous mission. Really dicey. Her training was probably adequate for deep cover work, but according to her file, she had no experience in it at all. Diving in headfirst was a hell of a way to get her feet wet.

She seemed to consider for a few seconds, then shook her head. "No. No objections. I want to do whatever I can." Still, she looked doubtful about why they wanted her in on it.

Eric turned to her and smiled. "The NSA trained all the trust right out of you, didn't they?"

She shrugged and issued a bitter half laugh. "Apparently not thoroughly enough. I trusted Bergen."

"Will you be able to trust *me,* Dawn?" he asked, using her Christian name for the first time, his voice brisk to cover the soft spot developing where she was concerned.

She had been betrayed by one of her own, a man she had trusted implicitly. Eric sympathized. It would be hard to place that much faith in anyone she worked with next.

He glanced at Jack Mercier, his own supervisor, fellow agent and friend, and could only imagine how he would feel if Jack had done that to him.

Dawn Moon stood, her fingertips splayed on the tabletop. The brown eyes hid behind her long lashes and the expressive lips tightened before she replied. "I have no choice but to trust you if I want to vindicate myself completely, do I?"

"None whatsoever," Eric agreed. "The trust has to begin now because we'll be joined at the hip for the duration of this op." He paused for effect. "In case Bergen wasn't working alone on this end, you'll need to stay off the radar. We're going to my place for the first stage of preparation."

She looked warily from him to Mercier and back again. "We'll need to stop by my apartment and pick up a few things."

"No. We'll take care of that," Jack promised. He cleared his throat and looked pointedly at Eric, then at her. "We'll take care of *you*."

"Absolutely," Eric added. He offered her his most confident smile.

Agent Moon was no fool. She knew where the road paved with good intentions led. She also knew there could be giant potholes and detours along that route.

Chapter 2

Dawn woke with a headache. She needed caffeine in the worst way. Sun streamed through the window. Squinting, she propped up in bed on her elbows. This wasn't her apartment. Not her room. Where the hell was she?

She was wearing nothing but her black sports bra and panties. When had she ever slept in a bra?

"Oh," she groaned and collapsed back on the pillow as memory intruded. She was at Vinland's place, an old federal-style house in one of the more exclusive sections of McLean. Though time was of the essence, he had brought her here for a few hours of sleep before they began their mission in earnest.

She didn't want to get up and face more questions. He would probably want her entire life story and everything she'd done since kindergarten. There were certain off-the-record incidents she'd just as soon not recall out loud, especially to him.

Bathroom first, then coffee, she decided. She remembered where the john was. Groggy and grumpy, she crawled out of bed and made it across the room, her bare feet all but dragging. She was incredibly tired.

She yanked open the door to the bathroom and froze. Vinland stood in front of the mirror, a towel around his hips, his face half covered with shaving cream, razor suspended as he stared at her. Looking past him, she saw the connecting door to the other bedroom standing open.

Again she groaned and turned around, pulling her door shut. He grabbed it and swept it open again. "Didn't you sleep at all? You look like hell."

She glared at him from beneath her lashes and growled, "Yeah, and you're so beautiful."

Okay, he *was,* all lean, corded muscles and beach-boy good looks. But male beauty didn't interest her at the moment. "Where's the coffee before I disintegrate?"

"Hallway, go left, downstairs and follow the scent." His sandy eyebrows lowered. "You're not sick, are you?"

That question didn't rate an answer. Of course she was sick. Sick at heart. Bergen's plan had probably ruined her career. This cloud of suspicion could follow her until she was forced to resign or was fired. Or worse yet, arrested and imprisoned.

She plodded to the door across the room and followed his directions to the kitchen. She was nearly naked, but why bother with more clothes? He had already seen her in her underwear and didn't seem greatly affected by it. Small wonder about that if she looked like she felt, and she *must.* He'd even said she looked like hell.

Dawn knew she had no choice but to work with these people, this man in particular. Sure, Vinland struck her as a little too cocky, but the National Security Agency had no place for an agent with a question of treason on her record. She needed to prove beyond a shadow of a doubt that Bergen had intended to set her up. They needed her to identify one of the players. That was the only reason she was getting this chance and she knew it.

Even so, she did not plan to assume an attitude of gratitude with these Sextant agents or simply play tagalong while they solved this. She had a job to do, and they might as well realize that from the get-go.

She wanted to do this for a number of reasons. There was the guilt she felt for not having a clue what Bergen had been up to, even though he had given her no reason to suspect him of anything. No matter how many times she replayed last night's mission in her mind, she could think of nothing that might have alerted her to his intent. Still, she felt a grave personal, and professional, responsibility to ensure that his attempt to sell state secrets did not succeed.

Though she had only known him for a few weeks, Dawn had viewed him as the quintessential agent in charge. All business, no banter, distinguished in both dress and manner, Bergen had neither lorded his seniority over her nor tried to be her friend. He'd simply given her orders and she had obeyed them without question, trusting in what she had been trained to do. Trusting him, simply because he had possessed the experience and the authority to run the operation.

Would she ever be able to obey like that again, without reserve? Not likely. This whole experience could wreck her career in more ways than one.

If the information that Bergen had stolen, ostensibly to sell, remained in terrorist hands long enough to be implemented, it could well be devastating. She had no clue precisely what it was and wasn't sure she wanted to know, but it had to be critically important to rate this much attention from Sextant.

The delicious beckoning of freshly ground coffee beans perking led her by the nose to his kitchen. She inhaled the scent that might make her human again, poured herself a cup and loaded it with sugar. She loved sugar.

Footsteps behind her indicated Vinland was risking contact again. She downed the remainder of her coffee and refilled the mug, pouring one for him, too.

He reached for the cup, and his fingers brushed hers as he took it from her. Dawn made a fist and struggled to ignore the tingling sensation that spread through her from that lightest of touches. The man was lethally handsome. He even smelled terrific. Could be tough or gentle and knew when to be which, a quality that appealed to all women. Small wonder she reacted the way she did. It was perfectly natural, and she could handle it.

She watched as he opened the cabinet and retrieved a box of doughnuts. Uh-oh, the way to her heart. Dawn squelched a smile. Trust him to intuit her weakness.

They took seats at the table where he proceeded to open the sweets. He didn't hurry. It was as if he taunted her a little. He lifted a doughnut from the box and held it out as if anticipating that first bite. "Jack called earlier," he said. "They ran the plates and the car was rented with a bogus ID. He will have ditched it. Soon as it's found, we'll have a lead to follow." Then he took a bite out of a chocolate-covered confection and pointed at her with what was left. "We'll get him."

Unable to resist a minute longer, Dawn reached over and snagged what looked like a lemon-filled doughnut. "Right. I'm sure he left a forwarding address in the glove compartment. Or maybe we can call in the psychics."

Vinland's brow furrowed as he swallowed and thunked down the remains of his doughnut. "Look, we need to get something straight before we get started."

"Oh, spare me the drill. I get it. I *know* you're in charge and I'm not in the habit of trampling male egos. You lead, boy wonder, and I won't even protest. I'll do whatever you say."

He looked a little taken aback, probably because she wasn't bowing at his feet for this opportunity.

"All right, then," he said finally. "Do you want to know what I'm going to do to you?"

That opened her eyes. "*Do* to me?"

His boyish grin didn't sit well with her. "Work with you so you don't sound and look so American. But first I need to talk to you a little more. Get better acquainted."

That might have sounded appealing, except for the way he'd said it. "I thought we did that on the way here." She waved a hand. "So talk."

"Look at me," he instructed, taking the seat across the small table from her. "Take my hand."

"Ha, right. Spare me the lame come-ons, will you?" Dawn scoffed. She didn't want to touch him and feel that tingle again. Or maybe she wanted it too much. Like a third doughnut she knew she'd better say no to. "Just get on with it and ask what you want to ask."

He took her hand anyway. Dawn started to retract it, but decided that so far the gesture seemed harmless enough. Maybe he was only trying to put her at ease. If that was what he had in mind, it sure wasn't working. She tingled in spite of herself. Her skin grew warm, and she was afraid she was blushing all over.

His hand was smooth, the nails clipped straight across and very clean. Calluses ridged the outer edges of his palm and his knuckles were slightly enlarged. All in all, nice hands. Large and warm. Hers felt hot and were probably a little damp.

He gripped her fingers tighter. What was with the hand-holding? If he meant to get any chummier than that, he had another think coming. But when she attempted to pull away, he held her fast, threading his fingers through hers. She glanced up from their joined hands.

His intense look surprised her. The bluest eyes in the world bored into hers as if seeking the secret of the universe. She couldn't look away. Hypnosis? No, she didn't feel the least bit woozy. As a matter of fact, the sugared coffee and doughnut were kicking in and the energy from them had perked her up. Or maybe he did that. The old hormones were alive and kicking, no doubt about that.

Yep, Vinland was a great-looking guy. Exactly the kind she wouldn't trust. She had learned that lesson all too well and twice over. She made herself remember what she'd love to forget.

Her first affair had been with a research assistant in her second year of college. Thomas had had a similar wicked grin, same golden-boy looks as Vinland, same know-it-all attitude, too. She'd found out too late it was a know-*them*-all attitude and ol' Tom was keeping score, a dumping offense if she'd ever encountered one.

Her second lapse of sanity involved a fellow student at the academy. Nice guy, Scott. She had begun to have wonderful visions of something permanent when she found out he had sugared up to her for tutorial reasons. So much for being loved for one's mind. As soon as he passed, she was history.

Given how Bergen had so recently dashed her ability to judge the character of a man, Dawn could no longer trust her professional assessment, much less her personal instincts, when it came to men.

She wasn't falling again, no way.

Vinland equaled danger if she didn't gear down and treat him like artwork. And he was a piece of work for sure.

Finely textured skin, slightly tanned. Those shoulders definitely saw the inside of a gym on a regular basis. His hair gleamed a sort of pale brown with blond highlights. Bottled lights? She wondered. His eyes mesmerized, an almost iridescent blue with long, sexy lashes any woman would covet.

The mouth looked a little too firm at the moment, but she remembered how sensuous it had appeared before when he was more relaxed. Didn't hurt to admire, though doing so did jack up her tension to an uncomfortable level.

Her feeling that way, she understood, but why was *he* so uptight right now?

"Can't you think of anything to say?" she asked. "You're the one who wanted to talk."

He shook his head a little sharply and glanced away from her. "Something's not… Excuse me," he said, releasing her hand and getting up. "I'll be back in a minute."

She shrugged when he left. Maybe he didn't quite know what to make of her. Despite her better judgment, she grabbed another doughnut, a yummy glazed one, swearing to herself that she would work it off later.

He returned in a few minutes clutching her black shirt. Though she was covered better than she would have been in a bathing suit, she *was* sitting there in her undies. Modesty wasn't a big thing with her. Maybe it was with him.

Dawn licked her sticky fingers and reached for the shirt to put it on, but he didn't let it go. Those blue eyes followed her every move.

"Sorry about that," she said with an embarrassed chuckle. Again, she tugged at the shirt. "I'll get dressed now."

"No."

"Yes!" she insisted, snatching the garment from his grasp. "What is it with you?"

Whatever it was, it didn't seem limited to lust. Vinland seemed worried, distracted.

"Would you mind sitting down again?" he asked politely.

"I really need to get some clothes on." She held up the shirt he had brought her. "I shouldn't have come down here in my skivvies. Guess I've lived alone too long."

He nodded relutantly and turned away. "Later, then."

"Is something wrong?" she asked over her shoulder.

He shook his head, but it didn't seem like it was in answer to her question. Instead, he was frowning and looked seriously puzzled about something, and she knew it had to do with her.

Dawn went back to the bedroom where she'd slept and put on the rest of her clothes. Vinland was one strange dude. If he couldn't even get it together to brief her on what they were planning to do, how could she depend on him to run this investigation?

Maybe she should have a word with Jack Mercier about it. Trouble was, she had no idea how to get in touch with his boss without asking Vinland for the number and telling him why she wanted it.

Oh hell, maybe Vinland also just needed a lot of coffee before he could function. She could understand that.

Eric had hoped that Dawn's blocking his attempts at establishing a telepathic connection was a temporary thing, caused by Bergen's blow to her trust. Shields definitely went up at times like that.

That's all it was, he decided. Once she got past that shock and her defenses went down, he'd read her like a novel in oversized print. This morning's repeated efforts didn't signal failure, only delay.

Touching her hadn't helped at all. In fact, it only

confused things more. He hadn't gotten anything from handling her clothing, either.

All Eric had to do today was get their ducks in a row. The first order of business was to get Dawn disguised, brief her about the details of the mission and get her adjusted to him and their new looks. Also, to get himself comfortable with *her,* Eric admitted.

The truth was, he felt a little out of control around Dawn Moon, on both a professional and a personal level. He felt different, less and yet more. Deprived of something, but somehow more complete. It made no sense to feel that way.

He rummaged around in the side pocket of his carry-on bag for the case containing his glasses. Maybe that was the key. He hadn't had his glasses on, either last night or this morning. On the flight into D.C. from Seattle, he had slipped them off to take a short nap and put them away. In his hurry to deplane and report for duty, he had forgotten about them since he didn't need them to see.

Over the years, they had become almost like a light switch that regulated his ability. Though they were nothing but very lightly tinted glass, they had always seemed to block, or at least filter, the thoughts of others that used to bombard him unexpectedly.

He thought back to his arrival at the interrogation. He had immediately picked up on Jack's belief that Dawn was not guilty. He had read Holly's sympathy for Dawn before okaying her visit to the ladies' room. But the inner thoughts of Dawn Moon had remained a mystery.

Since seeing her for the first time, he hadn't read anyone, he realized. There had been a crazy moment of sheer, unadulterated peace. Always, for as long as he could remember, he had endured background noise in his mind, something like constant static. Thoughts of others bombarding him from every direction, held at bay only by doing some blocking of his own. At the moment his eyes had met Dawn's, that had ceased like magic.

He had grabbed it like a blessed reprieve he couldn't bear to give up. It lingered even now. Even when he needed it to go away.

The specs were merely a psychosomatic screen—he knew that—but whatever worked, he had learned to use. He'd put his glasses on now, then take them off after he got Dawn used to being around him. Surely then he would have no problem knowing her every thought.

Eric knew the reasoning was somehow faulty. He also was trying too hard. And maybe loving that clarity of mind and near silence in his head a little too much.

"Hey, Moon, you dressed?" Dawn jumped when Vinland called out to her through the bathroom door. He knocked a couple of times, then opened the door to the guest room.

She was fully clothed, looking out the window, but turned when he entered. "Where are we going?"

"Nowhere, yet."

"Hey, better lose the granny glasses," she suggested. "They make you look like Brad Pitt in that movie where he played a wimp." Actually, he looked too scrumptious for words in those things. The glasses hinted at a hidden vulnerability that made him seem even more approachable, something she did not need at the moment.

He laughed at her insult and reached up, taking off his eyewear. When he had pocketed them, he looked directly at her, his expression growing almost fierce in its intensity.

A few seconds passed and he lightened up, shrugging and shaking his head as if what he saw in her disappointed him.

Damn the man, then. She tossed her hair back with one hand and could have kicked herself for the high-school-ish gesture.

For the remainder of the morning, Dawn shared the tension as they waited on the call from Mercier.

Vinland left her alone for a few hours, but he didn't go out. Instead, he stayed in his home office on the phone and the computer.

The door remained open. She gave him a cursory wave as she passed on her way to the kitchen, but she didn't intrude. What was it that agents like Vinland did to prepare for a mission? she wondered.

He joined her around four in the afternoon in his den, where she was clicking through the TV channels, finding nothing interesting to watch.

"Want some popcorn?" he asked, strolling over to thumb through his DVD collection. "How about pizza? I could order one."

"No way," she said, looking at him now instead of the television. He wore faded jeans and a T-shirt that simply said Navy with a tiny cartoon of a seal underneath the word.

"You don't like pizza? Now *that* is un-American," he stated categorically, shaking a finger at her. "You're obviously some kind of alien. Not a foreigner, but a strange being from another planet."

Dawn laughed and abandoned the remote. "I was going to say you'd better order *two*."

He clutched his chest and rolled his eyes. "Thank God."

With a flourish, he popped in a DVD without asking her what movie she wanted to watch. It was a chick flick, an old one. Dawn smiled at his consideration, though she really preferred action/adventure.

She didn't intend to watch it, anyway. This bit of

downtime was a perfect opportunity for her to find out what kind of agent, and what kind of man, she was dealing with.

So far, nothing about Vinland seemed consistent. One minute he acted stern and uncompromising, the next polite and considerate; then he'd tease her and make her laugh. Who was he, really?

She listened while he joked around on the phone with the pizza person and tried to con them into adding extra olives for free. He quirked an eyebrow at her, as if asking if she approved the request. Dawn nodded enthusiastically. He wound up paying extra, but apparently enjoyed the verbal exchange.

He seemed to enjoy practically everything, she noticed. Only once in a while did he go all serious, and then not for long. One thing about him: he didn't exhibit the wary reluctance to reveal personal things about himself that agents in their business usually did.

He obviously loved his house and spent a great deal on it. Expensive antiques looked very much at home here, complemented by exquisitely framed original art. She noted he preferred realistic to abstract, traditional over modern. Though masculine in tone, the style of the place felt welcoming, warm, friendly. Like Vinland himself. Or, maybe he had simply hired a good decorator, she thought with a shrug. There were photos everywhere, a great many of them of women. Beautiful women.

She pointed to one in particular. "Is that who I think it is?"

He nodded. "Bev Martin."

"The actress?" Dawn was impressed. "You know her?"

Again he nodded and added a grin. "She's a good friend."

More than that, Dawn would bet. Here was a man who had no trouble attracting females. Of all ages, judging by his collection of pictures. The one of the actress she recognized was no publicity photo, but a candid shot of sexy Bev relaxing in the very recliner that sat across the room. "She's very beautiful."

"Yeah, nice person, too," he admitted readily, then promptly changed the subject. Or maybe not. "You going with anyone in particular? I'm only asking in case you need to excuse your absence for a week or so."

"Not at the moment." Not in the last few years, but she wasn't admitting that much to him or anyone else. "What about you?"

"No excuses needed," he assured her without really answering the other part of the question. Maybe Miss Martin understood what he did for a living and knew better than to expect explanations for his absences.

Dawn curled her feet under her on the comfy suede sofa and lay back against the cushions, stretching her arm along the back. "I love your place. Have you lived here long?"

He glanced around. "Almost two years. Bought it just before I left the Navy."

"You're not from here, though," she guessed. His accent was pure Boston. Upper class, too. No doubt an Ivy Leaguer, a Princeton or Harvard man. "Massachusetts, right?"

"Good ear," he said, approving her skill. "And you…let me see…from New Jersey."

"Right," she admitted. "But you didn't get that from my accent. I don't have one."

"Right, you don't," he admitted with a smile. "Read your file." He plopped down beside her, his leg almost touching her knees.

"That is so unfair. I know nothing about you."

"Sure you do." He plucked at the front of his shirt. "I'm ex-Navy. I like old stuff," he said, glancing around at the antiques gracing his den. "Vintage movies and pizza," he added with a nod at the television. "And I've just revealed that I'm unencumbered socially. So what else do you want to know?"

"How'd you get into this business?" Somehow he just didn't seem the intelligence-agent type with that openness of his and the laid-back attitude. Or was that merely a front?

He pursed his lips for a minute, making her stare at their perfection. She hated it when a man made her gawk. He relaxed them and cut his gaze sideways. "Well, I kept getting seasick. The Navy tossed me out and Jack felt sorry for me, cast ashore like that with nowhere to go. Told me if I'd behave like a spy, he'd let me hang out with him and his team for a while."

Dawn laughed. "So you try to behave."

"Sometimes. I keep waiting for him to throw me back, but I guess he'd have nobody to razz if he did."

"Don't tell me you're the team screwup."

"No, but I do believe a sense of humor helps get you through the dark times. Take yourself too seriously and it's harder to roll with the punches, don't you think?"

Dawn did. Odd how he seemed to want her to understand him. He had divulged a lot about himself. "You take the job seriously, though," she guessed.

"Damn straight."

Right. She picked at the luxurious fringe on the pillow beneath her hand and caressed the woven tapestry fabric. She loved this room and everything in it. It suited him perfectly, or at least what she thought she knew of him now. "You have either great taste or a good decorator."

"Thanks." But he didn't indicate which.

Dawn suspected he had chosen everything in his house himself, and did it with an eye for comfort and quality. The painting above the mantel was of a woman who looked a bit like him. "Who's that?"

"My grandmother," he said with an openly affectionate look at the portrait. "Also my favorite person. She died a few years ago and I still miss her."

The woman in the picture told Dawn even more than Eric had. He was obviously from old money and from a family well established in society. She recognized his grandmother from articles in national news magazines and knew why Eric's features had seemed a bit familiar to her.

"Of the Boston Pricevilles," Dawn murmured under her breath, not realizing she had spoken out loud until he replied.

"Mother's people," he said. "The Vinlands are the outlaws."

Dawn laughed at his wry expression, loving the way his brow wrinkled in one spot, right between his golden, perfectly arched eyebrows. "Now that sounds interesting. A mésalliance?"

"A disaster, but that's a story for another day." He pushed up from the sofa, tapped his temple with one finger and headed out of the room. "Pizza's coming up the walk."

How did he know that? There was no window facing the front of the house and she hadn't heard a car outside. Still, the doorbell chimed before he reached the hall.

That was downright spooky, she thought, until the clock on the mantel beneath the portrait chimed, too. Twenty minutes since he had ordered. Of course. He was probably a regular customer. For a minute there, she'd wondered if he was psychic. Not that she believed in such things.

Chapter 3

For the rest of the afternoon and evening, they tacitly agreed to place thoughts of the job on hold and try to relax. The mission would be exhausting emotionally, perhaps even physically, and they both knew it. It paid to go into something like this with a cool head and senses firing on all cylinders.

They talked of their preferences and opinions regarding current events, books and movies, things a couple generally did when getting acquainted. Dawn wasn't certain why that thought came to mind. She certainly didn't want to be half of a couple.

That certainty slid right out of her mind when they called it a night, however. He took her hand to help her up from the sofa where they had been sitting a circumspect three feet apart for nearly two hours. His fingers interlocked with hers, he raised their hands and planted a kiss on the back of hers as their eyes met and held. Her heart stuttered and she leaned toward him, drawn by an unseen force.

Uh-huh, lust, she reckoned when he stepped back and released her hand.

"Good night," he said, gesturing for her to precede him out the door. "Breakfast is at six. Expect a long and busy day."

Dawn felt so rattled, she couldn't say a word. She quickly turned to go up the stairs and didn't dare glance back at him. If she did, she knew she would have a look of invitation plastered all over her face. He might take her up on it, and that would be bad. Then again, he might refuse, and that would be even worse.

She hardly slept at all and when she did, she dreamed of him. As dreams went, these were definitely rated X, fantasies originating in a Georgian town house, sweeping across desert sands and landing in a silken tent with a Valentino-garbed Vinland doing what old silent-movie sheikhs are prone to do. *Prone* being the big word for her, too.

The next morning, Dawn consigned everything that had happened the night before to a file in her mind labeled Forbidden. No way would she take it out and study it in depth, not after what she'd dreamed.

Vinland had only been managing her, she told herself. Mentor to novice, agent in charge to junior agent. If it had been a test, then she had passed, kept her hands and thoughts to herself.

Breakfast proved to be simple. Coffee, cereal chock-full of vitamins, milk and a banana were all ready and waiting for her when she came downstairs. They ate in silence, he as lost in his thoughts as she was in hers, neither mentioning that brief moment when the current of longing had zapped them. She knew he had felt it, and he surely knew that she had.

"Go on upstairs," he said when she had finished. "I'll be up in a few minutes. We need to get started."

She rose and escaped, or that was what it felt like. Maybe a few minutes alone would give her time to shore up her defenses. The man was majorly messing with her hormones, and she resented it.

He arrived ten minutes later, coming through the bathroom that joined their bedrooms.

"First thing we need to do is change your appearance." He held up a kit he had retrieved from his bedroom and plucked out a box. "You want to dye first or shall I?"

Dawn quirked one auburn eyebrow at him and her lips softened into a natural smile. The way he made her feel was not his fault. Vinland couldn't help being as handsome as he was and owning the drawbacks that went with it. She could be kind without losing her head over him. Look at all the practice she'd had.

"I'll go first," she offered.

"Leave your hair wet when you finish coloring it. I'll need to style it."

Somehow she could not imagine him as a hairdresser. "Multitalented, are you?"

"We'll see how you feel about that when I'm done." He grinned and tossed her the box of hair dye.

"Why are you disguising me? The guy didn't see me, I'm sure of that. He'd have killed me if he had. And if someone else at NSA was working with Bergen, they could identify me, disguised or not."

"No one will recognize you when I get through," he assured her. "Besides, no one at your agency will be in on this, except you. They're totally out of the loop until everyone who had contact with Bergen is cleared. Safe to say, you won't be running into any of your fellow agents where we're going."

"Where will that be?" she asked, wondering if he was sharing all he knew.

"Waiting to find that out, but I can almost guarantee it won't be this side of the pond."

Vinland grinned his wicked grin and pointed at the hair dye she held. "It's a good trick when going undercover, a self-perception thing. Changing your looks will alter your whole personality. See yourself differently and I guarantee you won't act the same." He spread his hands wide. "You'll be a blank slate when we're done, and become who I need you to be."

Oh great. "And just who is that?" she asked, fascinated by the concept, if not wild about participating in it.

"Wait and see," he said cryptically. Then he added, "And try to be open-minded, will you?"

Dawn almost laughed, and bitterly at that. He really didn't need to know all the things that crossed her mind when he was around.

An hour later, Dawn realized that her own father wouldn't recognize her. And Vinland wasn't finished with her yet.

Her hair was very dark brown now and straight as a stick. Vinland had expertly trimmed it in a blunt cut, several inches shorter than her former length, and used a flat iron to smooth out every vestige of curl. She'd been trying to do that for years. Amazing man.

She blinked at her reflection, getting used to the style he had created with such dexterity. Their breath had mingled as he'd drawn the scissor-like heated panels of the straightening iron through the sections of hair that framed her face.

He had lingered as he worked, touching her forehead, lifting her chin, caressing an ear. Those marvelous fingers worked their magic, both on her hair and her libido.

He had been so close then, her nostrils flared at the lime scent of his aftershave. And the damn pheromones he threw off along with it. Her cheeks were heated, and so were other parts she didn't want to think about. Five-alarm fire sirens were screaming like crazy in her head.

His hands could be so gentle, she had trouble visualizing them performing anything like defense. But those calluses along his outer palms had not evolved through pampering. Martial arts, probably karate, studied over a considerable period of time would have formed them. Hers were similar, only not nearly as prominent as his.

"You will need to undress," he announced abruptly, all business.

"In your dreams," she replied evenly. "You had your show yesterday."

He held up a spray can, shaking it. "Got to tan you. Don't want to miss any spots."

"Hey, I'm not all that fair. Won't I do?"

"Well, I can't get you any lighter than you are, but the hair change isn't enough. Let's go a bit darker."

Oh well, she could stand that. Obediently, she stripped down to her bra and panties again, praying her nipples wouldn't peak. It was anything but chilly in the room, so there was no excuse. Well, there *was* one, but she didn't want to reveal that to him.

"Straps down, please," he snapped impatiently.

Carefully, Dawn slipped her arms out of the bra straps and hoped the cups would cling to her breasts and not fall down around her waist. Not much chance of that, since she was almost too well-endowed, a fact he was now noticing without trying to be obvious about it. Oddly enough, she didn't mind.

Just for good measure, literally, she inhaled deeply. No reason why she should be the only one suffering around here.

He quickly focused elsewhere. "Okay, hold out your arms," he ordered, his voice gruff as he continued coating her with the spray. Dawn figured he was fighting a little battle of his own now, but she refused to look down his body to check whether he was. Didn't matter.

Did...not...matter.

He crouched and stroked her legs with the spray, clearing his throat as he nudged her knee so he could get to her inner thighs.

Oh...my...goodness.

Dawn felt laughter well up in her throat. She coughed to cover it. This was so ridiculous. Which one of them was more awkward with this? Well, it was Vinland's idea to do it himself. Let him deal with it.

He stood quickly and turned away from her, depositing the can back into his kit that sat open on the bed. "There. All done. In a few minutes, you'll be brown as a berry, a deep Riviera tan with no streaks. Leave your clothes off until it dries."

"Leave my clothes off," she repeated dryly.

"Hey, you can trust me," he replied. "Scout's honor." Grinning, he held up three fingers in the official salute.

"You were a Boy Scout," she deadpanned.

"Oh, absolutely. Got a merit badge for ignoring naked women." He sighed, a woeful sound. "Of course, I was about ten at the time. A couple of years after that, I had to give it back."

"I'll just bet you did." She frowned into the mirror of the dresser and flicked back one side of the dark waves that fell to her shoulders. "I look strange. But not exactly Middle Eastern, if that's what you're going for."

"No, it's not, but you *do* look very different. The idea is to change your looks. You'll be surprised at how that will automatically alter your behavior, mannerisms, everything. Works wonders," he told her.

"Oh, so now I'll be flighty, disorganized and dumb?" she grumbled. "Tell me, how is this good for the mission?"

He grunted a laugh. "Cute. Now for the makeup." With a deep and audible breath of what sounded like frustration, he withdrew a smaller case out of the large one.

Dawn barely squelched a groan. More touching. Time to call a halt to this torture, or one of them was bound to cave and do something really, really stupid.

She hadn't been this revved up sexually since high-school graduation night when Harry Forsythe seduced her in the back of his parents' van. Her skin tingled like crazy and her pulse must have doubled by now. The sweet memory of old first love Harry vanished completely in light of the hot fantasies this guy stirred up. Thomas or Scott didn't even come to mind long enough to warrant a dismissal.

Then there was the debacle of her trusting Bergen too much. Not that she had ever had any personal attachment to the man, but his overwhelming betrayal had undermined whatever vestige of confidence she had in her dealings with men.

No use making these comparisons. She was not, definitely not and no *way*, about to allow any slap and tickle with beach boy agent, no matter how thoroughly he stirred up her hormones.

There was too much at stake. Her career, to begin with. Her reputation. Her credibility. Engaging in anything like that with him, considering her circumstances, would be disastrous. And there were the other reasons, she reminded herself. Better and more personal reasons than screwing up on the job. She couldn't do the sex thing casually. It just wasn't in her, and she knew it.

It irritated her that she couldn't, because she didn't need or want a commitment at this point in her life, even if the guy was willing to commit. Which Vinland never would be, she firmly reminded herself.

"I can handle the makeup," she declared, snatching the zippered makeup bag out of his hand. "Go do…whatever you need to do to yourself."

She meant for him start on his own disguise, of course, but her guilty glance at his body's reaction to her and his fierce frown told her he had briefly thought she meant something else entirely.

She couldn't help grinning at him.

To her surprise, he didn't shoot back some smart reply. Instead, he took the rest of the kit and stalked into the bathroom, leaving her alone.

Eric had to lean on the sink for a minute to get his equilibrium back. What was the matter with him?

This was one of his specialties. How many female agents had he assisted with disguises during his years with Intel and with Sextant? More than he could count. But this one, even with all her clothes on, did something powerful and unique.

She screwed up his concentration. She overturned his priorities. She aroused him without even being interested.

Generally speaking, he required at least a modicum of interest from the other party. Otherwise what was the point in letting himself get excited?

He had kissed her hand last night, an impulse he had regretted immediately. She'd hurried away the instant he'd let go of her. Maybe she feared sexual harassment on his part, since he was technically running the op and she was the secondary. Still, he didn't have the power to affect her career at NSA since he worked for a different outfit entirely. Surely she knew that.

No, fear wasn't a factor. Dawn wasn't above a little teasing, but he could tell she wasn't up for a tension-relieving tumble. Neither was he, not with a fellow agent. He had rules about that and suspected she did, too.

He looked in the mirror and blinked at his image. Why wasn't she interested? Ordinary-looking guy, he thought. Nothing special, but something about him usually drew women to him, he knew that. They probably sensed his innate love and appreciation of them. He rarely met a woman who didn't have something great to recommend her.

Bev, his friend and sometime lover, once told him that his main attraction was that he truly listened when she talked, that the intensity of his look, the fact that he met her eyes and held them, communicated real regard. Little did she know that he was probing her mind for what she really meant instead of paying attention to the words that came out of her mouth.

He sighed and looked away. If women only knew what a fraud he was, how he played to their own fantasies. That had begun when he was a spindly tenth-grade swimmer instead of the beefy quarterback he had longed to be.

Even though he had never used his mind-reading talent to score with girls, he had used it to insure that they liked and trusted him as a person. Consequently, he felt he had never had a real relationship untainted by his advantage.

Dawn would be the perfect woman to begin one with if he could leave the mind thing alone, abandon all attempts to read her and play it straight. It really bothered him, how much he wanted to do that.

Unfortunately, their present situation made that impossible. He had to keep trying, to somehow get inside her mind and see whether she harbored some little something that might help with this mission.

Not that he believed for a minute that she was holding out details on purpose. It was just that people often knew things they didn't realize they knew. Ferreting those out was what he did best. Usually.

In spite of the necessity and as selfish as it was, Eric almost hoped Dawn would keep blocking him. How much he wanted a chance of something lasting with her surprised and daunted him. The thought, the very idea of that, was premature to say the least. He hardly knew her. And yet he felt he knew Dawn better than other people whose minds were wide open to him. Why was that?

He clearly had the hots for her, but his feelings seemed to go well beyond that even now. His protective instincts had kicked in the second he saw her, even though he knew she had to have been trained to take care of herself.

Something quirky about Dawn had hooked him like a clueless trout and he couldn't for the life of him figure out what it was. Maybe the fact that he couldn't read her mind contributed, but there had been others like that whom he'd shrugged off without a pause. Not her. No shrugging.

No shagging, either, he reminded himself firmly. At least, not while they were working this job.

He turned on the cold water and splashed his face several times, then scrubbed it fiercely with a towel.

"Grow up and quit bellyaching," he muttered to his reflection. "Keep your focus on the game."

Eric reached for the kit on the countertop and set about becoming someone else.

Maybe when he switched identities and cultures, he could temporarily change his attitude toward her while he was at it. If he couldn't, he knew he was in the worst kind of trouble.

Chapter 4

Dawn nearly jumped out of her skin when Eric walked into the den. Until he grinned, she thought a stranger had broken in. Nothing could disguise that grin with its almost-dimples and flash of perfect white teeth, but everything else about him had changed radically.

He had dyed his skin darker than hers and his eyes were so black she couldn't distinguish pupil from iris. Even his eyelashes were inky, their fascinating golden tips a thing of the past. The makeup job was fantastic.

He wore a stark white silk shirt and loose trousers that had to be tailored and looked very expensive. On his head was a linen cloth with a crown of black cord to hold it in place.

His bearing had altered, too. As he walked over to her, she noted how his elbows rested nearer his body, his shoulders were not quite as straight as before and his gait seemed more measured. He gave the impression of being much more self-contained and reserved. If it weren't for that grin.

It vanished abruptly and he regarded her with a serious expression. Now he had become another man entirely. Dawn stared, transfixed and amazed. What a dress rehearsal. She could tell he was enjoying her reaction.

He bowed. "Greetings," he said simply, his voice a caress hot as a desert in July. He added another soft musical phrase, this time in Arabic, lifting the dark eyelashes that had briefly covered his taunting black eyes.

Dawn quirked an eyebrow. "May Allah bless you with many camels. And deliver you from flaky mascara."

He broke up, laughing so hard the ghutra toppled off his head. Still chuckling, he pulled off the embroidered skullcap he had worn beneath it and collapsed on the sofa beside her. "I wonder if anyone would notice duct tape over your mouth under your chador." He ran both hands through his jet-black hair, causing it to stand on end.

"Under my what?"

"Your chador, the traditional veil and robe you'll be wearing." he explained.

She scoffed, crossing her arms over her chest. "I am *not* wearing one of those. I would suffocate or dehydrate from sweating."

Eric sighed. "Your eyes, nose and mouth needn't be covered if you'll remember to keep your head down. Modest western dress is acceptable sometimes, of course, but the chador will be good cover for you, no pun intended."

"So you found out our shooter is headed for Sand Land?"

He sighed, smoothing out the wrinkles on his disguise's headgear and folding it neatly. "No. We don't know yet where the chase will lead, but we do know a buy will go down. It stands to reason there will be a few from that neck of the woods who will want this technology. I plan to be one of them."

"I just don't understand why you are going to these lengths to disguise *me?* I know you think it helps with the personality switch or whatever, but I could act differently than I do without all this. Who's gonna know I'm American?"

"I'm taking every precaution I can think of to prevent anyone finding out. You're supposed to be Andorran, of Spanish birth, but a convert to Islam, therefore not a Western wife. Otherwise, my credibility would be shot with these people. Hell, *I* might be shot if anyone even suspects who you really are. And you surely would be. Or worse."

She picked up the ghutra he had laid aside, giving it a cursory examination as she spoke, studying the intricately braided cord crown that held the linen head-covering in place. "Okay, I can play this part, but even I know enough about customs over there to know I won't be allowed to attend any meetings with you. You can't introduce me or even talk about me to any other men, and I probably won't be able to communicate with any of the women. Why take me along?"

His lips firmed and he shook his head as he smoothed down his spiky hair. "My first thoughts exactly and I told Jack as much, right up front. It was his idea, but I do see his point, despite my objections. You're the only one able to identify the man who killed Bergen and took the information from him."

"What good will that do?"

"Maybe then we could identify some of his associates. Find out where he fits in the scheme of things. I talked to Jack and they've located the car he abandoned at the airport. They lifted a few prints, but none are in our databases, so he hasn't officially made our list yet. We're waiting on Interpol to see what they have."

Dawn shivered every time she thought about who they were after, a soulless criminal who had killed a man in cold blood at close range and dealt with the scum of the world. "Okay, maybe the chador thing's not such a bad idea after all."

"I'll get you one that's top of the line," he said, leaning back and crossing one leg over his knee, tapping the back of the sofa with his fingers. "You know the logic behind making the women wear them?"

She blinked slowly and scoffed. "Oh, there's logic to that, you think?"

"Sure. They say if a man leaves his treasure out in plain view, other men will think it's for the taking. So he must conceal it."

"Then the ridiculous custom should work both ways. How would you men feel if we put sacks over your heads to ward off the competition?" she snapped.

He seemed to consider that for a minute, then shook his head. "Wouldn't work. See, guys will never steal a pig in a poke. They want to see what they're getting for their trouble. But women? They just can't seem to resist uncovering a mystery. Curiosity killed the cat."

"Speaking of animals…" She slammed him with a sofa cushion and got up, crossing her arms, and looking down at him. "You're the pig, Vinland. A truly chauvinistic pig."

"Hold on a minute and don't stomp out on me yet," he said, replacing the cushion and leaning forward. "We need to get a few language lessons going while we wait for our traveling papers. You'll need to know a few phrases in Arabic. It would seem strange if you hadn't picked up any from your husband."

"I know a little. One of my suite mates at college was Jordanian. Her English was good, but I had to help her with colloquialisms. She tried to prep me for a future visit to her part of the world. I think I learned enough to shop and order food."

His newly darkened eyebrows flew up. "Well, hurrah. That's gotta be an omen."

She paused, throwing him a jaded look. "Omen? Don't tell me you're superstitious."

He grinned again. "Sure am. Omens, signs, especially predictions. My grandma, who had the sight, warned me that one day a sharp-spoken woman with red hair would turn my life around. All these years, I thought it was my tenth-grade history teacher who straightened me out by threatening to flunk me. Now I know better." He spread his arms wide. "Just look at how I've changed since I met you."

"I never know when you're serious. This is never gonna work."

"It'll work," he promised, losing the grin. "It has to. I'm deadly serious about this mission, Dawn. There'll be no more joking around once we're on our way."

She nodded, sighed and walked over to the window, looking out again over the quiet neighborhood. The very essence of upper-middle-class America. "I wonder where we will be going," she murmured. "Exactly."

"Doesn't matter as long as it's where he and the stolen information are," he answered, approaching, placing a hand on her shoulder in what seemed a reassuring gesture. She felt the heat of his palm nearly scorch her skin. "For starters, if Allah is with us, we make the deal where it's relatively safe, identify all the parties involved, eliminate the threat and get out before the showdown."

"Are you Muslim?"

"Nope, Methodist. You?"

"Presbyterian." She turned, her face scant inches from his. "And if God's not providing us an easy solution?"

He shrugged. "We go wherever and do whatever it takes."

"Do you know what was stolen and what the outcome

will be if we aren't successful?" Dawn asked, moving away from him so she could concentrate. Lord, he had a force field or something that she knew she needed to avoid. It wasn't that easy when it was drawing her in like heavy-duty gravity.

"Kenro Applications. Ever heard of it?"

"They do atmospheric studies and evaluate ecological conditions here and in space, right?" she guessed.

"Yeah, that's right." He gave her a look of approval and indicated she should sit down again. When she did, he sat opposite her in the chair, leaning forward, elbows resting on his knees. "They're a NASA subcontractor, not a large company, extremely specialized. Some of the stolen data was research they had supplied."

"I'm getting a scary picture here," she muttered.

"You're familiar with Halmann Electronics?"

"Radar." She thought for a minute. "If you're saying Zelcon was working with both, then this has to do with testing a technology that's already developed?"

"Yes," he confirmed. As if only half paying attention to their conversation, he took her chin between his thumb and forefinger and turned her face this way and that. "More kohl on the lower eyelids, I think."

Dawn pulled back absently and pushed his hand away. "So we have specialized atmospheric alterations from this Kenro Apps. And radar from Halmann. The plans must have to do with producing some sort of antiradar thing, maybe a shield of some kind."

"Not producing it. We already have it and it's called AHSADS, an atmospheric dome to prevent any heat-seeking equipment on satellites from pinpointing human activity on the ground. The software for testing it is what they took."

Dawn experienced a chill. She stared into Eric's eyes, seeing her concern mirrored there. "To use over weapons development sites? Training facilities? God, there are any number of uses. Everybody with anything to hide from the world will want that. They can reconstruct it from the testing data, can't they? That would explain exactly how it works, what components are used and so forth?" she asked. "And if they do, it would seriously hamper our efforts to locate terrorist training camps and troop concentrations." She paused, thinking about that. "Anybody's."

He nodded slowly, holding her gaze.

"We have to get it back before they disperse it all over the place," she declared, grabbing his arm. "Our satellites would be useless."

"And seriously impact our intelligence-gathering capabilities." He placed his hand over hers where it clutched his sleeve. "They surely realize that exclusivity of the information will make it much more valuable, so it won't be offered to just anyone. I think there will be a bidding war among several potential customers who would benefit from the technology. They'll be the ones who have big bucks and also the resources to recreate it."

"Bidders like you, in your alternate persona as this Arab?"

"Yes. My job is to outbid the others while taking names. Yours is to see if the seller is the same guy you saw. I'll give you odds he's either the same dude who offed Bergen or a very close associate who'll want to be present when the deal goes down."

"Why would you think so?"

Eric's eyebrows drew together, his face unfamiliar without the light of humor. "Greed. The more partners involved in this, the less hefty the cut."

Dawn rubbed her hands together nervously, then

looked up at him. "How do you find out whom to contact and where?"

"Your None Such Agency, of course," he replied, using the sobriquet some had tacked on to her outfit back in the days when it was not supposed to exist. "Thank goodness your people at the National Security Agency have a finger on the pulse of every transmission worldwide. We'll make use of that. Or rather, *you* will, since we're well aware of what you did for NSA before you switched to fieldwork and started crawling through vents."

She laughed bitterly. "Are you kidding? They won't let me near our electronic brainiacs, not with this cloud of suspicion over my head. No way to hack into their tracking systems, either, trust me on that."

He took her hand, lacing his fingers through hers. "I do trust you, Dawn. So does Jack, or you wouldn't be here listening to all this. And," he added, with a pause for effect, "we wouldn't share the passwords we acquired."

So now he had let the cat out of the bag. She wasn't really a suspect at all. They knew she was innocent, or they'd never allow her in on something as critical as this. Her relief was so enormous, it nearly eclipsed the buzz of tension his nearness caused.

Eric sat quietly and watched while Dawn concentrated, her fingers flying over the computer keys. She had been at it for several hours. She would type like crazy, pause, cuss a little now and then, hum with satisfaction when she met with success, then repeat the process.

At Mercier's suggestion, Eric had brought her to their office in McLean where she could use the secure connections on their top-of-the-line computers in the room they called The Vault. The place always made Eric a little claustrophobic.

The fifteen-by-twenty windowless space was lead-lined and outfitted with every available protection against intrusion, physical or electronic. There was only one seriously fire-walled line leading in and out, a secure connection on which they could access whatever they needed in the way of top-secret sites.

Jack had worked for NSA and the setup here was similar, but on a much smaller scale. His former affiliations served him well in other ways, too. The passwords, however he had obtained them, got Dawn into the bank of sites set up by various terrorist organizations that NSA kept tabs on regularly.

She was searching those that might indicate new technology for sale on the underground market. Word had already gone out to less secure sites that something had recently become available. The timing of that indicated it could be the stolen data.

"Pay dirt!" Dawn whispered with excitement. "Eric, I think this is it. Look." She clicked another page on the benign-looking Web site and moved to one side so he could see. "There it is, the invitation. Arabic, French, Farsi, I think, and English."

Eric slipped on his glasses to cut the screen glare and read what she had found. "This is it! I *knew* you could do it," he said with pride.

He picked up the secure phone to Mercier's office. "Jack? We're ready to RSVP. And we have a name. An alias, of course, but we'll need to run it through Interpol and see if anything kicks out. He signs himself Quince."

"I'll handle that and join you shortly," Mercier said. He hurried into the computer room in less than five minutes.

"Good moves, Moon," he said with a perfunctory nod. "How do we explain gaining access to their exclusive client list?" Dawn asked Mercier while Eric e-mailed his acceptance, choosing his words carefully. The characters of the Arabic font strung out across the screen as he typed.

"We don't have to," Eric replied. "I'm attending as Jarad Al-Dayal, oil tycoon and secret leader of a very select Iranian group, ostensibly based in Qatar. Al-Dayal gives no explanations for his actions or how he gleans his information."

"And what if the real Al-Dayal also responds to this?"

He looked up at her as he clicked on Send. "Not a problem."

"Eric *is* Al-Dayal," Jack explained. "He is also the *group*. It has a remarkably deadly reputation in the world community, considering it has done absolutely nothing in the way of terrorist acts."

The computer pinged. In unison, they turned, staring at the message on the screen.

"Bingo. We have a destination," Jack murmured softly, as if the messenger could overhear. "You'll need to get going ASAP."

Dawn's lips rounded in a soundless, "Oh." Then her eyes narrowed. "This says Leros. Isn't that Greek?"

"Leros is in the middle of the Aegean, between Greece and Turkey," Eric announced.

"A Greek Island?"

He nodded. "And a fairly large one with a big tourist population. It's a much better location than I figured we'd draw. My money would have been on Qatar or Jordan, at best. Maybe we can ditch the chador and buy you a swimsuit."

Jack cleared his throat and looked disapproving. "You know that Leros is probably only your first stop. My guess is one of the privately owned islands where it will be next to impossible to get backup to you."

Eric smiled slyly. "I trust you'll *try,* Jack."

Mercier spoke to Dawn, ignoring Eric's aside. "If you would, please back us out of the connection without leaving traces. The plane is waiting. I'll call about the flight plan."

"What about a change of clothes?" she asked, her eyes on the screen as she pecked away at the keyboard. "I am *not* wearing these for the third day in a row."

"Taken care of," Eric said, "Trust me, everything's been ordered and you won't lack for clothes."

He saw her chin come up, a sure sign of rebellion. "I'd rather have picked out my own stuff, thank you very much. And besides that, you could have given me a little more warning that we fly immediately. I might have had things to take care of before we left."

"We've paid your utility bill," he assured her. "And you don't have a cat. The plants can be replaced. Your dieffenbachia is dying, anyway. You overwater."

"Since you've never seen my apartment, I'm not even asking how you know that," she snapped. "We're not flying commercial, I take it."

Eric laughed. "With all my oil money? Are you kidding? Private jet. Straight flight to Athens and a hop from there to Leros."

She gave a mirthless little laugh. He noticed her fingers tremble slightly over the keys when she paused to wait for a prompt. Was she nervous, scared or just eager to get under way?

This mission was unlike anything she had ever been involved with. He wished he could give her a hug right now, take her in his arms and promise her that she would be fine, that he would never take her with him if he didn't believe she could pull it off. There was no point beginning their partnership with a lie, however.

Maybe it would help if he let her know that her personal safety was one of his main concerns. Or maybe it wouldn't help. It could throw her off her game. It could throw him, too. The mission had to take precedence, and they both needed to keep that foremost in their minds.

Mercier was watching them closely, his shrewd gray gaze flicking from one to the other. Eric gave him a thumbs-up and then placed a hand on Dawn's shoulder and squeezed. Her muscles tensed beneath his palm and he could tell what an effort she made to steady her breathing.

Dawn was no novice in this business. He needed to stop worrying about her and coddling her. Nothing would undermine her self-confidence quicker than that.

Eric suddenly experienced a pang of gut-wrenching apprehension, but quickly dismissed it. He couldn't function in this role if he lost his absolute belief in the success of the mission. He also couldn't operate efficiently if he kept allowing that lovely little body of hers to snag his attention and work him into a sweat.

She finished exiting the program, got up from the chair and stretched.

"I'll transmit whatever we can find on this Quince while you're in flight," Mercier said.

Time for a test, one Eric felt extremely reluctant to make, but it had to be done. The removing-glasses trick had not worked with Dawn. He had tried it twice and given up. But Jack was a good subject, one he'd never had problems reading before and usually without even trying.

Eric took off his glasses and looked directly at Jack, fully expecting to glean whether the boss had anything in mind he wasn't saying. Nothing. Not even the white noise that usually accompanied an unsuccessful attempt to read someone. However, the failed attempt didn't worry Eric especially in spite of the surprise it provided. Maybe it was the room itself hampering things. God knows it blocked out everything else.

He slid his glasses back on and shook Jack's hand. They didn't say goodbye. He noted that Dawn followed suit, merely inclining her head to Mercier. Her lips were firm, her stance confident. Together they left silently and hurried down the hallway.

"If you're Al-Dayal, what's my name?" she demanded as he ushered her out to the car. She still wore that obstinate look, one that warned him she might be masking fear with anger.

"Aurora, my second wife. It means Dawn."

"I know that." She frowned up at him as she got into the vehicle. "Give me a break. So where is number one spouse these days?"

He peered down, keeping his expression serious. "No longer with us. She refused to follow orders."

"Okay, hotshot. I get the picture," she snapped as she grabbed the handle and slammed the door, nearly catching his fingers in the process.

He rounded the car and got in. Dawn being a little angry was better than Dawn shaking in her boots, he supposed, but she would have to get over both reactions and do it pretty damn quick. When they arrived at their destination, he needed a calm, subordinate spouse who would stay in the background. Somehow Eric had trouble imagining that.

He sighed and shook his head as he looked over at her and stuck the key in the ignition.

She was probably nervous as hell, but she was concealing it pretty well. Everything about this mission would be as foreign to her as a trip to Mars. He wished she were better equipped, that he could prepare her adequately, but there simply wasn't time for a full indoctrination. He'd just have to help her wing it.

Dawn appeared anything but subservient, and he wasn't altogether sure she could fake that. "Look, you *can* do this, okay?" he said.

She yanked her seat belt across her slender curves, clicked it in place and huffed. "Of course I can do this. I'll just pretend I'm my great-grandmother."

Eric cranked the car and pulled away from the curb, laughing. "Honey, I can't believe the women in your family were servile even that far back."

"Well, she managed up to a point. Until about two years into the marriage, so I was told."

Did he dare ask? "What happened then?"

Dawn smiled, eyes narrowed menacingly. "Granny got fed up and nailed his butt to the wall."

"Figuratively speaking, I hope."

"She shot him in the behind with a load of bird shot. I hear he never walked quite right after that."

Eric winced. "Can you restrain yourself for a week or so, you think?"

Dawn shrugged. "Probably, but just in case, we'd better not drag this out any longer than we have to."

"Ten days, absolute max, I figure."

Eric fully meant to keep to that deadline, but not because he thought for a second she would blow her cool and endanger the mission. Despite her bragging about her granny's dubious antics, Dawn was too much the professional to act out when their very lives depended on it.

If the deal had not gotten under way within a week, Eric knew he would probably be a dead customer and Dawn along with him. It would mean they had been made.

Chapter 5

"How beautiful!" Dawn rarely gushed, but it was hard not to when flying fairly low over the blue Aegean and its green and white dots of paradise. "I'm coming back here for vacation one day."

"Yeah, you should take a yacht tour to Marathi. That's fantastic and fairly inexpensive," Eric advised. "Not too touristy or cluttered."

She turned to smile at him. "I take it you've been here before?"

He nodded and pointed out the window. "That speck off to the right is Horio, I think. Used to be a sponge-harvesting island, but most of that trade moved to Florida when the sponges died out here." He buckled his seat belt.

"Have you spoken with Mercier?" she asked, more interested in the mission now than the sight below.

"While you were sleeping. He ran the name Quince

through all sources and thinks he might have a hit. A Greek by the name of Stefan Cydonia, a mercenary known for his involvement in weapons dealing. He's dealt in uranium and some other components used to make WMDs, too. If it's him, he's an arrogant bastard. Cydonia is Latin for quince."

"So he's suspect because he's a Greek, his name means quince and this meeting is ostensibly set for somewhere in the Greek Isles?" she asked. "Makes sense to me."

"He was involved in an illegal arms deal years ago in Baden-Baden, Germany. We had some pretty good intel on that, but he managed to escape. That's how he got on our 'to watch' list and gained probable credit for some other deals in the same vein."

"I'm impressed. Do we have his address, by any chance?"

Eric shook his head. "No luck there. No usable photos, either. He has managed to stay off the radar for nearly a decade."

"What else do we know about him?" Dawn asked, intrigued and eager to know who they were up against.

"Very little, but Jack's working on that. We'll be landing soon."

No sooner had he said that than their captain announced they were approaching the international airport in Athens.

Two other men accompanied them on the plane, both very large bodyguard types wearing regular business suits and the traditional headpieces of Eric's bogus homeland. One was called Ressam. He was a dour man with darting eyes and quick movements. He reminded her of a ferret.

The other, Eric introduced as Clay Senate, a fellow Sextant agent also in disguise going by the name of Adil. It was impossible to determine what his nationality might be. He stood well over six feet tall, had a light reddish-brown complexion, wise gray-green eyes and faintly

oriental features. His formidable height and build were reassuring, and he was definitely an easy guy to look at. Pity
he was so stoic and never smiled. She hoped that was just
part of his current disguise and not his real demeanor.

When Eric warned her not to speak with either man except
in an emergency because it was forbidden, Dawn knew the
ruse had begun in earnest. She was now Aurora, wife of
Jarad Al-Dayal, wealthy oil magnate and closet terrorist.

The private jet impressed Dawn, as did the clothing she
had been provided. In the smaller piece of her Vuitton
luggage that he had told her to open, there were a couple of
the traditional robes Eric had warned her she would have to
wear, but also included were casual outfits appropriate for
a vacation in the warm climes of Greece and the islands.

At Eric's direction, she had napped in the cabin at the
back of the plane, which contained a bedroom with a king-
size bed sporting satin sheets. She had showered in the fantastic bathroom with its gold fittings and fancy soaps,
amazed that the bronze tan he'd sprayed on her didn't seem
to fade at all. Then she had applied her makeup—heavy on
the kohl shadow, as Eric had suggested—and dressed in
lightweight summer slacks and a pink silk tank top. Her
strappy little sandals probably cost more than her entire
wardrobe back home.

Eric was resplendent, dressed for show as a young oil
tycoon from the Middle East. The dark mustache was new
and looked perfectly real and at home above his finely
sculpted mouth. What a change from the handsome but
terse government agent she had first met in that interrogation room. Then later, at his place, he had become that
teasing, slightly rowdy blond jock. Was that his natural self,
or yet another guise?

She reminded herself once again that she must keep in

mind how easily this guy switched gears. How could any woman ever trust a man like Vinland? She still had no idea who he really was at heart or what the heck he was going to do next. Maybe that was the main part of his charm, that unpredictability.

But for now, Dawn knew she was completely in his hands whether she liked it or not. "Where do we go first?"

"Through security, then customs. Then we reboard for the flight to Leros."

Eric adjusted his ghutra. "Remember you are supposed to be Andorran. When you speak, use English with a Spanish accent. English will be our common language since it's the one I would be most likely to know with my Oxford education. You'll have to suit up before we deplane. Where's your stuff?"

"In the bedroom, laid out on the bed. You'll have to show me what goes where."

He smiled rather evilly, teasing her again. Dawn knew it was his way of trying to put her at ease, so she didn't even pretend to take offense.

"You'd better wear this, too," he said, reaching under his robes to retrieve a small box. In it were a gold band and an enormous diamond solitaire. He slipped both on her finger.

She stretched out her arm to view the rings from a distance. "Tell me this rock is not the real deal."

"Oh yes, darling. Only the most ostentatious for my missus," he assured her. Then he grinned. "On loan with the rest of the bling-bling, so don't lose anything down a drain or you'll be in hock for life."

"The clothes are loaners, too, right?" she asked.

"No, those are yours."

Dawn's eyes widened as she looked at him in wonder. "Really?" She ought to protest, but couldn't bring herself to do it. Though she had seen only a portion of the things someone had packed for her, those she had seen were absolutely fantastic. Expensive. Gorgeous. Made her feel like a million. Looking that way was the whole point, of course.

She chalked it up to a clothing allowance that beat all. Or maybe hazard pay. She'd probably earn the new duds in spades before this was over.

Twenty minutes later, they landed and were greeted by several official-looking men wearing suits.

Covered head to foot in blue, heavily embroidered flowing silk, Dawn kept her gaze lowered. Her face, hands and feet were the only parts of her visible to others. She stayed in Eric's wake while he hammed it up in his new role. He gave the word *pompous* new meaning, but certainly looked grand enough to carry it off with panache.

After they entered the building, she experienced a few minutes of apprehension when they were separated. A female attendant guided her to a private room where Dawn was politely, but very thoroughly, searched. Not a pleasant experience, but tolerable. The wait to get back to Eric and their two bodyguards seemed interminable, but she guessed that was to be expected, too.

She thought she noted a look of relief in his eyes when she rejoined him later. Or maybe he was only squinting from the contacts he was wearing. She missed the glasses.

She blinked and looked down at her hands with their newly tanned skin, natural-colored nails and enormous diamond, and didn't recognize them as her own. This was too weird.

The short flight to the island of Leros and limousine trip to the Milos hotel proved uneventful and was virtually silent. Surprisingly, she missed the easy banter with Eric. But the bodyguards sat across from them, vigilant and fierce-looking as Dobermans. Even though Dawn knew whose side they were on, their somber presence discouraged any conversation.

When she and Eric were alone at last, Dawn quickly removed the confining outer garments and drew in a deep breath. They were staying at a new and very exclusive hotel near the black-sand beach. The place must have been constructed especially for visiting royalty. Though the outside looked relatively modest and in keeping with the simple local architecture, the interior was downright fantastic.

"This place would wow Trump," she muttered.

Eric tossed his head-covering onto the sofa of the sitting room and glared at her. "Silence, woman!" he snapped, then covered her mouth with his hand to keep her from spouting the sharp comeback she had in mind.

Dawn realized at once he thought the place might be wired. He moved his hand and gestured to one of the doors leading off the sitting room. In the bathroom, he turned on the shower and left it running.

Immediately, he moved close to her, embraced her carefully and whispered into her ear, "Wherever we are, assume that everything we say and do is monitored. Especially here. The Milos is the only five-star around and the one in which I, as Al-Dayal, would be most likely to stay. If our rooms aren't bugged, then we're dealing with amateurs."

Dawn nodded, trying to ignore the closeness of his body, his exotic scent and the feel of his palm on her cheek. She could kick herself for not thinking of wires first thing. It was a simple matter for a bribed employee to plant listening devices. That could have been the porter who accompanied them to the room with their luggage, a concierge ordered to dash up to see that all was in order, or whoever had delivered the fresh arrangement of flowers minutes before they arrived.

Eric continued, his voice barely audible, his fake mustache tickling her ear. "Stay in character. *Always,* unless I invite you out of it. I'll decide when it's safe."

She nodded again, not minding his orders in the least. He was running the op and he knew best.

Eric drew back, still holding her, and gave her a tight smile. "All right. Do not forget." Then he drew his bottom lip between his teeth and looked pensive. Tension played between them like a high-voltage current.

Dawn became very aware of his hands on her, the subtle catch in his breathing, the intoxicating sandalwood scent of him this close to her. His gaze prowled over her like a hungry lion.

Suddenly, he released her and left her there alone, quickly closing the door behind him.

Something had happened in that brief span of time and Dawn could not explain it. Sexual attraction peaking bigtime, of course, but more than that. It was as if she had felt his thoughts, his worry, even a fear that he was getting too close to her and yet not close enough. Or maybe she was projecting her own thoughts onto him because she was so reluctant to admit they were hers.

She shook her head to clear it and went to the sink to splash cold water on her face. Must be a bizarre case of jet lag, she figured. That man was seriously meddling with her objectivity and professionalism. It had to stop.

Eric felt a little more in control as he set up the laptop he'd brought with him. He sent e-mails to several contacts in Iran, a few to Saudi Arabia and a couple to various places in Europe. The messages were not important, merely for show should anyone tap into what he was doing. Unnecessary detail, maybe, but he liked to be thorough.

Later tonight, he would log on to the address furnished in the message from the seller. Instructions for the next leg of their trip could come through, then. If not, he would know he was being checked out very thoroughly. His identity would be verified with former photos and disinformation Sextant had circulated for this very purpose.

Someone would surely be comparing the fingerprints that were on file as Al-Dayal's with those he had provided on everything he had touched since entering the hotel. Dawn's had been erased from her actual records completely and replanted in all the right places. If the one doing this deal had the resources, this portion of the mission could take several days.

The concierge called and offered to set up a sight-seeing expedition for the Al-Dayals tomorrow. Eric pretended to vacillate. Should he allow his beloved wife the exposure? He even asked how private they would be.

The concierge insisted they would not be troubled by the rabble of tourists or jostled by the locals. In the end, Eric reluctantly agreed to a day of fun, sun and freedom from his spouse's usual confinement. He was the soul of benevolence, the man had told him.

Yeah, right. Eric figured Dawn would kick his butt if he left her in the room while he went out to play sheikh. Besides, this could be the setup for contact with Quince.

"Aurora!" he called to her through her bedroom door. "I have wonderful news. Come here."

She entered, wearing a bright summer shift the color of raspberries. He smiled at her as a fond husband might. "Would you care to go sailing?"

"Oh yes, master," she answered with only the smallest trace of sarcasm.

He shot her a dark look of warning.

She smiled innocently and sat beside him, her hands folded primly on her knees. "Where shall we sail, Jarad?"

"About the islands," he replied. "Perhaps we shall find a secluded beach and go for a nice swim. Would you like that, my heart?"

"Oh, above *all!*" she cried, threw her arms around his neck and kissed him soundly on the mouth.

Eric could have spanked her. Damn, she was overacting. Overacting to a wild and delicious degree, he realized as he abandoned himself and enjoyed her mouth to the fullest. His entire body reacted with a vengeance, blood rushing south from his brain like a tidal wave.

He broke the kiss, then took another angle, pressing his chest to hers until they were nearly reclining on the sofa. Only when he felt the increased pressure of her palms against his chest did he relent.

Damn, she was hot. And he was hotter. Both were hyperventilating.

She laughed as she escaped his clutches and danced back into her bedroom, shaking her finger at him over her shoulder. A quicksilver imp, that girl. And wicked.

For a minute, he was tempted to follow, just to see where things might go. But he knew how out of hand he had gotten with just the kiss, so he stayed put.

No matter how many days it lasted, this was going to be a long, long assignment.

The next morning, in deference to her role, Dawn donned modest white slacks and a loose, flowing shirt that covered her arms. She knotted her hair in a bun at her nape and covered most of it with a floral scarf in soft pastels—colors she could never have worn comfortably as a redhead.

From the jewelry case someone had provided along

with the new wardrobe, she chose gold hoop earrings and numerous bangles for her wrists. She looked prim but fashionable, she thought, as she examined her image in the mirror. Rich, too. The clothes were fantastic, their labels indicating that whoever bought them had pulled no punches where price was concerned. Had Eric chosen these and ordered them? The only opportunity he'd had was when she slept at his house. Maybe Mercier was responsible.

When she emerged from the bedroom, he smiled his approval, slipping a cell phone into his shirt pocket. He had also dressed in white, wearing shorts, a knit shirt and sneakers. It emphasized the darkness of his skin. The man looked scrumptious, but she decided she preferred him blond and without facial hair.

He stood immediately, resting his hands on his hips as he appraised her. "Excellent choice of apparel."

"Gracias. May we go now?" Dawn could not wait to get out of their rooms, or the goldfish bowl, as she was coming to think of it. Having to be seriously conscious of every single move and sound she made was driving her crazy.

He reached for her hand and she gave it. The warmth of his palm and those long, strong fingers laced between hers felt reassuring. Confidence seemed to emanate from his pores and bolster her own. Not that she didn't think she could handle the mission, but she knew she could never have done it on her own. He knew all the ropes. Master, indeed.

Clay Senate, or Adil, as he was to be called, and Ressam joined them at the elevator. Dawn lowered her gaze to the floor, but only after a lightning-quick assessment of the men who would protect them. Ressam had left off his ghutra. Clay kept his. Both men wore slacks with floral cotton shirts worn untucked to hide the weapons she knew they carried. Covered up as she was, she felt naked without hers.

She remained silent while Eric barked a few terse instructions to the men in Farsi. Were there cameras in the elevators, too? she wondered, then decided they were assuming so just in case there were.

Maybe with so many international travelers and no rules governing surveillance, the nooks and crannies of everywhere contained wires and cameras.

God, this was not what she had expected or trained for. Undercover work was not her forté. She much preferred doing sanctioned breaking and entering. Even the official hacking she had done on the computers back at headquarters before being transferred was preferable to this.

Surely on the sailboat it would be safe to be themselves again, at least for the duration of their day trip.

As if he had read her mind, Eric spoke. "Live it, Aurora," he said quietly as they exited the hotel and headed for the car that she supposed would take them to the marina.

Well, that killed that hope, Dawn thought. She had to become Aurora with no hope for a rest until this was over. "Yes, Jarad," she replied softly. "With relish, I promise."

"Good little wife," he replied under his breath. "Allah be praised."

Necessary role-playing aside, Dawn heartily wished she could kick him in the shins.

Chapter 6

"The *Angeline?* What a lovely name for a boat," Dawn said softly as she stepped carefully on board the sailing yacht. "She is very beautiful."

Eric had gone ahead of her. Ladies first did not apply as far as he was concerned. He appeared to be enjoying this charade of theirs to the max.

Dawn had kissed him last night, not just for any cameras that might be running, but also to show him he wasn't calling *all* the shots, at least not between them. The problem was that the kiss had backfired on her and she had almost lost control of it, along with her good sense. The man was no novice when it came to lip-locks, that was for sure.

He grasped her waist and lifted her onto the deck. "A top-of-the-line, forty-two-footer," he replied to her observation about the boat. "Do you know anything of yachts, my sweet?" he asked, steadying her as if she were fragile.

Dawn shook her head. "No, I have never sailed." The absolute truth. All her life, she had hated deep water. It was not a phobia, exactly, and she could swim very well, but all the same she didn't like deep water.

She glanced warily at the man standing several feet away, watching him through squinty eyes. The brown face beneath his captain's cap looked weathered, his body, lean and mean. His khaki shorts and shirt resembled a uniform. The white cap looked too new. She quickly lowered her gaze and covered her mouth with her hand as if automatically attempting to hide her face from him.

"Our captain, Mr. Kerosian," Eric announced, stepping between her and the man. "If you would go below, my dove, we will cast off. You may return to deck in a while when I come for you."

Dawn did as ordered, trying all at once to remain regal while hurrying to obey. She thought she had performed pretty well. Eric should have no reason at all to fuss about her stepping out of character.

Once in the salon, her curiosity got the better of her. She tossed her tote bag onto one of the suede-upholstered lounges, then plundered through every inch of the efficient little kitchen, the head and the two sleeping cabins. It wasn't on the scale of the private jet, but it was very luxurious for a relatively small yacht.

Though this was supposed to be a day trip and they would not be sleeping aboard, Dawn figured she might never get a chance to examine a pleasure yacht like this one again unless she found she loved sailing and then won a lottery. Neither seemed all that likely. The boat was sleek, serene and ultracomfortable.

"Is your stomach surviving, little landlubber?" Eric asked.

"Admirably," she answered, greeting him with a lift

of her chin. "I believe I am a, how would you say it, an old salty."

He laughed and glanced around the salon, taking it all in much more quickly than Dawn had done. "Well done. Come above and we will watch together for dolphins."

Dawn retied the scarf to cover her hair and buttoned her shirt up to her neck. She didn't want to risk sunburn through her artificially darkened skin. And there was her newly acquired modesty to consider.

He took her directly to the bow where they stood against the rail facing forward, Eric's arms braced on either side of her as he held the steel railing. She remained very still when he bent down and placed a kiss on her cheek, then settled his mouth next to her ear. "This is no ordinary sailboat for hire."

"I noticed," she replied, not daring even now to abandon her persona. "You are a very important man who would never settle for the ordinary, even temporarily."

"No one can hear us here. The *Angeline* is custom-made, outfitted for a private and very wealthy owner, not for tourist day trips, even for one such as Jarad Al-Dayal. I want you to be prepared. I'm certain Quince arranged for this. We might be sailing directly to his stronghold now, wherever that is. Unless this trip is simply a diversion to keep us busy until he has verified my identity. I don't believe Captain Kerosian knows which yet until he gets a call."

"I wish I were armed," she said.

One of his hands disappeared from the rail and a second later snaked around her waist to the buttons at the middle of her shirt front. Cold steel and a warm hand slid inside the gap he had unfastened. She sucked in her breath and he tucked a pistol beneath the waistband of her slacks. He smoothed the fabric down over the weapon. Dawn's heart fluttered.

"Your security blanket," he murmured with another kiss near her ear.

Dawn sighed her thanks and rested her head back against his chest, slipping back into her role as Aurora. For a long time they stood there, gazing out over the Aegean.

Suddenly, she saw them. "Look! Dolphins!" she cried, pointing. "Just as you predicted."

"What a sight," he declared as she turned to meet his gaze. "You are almost as beautiful as the moment I first saw you."

"Almost?" she asked, frowning at him.

"But not quite," he answered. "That *is* a sincere compliment, by the way."

"Then I thank you."

Why had he said that? Probably to insure that she didn't screw things up because of her independent nature. And maybe he figured she needed to hold on to her real identity. He must know how much she hated acting subservient.

"You are doing great so far," he said, corroborating her assumption about his praise. Yep, he was pulling strings. Handling her like a pro. What else should she have expected—that he was really interested in her as a woman?

Having him take a serious interest in her was not one of her ambitions, anyway. As it stood now, she had only two goals. She wanted to be known as the best damn intelligence agent in her group, and to help enhance the world's opinion of her profession, specifically female agents. To that end, she used every skill she had learned and threw herself into every mission, regardless of the personal danger. Her second aspiration did deal with men, in a way—she intended to steer clear of them emotionally and restrict her trust, at least in the personal areas of her life.

She seemed to lack the necessary intuition that most women had, and therefore had suffered not one, but two relatively sharp kicks in the teeth. She simply was no good at figuring out men and how they thought, and this particular man gave new meaning to the word *enigmatic*.

She didn't need Vinland's interest or his compliments, only his leadership on this mission and his respect when she did her job as ordered. This was business.

Dawn looked back out to sea where the dolphins leapt in unison and admired their ability to stay in synch. She hoped that she, Eric and the others could perform as precisely as those dolphins did and get this mission completed.

She could stand being Aurora, his compliant little wife, for a little while, but was in serious danger of losing herself in another way if the job with this specific Sextant agent lasted too long.

The day wore on as they tacked around the islands. Dawn tensed a bit when they docked for lunch at a quaint little bay on Kos. She hardly tasted the food that Eric consumed with gusto. However, when they reboarded the *Angeline* a couple of hours later, no one had approached them about a meeting with anyone.

Eric remained on deck and gestured for her to join him. "Shall we go for a swim? The captain says there is a perfect and very private inlet on an uninhabited island he knows about. We're headed there now."

"Your idea?" she asked quietly.

"Yes, but his choice of island," he admitted, letting her know that this could be the rendezvous point with Quince if that was what the captain had been hired to arrange.

"Sounds lovely. Shall I go and change?" At his insistence, she had brought a bathing suit and beach cover in her tote.

"No, we will change after we get out there." He got up and took her hand.

She was getting way too used to holding hands with him, Dawn thought. But to anyone watching, she figured it would seem a natural thing for a recently married couple to do.

Dawn hung back while the captain advised Eric that he would drop anchor just offshore and let the two of them swim to the beach. Damned difficult to do without someone noticing a gun tucked in your swimwear, she thought.

"Impossible!" Eric declared, red in the face and spouting the proper outrage. "I insist you lower the inflatable for us. I will not allow another man's eyes to view my wife uncovered enough to go swimming!"

The captain shrugged as if it didn't matter to him and set about doing as Eric demanded. Ressam gave him a hand with the inflatable, then stood away.

In moments, she and Eric were motoring to the pristine, unspoiled beach that appeared to be shielded completely by rough, rocky cliffs.

He cut the motor and they stepped out into knee-deep surf. She helped him tug the rubber dinghy up onto the shore where it would not be washed back out by the gentle waves.

"So what do we do now?" she asked, her hands propped on her hips.

"Stop looking so saucy and get out of sight behind that outcropping over there while you change." He mugged at her and mouthed the word parabolics.

Was he kidding? Parabolic mikes? Out here? She must have shown her disbelief because he nodded emphatically. Maybe he wasn't paranoid. Or even if he was, who was she to knock that? It would probably be what kept them alive. She obeyed, as usual, and went behind the rocks. But she did not undress right away. What if there were cameras, too?

Nonsense. Parabolic microphones that could aim and

eavesdrop at a distance, she might buy, but video was a reach. Still, she scanned the cliffs very carefully, then looked out to sea. The *Angeline* was the only craft visible.

That was when she saw Eric climbing up the face of one cliff, already about three-quarters of the way up. No rope, no belay pins, nothing but his bare hands and feet.

Dawn covered her mouth to keep from crying out, startling him and causing him to fall. Instead she watched, fascinated by the play of muscles in his calves and forearms as he gripped, reached and gripped again. Terrified for him, she held her breath and prayed for his safety.

The moments crawled by like hours. Finally, he hefted himself up onto the ledge and stood, surveying the portion of the island hidden from her view.

He turned and looked down, waving. She raised her hand tentatively and waved back. Surely he would find an easier way down. Hope fled when he dropped to his stomach, legs hanging over the edge, feet searching for purchase.

"Idiot," she whispered to herself. "What the devil is he thinking?"

Well, whatever that was, she refused to watch any longer. Instead, she whipped off her shirt. Careful to keep the large rock outcroppings between her and those who might view her from the yacht, Dawn had changed and reached the water's edge by the time Eric joined her.

"The place is clear," he assured her. "I could see the entire island from up there and it's uninhabited, only rocks and seabirds. No mikes and no cameras. I believe this is a test and also a diversion to keep us busy until Quince can check us out with his sources."

He zoomed past her and splashed into the water. Dawn followed. When he surfaced next to her after a dive, he said, "Might as well enjoy ourselves while we wait for the real summons. I figure we probably have a couple of days to kill."

She was in over her head in all respects. He looked so damn good with his muscles all wet and shiny, his teeth gleaming when he smiled, his eyes twinkling. She missed the incredible blue of his eyes that was nearly the same color as the azure water in which they swam.

His hands gripped her waist as she treaded water to stay afloat. "Dawn, are you all right? You haven't said a word. No one can hear us here."

She blew out a breath and raked her wet hair off her face. "Shouldn't we be making a plan? Deciding what we should do when we meet with Quince?"

"I told you already before we flew out. I make an offer, buy the gizmo with the information on it and we leave. Someone else will do the actual cleanup. My job is to get in, get the goods and get out. Yours is to identify the shooter if he's there."

She moved her legs, brushing against his, wishing he would turn her loose so she could breathe evenly and get her equilibrium back.

"You stay out of the confrontation so you can maintain this disguise for the next time something like this comes along?" she asked, trying hard to concentrate on aspects of the mission and not the proximity of that heat-seeking missile she felt against her stomach.

He shrugged one shoulder and smiled. "Jarad's persona has come in handy a few times. Hate to ditch a good alternate identity just to collar Quince myself."

"What if he's copied the information? Suppose he intends to sell it more than once?"

"He advertised exclusive use of it when he put out the word. He's gotta know he'd get himself killed for double-dealing. No, all his bidders will be in one place and our people will make sure none of them leave with what they came after. I'll outbid them all, anyway."

It sounded too easy to her. "So we just...buy it and go?"

He smiled, looking straight into her eyes. "*I* buy it and we go. You remain in the background, very low profile. Your only job is to see whether Quince is the one who killed Bergen or if it was a close associate of his who is present when we have the meeting."

She pushed at his hands until he released her. "I'm not in the mood to swim. Let's go."

He turned her around so that she faced the beach. "Stay in front of me till we get behind the rocks. Jarad can't let the others see that lovely bod of yours from the boat."

"They probably saw me get into the water," she reminded him. "Jarad didn't seem to care then."

"Yeah, but that thong is way too enticing to give them a rear view."

"It is *not* a thong!" she argued.

"Close enough. That's the one thing I didn't choose for you. I asked for a modest two-piece swimsuit. Maybe they don't even make those anymore." He sounded so disgruntled.

She half turned to glare at him. "You picked out the clothes? When?"

"While you were sleeping. Now get a wiggle on. We've got to sit behind those rocks long enough for me to have my wicked way with you."

She shrieked in protest when he goosed her waist.

"Not really," he assured her, laughing. "Just for show."

Right. Dawn wished her pulse would quit racing. Her blood just would not behave when he was this close, especially not when he was talking so casually about having sex. Even the pretense of having it.

"I can handle this," she said to herself. "I can."

"Sure you can. Never doubted it for a minute," he said, following close behind her as she waded out of the surf. "Now get your pretty little butt behind that rock. The captain's binoculars are probably glowing red with the heat from his hands."

Dawn laughed with him. "You are impossible!"

"Possible," he argued. "Very possible. Try me."

"Not on a dare," Dawn muttered. Not on a double-dog dare, she added to herself.

They remained behind the rocks for about half an hour. Eric stretched out on the sand, head resting on his hands, and fell sound asleep. Dawn sat there fuming. The least he could have done was talk to her while they knew they had no listeners.

She spent the time brushing off sand and donning her slacks and shirt. When he woke, she was dressed and more than ready to climb into the inflatable and get back to work. Damn the man.

Back in Leros at the hotel, Dawn passed the time watching television she couldn't understand and looking at pamphlets on the local sights and those on the mainland of Greece. The area had never been on her list of places she wanted to visit until now. How beautiful it was, a veritable paradise.

Eric went out periodically and left her alone in the suite. The first time he did, he put on his superprotective husband attitude and gave her a weapon. "If anyone enters, shoot them," he ordered. Dawn's mouth had dropped open in surprise and disbelief that he would say that aloud. "I have left precise instructions that no one is to knock or come into our rooms. If they do so, you are to shoot them, do you understand?"

She already had the pistol he'd given her on the boat tucked away in her purse. This one must be for show, a warning to anyone listening, that she was armed. She held the gun loosely in her hand, as any wife without weapons training would do when handed one. "But why?" she asked meekly.

He glared at her, looking for all the world like the man he was supposed to be. "You must know how vulnerable you are to abduction. I am a wealthy man, Aurora. It would be a simple matter for someone to snatch you away from me and demand a fortune. If that happens, I warn you, I will not submit to it. So protect yourself."

"Very well, Jarad," she said, laying the pistol on the cushions next to her. "But what of you? Have you another one of these?"

"Of course," he replied with a condescending smile. "Not to worry. I shall return in a while. One day before we leave, I will take you around the town so that you might shop. Would that make you happy?"

"Delirious," she cooed, beaming up at him, going for coy. "I shall choose something wildly expensive!"

He laughed, but it sounded forced. "A woman of simple tastes. Silks and diamonds. What was I thinking when I married you?" With that, he leaned down and kissed her briefly on the forehead. "Be good, Aurora."

"As if I have a choice," she murmured under her breath as he left. She heard the click of the automatic lock when he closed the door and felt trapped in a gilded prison. What she wouldn't give to put on shorts and a halter top and stroll the streets of Leros by herself.

A wife such as Aurora Al-Dayal would feel the same if an overbearing and authoritative husband ordered her to stay put while he took in the glorious sights outside. A woman like Aurora might even slip out of the hotel and risk the consequences of her husband's anger if tempted that way. But Dawn knew better than to entertain the thought.

Strange eyes might be watching, ears listening, her every move monitored. Defiance would be highly unprofessional, not to mention possibly fatal. With a sigh, she went back to her magazine with the enticing pictures of all she was missing.

After two full days of seclusion, Dawn's nerves were on edge. When Eric returned that afternoon, Aurora made a few demands of her own. "Take me out as you promised, Jarad. I wish it."

He cocked a dark eyebrow and smiled the patronizing smile she hated. In her mind, she knew it was only part of the role he played, but the entire ruse was becoming somehow real to her. She had begun to feel more like Aurora than the fiercely independent Dawn Moon.

"Now?" he asked idly, strolling over to the window and parting the drapery to look out.

"Yes," she said, almost desperately, almost forgetting her accent. "Today. This moment."

"Put on your chador."

"Must I?" she asked, risking his anger. Rather, Jarad's anger, she reminded herself. Eric would understand.

"Yes, you must," he answered curtly. "This is not Andorra and you are no longer a schoolgirl. There are rules and you agreed to them when we married."

Then he sighed and dropped the curtain back in place, turning to her with outstretched hands. "I know things are changing. Perhaps I cling too fiercely to the old ways." He pondered for a minute, rubbing his chin. "All right, you may leave it off, but only for today."

"Thank you, husband," Dawn murmured, wanting to smack him upside his head. "You are generous to a fault."

She wasted no time getting dressed. Blue raw-silk slacks and a matching shirt looked smart and felt comfortable as well as cool. Instead of a scarf, she tucked her hair beneath a crushable straw hat of bright white that would shade her face. For good measure, she added dark sunglasses and the Beretta to a white crocheted sack purse and went to stand inspection.

"Very cosmopolitan," he commented dryly. "At least you are modest."

Together they went out into the bright afternoon. Dawn wanted to crow with delight. The air didn't get much fresher than this, she thought.

With a spring in her step, she marched along beside Eric as he took her straight to a jeweler and purchased her a bracelet that would wipe out a year's salary if she kept it.

"Image," he whispered, as if he needed to remind her why her wrist was dripping with precious stones. Everything would be returned, of course. She knew that. Even the clothes, no matter what he said or what she wanted. She could not, in good conscience, keep those designer labels bought with government money, no matter how slushy the black op funds might be.

Dawn promptly forgot all of that as Eric drove her around the island in their rented vintage convertible. The two bodyguards rode in back, eyes forever scanning the streets, storefronts and roadsides.

There were people around, ostensibly tourists, who kept turning up at the same sites. They weren't too numerous, but enough so that it was difficult for her to determine whether any of them were actually following to keep up with Eric's little sightseeing expedition.

They climbed to the castle built by the fourteenth-century Knights of St. John as a defense against invaders. "It's so huge! And so old," she whispered. "Awe-inspiring."

"At night they light it. Glows like something you would imagine in a fairy tale," Eric told her. "Can you fathom the difficulty in constructing something like this here on such a small island over five hundred years ago? Think of the manpower and engineering it would have taken."

They did not enter the church built within the castle. Though she truly wanted to see inside it, she did not ask. They were supposed to be of the Islamic faith, not Christian. To enter there would be forbidden. Later she would come back, Dawn promised herself.

Together they visited several of the inlets on the island with their picturesque villages of white houses trimmed in blue. Hand in hand, she and Eric strolled along the beaches barefoot while their well-armed shadows followed, ever vigilant for a threat of any kind.

When dusk came, they headed back toward the hotel, tired and hungry. Eric stopped at a small restaurant in a village that was inland, well back from the coast. "I'm famished," he announced. He ushered her out of the car and into the humble structure. Clay and Ressam remained outside.

"We need to talk," he told her when they were seated. "Here we won't be overheard."

"You're sure?" she asked, looking around them. One old man wearing an apron scurried toward them. The only other customers sat well across the room out of earshot, a couple who were obviously enthralled with each other and had been for a while.

"Certain." Eric greeted their server and ordered.

This was the first meal she had consumed in public since they had arrived four days ago. Already she had her favorites among the local dishes, thanks to room service.

"Tonight, something new," Eric told her. "You must try the tzatziki."

"Not snails, is it?" she asked, wrinkling her nose.

"Yogurt and cucumber dip. With pickled octopus, of course."

She grimaced again. "You said that with a straight face. You really eat that stuff?"

"You can't live on salad alone. We're having moussaka, too. You'll like that."

She recognized the eggplant-and-meat dish she had grown quite fond of. "Wish I could try the ouzo since I've heard so much about it."

"No booze. Sorry. But I promise no more goat's milk. I ordered tea."

When his hand moved over hers, she didn't pull away. At this point, she needed a human touch more than she needed food. He had not really touched her, except inadvertently, in a couple of days now.

If someone were watching them every minute at the hotel, wouldn't they find that odd? She couldn't ask him that, however. If she did, he might think she was suggesting they actually do something married people would do.

His fingers played with hers as their eyes met over the small table. "How are you holding up?"

"Going bonkers with the waiting. Will this show ever get on the road?"

"Soon. We're leaving for Kos tomorrow."

She sat up straight and gripped his hand. "You heard from him?"

Eric nodded. "He called this morning and left a message at the desk. The instructions were very precise. We're to go on the *Angeline*."

Dawn considered that. "So you were right. Our sail was a test."

"I think we've passed on all counts. The invitation indicates that. Or else he has us pegged and intends to kill us. You ready to rock and roll?" He grinned and wriggled his eyebrows, letting her see the old Eric behind the usually stern, brown-eyed mask of Jarad Al-Dayal. The sight was disconcerting, to say the least. It also proved to be comforting.

Dawn ate with relish when the meal arrived, fueling up for the action. Adrenaline would probably keep her from sleeping a wink tonight.

Clay was gone when they exited the restaurant. Dawn didn't ask where he was and Ressam didn't say. He never said anything. Eric did not appear to be concerned. The ride back to their hotel was short and uneventful.

When they reached their floor and got off the elevator, Clay was waiting. He spoke with Eric for a minute, his voice so low she couldn't hear a thing he said. Then he accompanied Ressam down the hallway, leaving her and Eric alone to enter the suite.

"You have what you wanted. Go to bed now," he ordered, fully into Jarad mode. However, when she obeyed without question, he soon followed her into her bedroom and shut the door.

Dawn looked the question she wanted to ask, but didn't speak. "We can talk freely in here," he told her. "Clay swept the rooms. There are no cameras, except outside by the elevator to keep tabs on everyone's comings and goings. He left two mikes working in the sitting lounge and my room and deactivated the one in here. I thought you might rest better and you *will* need a good night's sleep."

"Won't whoever is listening in suspect something's up?"

Eric made himself at home by flopping down on her bed, his head resting on his hands. "If Clay had done this to begin with, they probably would. Now they'll think it's an equipment malfunction since it's only the one mike he tampered with. He's very good at what he does."

Dawn sat down on the edge of the bed and kicked off her sandals. "It was a lovely afternoon and evening. Thank you for that." His smile drew her like a warm caress.

No sooner had she thought that than he reached out and touched her arm, his palm and fingers hot against her skin. "You needed it. You were wound tight as a top string."

This was only her third mission in the field and on the other two, her life was never at risk. She had barely gotten started in fieldwork. Dawn felt justified in being a little nervous about it.

"I know this kind of thing is new to you," he said, "but you were trained well and you're doing fine."

"For someone inexperienced?"

"For anyone. You're a good actress. You won't slip up. I know it. Your record with NSA is excellent."

"That's hardly fair. They should have let me read yours."

He rolled over on his side so that his stomach rested lightly against her lower back and propped his head on one hand. She felt the hand that had caressed her arm come to rest between her shoulder blades, rubbing lightly. "This is not a come-on, by the way," he said seriously.

She turned a little and faced him, feeling bold as she looked into his eyes. "Why not?"

His smile was wry and a little regretful. "I think you know why not."

Dawn felt such an affinity for this man. Such a connection. And such an overpowering need to get closer. She figured that this tension between them was as wicked a distraction as anything. Relieving it could only help, she rationalized. Once they put out the fire, maybe she could think straight. On impulse, she leaned down and met his lips with hers, then drew back to look at him again. "That *was* a come-on, by the way."

"I know," he whispered, still stroking her back. "This is a distraction we can't afford, Dawn," he warned, but his expression displayed another message entirely.

"I can," she told him, feeling bold and incredibly turned on. Oddly enough, she felt she could say anything, no matter how outrageous, to him. Caution flew right out the window, just like that.

Chapter 7

Eric stifled a groan of frustration. The point was to do the right thing here. The thing he had intended when he had instructed Clay to find any listening or surveillance devices in the room. If he'd had any sense, he would have begun doing that the moment he closed the door instead of taking a while to get her comfortable and reassure her.

She wanted him. God knows he wanted her more every second he spent with her and that wasn't going away, no matter how hard he tried to deny it. But Dawn didn't really know him, couldn't even guess what he was capable of. But she needed to.

She only saw the chameleon. That had sparked some interest, maybe. Could be that she saw him as a sort of mentor, too. He had been doing undercover work for quite a while now. This was not only Dawn's first mission outside the scope of her regular security duties, but also her first international assignment. That made her dependent on his expertise.

The real truth about him would probably scare her or at least put her off. He doubted she would believe him at first, but he could convince her. She deserved to know the truth before they went into the final phase of this mission. It could save her life, or his. And she certainly should know what she was up against on a personal front. That was only fair.

Resolved, Eric sat up and took her by the shoulders and looked into her eyes. "There's something I have to tell you, Dawn."

She blinked and looked away. "I knew it. You're already involved. Or married?"

"No way, not even close. I would have told you that in the beginning." He took a deep breath and went for it. "You have to know what I'm about to tell you because it's who I am. If you don't know it, then you don't know me."

"So let's have it. What are you?" she asked, tracing his chin with her finger. "A vampire or something?"

He shook his head. "I'm able to *see* certain things normal people can't."

One corner of her lips rose in a very wry half smile. "Oh, fascinating. You see dead people? Find missing objects? What?"

Eric released her and pushed himself back against the headboard, crossing his arms over his chest. "Both, if conditions are right. I'm a telepath and a clairvoyant."

She rolled her eyes and laughed. "This is absolutely the worst line I have *ever* heard for sidestepping an unwanted advance. Stop it."

"This has nothing to do with sidestepping anything. I'm telling you that I'm a psychic, Dawn."

Tongue in cheek, she regarded him closely. "All right, Kreskin. Then tell me what I'm thinking right now."

"You'd like to strangle me with my own tie?"

"You aren't wearing a tie," she reminded him, leaning back on her arms, kicking one foot idly, or maybe nervously, against the bottom edge of the bed. "But that would be a natural reaction to a man explaining to me why he's unavailable, wouldn't you say? Especially when the reason he gives is so weird. No special skills needed to figure that out."

Again he sighed, and nodded. "Yeah, I guess it would be. See, what I would like to do with you is not possible, at least not right now."

Her gaze narrowed. "Try not *ever*. This is so lame it's funny. All you had to say was no. I'm not so dense that I need some fairy tale excuse for a turndown."

"If I'm freaking you out with this, I'm sorry, but it is true."

Her lips firmed, then relaxed as she spoke and cast him a sidewise look. "Speaking of mental vibes, you've been sending me signals since the minute I first met you, Eric. All those little touches, looks that could scorch, kissing me back the way you did. Tell me I read all that wrong."

"You didn't." He ignored her rising anger and continued explaining. "I want you, Dawn, make no mistake about that. But if you and I get too into each other, it could really interfere with my perceptions of other people, like Quince."

She got up and walked over to the bathroom, turning, with one hand on the door frame. "Tell you what, just in case your wavelengths are not fully operational at the moment. You go to your room and mind-meld with anybody you damn well please while I take a shower. Then I'm going to sleep and forget you exist, okay?"

"Wait, Dawn. This has to do with our mission, too. You need to let me finish."

"You *are* finished. Seems like you would have divined that already since you claim to be so *perceptive*."

"It's why I'm in Sextant," he added anyway. "All of us have some form of special powers, even if it's just lucky hunches that always play out. My particular aptitude exceeds that. I—"

"So go bend a spoon!" she snapped, then whisked into the bathroom and slammed the door.

Eric stared at the barrier between them and exhaled the breath he'd caught and held at the exceptional sight of Dawn in full-blown fury.

"That went well," he muttered to himself and got up off her bed where he had no business being in the first place.

An hour later in his own room, he closed his laptop. The coded message he had sent Mercier and the answer to it had done nothing to further the mission.

Quince remained a mystery. No one knew where he was. No objects were available that he might have touched that could conduct the necessary energy for Eric to locate him. Until they actually met, Eric had no way to get inside the man's mind and determine the extent of his plans.

He realized he could think of no way to prove to Dawn that he had the capability to do that. Eric had never been able to read her at all unless what she was feeling appeared on that lovely face of hers for anyone to see. Maybe he could fake it that way.

Somehow, he needed to get past Dawn's defenses and make her believe him. The more he thought about what had happened between them, the worse he felt.

Hell truly had no fury like a woman scorned, and that was what Dawn felt he had done, scorned her. However, if he had made love to her the way they both wanted and she found out what he was like later, she would probably hate him. And as he had told her, there was a distinct possibility that it might skew any readings he got from anyone else if his mind was preoccupied with her.

It bothered him that he'd had no luck reading the concierge or the captain of the *Angeline*. Clay was usually a snap. Ressam was sometimes a little difficult, but not impossible. Eric hadn't fully tested his ability on them, not since he had met Dawn. Suppose it didn't work? What would he do when he needed to read Quince or others who were critical to the mission's success?

What if his only hope of getting his powers back was to break down Dawn's defenses? Could he make himself do that? Was he even able to? If he did, how could they hope to have anything approaching a normal relationship? He would have too much of an advantage and she'd soon come to resent that, not to mention how she'd hate the invasion of privacy it involved.

However, her safety, maybe even her survival, might depend on their being able to communicate, and he couldn't ignore that. Tomorrow was D-day and he suspected he had left giving her this information until it was too late. They would not be able to deviate from their new personas once she came out of her bedroom tomorrow morning. If he was to have any success in letting her know how he intended to work this op and what his real mission was, it had to be tonight.

He tugged on his robe and headed back to her bedroom. The door was locked, but he had expected that. He slipped the credit card he'd tucked in his pocket between the door and frame and entered. The lights were off, the curtains drawn, the room black as pitch.

"Dawn?" he said softly.

"Good way to get yourself shot," she replied out loud as she punched the light switch, nearly blinding him.

Eric blinked and turned. She stood behind him, weapon in hand, wearing the slinky little slip thing he had ordered for her travel wardrobe. It was teal, setting off her fake tan and dark hair to perfection. In his mind, he pictured how much better it would complement her fairer complexion and red hair once she could abandon her disguise. But the pistol she held intruded on that thought. He could be entertaining a bullet if she hadn't hesitated.

"Get out," she advised him. Her tone sounded soft, but deadly. "Now, Vinland."

"Unless you plan to shoot, put that thing away. I have to talk to you, and this is no time for either of us to let personal feelings intrude. That's an order."

She lowered the gun and shrugged. "Official and offensive. Try to stay that way."

"Sit down and listen to me, Dawn," he demanded.

"Make sense and I will," she replied, in full command of her emotions, by the look of her.

They marched to the sitting area of her room, two comfy chairs flanking a round, skirted table. Eric waited until she sat, then joined her.

He clasped his hands together, resting his elbows on his knees as he leaned forward. "Look, I know how far out this sounds to you if you've had no prior experience with paranormal events, but I swear I'm being straight with you."

Dawn studied his face carefully, examining his every feature. He could feel her disdain like a pinch. She inhaled, then released it. "I'm aware that the intel agencies have done some studies in that area. I'll give you the benefit of the doubt here. But if I find out you're putting me on about this, Vinland, you're in deep trouble."

"No. I do read thoughts," Eric said seriously. "That is no joke. I'm for real."

She shifted in the chair, crossing her legs, apparently not in the least concerned about how seductive she appeared wearing that little confection she had on. He looked away, trying not to get any more distracted than he already was.

Obviously she planned to use that old trick of making him want to fill the silence, so he went ahead and bit. "I understand that you're a skeptic. That's okay. I've lived with this all my life and sometimes I forget how difficult it is for some people to buy into it if they've never encountered anything like it before. You haven't, have you?"

"I guessed the number of marbles in a jar once. That's as close as I've come, so don't expect much."

He nodded. "Okay. I am able—sometimes, most of the time, actually—to connect to people as they're thinking. If they think in words, I hear them. If not, then I get their general mood, hints of their intentions, specific feelings."

"Like mine?" she asked wryly. "Are you getting my general mood?"

He nodded. "Yes, anyone could see you're still mad as hell. I don't have to be psychic to know I blew it. But I can't read your mind and never could."

"Why not?"

He shrugged. "You have a natural block, I guess, or really good defenses. Some people do."

"Whew, what a relief," she said, sounding bored. "But I suppose you'll have no problem with Quince? Is he an open book, too?"

"I don't know yet. I won't until I meet him."

"So, tell me, what other tricks do you do?" she asked with a mirthless smile.

Eric decided to lay it all out there and see if she would buy any part of it. Maybe in the meantime, he could figure some way to demonstrate his abilities so she would drop the sarcasm and patent disbelief. "Remote viewing, are you familiar with that?"

"Oh yes, from television. You see things that happen, a little videotape in your mind. Flashing and in fragments, of course, like the results of bad camera work. It's a great hook in the world of fiction."

"That's pretty close to how it works. Don't smirk. I can sometimes see hidden objects or even people if I can touch the place where they lay or clothing they wore before they went missing."

She got up and began to pace. "Sometimes? Not an exact science, then. Pity. It would sure make our life simpler if you could have touched that computer and pin-pointed the location of that gadget with the information on it, wouldn't it? Wow, think of the manpower and money that could be saved if your little talents were consistent."

"Stop it. You know paranormal phenomena exist, Dawn. You admitted yourself that the government has been studying this. They have, in all its forms, for decades. I am a telepath, more consistent than most."

She stopped pacing and faced him with her hands on her hips, her jaw set. "I don't believe you. Is that clear enough?" She flung out her hands. "It's hooey. So go to bed. I promise you there's no need for you to worry. What I felt was a momentary jolt of lust. You're a good-looking guy, Eric, and it has been a while since I've been alone in a bedroom with one, but I'm not quite desperate enough to jump you in your sleep, okay?"

He was already on his feet and unable to stop himself. He grabbed her and kissed her before she knew what was happening. For a second, she froze. Then she relaxed into the kiss for all she was worth.

The next thing he knew, he was flat on his back on the floor, Dawn straddling his waist with her sharp fingernails biting into his neck. "You move one inch and I'll open your jugular and laugh while you bleed out. Got that?"

Eric knew better than to smile. "Got it."

She didn't budge. "Now you listen to me, Vinland. I've about had it with you. You have one chance to make this right. When I release you, get up slowly. Walk directly out of this room and when I see you first thing in the morning, this night never happened. I don't want to hear any more about how you *see things*. Not one more word. And you will never—I repeat, never—kiss me again."

Eric, perfectly relaxed, grabbed the hand that gripped his neck, flipped her easily and reversed their positions. "You want to do this the hard way, okay. No, nothing sexual and no more kisses tonight, but you will listen to me and you will believe what I say."

But for the life of him, he couldn't think of a single thing he could do that would convince her he was telling the truth.

For a long moment, they glared at one another, breathing hard with exertion and bold remnants of unwanted lust. Then she spoke.

"I read once that some prominent scientist has a standing offer of one million dollars to anyone who can prove this exists. Why haven't you collected if you're for real?"

"Maybe I already have a million dollars."

"Let's say you do. Then tell me where I lost my grandmother's ring," she challenged. "It was on my ring finger, right hand, for years. Where is it now?"

Eric slid his hand from her wrist up to her fourth finger and touched the place, closing his eyes. It came to him as easily as anything ever had.

"There's a pool. The ring… It's in the drain. It's in the drain of that pool."

He opened his eyes and smiled down at her, still full of the delight she had experienced in that long-ago moment. "It's a very small size. You were a kid when you lost it, right?"

The look of shock on her face was priceless.

"Oblong, diamond-shaped. It has one stone surrounded by chips," Eric told her.

Her gaze narrowed with suspicion. "How do you know that? How could you possibly know?"

He released her other wrist and sat up, moving off of her. "I saw it."

"So where's the pool with the ring?" she challenged.

Eric reached down to give her a hand getting up. "I have no clue, but surely you can remember the day and where you went swimming."

It wasn't telepathy. He considered it little more than a parlor trick. Still, it had come in handy in a lot of instances. Inanimate objects were usually a piece of cake, the more insignificant, the easier they were to locate. Still, this little success gave him a swell of relief. He hadn't completely lost his powers.

Her body relaxed beneath him. "Leave me alone until the morning, will you?" she asked quietly. "This is a lot to digest and I'm still not sure I trust what you're telling me. If you can do all this, why are we here? Why don't you just zone in or whatever it is you do, and send in a contingent of special ops to grab Quince and the others?"

"Would that it worked that way," Eric admitted, shaking his head. "I need to explain a little more about the specifics of what I plan to do and how it might affect you, okay? Then I'll go."

She nodded wordlessly, looking at him with suspicion.

"The idea is to glean whatever I can from Quince about his intentions for the stolen information and whether he's made copies of it. If so, where he has those stashed. Anything I can get. I'll try to pick up on any names associated with the theft and how he chose these particular bidders to deal with."

Dawn had no expression whatsoever on her face. She did not believe him. At least not now.

He continued. "I'll transmit this information to you, so that one of us has it in case the other can't make it off the island for some reason."

"Say what you mean. One of us could die."

"Yes. But if we play out our roles, we should be safe enough. Quince is no fool. His intention is to sell what he's got. If he behaves himself, he can deal again next time. Only we won't give him that chance, of course."

"What if…"

"What?" Eric prompted.

"Suppose this Quince is similarly talented and figures out what you're doing? What if he reads you better than you read him?"

Eric sighed. "Then kick off your high heels and swim like hell because we won't stand a bloody chance."

"Go to bed, Eric," she said with a shake of her head.

He left the room and closed the door.

"Now *that* went well," he said to himself, strolling casually into his bedroom, almost satisfied. Not physically, of course. He was trying to ignore his heightened state of arousal.

He couldn't have her and he knew that. A little corner of his brain wouldn't quite accept it, though. That part kept urging that after this was all over, then maybe…

* * *

Dawn did not argue when Eric advised her to don the chador the next morning before leaving the hotel. Beneath it she wore a white sleeveless cotton top and slacks. Her shoes were leather with intricate embroidery on the toes that matched the blue color of her robe.

Together they preceded the porter who pushed the brass trolley holding their luggage. Clay and Ressam followed the porter. Their bags would be delivered to the *Angeline* in time for them to sail at noon.

She remained as unobtrusive as possible when they boarded the boat, going directly to the deserted salon without a word from Eric. He wore the role of the haughty Jarad Al-Dayal as if born to that name and station. She attempted to match his effort with the same ease.

One hour into the trip, he beckoned to her from the steps leading up from the salon to the deck. She rose obediently and joined him.

"Dolphins again. I thought you would enjoy them."

Dawn nodded and walked with him to the rail. She noted the captain ducking into the cabin. "Making a call?" she asked Eric.

"Looks like it. Are you all right?"

"Of course. Are you? How's the old gray matter receiving today?"

He didn't answer directly. "I think the captain will troll us around until dark, then disorient us with a few wide turns before making landfall."

Dawn could figure that much without the benefit of telepathy. It's what she would do if she were the captain delivering them to some secret destination. "So we keep an eye on the stars to determine where we are, right?"

"Clouds expected and probably a storm. That's why

this is happening now. Good news, though. That means Quince still plans to let us go later or he wouldn't bother trying to conceal his whereabouts."

"How will our guys find out where he is if they don't know where we went for the meeting? Unless this Quince is an idiot, he won't allow you to bring your laptop or cell phone."

Eric smiled a cat's smile. "Under the skin on my left shoulder is an implant that gives off intermittent signals. They can follow wherever I go. Soon as we are ready for it to happen, they'll strike."

"And how will they know that we are ready?"

"I'll contact them, don't worry."

"How? With a mind link?" she asked, not bothering to mask her skepticism.

"Hey, we have running conversations sometimes. Better than a telephone." Now he was joking, she could tell by his grin.

"Excuse me if I prefer Ma Bell."

"*Shhh,* captain's coming back. Ooh and ahh at the dolphins a little, then go below. I need my mind on what I'm doing and you look entirely too fetching in that table-cloth. Blows my concentration."

Dawn did as he asked, then spun neatly out of his grasp, actually enjoying the swirl of the robe around her ankles.

Could he actually do what he claimed? She had never met anyone who claimed to possess psychic abilities. He wouldn't be that confident if he wasn't sure his worked, would he? Would she actually find that ring he told her about? Dawn knew she would have to try, just to see if it was where he said it was.

She exhaled sharply and headed for the salon to pour herself a cup of coffee. Maybe he was delusional and they would both die as a result. How had she gotten herself into this mess?

She passed near Clay as she reached the door to the cabin. "Open your mind," he said emphatically in a deep, but nearly inaudible voice, the first words she had ever heard him speak. "Trust him."

Before she could respond by gesture or word, he hurried away. A servant realizing he had passed too close to the *mamsahib,* or whatever the boss's wife was called.

Okay, she decided. She would make herself trust. As if she had any options. Maybe a little meditation would calm her.

A good old Presbyterian prayer might not hurt, either, she thought with a heavy sigh.

Chapter 8

They sailed all afternoon and on into the night. The reason for that was a given. The location of the island was to remain a secret. That indicated it might be Quince's permanent home, or at least his usual base of operations.

The captain looked mighty smug and had an evil glint in his eye. He was probably making plans to get rid of the "bodyguards" Al-Dayal had brought along.

Dawn should be safe enough, though. How much trouble could a woman be anyway, the captain would figure, especially one as meek as Al-Dayal's wife? Eric almost laughed out loud. She had played her part so perfectly that no one could see her as a threat.

"We'll anchor here for the night," the captain said as he approached Eric. "If you and your men could give me some assistance."

They must be close to the rendezvous. Eric nodded and beckoned to Ressam and Clay.

Once the sails were furled and the anchor dropped, the captain bade them good-night, informing Eric that he would remain topside while Eric and the others were to use the cabins fore and aft.

"You are too kind," Eric said, shared a meaningful look with his men, and went below as the captain suggested.

Dawn was already in the forward cabin, reclining on the bed with a book. She glanced up as he entered. Since he had only a couple of feet of floor space, he kicked off his deck shoes and crawled onto the king-size bunk beside her.

"Are we there yet?" she asked with a saucy smile, turning down the page to mark her place and then tossing the novel aside.

Eric glanced at the author's name. Ian Fleming. "We will go ashore in the morning, I expect. So you are a James Bond fan?"

"Not really. I found it in the salon."

He laughed. "Decadent western novels, scorning your protective attire and taking the tone of a liberated woman. What are you coming to, Aurora? Will I have to take you in hand?"

"Have you the time for that before we disembark?" she asked playfully, all the while glancing curiously around the cabin and pointing to her ear.

"It's okay," he told her. "Clay swept the place. There are mikes hidden in the salon and in certain locations topside, but the cabins aren't bugged."

She grimaced. "Then why are you being such a jerk when you don't have to?"

He grinned. "Sorry, just yanking your chain. Are you ready for tomorrow?"

"Absolutely," she declared. "All this lounging around is boring as hell."

He lay back, linking his hands behind his head. "There'll be more of that once we get there, at least for you. But we could have some fireworks tonight if the captain tries to unload Ressam and Clay. No doubt Quince ordered him to."

"How do you know that?"

He quirked an eyebrow. "Wouldn't you if you were him?"

Dawn grabbed his arm and leaned close. "You think he means to kill them in their sleep?"

Eric grinned up at her. "The day they can't handle one spindly-legged, fifty-year-old wannabe pirate, they'll deserve what they get."

"We should keep watch or something in case they need our help."

"Relax. They'll be fine." He loved the feel of her hand on his arm, the concern he felt emanating from her in waves. She had a good heart and was a fine agent. Even though she barely knew Clay and Ressam, she would go to the mat to save them.

Though he sensed her goodness and her worry, it was not extrasensory perception at work, only normal observation. *Normal.* Dawn made him feel that way, and he couldn't help but love it. She saw him as a man, not some strange, inexplicable phenomenon. Maybe that was the reason he wanted her so much. But was that the only reason? Somehow, he didn't think so.

At a very young age, he had learned to brush off the awe people sometimes felt at what he could do. He did it with humor, merciless teasing and, if that didn't work, outright avoidance. Not many bothered to get to know the real Eric Vinland. He wasn't even certain he knew himself as well as he should.

His life had been mostly smoke and mirrors, a series of acts to either use or to cover his powers, depending on the situation. With Dawn, he felt he could be himself, providing he could figure out just who that was.

"I have you all figured out," she said, jerking him to attention with her words. God, was she reading *him* and not realizing it? "You observe body language and expressions really well," she continued. "Then you combine that with things you learn from your sources. For instance, you made a good guess that I lost my ring in a pool somewhere. How could I ever prove or disprove that?"

"Find the ring, maybe?"

She scoffed. "The pool is probably no longer there."

"Ah. So I'm like the fakers who wow folks at carnivals, huh? Or maybe a con artist on the psychic hotlines?"

She shrugged.

"I get that you don't believe me," he said.

Her expression was kind. "I believe that *you* believe it, like celebrities who begin to believe their own press. It could be dangerous, this overestimating what you can do, Eric."

"Thanks, I'll keep that in mind," he said dryly, now a little miffed that she thought he was so self-delusional that he would risk their lives.

"Hey, don't be mad. I'm trying to help."

Eric rolled over, giving her his back. "Okay, thanks. Get some sleep. Tomorrow's gonna be a big day for both of us."

"C'mon," she urged. "Don't pout. You're ruining your image. Or have you suddenly run out of jokes?" Her hand closed over his shoulder.

It was too much. Entirely too much to tolerate when he was already hyped up to kiss her. One kiss. That's all he'd do, to shut that smart little mouth of hers.

He rolled back to her and sealed his lips to hers. Only

hers were open in surprise, giving him full access, tempting him to explore her fully while teaching her a lesson in tact.

Tact went right out the window, along with any subtle punishment he'd intended. How sweet she was, and how perfectly fitted to him. He embraced her full length, planning to enjoy every second until she cried wolf.

But Dawn didn't cry wolf. She didn't push back, and she didn't protest in any other way. Instead, she shifted against him, stoking his need even higher and harder. Damn, he wished she would hurry up and learn her lesson, give him a hard smack on the head or something, because he couldn't seem to stop himself as long as she was cooperating.

The little groan she made reverberated through him like a plucked string. An electric, erotic note, one that played over and over in his head, drumming out coherence, vibrating, sending all the blood in his brain to parts of him that never thought for themselves.

Her hands grasped his shoulders, slid down his back, firmly gripped his butt and urged him closer. She wants this. She really, really wants this, cried that devil fighting his conscience. And he wanted it even more than she did, too keenly to resist.

He slid a hand beneath her blouse and found bare skin, firm and welcoming, burning with the same fever that gripped him. He felt the budding of her nipples, caressed them with eager fingers and both heard and felt his reward in her response.

She was so damned responsive it blew him away. He had to taste her, touch her everywhere, inhale her, be a part of her in every way possible. This intense need for total possession shocked him. He had never wanted to *own* a partner before, but Dawn was not just a partner. This was not just sex. This was everything at the moment, everything he had ever wanted or would ever want. No, he knew it was not a momentary thing at all. He might never recover and be what he had been, but he didn't care.

Dawn filled him up somehow, occupied all those vacant places he never realized existed in him. This phenomenon had been at work for days now, about to culminate in this unstoppable act. The sheer power of his feelings and this new vulnerability scared the hell out of him, but he knew he had no defense. Didn't even want one. He only wanted *her*.

"Mine now," he murmured against her mouth.

Hardly breaking the kiss, they tore off clothes and came together in a rush of heat. No way to stop, no way. Fractured thoughts tried to intrude, but he drowned them out with a growl of pleasure so intense it nearly hurt. She met his every move, urging him on, banishing any coherent thought he had left.

Her soft exclamation rushed out against his neck when he thrust inside her and took her with all the finesse of a novice.

Regret wouldn't register. He didn't care about technique, about anything but becoming one with Dawn, living, breathing, being a part of her. And he was. For a few minutes, it seemed as if her every feeling rushed into him and expanded his own.

Faster and higher, keener and sharper, the ecstasy mounted until they exploded together in a cry of completion.

But once he withdrew, Eric realized he was no longer complete. Something would always be missing unless he held her as close as could be, unless he was part of her and she a part of him.

Breathless and confused, he couldn't seem to let her go, to give her space to recover. Instead, he pressed her closer and buried his face in her neck, reluctant to discuss what had happened.

"Now I can sleep," she murmured, placing a soft kiss on his temple. "Don't talk."

Well, damn. What kind of woman was she that she didn't want to dissect what had happened and ruin the magic?

Eric smiled and caressed her naked back with his hand, letting go just a little, certain that he could get the magic back again once they had rested. Dawn amazed him. She just amazed the hell out of him.

Drifting into oblivion was the last thing he wanted to do. She had gone there before him, her breathing already becoming even and her heartbeat calm. His one thought was of how happy he was. For the first time in memory, truly happy. How rare was that, to experience it and know it as it was happening?

Happiness made little sense, knowing what they might face in the morning, how they might not survive if Stefan Cydonia, the indomitable Quince, guessed who they really were. Eric could die a happy man if he expired right now, but he wasn't ready to go just yet. And he could never let any harm come to Dawn.

Things had to go perfectly. Had he considered and prepared for every eventuality, every contingency? God, he hoped so. He prayed so.

In the aftermath of their lovemaking, Dawn feigned sleep. It was too soon to talk about what had happened between them. Maybe she wouldn't discuss it at all. If she could pass it off as an impulse, that would be best. People in dangerous situations often did reckless things they wouldn't ordinarily do. But if she were completely honest with herself, Dawn had to admit she might have done it under any circumstances.

She couldn't bring herself to regret it, not when her body still glowed with pleasure. There was another feeling as well, the sublime comfort of truly connecting with another person.

She and Eric were special together, even though she knew in her heart that it was only temporary. Eric Vinland wasn't the type for a girl to pin any long-term hopes on, but that was all right with her. Nope, no regrets at all, she decided.

What if they had never found another chance? They certainly wouldn't on that island, where they would surely be under constant surveillance. And after the mission was over, assuming they survived it, they would go back to their respective jobs and probably never see each other again.

He was not the marrying kind, and Dawn knew it. Not that she had even entertained the thought of that. Not seriously, anyway. It was just that she had experienced something, however brief, with him that she never expected. That feeling of belonging, of being part of another.

She sighed and snuggled against him, still pretending to be asleep. Maybe it was only great sex that made her feel this way. That was something she hadn't experienced before, either. All her adult life, she had wondered what the fuss was all about. Well, now she knew.

For the rest of tonight, she planned to luxuriate in the pleasure of being her own well-satisfied self, lying beside her evanescent lover and partner. Tomorrow, she must become Aurora again, a completely cloaked shadow in the wake of the great Jarad Al-Dayal.

Eric sat straight up out of a sound sleep. Whether a sound or a premonition had awakened him, he couldn't tell. He placed a hand on Dawn's shoulder and gave her a gentle shake. "Wake up. Something's going down."

He hurriedly yanked on his loose trousers and crept barefoot through the salon, sensing Dawn right behind him. He hurried across the salon to the other sleeping quarters.

The aft cabin door stood open. Clay rushed out, glanced around the salon, then pointed to the deck. When they were topside, Clay leaned close and spoke. "I killed the captain. I couldn't avoid it."

"What happened?" Dawn asked.

"Ressam, since he's smaller, hid in the salon. We figured the captain would come after us, so we made a plan. Ressam would grab him from behind when he started for our cabin. I'd be inside, ready to assist. But the door opened and I saw a blade coming at me. I kicked him in the chest. Then he just fell across the bunk, dead to the world. No pulse."

"You tried to revive him?"

Clay nodded. "The kick must have stopped his heart and I couldn't start him up again. We need to find Ressam."

The clouds had passed and the moon beamed down on them, throwing an eerie blue cast over everything on the deck. The scene looked surreal.

The three of them searched. Ressam was missing, but there was blood on the deck, a trail of it leading to the side of the deck. Eric looked down into the water. Though there was nothing to see but black waves calmly sloshing against the side of the *Angeline,* he knew. "Ressam's dead."

"The phone in the salon's ringing," Dawn said.

Eric strode past her and went inside. Dawn and Clay remained on deck.

He picked up the receiver and listened. "Kerosian?" a low-pitched voice asked. "Are you there?"

Eric took a deep breath. "This is Jarad Al-Dayal. Are you Quince?"

"Put Kerosian on."

"He is no longer with us," Eric admitted. "The poor fellow suffered heart failure and expired despite our attempts at resuscitation."

A long silence ensued before the voice spoke again. "Then you must complete his task."

"I am no sailor and have no idea where we are at the moment. I was seriously contemplating ringing up the authorities to come and rescue us."

Bitter laughter sounded on the other end.

"Unless you have a better suggestion," Eric said, using his most condescending tone.

"You can guess what must be done, so do the deed yourself, Al-Dayal. No one else must be privy to this arrangement. Dispose of your remaining watchdog. After you are finished, weight the body down and put it over the side. I have infrared and will be observing. And listening."

Eric pretended to consider it. "And if I refuse? He is a loyal retainer and can be trusted."

"Not by me. I shall terminate the plans for your visit and you will have no need of sailing experience when you depart. And with regard to your wife…"

"She knows nothing," Eric assured him, "and will do as I command."

"Your Aurora is of little consequence other than as a beautiful asset, I know. But I would like her involved in this bit of business on the yacht. If she could be implicated in getting rid of your bodyguard, then she is less likely to report the tale to anyone later, wouldn't you agree?"

"Leave her out of this. What can a mere woman do anyway?"

"As you said, whatever you order her to. I will ring you again when I see you have done as instructed. You and the woman will take the inflatable and come ashore. If there is evidence of life on board the *Angeline* after you leave it, you will never return to it or to the mainland. Are we understood?"

Eric hesitated a minute for effect, then agreed. "It shall be done."

He replaced the receiver and went topside to rejoin Dawn and Clay. "Adil, prepare the inflatable for us and load our bags into it," he ordered Clay. "We are to go ashore soon."

Dawn looked at him curiously. He wished he had time to tell her what was to happen, but maybe her natural reaction to it would satisfy Quince. Then Eric wondered if he would actually get the response from her that a woman such as Aurora might give.

To insure that, he muttered to her as he passed her on deck. "Trust what I'm about to do. He has a night scope trained on our every move. Act appropriately."

Eric stood idly by and watched as Clay prepared the small boat as ordered. Then his friend retrieved their bags from their cabin and put them aboard. "Ready to go," Clay told him.

Eric beckoned him back on board, then glanced out over the water to the blue-gray island, now barely visible on the horizon. He pulled the nine millimeter out of his belt and aimed.

Clay nodded once, holding up his hands as if pleading for his life. Eric fired, one miss, one hit.

Dawn screamed. "What have you done?" She ran toward the fallen body.

Eric grabbed her arm. "Get something heavy to weight him down!" he shouted.

"No!" she screamed, batting at him with her hands and arms.

Eric shook her and pretended a slap. She recoiled, went

reeling like a practiced stunt woman and screamed again. That one would surely reach the mikes, Eric figured. It probably reached the mainland without a microphone. His ears certainly were ringing.

He leaned forward to help her to her feet and murmured low, as his head neared hers, "Scuba gear's in that hold over there." He guided her with a look. "Go in and grab a bedsheet first to disguise the tank. Put on your garb while you're in there."

She nodded, then scurried back inside.

Meanwhile, Eric had noted that Clay was not moving. He rushed over to make sure the bullet hadn't penetrated the vest Clay always wore. "You okay?"

Clay cursed, still not moving. "I *hate* this job."

Eric snickered, keeping his voice low. "Quit belly-aching, you're on vacation in Greece, dude. How's your Houdini act?"

"Rusty. Don't do the knots too tight or you'll damn well be on your own."

"You aren't bleeding anywhere, are you? Hate to give the sharks a snack."

"Had to mention them, didn't you?"

"Hang on to the inflatable and we'll tow you as far as we can. I'll veer right as a signal for you to let go. Sun's about to come up. Great timing. Quince's infrared will be practically useless in this much light, but it's still dark enough that a telescope won't show details. Let's get you outfitted."

Dawn returned, properly covered in a dark blue robe and matching head-covering. She deposited the air tank nearby and began to help Eric buckle Clay's motionless body into it. He was well over six feet tall and as heavy as lead. Eric wondered how the two of them would heft him over the side.

"Catch you later," Eric said as they managed to drag Clay upright and bend him forward over the rail. Then Eric stepped back and motioned imperiously for Dawn to tip up Clay's legs and send him into the drink. She grunted with the effort, but performed admirably, he thought.

With a satisfied nod, he guided her down into the inflatable Zodiac. Three bumps on the rubber side of the boat and the appearance of air bubbles told him Clay was good to go. "Let's do this," he snapped, and they were off for the island.

Several hundred yards offshore, Eric turned right, ostensibly to approach a better section of the small beach. Less drag on the boat told him Clay was now operating on his own.

The craggy section of rock to the left would provide perfect cover for Clay's secret insertion. The waves dashing against the rocks worried Eric, but Clay Senate was the ultimate warrior, an excellent swimmer. Now was not the time for a mind link, but Eric gave it a shot. All he picked up was solid determination mixed with a smidgen of annoyance. Or maybe those were his own feelings.

Reluctantly, Eric deliberately quit trying to connect with Clay and concentrated on their own landing.

The welcoming party was well armed with automatics. Eric approached as far up on the beach as possible. Two of the four men slung their weapons' straps over their shoulders and waded out to meet them. Eric climbed out first, ignoring their greeters. Then he caught Dawn up in his arms to carry her ashore.

"Here goes nothin'!" he muttered in her ear.

"Eric, about what happened between us…" she began. "It was just…"

"Fantastic, I know. Now hold that thought until we get off this island," he ordered.

She pinched his neck. "I was going to say it was a freak mistake and we ought to put it out of our minds."

"Okay, go ahead. I can if you can," he replied without a touch of bitterness.

"Sometimes I could just shoot you, Vinland," she huffed.

"Yeah, well, you might have to get in line behind those oafs with the Uzis. Now morph into meek mode, will you? We've got a job to do here."

Chapter 9

There were steps carved in the sloped crags that surrounded the crescent section of beach. Eric deposited
Dawn on her feet and left her to follow him. He briefly
noted that the men who had dragged the Zodiac ashore
were now collecting the bags out of it. The two remaining
kept their weapons trained on him. The swish of wet fabric
behind him assured him that Dawn was keeping up with
his long stride.

He allowed one of the men to run a metal-detecting
wand up and down the length of their bodies without
actually touching them. It was to be expected. They had
left their weapons aboard the *Angeline* since the hardware
would have been confiscated anyway.

At the top of the steps, he paused. What a layout Quince
had here. A virtual castle of natural stone blended beautifully with the island's natural vegetation. From the air, it

would probably go unnoticed. Up close, the attention to detail was impressive.

The care with which the surroundings were cultivated proved Quince had good maintenance help. That probably meant a large staff beyond these guards he had sent to meet them.

"This way," one of the men instructed in Greek, stepping around Eric and pointing to the right.

Eric followed, listening for Dawn's footsteps on the flagstone path behind him.

When they neared the double doors of the entrance, one panel opened, then the other. A white-coated servant gestured them inside and led the way to the curved staircase. The majordomo, Eric supposed.

The older man smiled. "Madame is to go to her rooms with the baggage, sir. If you will come with me?"

"I will see her to our room. *Then* I will come with you," Eric announced, at his most imperious.

"As you will, sir. This way."

The rooms proved to be more than adequate. They were adjoining, large and airy, containing identical king-size beds draped in white gauze. The rest of the furnishings looked antique and very expensive. "This will do," he said, deliberately exhibiting impatience.

He watched the hirelings deposit their bags. One disappeared with the case containing Eric's laptop, an expected act.

Then he addressed Dawn, not bothering to lower his voice. "Remain here. Lock the door.

"Out," he ordered the others and waited until they left. He stopped outside in the hallway and listened for the snick of the lock. With a satisfied nod, he followed the servant who had requested he do so.

A feeling of excitement pervaded his every nerve. Now

he would meet this Quince and see what they were up against. Dawn was probably seething at being excluded from this first meeting, but Eric felt a little relieved that he could scope out the situation first. Then again, he didn't much like leaving her alone in the event Quince was on to them. Not that he thought Dawn was helpless, but she might be if caught unawares.

Worrying about her could be deadly in itself, preventing him from doing what he came to do. He had to stop that now before he met Quince.

"Here we are, sir," the servant murmured as he tapped twice on the highly polished door and then opened it. "Mr. Jarad Al-Dayal," he announced.

Distinguished was the word Quince brought to mind. He reminded Eric of a silver-haired actor he had once seen in the vintage movies he loved to watch. Stewart something-or-other. Piercing gray eyes that held a coldness. Dark, expressive eyebrows, one now quirked as he examined his guest.

He rose slowly from the luxurious leather chair and extended a long-fingered, well-manicured hand. "Greetings," he said softly. "Won't you sit down?" He gestured to the matching chair facing the one in which he'd been sitting.

Eric swept his robe back and sat stiffly, regarding Quince with his most imperious glare. "Shall we get to the business at hand?"

Quince smiled. "Patience, my friend. I have always heard that men of your persuasion preferred a bit of social discourse before discussing weighty matters. We have the entire weekend for business. And longer if we need it. Would you care for a drink?" He inclined his head toward the elaborate wet bar that filled one corner of the study.

Eric narrowed his eyes. "You must know that *men of my persuasion,* as you so delicately put it, avoid alcohol."

"Perhaps a coffee, then?" Quince suggested, oozing hospitality, charm and sophistication.

Eric sat back, tapping his fingers on the arms of the chair. "Orange juice."

Quince smiled and sat down as he spoke to the servant. "Two juices, Conroy."

They waited, observing each other without any subterfuge until they had been served. Then Quince said, "We will breakfast in the dining room in a quarter hour, Conroy. Inform the lady and have her join us."

"She will not," Eric informed him. He sipped the fruit juice from the expensive crystal.

"Why not relax the rules for the duration of your visit, Al-Dayal? This is a new world, and too much adherence to tradition impedes progress. Come now, I insist. Your wife will be perfectly safe." His smile was almost a smirk.

Eric returned it in kind. "I meant that she will not come if I do not order it personally. Unless you intend to use force upon her, which I would not advise you to do."

Quince laughed. "Is that a warning against the lady herself or repercussions from you?"

"Both," Eric stated without pause.

"Then please, go with Conroy and fetch her. If you do not trust me to share a simple meal with your wife, how am I to believe you would trust me in any important transaction?"

Was that an implied threat? Eric studied the man's beatific expression but could not see behind it. However, Quince was providing the perfect opportunity to introduce Dawn to him so that Eric could add her reactions to his own. Dispensing with Dawn's isolation would be convenient. The question was, how would it benefit Quince?

Eric shrugged and took his time finishing his juice.

"Very well," he agreed. "It is no great concession. My wife was born in the West and is familiar with your customs."

"Excellent," Quince said smoothly. "I am happy to see that you yourself are adaptable to Western customs when the need arises, Jarad. I may call you that?"

"Of course, Quince. Or have you a *Christian* name you would like me to employ?" Eric asked with no small amount of sarcasm.

"Quince will suffice."

Eric left the study, carefully concealing a frown of consternation. Their adversary was Greek, as the identity Interpol had for him indicated. He had learned his English in England, perhaps attended school there. He was absolutely fluent and well-spoken. That didn't gibe with other indications of his social status, however. Middle- to lower-class Greeks didn't usually have access to a public school education abroad.

Maybe Quince had not been born to wealth, but he possessed it now, that was for sure. This place had cost several fortunes. Quince worked hard at giving the appearance of old money, but little things gave him away. A few statues that were too Romanesque to mix well with classic Greek. Furnishings that were not quite eclectic enough to have been gathered at leisure over decades. This place had been thrown up all at once, accessories bought in bulk and the entire estate done up for show. Like Quince himself, whose sophisticated exterior sported a few telltale cracks in the facade. He was an actor who had done exhaustive research for the role but neglected to immerse himself in it or, perhaps, didn't quite know how.

While observations might be helpful, Eric regretted he had not penetrated a single thought of Quince's the entire time he was with the man. Not even when they had shaken hands.

First, Dawn had blocked him without even trying and now Quince seemed to possess a solid mental barrier. Eric found he couldn't even read old Conroy's thoughts. The servant was most likely cursing the need to climb the stairs again. His arthritis was giving him fits. But it was not from the man's thoughts that Eric divined that information.

Maybe the problem lay in trying too hard, Eric decided. He was too uptight. That had to be it. Dawn's fault, of course, though he could hardly blame her. She hadn't asked him to obsess over her the way he was doing.

He shook his head and tried to clear it, but it seemed too filled with thoughts of her and whether she would be as relieved to see him as he would her in a few seconds.

What a helluva time for him to fall like a third-act curtain. The play had barely begun.

Dawn dressed casually for breakfast. She wore a white long-sleeved blouse, embroidered about the neck with a red Greek key design, and a calf-length flowing skirt cinched with an intricately woven belt of red cord. Dainty red sandals completed her ensemble. She quickly fastened her hair in a knot at her nape and went to present herself to Eric for his approval.

He frowned up at her when she entered his room. "For the length of this visit only, I shall allow you to revert to your European customs because our host expects this. Do not make me regret it, Aurora."

Of course, he was performing for any audio or video surveillance installed in their rooms. But even knowing that, it amazed Dawn how that tone of his ruffled her feathers. The man was entirely too good at acting the chauvinist.

She granted him a tight little smile. "Whatever you desire, of course, Jarad."

"Come." He led the way out of the room, then held the

door for her. The old servant was waiting for them in the corridor. Silently they followed him back down the stairs to the dining room.

When they entered Dawn had her first glimpse of their adversary. Her breath caught in her throat. She had fully expected to see the man who had committed murder right before her eyes. The one who stole the information. It definitely was not him. But surely this guy must have hired someone to have it done.

Quince rose and smiled at her. He was an incredibly handsome man, tanned and fit, impeccably dressed in a pale blue cashmere pullover, gray pleated slacks and sandals.

"Welcome to the island, Mrs. Al-Dayal. Would you mind if I call you Aurora?"

Dawn shot Eric a questioning look, as if asking his permission, and watched him nod once, his imperious frown darker than ever.

She turned back to Quince. "Yes, of course. Thank you, Señor Quince," she said, employing her Spanish accent.

"Just Quince will do." His smile widened as he gestured to the table. "Please, join me, both of you. The others will arrive momentarily, and in the meantime, we will have coffee."

Others? Dawn resisted voicing the question, but she was eager to see who else and how many had come to the island to bid on the information.

There were only six chairs at the table, though it could comfortably seat fourteen. Was that significant?

Their host sat at the head of the table, Eric to his right, she to his left.

Dawn stirred cream into her coffee and kept her eyes averted from Quince, as was proper. His deep voice rambled on about the weather.

In less than five minutes, two men and a woman arrived. Quince greeted them as cordially as he had Eric and Dawn, then proceeded to make introductions. "Carlotta Vasquez from Colombia," he said, bowing to the tall, sultry woman whose sharp brown eyes raked Dawn with blatant curiosity. "You and Aurora should get on remarkably well since you share a common language. She is originally from Andorra," Quince continued.

Dawn nodded shyly and murmured a short, formal greeting in Spanish, which gained her no response at all.

Quince turned then to a man who was extremely dark and sinister looking. "Obaya Minos from Tanzania."

That one said nothing, merely kept his thick lips pressed firmly together, his hands clenched by his side and appeared to be holding his breath. A portly man with a cleanly shaved head, Minos had elected to dress formally in a suit and a tie that must be choking his thick neck. Obviously, he did not like the atmosphere of bonhomie their host was attempting to instill.

"Last, but certainly not least, we have Sean McCoy from Dublin."

The Irishman nodded and pulled out a chair for Carlotta, who pierced him with a disdainful glare over her shoulder. Whether that stemmed from the fact that Carlotta liked to do things for herself or because McCoy looked like an unmade bed was anybody's guess. The man had a certain wild charm, Dawn guessed, if you liked spiky hair, thrift-store apparel and a probable connection to the extremist element of the IRA.

"Jarad Al-Dayal and his lovely Aurora complete our party, my friends. Please, feel free to chat and get to know one another. We are a select group, all in the same line of work, as it were, though I do not like discussing business matters until the time is right."

Silence ensued as a white-coated servant poured more coffee and another began serving. The plates of fruit were fresh and beautifully presented with sprigs of mint and candied violets. Pastries gleamed with their golden crusts and sweet glazes.

Dawn's mouth watered as she kept her hands in her lap and waited for Quince to begin.

Tension grew as thick as the honey Quince started spooning on his croissant. Everyone at the table must be wondering the same thing, of course.

Sean McCoy took a deep breath and treated them to a crooked grin before addressing Quince. "I'll ask for us all, then. Why would you be revealing our names?"

"Insurance," Quince replied evenly, taking a bite.

"I don't understand." Eric leaned back his head and stared down his nose at Quince. "We are competitors, at least in this transaction."

"But you need not be," their host said smoothly, lifting his cup. "Have your coffee, eat. There is a method to my madness, as you shall see later. For now, enjoy the meal."

The African stood abruptly. "I shall *not* make this pretense. Summon me when you are prepared to do business."

Quince stood, too, splaying his fingertips on the table-top. "Sit *down,* Minos. Now!" His curt command left no room for quibbling.

Minos paused only two seconds, glaring, then dropped his gaze and resumed his seat.

So did Quince. "Thank you. Now eat. There are activities planned for today that you will not wish to miss."

"Ridiculous farce," muttered the exotic Carlotta. "And dangerous." She poked at her fruit with her fork, speared a ball of cantaloupe and chewed it viciously.

Eric shrugged and began shifting the strawberries on

his plate to one side as if they were slugs. His eyes met Dawn's, a brief connection offering reassurance he didn't try to conceal. His little know-nothing wife should be wondering what the hell was going on, Dawn figured. After all, she was the only one at the table not directly involved in the imminent bidding war.

Never one to pass up a chance to fortify her strength, she dug into the luscious fare Quince had provided and satisfied her hunger.

Might as well seize the moment. It was rapidly becoming the creed she lived by. She had certainly done that with her partner in the early hours of this morning. There would be no further assuaging of that particular hunger any time soon.

She should kick herself for it, but she wouldn't. The slip-up had hurt no one. Not yet, anyway.

Their meal concluded with Quince's announcement. With a clap of his hands, he stood. "I have a fishing expedition planned for the morning. We will hike to an inlet where my thirty-two-footer is docked and—" he leaned forward eagerly as he spoke "—hopefully bring in a noteworthy marlin."

Everyone glared at him except Dawn. She had no problem looking puzzled. It was Sean McCoy who protested. "A waste of time, Quince. What are you tryin' to do here, make us all mates or somethin'?"

"I did not travel halfway around the world to fish," Carlotta snapped. "This is absurd."

Minos remained silent. So did Eric. Dawn looked to him for direction, as a wife should, but he was studying Quince intently. Could he divine what the man had in mind here? No, she still didn't quite believe Eric could do that.

They could be in big trouble if Eric was relying on that

dubious ability to get what he needed from Quince. Not to mention what a problem it could be if he intended to use whatever mind-melding talents he thought he possessed to call in the cavalry if things got hot.

Quince must be playing for time, delaying the bidding for some reason. But what could that be?

Suddenly Eric stood. "The sooner we leave, the sooner we can return. I am ready."

"Wonderful!" Quince crowed. "Aurora? Have you ever fished before?"

She ducked her head shyly, then shook it to indicate she had not.

"Fine. It's an uplifting experience, I can tell you. Nothing like a day in the good salt air to boost spirits."

Carlotta huffed audibly. "I am not dressed for this…fishing," she complained. It was true. Her shirt and pants were silk and she wore three-inch heels.

"Go and change, anyone who needs to," Quince said. "The rest of us will wait in the courtyard. But hurry. It will be an eventful trip, I promise."

None of them dared miss the outing, of course, even though nobody wanted to fish. Who knew what business would take place on Quince's yacht? Anyone left behind could be at a disadvantage if he decided to conduct the bidding there.

She needed to let Eric know Quince was not the one who had killed Bergen after he stole the information on the radar shield. That fact meant there was another man involved in all this, perhaps even on this island, keeping out of sight. Maybe with plans to eliminate all the disgruntled bidders after the deal went through.

As Quince led them down to the courtyard to wait for Carlotta and Minos, she addressed Eric. "I had so hoped we would see our friend again while we were on vacation. Odd how he's disappeared when we expected to see him."

Eric cleared his throat and glanced at Quince who was busy chatting with Sean McCoy about fishing in Ireland. "He will probably appear again before we return home."

"You think he will surprise us?" she asked with a sigh.

Eric's lips quirked in a half smile and he reached for her hand as they walked. "No doubt. I'll have another friend try to find him."

Dawn squeezed his hand. "Good. I would feel much better if we knew what happened to him." And infinitely better if he didn't pop up somewhere with a weapon trained on them.

"So you have never fished?" Eric asked.

"Doesn't one use worms for this?"

He threw back his head and laughed heartily, attracting Quince's and McCoy's attention. "No, my dear. I promise we will use no worms today."

The other men joined the laughter at her naiveté. All except Minos, who remained grim. Dawn blushed appropriately and ducked her head again, biting her lip to keep from laughing, too.

God grant her a chance to hold that fishing rod and she would show these yo-yos how to land the big one. Gramps hadn't dragged her down to the coast every summer for nothing.

Eric, however, had seen the gleam in her eye and issued a wordless warning by pursing his lips and giving an infinitesimal shake of his head.

Dawn sighed, shrugged and looked out across the placid and incredibly blue waters. How could evil exist in such a beautiful haven? Why would anyone desire any more wealth than a place like this island, especially if it meant conspiring with terrorists to create more havoc in the world?

* * *

The afternoon proved pleasant, considering the circumstances. No one other than Quince seemed to know exactly what those circumstances were. What was his plan?

Dawn noticed that the *Angeline* was nowhere in sight as they left the island. There were eight in all aboard the *Diana,* including Eric, herself, Quince, Carlotta, Sean, Minos, the Greek captain Helos at the wheel and a young fellow called Paulo who remained below unless he was serving drinks. Everyone else lounged topside.

Dawn relaxed in the sun beneath a wide-brimmed hat Quince had offered her from the salon below. They sped out across the Aegean, ventured very near the coast of Turkey and then trolled the deeper waters for the marlin Quince said they were after.

Carlotta grumbled periodically, her voice nearly as harsh as the prominent bones of her face and the slicked-back hairstyle that made her ebony hair shine with cold blue light.

Minos remained silent and avoided the others as much as possible, biding his time until the expedition was over, Dawn supposed.

Sean McCoy, on the other hand, threw himself into the expedition with gusto. But it was Eric who snagged the fish.

They were off then, giving the marlin its head while Eric's rod bent under pressure and the tendons in his bared forearms accepted the strain. His delighted grin looked genuine, his euphoria was contagious.

Dawn felt mesmerized by the sight of him locked in an elemental struggle with a creature easily triple his size and weight.

Quince hovered, offering sage advice, his gaze never leaving the prey. Periodically it would jump clear of the water, writhing with strength and grace, then splash down again and tear forward, still firmly hooked. It seemed a shame to catch and kill this beautiful denizen of the deep, but Dawn felt the excitement anyway. A paradox, for sure.

When the fish tired, Quince shouted for the others to come and help bring it aboard. Carlotta approached, wearing a cat's smile as if she planned to devour the thing then and there. Sean hopped around like a seasoned deck hand used to such chores. Minos was conspicuously absent.

As soon as they had secured the fish and everyone remarked on its size and power, Eric glanced around the deck. "Where is the African?"

Quince shrugged. "Probably below with Paulo."

But he was not. Paulo appeared with cold drinks and declared he had not seen Minos. A search of the entire boat turned up no sign of the big man from Tanzania. As the old gangsters used to say about their victims who were disposed of in the water, Dawn would bet he was *sleeping with the fishes*.

"Perhaps he fell overboard! We should go back for him!" Dawn said, stating the obvious to see what sort of reaction she'd get. They all looked at her as if she were the token imbecile.

"Back *where* precisely?" Carlotta asked wryly. "I say good riddance."

Sean's quick gaze glanced off each of them, but he said nothing.

"Shouldn't you call for a search?" Dawn asked Quince, wide-eyed.

Eric's arm slid around her and drew her close. "This is not for you to worry about, Aurora. Be silent now."

Though his voice sounded gentle, the command was firm. Dawn dropped her gaze to the deck and sniffled for effect while her mind raced, trying to recall where everyone had been during the last hour or so.

Unfortunately, her attention had been so locked on Eric's battle with the fish, she had not thought about keeping track of the other members of the party.

Quince had remained beside Eric, of that she was certain. The captain had been occupied at the wheel. And if Paulo had come on deck, she would have noticed. Wouldn't she?

It was a cinch Minos hadn't taken a dive over the side of the boat on his own. Either Carlotta or Sean must have given him some help.

Surely no one, with the possible exception of Quince and the captain, was armed, but she would bet her last nickel they were all trained to disable or kill bare-handed.

She should have been watching them all. But who would expect anyone to disappear off a boat?

Quince had expected it, though, she thought suddenly. He didn't look at all surprised when they noticed Minos was missing. Now she realized what he must be doing. He was giving them the opportunity to eliminate the competition.

Was this a game for his amusement or simply a business decision? All Quince had to do was issue the invitation to bid, see who responded, run financial checks of their organizations and determine which one was likely to pay the most for what he had to sell. Then he could give that one the best opportunities to kill off the competition.

If they were all dead but the buyer, Quince would remain safe on his uncharted island, his whereabouts unknown. It would be much easier to transport the lone survivor, the one who actually bought the information, back to the mainland without revealing the location of this place than to arrange for all of them to return. Less chance of betrayal that way, too.

Those who were not successful at getting what they had come for might want a little retribution. Or their respective organizations might.

Captain Kerosian, who had brought Eric and her here, had probably been the one to transport the others to the island. Now he was dead. Would Helos be next? As far as Quince knew, Eric's two bodyguards were out of the picture. The other bidders seemed to have none accompanying them, either.

"How unfortunate we are in no position to call for help," Quince said without conviction. "We will naturally return to the island by the same route we traveled, but I seriously doubt there is much hope of locating him now. Captain Helos? Set the appropriate course."

And the captain would, Dawn thought. They would return with all the many twists, turns and diversions that brought them to the spot where the marlin were plentiful. Who but someone tracking it on the charts would know if it was the same?

The fishing expedition was over and the bidders reduced to three, plus one unnecessary and highly expendable wife. She looked up at Eric, then at the others. They had figured that out, too. Who would be next?

Chapter 10

Eric marveled at Quince's ingenious plan. It was dastardly, yes, but you could hardly expect more from one who made his living off terrorists.

Quince had to be aware of the financial standing of the groups represented in the bidding war or they wouldn't have been invited here. When each of the losers returned unsuccessful, there could be repercussions. If they didn't return at all, that might also be the case, but by then he would bet that Quince would be impossible to find.

Dawn looked worried, as she should. Quince had noticed her consternation. Some of that worry was real, Eric knew, and at least a part of it was for him personally, not just the outcome of the mission. Though there was still no direct mental communication between them, he felt very strongly that she cared. If not romantically, then surely the way she would in covering a partner's back.

They were guided below where they lounged in the cabin with cold drinks. With the sun directly overhead, it would be impossible for anyone to gauge their direction on the return trip even if they remained on deck.

Quince had choreographed everything. How he had gotten the marlin to cooperate was anyone's guess, but it had gone down like clockwork, Eric had to give the man that much. Or maybe Quince was just lucky things were working out as he'd planned.

He sipped his soft drink and placed a protective arm around Dawn. As little Aurora, she performed beautifully, looking up at him with those soulful doe eyes, letting her sensitive lips tremble just a little.

God, he would have given his eyeteeth to kiss her, but an open display would be totally out of character for Al-Dayal. Instead, he squeezed her shoulder and released it. "Get me another pillow. My shoulders ache from all that exercise."

She hesitated only a second, then obeyed. Eric noted Quince's gaze flick from him to Dawn and back again. Then he smiled. "You are a very lucky man, Jarad."

Eric frowned, then folded his hands across his stomach. "So it is said. Perhaps a man makes his own luck."

Quince shrugged. "Some think that's true and in the event of good luck, it might be. I've found that bad luck, however, usually takes us totally unaware."

"It is how one reacts to any luck that determines his ultimate fortune," Eric replied evenly, adjusting the cushion Dawn placed behind his neck. She sat down beside him again, ever the dutiful wife.

"Enough stupid philosophy," Carlotta snapped, addressing Quince. "I need to have done with this now and fly home. Why can we not present our bids now and have you drop us on the mainland?"

She clunked her glass down on the table and stood, rubbing her upper arms with her palms as if she were cold. Or frightened.

"Patience, my dear," Quince said with a toothy smile. "All in good time."

He reached behind him and hit a switch. Music flooded the cabin. "*Rebetika*," he explained. "Sad, isn't it? For a time, this music was outlawed by the government because it so often deals with poverty and suffering, but now it is becoming prevalent again."

He listened to the plaintive, haunting strains for a time, then added, "Governments come and go, but the people themselves will prevail eventually."

"Now there's a freakin' message to live by," McCoy agreed, his voice rife with feeling.

Eric felt, aside from his and Dawn's reasons, that the Irishman was probably the only bidder present whose motives for acquiring the radar-shield plans were in any way connected to patriotism. However extremist their views were, the members in Sean's sort of group almost always possessed passion and dedication. He would die for his cause, but he would rather kill for it.

Carlotta rolled her eyes at Sean's comment and sat down again, resigned to endure whatever Quince arranged. She had little choice. Her motive was power. She got off on control, too, and now she had none. He didn't need her thoughts to know this woman was determined and deadly.

He wished he hadn't been forced to bring Dawn along on the mission. Though he wouldn't have had the chance to know her if he hadn't. Her presence put her at tremendous risk, and seriously hampered his goals.

Eric was unused to fear while on the job. Only a fool was never afraid, but he had never let it become a problem for him. Mostly he ignored it, but now he couldn't. He was afraid for Dawn.

Sure, she was good at testing security. Her record showed she was great at hand-to-hand and an expert shot, but he knew she had never come up against these sorts of international hard-asses before.

If McCoy or Carlotta managed to take him out first, she would be left a lamb among wolves. She had no weapons except her wits. He prayed those were as sharp as they appeared to be. Maybe he should plan to strike first and eliminate the risk of leaving her vulnerable.

Eric tried again to read Quince, hoping for some indication of what was on the agenda when they reached the island. He drew a blank. Quince merely smiled at him, nodding in time with the sorrowful strings of the bouzouki.

Neither could he read the others. Maybe Quince's block had shaken his confidence in that regard. Maybe Dawn had. Maybe he had simply lost the ability. He could function without it, he assured himself. Somehow.

A little over an hour later, they were back at Quince's estate having a light luncheon on the terrace. No one ate at first. They didn't touch a dish at all until Quince himself had eaten some of it.

Eric and Dawn were no exception, though Eric was doubtful Quince intended to do away with any of the bidders himself. No, he apparently planned to let them take care of each other. The man was enjoying himself, that was plain to see.

Carlotta kept casting sly looks in McCoy's direction. Maybe she planned to join forces with him if she could arrange it. Two of them working together could dispatch ol' Al-Dayal in a heartbeat. Even now, she was most likely thinking about the cold-blooded seduction she had planned for the Irishman tonight after everyone else had gone to bed. Eric switched his attention to McCoy and figured that Sean would be wise to such tricks. Had he decided what he would do about it?

Eric concentrated on the excellent souvlaki. Greece was famous for the skewered meat, grilled and sliced thinly, then tucked inside pita bread. He absolutely loved the stuff Dawn had jokingly called goat burgers. She was daintily wolfing hers down now, obviously famished after their morning outing.

"Why not go for a swim after lunch, eh?" Quince suggested. "There are suits in the cabana that should fit everyone."

The pool looked inviting and the heat had become almost oppressive. The high walls that surrounded the terrace, pool and gardens blocked the sea breeze that might have cooled it a bit. The fans only stirred the hot air.

"I'm for it," Sean announced, tossing down his napkin. He chucked Carlotta under her stubborn chin. "If the little chili pepper here promises not to try to drown me."

She jerked away from his touch and gave him a haughty glare. "Go straight to hell, McCoy."

He laughed merrily and sauntered off to change. Moments later, they watched his expert dive into the pool. "Water's fine," he crowed, daring Carlotta with a look. "Cool," he added provocatively, drawing out the word.

She tossed her braid over her shoulder and went to change into a suit.

Quince raised a brow. "Jarad? Do you not swim?"

Eric pretended resignation. "If you insist. Aurora, you will remain here where I can see you."

It went without saying that Al-Dayal would never allow his wife to swim in the company of other men.

Even Quince did not bother to suggest that. Instead, he offered to keep her company. "I promise to be a perfect gentleman, Jarad. Go have your swim. You have nothing to worry about."

With a warning glower, Eric went to the cabana, reluctantly leaving Dawn alone with their host. He trusted she could handle herself in broad daylight with him less than fifty feet away. Maybe she could get something out of Quince about what he had arranged for the evening.

Dawn watched Eric's controlled laps as Sean and Carlotta splashed around like dolphins. She ignored Quince, even though she could feel his cold gaze fastened on her.

"You would like to swim, too, wouldn't you, my dear?" he asked, all tea and sympathy. "What a pity Jarad is so mired in the old ways."

She shrugged and continued observing the pool.

"You strike me as an independent woman at heart, Aurora," Quince announced, his voice low and persuasive. "I'd wager you didn't know what you were getting into when you married him, did you?"

"I knew he was a Muslim."

"But not that he would stifle your every impulse and thought. That has to become tiring after a while."

"I am a faithful wife, Señor Quince. And a faithful Muslim since I converted."

"Ah, and a retired Catholic, if there is such a thing," he said, nodding. "So you love the man that much, eh?"

Dawn cleared her throat and looked away, out at the controlled riot of flowers, the elegant frangipani trees and the sweep of manicured lawn. "Of course."

He laughed. "Of course *not*," he corrected. "If you want out, I am the way."

She turned to look directly at him and hesitated a couple of seconds for effect. "What do you mean…out?"

"Of the marriage. I could help you escape him. You must know what he is…what he *does*."

"He is in the oil business. And he *does* very little," she replied.

Quince's eyebrows drew together, and he sighed loud and long. "My dear, he is a terrorist, a leader in a movement that is bent upon destroying Western civilization as we know it. Surely you've become aware of that during your time together."

Dawn swallowed hard and ducked her head as if in shame.

"I will give you the means to end your servitude to this arrogant man permanently if you say the word."

For a long time, Dawn continued to watch the swimmers. Then she turned and asked in a whisper, "What word?"

Quince smiled. "Patience, little one. As I said to Carlotta, all in good time."

Lord have mercy, Dawn thought, carefully schooling her expression of awe, Quince meant for *her* to kill Eric, or at least his alter ego, Jarad.

"If you tell him of this conversation," Quince warned, "he will never trust you again. Always, he will be expecting you to act on my suggestion. I advise you to keep this to yourself for your own good. If he asks, we have been discussing the garden and grounds."

"Yes," she agreed. "The fragrance of the frangipani and the recipe for controlling snails."

"That would be beer?" he asked, smiling sweetly.

"And salt. Now we need not lie about the subject of our talk. At least not entirely."

"I like you, little one," he said gently. "And I want you

to leave this island in a better spirit than how you arrived. You deserve that."

"Thank you," she murmured, wondering whether Quince meant *spirit* as in frame of mind, or *spirit* as in ghost.

As it happened, Eric, Carlotta and Sean survived their swim and soon were back at the table.

Dawn could hardly keep her eyes off the expanse of smooth brown skin exposed in the brief suit Eric was wearing. The ruddy-faced Sean McCoy was pale all over, fairly buff, but, she would guess from his muscles, not as efficiently trained as Eric. Also, he lacked the tensile, athletic grace Eric possessed.

Carlotta's bikini left little to the imagination, though Sean kept eyeing her as if his might be working overtime. She was stacked, to put it mildly. Her body was long-limbed, and she moved as fluidly as a jungle cat, with muscles concealed under a slick, firm exterior. Dawn thanked her stars she hadn't had to don a swimsuit and compete with that body today. That would have been enough to give a girl a complex.

Relief poured over her when Quince finally suggested they retire to their respective rooms for a siesta, or whatever the Greek equivalent of that might be called.

Quince reminded them for the third time that dinner was at eight and there would be entertainment. Then he walked on ahead of them to speak with his man, Conroy, who waited just inside the open doors.

"Probably planning a public execution or something," Dawn muttered under her breath as they crossed the terrace to the French doors leading in. "He virtually offered to help me kill you."

"Shh," Eric warned. "Play along with whatever he suggests."

Dawn wondered if that included taking a knife to his jugular while he slept.

Eric clasped her hand in his and began questioning her loudly about her short visit with Quince. She dutifully told him about snails, unfamiliar perennials and tamarind trees, noting the satisfied gleam in Quince's eyes when he glanced over his shoulder at them.

When they reached their rooms, Dawn headed to the bathroom where she systematically searched for any concealed mikes. It was the smallest room and would be the most difficult to wire. But it was wired, of that she was certain. Anybody with any half sense would go in here and turn on the water to conceal any conversation. That was basic stuff. She had the water on now, to hide any rustling sounds she made.

There was no camera. She had looked for that first. Either Quince had a jot of decency left in him or hadn't been able to figure out how to hide one in the john.

She discovered the mike, minuscule and sophisticated, top of the line. It wouldn't do to deactivate it right now. She only needed to know where it was.

She continued probing every possible spot where she might find another. Bingo. On the frame of the mirror above the sink, away from any noisy jets of water, and at mouth level with anyone standing nearby.

Okay. Threats identified. Just to be sure, she completed her organized search of the entire room until she was satisfied there were only two microphones. Realizing she'd have to wait to tell Eric about her conversation with Quince, Dawn gave way to mental exhaustion and slept like the dead.

She knew Eric would be keeping watch. A few hours later, she woke and took her turn while he caught a few winks. Who knew what the evening would bring?

Dawn donned one of the beautiful gowns that had been packed for her. The pale green satin flowed like soft liquid against her skin, revealing her arms and shoulders, swirling about her ankles and tickling the tops of her matching pumps. If their ruse were real, a gown such as this would be worn in private for her husband's eyes only. Dawn wondered what Eric's true reaction to it would be. Feeling pretty sexy, she swept her hair up into a twist, secured it and added a small spray of diamonds to cover the pins.

Eric looked elegant in his dinner jacket and black slacks. The snowy white shirt complemented his fake tan to perfection. His teeth gleamed when he smiled. With panache, he produced a delicate diamond bracelet and fastened it on her wrist. "For my precious gem," he crooned in Al-Dayal's possessive manner.

Dawn sighed, wishing for a second that he was simply Eric, clipping a rhinestone bauble on her just because he liked her. She examined the stones and nodded. "Thank you, Jarad."

"You are most welcome, my dove. Tonight I must share your loveliness with others and I hate the very thought. When this business is finished, I shall have you all to myself again. Only then will I be content."

How could he look so sincere and say things like that? Dawn almost laughed to think any female would treasure such a possessive relationship. And yet, she had to admit there might be a certain comfort in knowing a man would go to such lengths to protect his woman from the leers of other men.

There had actually been times she wished she were wearing the concealing robe and veil. At least when she had it on, she didn't have to worry about schooling her reactions. In spite of what most people thought, it did give a woman a kind of freedom from pretense.

At precisely eight o'clock, they went downstairs, arm in arm, to join the motley crew that made up Quince's house party. Conroy met them at the bottom of the staircase and directed them to the lounge, as he called it.

It was the living room, of course, beautifully decorated in a Tuscan style with tones of amber and gold. The glow of candles lent an old-world charm, though the furnishings looked rather new to Dawn. The others were already there, standing around with drinks in hand.

Sean had cleaned up nicely, but hadn't completely ditched his rough-edged appearance. His spiky blond hair stood on end, probably without the benefit of gel. He had shaved, but not closely, leaving a slight stubble.

McCoy's lively green eyes danced when he assessed her and his lips quirked appreciatively, drawing a warning growl from her *husband.*

Carlotta wore a crimson chiffon wrap that bared the top half of her generous breasts and one long leg, emphasizing her height. Her hair fell straight and thick, caught behind one ear with a matching silk flower.

Dawn suddenly felt totally eclipsed. She shouldn't have minded, ought to have felt relieved, but she couldn't help but wonder how her own appearance held up in comparison, at least in Eric's estimation.

For the first time, she was playing in the big leagues and wanted to measure up. Little Dawnie Moon from Middlesex, New Jersey, recently inducted into the world of espionage, wanted to be a Bond Girl.

The thought made her wince. What was wrong with her? Did she really want to be like Miss Galore over there?

At least her boobs were as big as Carlotta's. That was something. However, her genes dictated her legs were several inches shorter than the long-stemmed Latin beauty's. That was okay, Dawn decided. She visualized her precious marksmanship medals and the days in training when she had taken down male agents who were twice her size. Yep, she could hold her own where it counted, she was sure of it.

At that moment, Eric squeezed her hand and beamed down at her, ignoring the woman who shone like a red neon sign advertising sex for sale. His regard made Dawn feel better. But then again, he *was* pretending at everything else. She shook off the thought.

Quince approached from the mirrored bar with two glasses. "Nonalcoholic wine, especially for you two," he announced.

They accepted the drinks without tasting them. Poison was a distinct possibility, Dawn realized. But then, Quince could simply shoot them, or have them shot, and bury them on the island if he wanted them dead right now. No, he wanted to watch them all match wits, she figured.

"Since it's quite impossible to import any talent to the island for the purpose, I've decided that we will entertain ourselves tonight after dinner," Quince announced. "Sean here is an accomplished tenor."

Sean's smile vanished and he set his drink down on a marble-topped table.

"Surely you realized that I would delve into your pasts extensively," Quince said with a clever grin. "Can't have strangers hanging about when the stakes are this high."

"I won't sing," Sean said.

Quince's grin disappeared in the instant. "I encourage you to humor me, my boy. If you refuse, or if you haven't a tenor voice that rings true to form, I will have to wonder whether someone has seen fit to replace the real Sean McCoy with an imposter."

"That's absurd," Sean remarked, shaking his head.

Quince pursed his lips and shrugged. "Surely you understand that it pays to be thorough in these matters. Let's call tonight's event a verification of sorts."

Sean threw up his hands and surrendered. "Aye, I'll sing, then, if it'll make you happy."

Carlotta laughed. "What do you sing, McCoy? Sad Irish laments?"

He forced a grin. "'Danny Boy', wouldn't you know?" he replied. "A favorite of yours, Lottie?"

She tossed back the remainder of her drink. "Oh please, spare me. Or at least pour me another scotch first."

Quince turned to her. "And you are an incredible dancer, so I am told."

Carlotta inclined her head in a pretense of modesty. "I do try." She raised a jet-black brow at Eric. "And what does our esteemed sheikh do, I wonder? Camel calls?"

Eric shot her a nasty look that included Quince. "I do not perform," he stated categorically. "Ever."

"But you have," Quince argued. "When you attended Oxford, you were known as an excellent pianist." He gestured to the baby grand that occupied one corner of the room. "We would be honored if you would play for us." He paused, then added to all of them, "As I said to Sean, this would certainly establish your backgrounds as genuine."

"Come now, Jarad," Carlotta said provocatively. "If I dance, then you must play. What else is there to do in this godforsaken place?" She cast a dismissive look at Quince. "Until our erstwhile host decides to end our captivity and allow us to get on with our lives?"

Then she seemed to remember Dawn. "What about her?" She flicked a red-tipped finger in Dawn's direction.

"Oh, Aurora sings, too," Quince said. "At the École de Fleur in Nice, she sang with the choir. I'm quite sure she would be happy to grace us with a song. Perhaps Jarad will accompany her on the piano?"

Dawn's heart plunged to the pit of her stomach, but she retained her placid expression. Someone in charge of their cover identities had invented a persona for Aurora that listed *choir,* of all things?

She hadn't sung a note since high school when she entered the contest for sweetheart of the FFA. Even the Future Farmers of America had been discriminating enough to recognize a shower singer when they heard her. She had lost to Susan Zimmerman, who wasn't very good herself.

Quince didn't quite trust that they were who they said they were. Okay. She could do this if it came down to the wire. What could she sing? Her old rendition of "America the Beautiful" was definitely out.

Something easy, then, that didn't require much range. Nothing recently popular in the West. An old song that had probably made it to Europe. Peggy Lee's "Fever"? She glanced surreptitiously at Eric. Okay, maybe not "Fever." *Jarad* would have a fit.

With a shy smile, she looked to Eric for help. "Is this allowed?"

She noted the surprise he instantly masked with disdain. "Nothing of a religious nature," he warned, referring to the fictional Aurora's Catholic school education in France.

"Secular, of course," she replied. "Perhaps something French? 'La Vie En Rose'? Do you know it?"

"Edith Piaf?"

"She is a favorite of mine," Dawn answered. "You have

heard it, then?" She injected a saucy note into her question that drew a reprimanding frown and a reluctant nod.

"Excellent!" Quince said, clapping his hands. "Off to dinner, now. I see Conroy is about to announce it. Come along, all of you. Aren't we famished?"

He herded them to the dining room where they were expected to enjoy the fruits of his chef's labors. Dawn tried to relax. Her nerves were strung so tightly, she was afraid she couldn't eat a bite. However, everyone's mood seemed to have lightened and hers did, too, eventually. Even the dinner conversation exceeded her expectations.

All the while, Dawn wondered just how Quince had managed to get them psyched up to show off abilities beyond their regular occupations.

Carlotta was bragging about the places she had danced when she was a girl. Sean kept trying to top her stories with anecdotes about the clubs in which he had sung.

Egos were odd things and reared up at the strangest of times. She was actually looking forward to trying her hand at being Edith Piaf and leaning on the piano while Eric played.

Jeez, she *hoped* he could play, and if he could, he was probably hoping just as fervently that she could sing.

As distractions went, the imminent program of entertainment served admirably. She could almost forget for whole minutes that one or more of the group might not survive the night.

Chapter 11

God help her, she was next. Following Carlotta's erotic heel-clicking routine that had shown off so much prominent bosom and leg wouldn't be easy. The girl had some great moves, Dawn had to give her that. The flashy red dress hadn't hurt the performance a bit. Had to make you wonder if she knew ahead of time she'd be cutting a rug.

Poor old Sean had to reel in his tongue when she stopped. Eric had applauded, too, surprising them all. His appreciation apparently whetted Carlotta's ham factor and caused an immediate encore. Now a thin sheen of sweat coated Carlotta and she'd had enough adulation to do her a while, Dawn guessed.

Quince was fiddling with the stereo system that had provided the rousing bambuca music.

Eric rose and offered his hand to Dawn. "Shall we?"

She stood and trailed him across the room to the piano.

"What key?" he asked under his breath as they approached it.

"You choose," she whispered, now terrified and trying hard to mask it. She didn't even read music, much less know what key she sang in, but she couldn't admit that in front of Quince. She was supposed to have been in a choir.

"You begin and I'll follow. Whatever key is comfortable for you." He squeezed her hand. "Relax, Aurora. I'm certain you will be fine."

Dawn swallowed hard, blew out a breath and sucked in another. "I was never a soloist," she admitted to Quince, "but I shall do my best."

She had been running over the words in her mind. Her French was fair and she did love the song. She had heard a scratchy recording of Piaf singing it on television.

All eyes were on her now—Carlotta's mocking, Sean's curious and Quince's ready to assess. She looked at Eric for reassurance, and his smile did the trick. He hit several chords, pausing between each, then waited for her to begin.

She closed her eyes and leaned against the piano, feeling the smooth hard surface beneath her forearm.

You're in the shower. All alone. Doors locked. No one to hear but you. Dawn imagined the water pulsing down on her, soothing, warm, relaxing.

She began with a breathy talking of the first line of lyrics, then found her way into it, raising her voice as she let loose. The vibrations from the instrument's strings reverberated through her, giving her confidence.

Words poured out almost without effort and before she knew it, she reached the last note and held it, knowing it sounded sweet. She was a chanteuse!

When Eric's music trailed away to nothing, she heard only dead silence.

Oh God, she had blown it. Dread held her immobile as she forced her eyes to open.

Sean stood and began to clap, his face rapt and his smile wide. Quince followed suit, grinning from guest to guest. Carlotta merely rolled her eyes and gulped her scotch and water.

Unable to help herself, Dawn turned to Eric. He smiled, too, plunked a resounding chord and added a trill of notes. "Very nice, Aurora," he said almost inaudibly.

Quince sat down again and waved an autocratic hand at Sean. "Top *that,* I dare you!" he said with a gruff laugh.

Dawn's knees were absolutely too weak to walk back to her chair. Eric seemed to realize it and got up to escort her, his strong forearm and hand supporting hers. She would have killed for the remainder of Carlotta's scotch and she didn't even like the stuff.

Eric returned to the piano to accompany Sean on the ballad. He did "Danny Boy," probably to annoy Carlotta, Dawn thought. His voice was clear and sweet, reaching notes that sent goose bumps chasing up and down her arms. The boy had missed his calling. What a waste of talent. Or maybe he had talents on the terrorist front that surpassed his music. God only knew.

Eric remained seated after Sean's offering and gave them a small taste of Beethoven. Just a dash of culture that supposedly wasn't his but had been necessary to acquire while he had been a foreign student.

Dawn smiled with true satisfaction. He played both the piano and the audience to perfection, she thought.

Everyone had convinced Quince they were who they proclaimed to be, that was obvious. He looked very pleased with himself and with their efforts as he got up from his chair and suggested drinks on the terrace.

The whole evening seemed surreal.

Dawn grasped Eric's hand in a death grip as they climbed the steps that led up the high wall that surrounded the terrace. The scent of the blooms below swept up and enveloped them in a swirl of heady perfume tinged with salt air. Wind off the sea tossed her hair in every direction, all but blinding her.

He stopped and sat down a few steps from the top where they had an excellent view of both seascape and the terrace where the others were sitting with drinks.

"Let's play newlyweds," he suggested quietly, turning her so that she lay back against his chest with his arms around her to ward off the night's chill. He placed his lips near her ear. "Keep your voice low and no one can possibly hear us up here if you have anything you want to say."

"Parabolics?" she asked, reminding him of the possibility.

"They'd be useless with this wind, but there won't be any set up out here anyway. The house isn't even properly bugged." He hugged her. "It's okay."

"I hate having to interact with them," Dawn whispered, eager to share her thoughts. "In some respects they seem almost normal at times." She turned her head so that she could see his expression as they talked.

"Yeah, we'd rather think of them as monsters without conscience, things with no feelings or emotions. But they are people, too, you know," Eric said with a sigh. He smoothed down the sides of the fake mustache and regarded McCoy, who was laughing merrily at something Carlotta had said. "You know as well as I do that people are seldom all bad or all good."

"You believe that?" Dawn had known people who were definitely all bad. And her grandmother had been good clear down to the marrow of her bones. "One of them is a killer."

"And definitely more bad than good," Eric admitted with a grimace. He lifted his chin in McCoy's direction. "Take Sean there. Given his behavior toward you and Carlotta, I'd be willing to bet he was always kind to his mother. Loved her. But he was raised in a society filled with hatred for the opposition, and war has always been a way of life for him. He thinks he's honoring his family with what he does and they may think so, too. No doubt he's loyal to the death when it comes to his cause and his comrades. Likable fellow under the right circumstances."

"These are not those," Dawn muttered darkly. "I suppose you see redeeming qualities in Carlotta, too."

He chuckled and took her hand, teasing her fingers with his lips. "The girl can dance, you gotta give her that."

"Big deal. And Quince, what about him? I swear I can't get a handle on that guy. Why is he playing at this and dragging it out this way? You'd think he'd be anxious to be done with it."

Eric seemed to be assessing their host as she spoke. For a long time, he said nothing, then shook his head. "Something's not right about him. Have you noticed how tentative he seems at times? He'll be totally in command, marching all of us around like chess pieces and then you see this hesitation, like he's not quite sure what to do next."

Dawn nodded. "Exactly. I think he's the front man. Somebody else is running the show, someone who doesn't want anyone to see his face." She sighed. "Anyway, that's my take on it."

"Astute. I get the same impression."

She leaned even closer. "Impression? What happened to your mind-reading talent? Can't you delve into the old gent's thoughts, or won't he cooperate?"

He didn't want to answer, she could tell. After a long moment of silence, he replied. "I can't do it anymore."

"C'mon," she teased, certain now that he had been feeding her a line of bull about it from the beginning. "Not at all?"

"No. I could before and now I can't, except when…" His voice trailed off as if he'd said more than he meant to say.

"Okay, except when?" she prompted, sure it was a game.

"When we made love. I could see right into your soul," he told her. He looked so deadly serious, he had to be joking.

Dawn laughed. "Wow. Good one. Was it a pretty sight or did you have to wrangle with my dark side?"

He grasped her chin and kissed her thoroughly, erasing every thought she had except how much she wanted him. And he didn't stop. Her body hummed, shot through with a current of longing so intense it scared her.

Before she knew it, he had twisted her around so that they embraced fully. If not for the fact that they were outside, balanced on a steep stone stairway with terrorists looking up at them, Dawn knew they would have made love then and there.

When he finally relented, she had trouble catching her breath and recalling what had prompted him to kiss her in the first place. "Wow," she said on a protracted exhale.

"Yeah," he agreed. "Wow."

"You're angry?" she asked, smoothing her palm down the front of his shirt.

He caught her hand in his and squeezed. "Not with you. Let's get down from here and cut this out before I lose what's left of my control."

On the way down, he preceded her so that she was about

level with his ear as she whispered, "Could you read my mind when you kissed me?" Teasing him seemed to be the only way she might coax him into a better mood.

"Silence," he snapped, his voice gruff and definitely Jarad Al-Dayal's.

Dawn made a face at the back of his head, drawing a hoot of laughter from Carlotta, who was watching them.

He turned quickly, his dark eyebrows drawn together in a warning frown. Dawn gave him a bland look of pure innocence and Carlotta laughed again.

"Perhaps we should say good-night now," Quince announced as she and Eric reached the terrace. "We have a big day tomorrow."

Carlotta stood. "Wait a minute. How long is this going to continue, Quince? You asked us here to bid on the damned plans. I can't speak for the rest, but I have other commitments. Could we finish this tonight?"

"No," he said simply. "If you no longer wish to participate, I will arrange for you to leave."

That shut her up. Her lips firmed, probably to hold in an epithet.

"Well?" he asked, one dark eyebrow raised in question.

"I will stay," she declared with a huff of frustration. "You know how important this is to me."

He nodded, and left them without another word.

Sean went to the bar and poured himself another drink, then relaxed back against it and held up his glass. "Well then. Here's to us and those like us. Damn few, and they are all dead." With a snap of his head, he downed the whiskey and plunked down his empty glass.

"A stupid toast," Carlotta remarked. "What does it mean?"

Sean grinned. "You have to be Irish to understand it."

"Thank God I'm in the dark, then," she replied.

"Speaking of a beckoning darkness, would you care to take a stroll in the gardens before bed?"

She hesitated only a moment, then pasted on a patently fake smile. "I would like nothing better."

They left without saying good-night.

"Interesting evening," Dawn commented when they were alone. Not really alone, she remembered. Almost certainly there were ears listening and probably hidden cameras watching.

She wanted to ask Eric whether he thought it would be Carlotta or Sean who would return from that walk, but she didn't dare. After listening to them banter and watching them perform, they had become individuals to her, real people, not simply faceless terrorists. She had to make herself remember who they really were and what they did for a living. One of them had killed Minos on the boat today while everyone else's attention was on Eric landing that fish. She was sure of it.

Eric frowned at the couple disappearing down the path. "You should go to bed now."

Yeah, right. As if she would sleep a wink wondering what was going on in that garden. Would one of them have disappeared by breakfast? Or would Carlotta and Sean join forces to try to get rid of Eric?

"You will come with me?" she asked. More of a demand, really.

"Not yet. I plan to take a walk myself."

Dawn grasped his arm and shot him a warning look. "I don't like to be alone, Jarad. I'll come, too."

"No." He smiled down at her and pulled away from her grip as he stood. "Don't worry. I will return before you know it." He glanced at the open door to the hallway. "Go up to our rooms. I'll watch from the hall until you are safely inside. Remember to lock the door."

With one further plea in her eyes, Dawn realized she had no way to keep him from going out there and that he wouldn't let her come with him, no matter what she said.

When she reached their quarters, she set the lock and leaned back against the heavy portal, praying he would stay safe. He would try to prevent whatever Sean or Carlotta were planning to do, whether to each other or to him. Hopefully, his friend was out there somewhere keeping watch. If Clay had made it safely ashore. Eric had not seemed too concerned about that, so maybe he knew something she didn't.

She pushed away from the door and started across the sitting room to her bedroom.

"You shouldn't worry about him, you know," a deep voice said, scaring her out of ten years' growth. She whirled around to find Quince standing in the room with her. Where the devil had he come from?

He gestured to the panel behind him that appeared to be part of the wall when closed, answering her unspoken question. "Forgive me for intruding, but I thought we needed to talk."

She pressed a palm firmly against her midsection. "Jarad will kill me if he finds you here," she whispered.

He chuckled and sauntered over to the formal sofa that sat in the middle of the room. He took a seat and patted the cushion beside him. "No doubt he would. This husband of yours is a violent man, Aurora. And so suspicious! You must know it's only a matter of time before he gets rid of you. All it will take is his meeting another who intrigues him more than you do. Any trumped-up charge against you would vindicate him in the eyes of his law. He'll either divorce you or find a more permanent solution. Why not arrange a preemptive strike? I'll help."

She widened her eyes and touched trembling fingers to her lips. "You want me to…do something to him first?"

Quince clicked his tongue. "Makes sense, wouldn't you say? Here is the perfect place to do it. There are no authorities to call his disappearance into question."

She pretended to digest the thought and come to terms with it. "How?" she asked, her voice still a whisper.

He got up then and headed back to the panel which opened as if by magic. Or perhaps a remote he carried in the pocket where his hand had disappeared. "I will work that out for you if the others are not successful."

"The others? You mean Carlotta and Scan?"

"Of course. If he returns, try to act normal so you won't give yourself away. Remember," he said seriously, dropping the attitude of amusement, "if he suspects you plan to betray him, he might kill you before you have a chance to act. If that happens, there is no one here who would even think about bringing him to justice. Even *I* wouldn't, so be warned."

"But why do you want this? His death, I mean? I thought you wished Jarad or one of the others to buy something from you, to pay you a fortune for whatever they came here after."

"I will be compensated," he assured her.

"What of me, Quince? When you are finished with your games?"

He shrugged. "You are an innocent, caught up in a web not of your making. If I can, I mean to save you." Then he smiled at her, not a baring of teeth, not taunting, either. A real smile that looked sincere.

Dawn watched him leave. The panel slid soundlessly back into place and the wall looked as solid and impene-

Straight Through the Heart

trable as the rest. She sank down onto the sofa and sighed loud and long, not caring who heard or observed.

What had he meant, *he would be compensated?* Was someone paying Quince to get rid of the bidders? If so, why not just kill them all and be done with it? Or at least kill them all but the one lucky winner who got to buy the plans from him?

But maybe he wasn't selling the plans after all. It sounded more and more to her as if he had set a trap with the offer just to get them to the island.

She needed to discuss this with Eric and get his thoughts on it, but there was no way they could speak openly. It wasn't safe to talk. She wished he really did have that handy mind link thing going on.

So here they were, acting up a storm, while everybody tried to murder everybody else. Except for Quince. It seemed he intended to keep his hands clean and let the others—and her, of course—do his dirty work for him.

Eric stood in the shadows near the pool, observing Quince, who strolled the terrace while smoking a cigar. Try as he might, Eric could not tell what the man was thinking. What an enigma.

He was just about to reveal himself and see whether he could get anything from Quince with a one-on-one conversation, when Conroy appeared.

"Have the new bidders arrived on the mainland?" Quince asked quietly.

"Yes, just this afternoon. They should be arriving here the day after tomorrow if that is still your wish, sir."

"Fine. This group should be out of the way by then. If not, we will combine them and see what happens. Carry on, my friend."

Conroy nodded and went back into the house.

There were others coming? What was going on here?

Eric had followed Carlotta and Sean, knowing that Carlotta was planning to seduce the Irishman into helping her get rid of the competition, namely himself.

But Sean had other ideas. Eric listened as they had a heated argument. Sean said he hated all she represented. The organized manufacturing and marketing of drugs worldwide was anathema to him. Her blatant sex appeal and the way she used it went hand in hand with the seductive powers of her product, as far as Sean was concerned. McCoy was an idealist at heart.

When the two had separated, Eric had returned to the terrace. Somewhere out there in the darkness, one of them would probably die. Eric hoped Clay would be able to prevent it. If he could secure one or both, they could be taken into custody for questioning later when the Sextant team arrived.

However, now there would be others arriving soon. It made no sense, unless Quince was systematically getting rid of terrorist representatives, or at least arranging it so they could conveniently knock off one another.

Where was the profit for him in that? What was his game? Maybe Quince saw himself as one of the good guys. Eric walked out of the trees onto the terrace.

"Come join me, Jarad," Quince said, a smile in his voice. He puffed on his cigar and blew a stream of smoke upward, watching it dissipate into the humid night air. "Smoke?"

"No," Eric answered, sauntering over to take one of the cushioned lounges. He sat down on the edge of it, leaned forward and clasped his hands. "What are you planning, Quince?"

"Why, nothing," he replied. "There is very little more to offer here on the island in the way of entertainment that we haven't already done. Brilliant fishing today, by the way."

"One of them killed Minos and you know it," Eric stated.

Quince nodded. "It is a cruel world, Jarad. In your line of work, you come to expect death to rear its ugly head fairly often, as do I. In my opinion, Minos is no great loss."

"His people might disagree, and they knew he was coming to you for this deal."

Quince smiled. "I expect and hope for a response to his death when they learn of it. The same with the woman and the Irishman." He grinned and pointed at Eric with his cigar. "And you, too, of course, if you are a victim."

Eric laughed, a bitter sound. "You plan to kill me, too?"

Quince affected a wounded expression. "But I have killed no one, Jarad. Each of your organizations will be informed of how their delegate met his or her end. The repercussions will fall on other heads, you see."

"Ingenious, but not too lucrative," Eric remarked, pushing back on the lounge, linking his hands behind his head. "Why the advance warning? You have put me on guard against the one who returns tonight."

"And you will prevail, I'm certain," Quince agreed. "Maybe you will survive to make me a fabulous offer and then go home with what you came here for."

Eric knew that was not in his plans. Quince thought he had a deal with Dawn, as the unhappy Aurora, to get rid of the offending husband. The bidders would all be dead if he had his way.

The new group coming in would probably repeat the scenario. How long did Quince plan to keep this up? And had he been at it a while already, changing the bait as necessary?

Eric got up and leisurely headed for the French doors. "Good night, Quince."

"Good night, Jarad. Sleep well." A chuckle accompanied the suggestion.

Had Quince already provided Dawn the means to take him out? She must be jumping up and down to share what had happened in Eric's absence, but there was no way they could talk about it.

The microphones in the suite would be of the best quality, able to detect the slightest whisper. Quince had a fortune at his disposal for such things. He would employ them, too, to stay aware of any side deals made by his guests.

Whatever was going on with Sean and Carlotta would probably be caught on audio if not on tape. How else would Quince convince their respective organizations that he wasn't the one who had gotten rid of their valuable representatives? No, he was pitting not only the buyers he had invited to the island against one another, he was extending the battle to their respective fraternities.

The chaos created by that could only benefit mankind in the long run, Eric thought to himself. But it was still vigilante justice anyway you looked at it. If, indeed, providing a little justice was Quince's intent. God, he wished he knew the man's mind.

Chapter 12

"Aurora?"

Eric was back at last, thank God. She hurried out to the sitting room and walked into his waiting arms just like a good little wife should. Dawn had to admit she didn't mind this part of the charade at all. Eric didn't seem to, either.

"I was afraid for you, Jarad," she said, laying her head on his shoulder.

He caressed her hair, smoothing it, soothing her. "No problems. After you left us I saw no one out there but our host. You should be in bed." He smiled down at her, his eyes gleaming as he eyed the pale yellow satin nightgown she'd donned and plucked away the clip she had used to pin up her hair. "You smell of jasmine."

"I am just out of the bath," she explained.

"I should have returned a bit sooner. I could have joined

you." He bent to nuzzle her neck. His lips sent delicious shivers down her spine.

She pulled away. "Have your bath now. I'll assist you." She took him by the hand and led him to the bathroom, allowing herself to frown after she turned away from him, in case Quince was watching them.

Once they were in the bathroom, she turned and mouthed the words, "There are no cameras here. Two mikes," she said, pointing to the locations.

He smiled and nodded his approval. "I hope the water is hot. My legs ache from the long walk. Perhaps you could help relieve that."

She turned on the water in the tub, then faced him again. He was scanning the room, probably wondering how thorough her search for cameras had been.

"I'm very good at it," she assured him, following the path of his scan with one of her own.

"I know," he replied, and began shucking his clothes, apparently trusting that she was talking about the physical security of the room, not her leg-rubbing skills.

But how could they communicate unless she deactivated the mikes? She really needed to talk to him.

Suddenly she had an idea. Hadn't he mentioned being a Scout? She knew they had the finger-spelling alphabet in the Boy Scout manual. Her cousin, who was deaf, had proudly pointed it out to her once. But then, Jim was older than Eric. Maybe it wasn't in the handbooks Eric had used. Still, it was worth a try.

It was a long shot, she knew, but Eric was supposed to be very proficient in a number of other languages. Dawn had learned to sign as a child in order to communicate with Jim. Maybe Eric had been as fascinated with the language as she had been. "Do you understand the alphabet for the deaf?" she spelled out slowly.

Eric looked surprised, then smiled and gave her the sign for *yes*. He finger-spelled the word *genius* and pointed to her. Then he proceeded to tell her, in ASL, the American Sign Language, that they should have thought of this sooner.

Dawn, stared, openmouthed, while he then removed the rest of his clothes and got into the tub.

She caught herself ogling and turned away slightly, but continued to steal glances at him. It was impossible to ignore his nudity, and he obviously thought it funny that she would try.

They had been intimate the night before, but somehow this seemed even more so. His muscles rippled as he began to soap himself, watching her all the while as if daring her to join him. She forced her gaze to remain on his face.

Dawn was sorely tempted, but knew exactly how that would end. They would make love in that enormous tub. Enticing as that was—as *he* was—at the moment, she knew they needed to talk. Besides, she didn't exactly relish having a listener or listeners at tubside while they frolicked in the suds.

Signing comfortably, she told him of Quince's visit to her room through the concealed doorway and explained what he wanted her to do.

Eric revealed what Quince had admitted to him, and the possibilities that brought up. Quince would have to silence her, too, eventually. They agreed on that.

Even if the man's motives were lofty and he let her live, she would never be allowed to leave the island if he succeeded in what he was doing. Their mission had to succeed and the team would have to arrive soon to accomplish that.

Eric's command of the language was imperfect, interspersed with many more spelled-out words than she used, but it proved fully understandable.

Every now and then, he would speak out loud as Jarad, ordering her around, sounding suggestive and teasing. Finally, downright provocative. Dawn got the feeling that he meant at least half of it.

She watched his hand rise and approach her breast. With one wet finger, he touched her through the gown and smiled into her eyes. His lips formed the words, "I want you" while he made the sign for it.

Her heartbeat raced even faster. What would it be like to take his dare, to slip off the satin and slide into the warm water beside him? Her imagination ran wild. She knew exactly what it would feel like. Dawn needed to be held. And he wanted to hold her, that was very clear.

Their gazes locked. What was left of her resolve melted. She stood, peeled off her peignoir and gown and stepped into the huge marble tub. He reached over and pushed the button to turn on the jets of water, surrounding them with warm, powerful streams that seemed to force their bodies closer.

Not that she needed a push. His hot slick skin slid against hers when he embraced her, firing her to fever pitch as his lips met hers in a devouring kiss. Damn the mikes, she couldn't contain the groan that rose from her throat, merging with his.

He lifted her slightly and entered her without breaking the kiss. *Complete,* she thought. *I feel complete.* Nothing mattered but this, this incredible oneness.

He felt the same and she knew it somehow, sensed that he had abandoned all caution, all thought of self-preservation, all pretense. This was as real as it got. And as profound a feeling as she had ever experienced. Nothing compared.

Dawn moved sinuously, grasping for more, winding her arms around his neck, sliding her fingers through his hair and holding on for dear life. The sensations bombarding her stole what breath she had left. Strong pulsating jets pummeled the base of her spine and the middle of her back. Powerful legs entwined with hers.

The scent of him, earthy, exotic, mingled with the sandalwood soap that half coated his body. His growl of pleasure reverberated through her while his hands glided over her, now gripping firmly, then searching madly.

Higher and higher she flew until he splayed one hand against her lower back and pressed her to him for a final, shuddering thrust. She must have cried out. His mouth covered hers and took them under the water for a second. That did anything but douse the pure glee that welled up inside her.

They surfaced, sputtering and laughing, bodies still joined. His expression grew tender as he brushed the wet hair from her eyes and looked into them, the sign for *I love you* on the hand he used for the caress.

Did he realize that? It was a fairly common position for a hand to take, thumb and fingers extended except for the middle and ring fingers, which were folded down.

This was no time to think about love. She was lying in a bathtub wired for sound, glowing in the aftermath of the greatest sex she'd ever had, and in the greatest danger she'd ever encountered in her life.

Slowly he lifted her off of him and sat up. "Later, then," he muttered, sounding very sure of himself.

His on-the-mark comment shocked her a little. No, he couldn't be reading her mind, but he sure wanted her to think he was. What she was thinking was probably written all over her face with her defenses down the way they were.

Dawn scrambled out of the tub as gracefully as she could and grabbed a towel. She tossed him one, too. Hit him in the face with it and grimaced when he raised both eyebrows and offered her a satisfied grin.

"I hate you!" she signed with fake vehemence.

He laughed soundlessly and began to dry off.

Dawn had a feeling she wasn't going to get out of this with her heart intact even if she did survive the mission. If she had any sense, she would rebuild her barriers even higher and denser than before. She did not need to fall in love with Eric Vinland. She *wouldn't*.

Eric's certainty about Dawn's feelings began to fade as soon as she left the bathroom. He wrapped the towel around his waist and watched her march across the sitting room and enter her bedroom. She didn't slam the door, but she closed it firmly, letting him know she wanted to be alone.

He wasn't used to this. Oh, he occasionally ticked women off, sure, and most of the time it was on purpose when they got too involved. But he knew Dawn wasn't really angry with him. Embarrassed, maybe, or upset that she had sort of lost control. Hell, he had, too.

He shouldn't have seduced her in there, not with microphones stuck all over the place. He hadn't intended to carry through and actually have sex with her, but things had gotten out of hand in a hurry. Not that they had made much noise.

She probably wondered if he had done it on purpose, staking his claim so Quince would know they were being intimate. To tell the truth, he hadn't so much as thought about their host or hidden mikes or anything else once he had begun to kiss her. There could have been cameras running and he wouldn't have cared.

Well, he would have *cared*, of course, but probably after

the fact. He gave a mirthless little chuckle. So much for professionalism. Damn, the woman had him off center. She had wrecked his confidence in his psychic abilities. Or destroyed them. He wasn't even picking up any thoughts when he tuned in on the others, only reading their body language and expressions as anyone might do.

As a quick check, he tried to connect with Clay who was somewhere out there lurking in the trees and rocks.

Nothing. No matter how hard he concentrated. Not one damn thought. Of course, Clay could be asleep. Eric tried to visualize. Most of the time he could do that, get a brief glimpse of a person's surroundings in real time. *Nothing*.

He had picked up a brief warning out there in the dark when he was on his walk. *Go back to the house.* However, that could have been his own alarm system kicking in and not anyone else's thoughts at all. Dawn had been alone with Quince, and he hadn't liked leaving her.

Everything always came back to Dawn. She was his primary concern and that shouldn't be the case. The mission was the all-important thing here. He needed to remember that.

He thought about linking with Mercier, sending a concentration of energy that would serve as a green light to ending all this. But there was a new group of bidders arriving tomorrow. Better that they were already on the island with less chance to escape capture. No, he couldn't endanger the mission merely to test his powers.

He cursed under his breath and went to his own room to put on some clothes. And he was *keeping* his clothes on until this thing was over and they were back on the mainland, he firmly promised himself.

Damn Dawn's pretty little hide, she had probably ruined him for this kind of work. He might wind up teaching languages at Podunk University one of these days instead of what he was doing now, but he couldn't for a second regret what he felt for her, despite that. She was worth any price he had to pay if she loved him, too.

He had been so sure she did in those intimate moments. It was as if he could reach clear into her soul and experience every nuance of her feelings right along with her, a sharing such as he had never known before. Now he wondered if maybe he had been indulging in a fantasy.

The time had come to get his act together and put his personal life on hold, or he and Dawn might not have lives to straighten out later. Whatever Quince's objective was, he meant business.

Breakfast was at nine on the terrace. Eric and Dawn were seated having coffee when Quince arrived, for once unsmiling. He sat down, leaned forward and clasped his long, slender hands on the tabletop, looking from one to the other. "Carlotta and Sean are gone. No one can find them."

Eric heard Dawn's gasp and wondered if it was real or for effect. He wasn't all that surprised and she shouldn't be. Quince didn't exactly look broken up by the news, but there was a shade of worry in his eyes.

"Maybe they found a way off the island," Eric suggested.

"No," Quince assured him. "Carlotta did not leave. Not the way you mean."

The minute Carlotta and Sean left for their *walk,* everyone figured that one of them would not be coming back.

"Then what do you think has happened to her?" Dawn asked.

Quince shrugged and sat back, allowing Conroy to pour his coffee. "It appears that she fell from one of the rock faces. There were signs of a struggle. One of her shoes was found on a ledge ten feet down. There are jagged rocks lining the shore at the bottom of that cliff. She probably fell and was washed out to sea."

"And Sean?" Dawn asked.

"Missing," Quince admitted, biting off the word as he raised his cup to his lips.

"Not for long, I'm certain," Eric commented. "I shouldn't think there are many places to conceal oneself on an island of this size. Besides, he will return in order to make his bid."

Quince said nothing further as they finished their morning repast of delicious pastries and fruit. Then he excused himself and left the house.

Dawn quickly slid out of her chair. "I think I will go upstairs and read for a while."

"I'll come with you."

When they got upstairs, they headed straight for the bathroom. She whirled around and signed to him. "We should find out whether this group arriving today will really be the last."

Eric agreed. "We need the list. There's a computer in Quince's study where I was taken when we arrived. If we could somehow bypass the cameras, maybe we could get into his files. He will delete everything if our people lose the element of surprise when they come in."

She nodded and sat down on the edge of the platform around the tub to think. "There has to be a base of operations somewhere in the house. The trick is finding it without being seen." She brightened, making the sign for *idea*. "The secret door Quince used to come in here! Maybe the corridor inside the walls leads to the control room."

Eric picked up his shaving cream container and went back to the sitting room. Casually moving a chair to the outermost wall near the window, he climbed up and squirted a little glob of foam into the hole that was the size of a quarter. That was the only camera in the room and by staying near the wall, took advantage of its limited scope. "There," he signed.

Dawn gave him a thumbs-up and began searching for the release mechanism where Quince's hidden door was located. But it was nowhere to be found. She and Eric punched and prodded every possible location and nothing happened. "Remote control," she mouthed and then shrugged.

Well, it had been a great idea as far as it went, Eric thought, disappointed. He would just have to get into the control room another way.

Someone rapped on the door to the hallway. Eric went to answer. It was Conroy. "More guests have arrived, sir. You and the lady are requested to attend Mr. Quince in the lounge."

Eric nodded and beckoned to Dawn. They followed the butler down the stairs. Seated in the room with Quince were three men in business suits.

Quince stood. The others remained seated. "Ah, Jarad. Come and meet Cal Markham. He has come all the way from the States. He runs an organization that plans to better the fate of Americans." Then he slid his jaw to one side in a wry look. "*Selected* Americans, of course."

Markham shot Quince a killing look. Their host ignored it and proceeded to introduce another of the men. "And here we have Boris Korkova, who intends to reorganize the Kremlin." Quince issued a little chuckle. "And finally Ali Mohandra. He hails from the Sudan. Allah only knows what he's up to because he insists on secrecy. But we can guess, can we not?"

"Damn you, Quince!" the man shouted as he leapt to his feet. The two armed guards raised their weapons.

Quince lifted his eyebrows and smiled. "Please resume your seat, Ali." He then turned to Eric and Dawn. "I would like you all to meet the esteemed Jarad Al-Dayal and his lovely wife, Aurora." He made a slight bow in Dawn's direction. "Jarad is well-known for his unorthodox methods of warfare against the Western powers that be. I hope no one here takes offense at that." He looked pointedly at Markham, who was grinding his teeth. "After all, Cal, he is abetting your contretemps with your American government."

Boris rose slowly from his chair. "Now that you have done your social duties, Quince, I see no reason to delay. Let us get on with the bidding."

"Not today," Quince replied, strolling over to take Dawn's arm. "I don't like skipping the amenities. First, we shall take a tour of my home so you will all feel comfortable. Then we will take a turn around the island."

"Now see here…" Cal began to protest.

"Come along," Quince advised, pointedly gesturing to the two armed guards. "Now."

With Quince and Dawn in the lead and the others in tow, the guards brought up the rear as they wound through the downstairs rooms, suffering Quince's running dialogue as he admired his own art objects and antiques, inviting comments.

No one provided them but Dawn, who said all the right things and kept her arm linked with Quince's.

Eric trusted Dawn would keep the man's attention off him while he tried to figure out where Quince's control room was located.

He also noted the position of the cameras. No way those could be avoided in an out-and-out search of the place. They had to find out how to get into that hidden passageway. He wondered if anyone had noted yet that the camera in the main room of their suite was no longer operational.

When they toured upstairs, he saw a jog in the wall of the hallway that shouldn't be there, according to the shape of the rooms they were allowed to view. That must be Control.

Dawn turned slightly and met his gaze. She had figured it out, too. Even that feat didn't account for the smug little upturn of her lips. What was she up to now?

He begged off the tour of the island, which he and Dawn had already been through the day before. To his surprise, Quince allowed it.

Who would be missing on their return? Eric wondered. Not that he cared. Dump *all* these guys off a cliff and no one would be the worse for the loss.

As soon as they were alone again, seated in the lounge with a glass of juice, Dawn toyed with the scarf she wore around her neck, surreptitiously finger-spelling the word *remote*. Then she patted the pocket of her skirt and winked.

Damn! She had lifted the remote control right out of Quince's pocket! Eric suggested they retire to their rooms immediately.

"What a cream-fed expression you wear, little cat," he said as he escorted her up the stairs. "It makes a man wonder what you have in mind."

She wisely didn't reply, but flashed him a droll look as they reached the door to their suite. He hoped anyone watching them would think they had come upstairs with sex in mind and would leave them alone for an hour or so. He also hoped that if anyone was minding the cameras, they didn't intend to stick around for the show.

Chapter 13

As soon as they reached their rooms, Dawn systematically found and disabled the two mikes she knew were in the sitting room. They were exactly where any novice would have planted them, which sent up red flags in her mind. Quince was no beginner at this. She kept searching, as did Eric.

When Eric grunted with satisfaction, she turned to see him taking care of another that had been placed in the side hem of one of the drapes. He gave her a nod. "That's all."

She smiled and pulled the remote out of her pocket, waggling it in front of him.

"Dangerous," he commented, but she could see he was impressed with her pickpocketing ability.

Hopefully Quince wouldn't miss the thing until he got back to the house. By that time, she hoped to have placed it somewhere that he might have inadvertently lost it.

"Stay here," she whispered. "Make some noise in the

bathroom so they'll think we're in there. If anyone's listening, I'll need them distracted." She kicked off her shoes so she could move soundlessly.

"Don't worry. I know what I'm doing." With a flourish, she pointed the remote at the wall and pushed the button. A panel slid back, just as it had when Quince was there.

"Be careful," he warned. "Leave that door open and yell if you run into trouble."

She blew Eric a kiss and stepped into the narrow corridor to explore.

The passageway, less than two feet wide, had not been finished on the inside and she had to take care not to snag her dress on the rough timbers.

If she went right, she knew it would lead to the quarters of the other guests. Since their rooms were closest to the irregular wall they had seen, she went left. She tried to visualize where it was leading her, though she knew roughly where the control room must be from her earlier observations. It couldn't be very large, possibly only six by nine feet. Close quarters for a confrontation if anyone was in there.

She crept forward as quickly as she could, running out of light from the open door after she turned the corner. Feeling her way along, measuring the distance by the protrusion of the studs placed at four-foot intervals. Suddenly, the floor seemed to fall away, but her foot caught on a step as she grabbed one of the timbers. There were stairs! Quince's control room wasn't on this floor after all.

Cautiously she descended, the darkness total now, and came to a closed door at the bottom. Dawn felt carefully for a knob or handle. There was none. She took a deep breath, almost coughing at the stuffiness of the air. Then she fished the remote out of her pocket, backed up a few steps and pushed the button. The light almost blinded her.

She bent double and head-butted the figure that had stood to greet her. A loud *oof* resulted. Without a pause, she fell back and kicked upward, catching him just beneath the chin.

Thank God he wasn't one of the beefy armed guards Quince employed. A computer geek, she guessed, not trained in hand-to-hand.

Before he could recover, she popped his ears with the flat of her palms, then chopped the back of his neck like a cinder block in karate class. He fell and lay motionless at her feet.

The first thing Dawn did was find his weapon, an automatic pistol, loaded. It was cheaply made and showed signs of neglect, but she immediately felt less vulnerable. Next, she felt for a pulse and found one, then looked around the room for something to tie him with. Nothing but computer cords.

Well, she'd just have to hurry and finish before he came to. Then she would have to hide him somewhere until Sextant sent the team in. Or kill him outright, which she wasn't entirely sure she could do. Defending herself was one thing, but the man was out cold.

All the while, she had been scanning the bank of computer screens set up around the room. There were only eight, which meant there weren't as many cameras as she had figured. One showed the terrace to keep track of the comings and goings in and out of the house. One pictured the cove where they had landed. The other six were set up in the guest rooms. No movement anywhere at the moment except from the one guard watching the beach.

Dawn systematically disabled all the surveillance equipment.

She noted another door and headed directly for it. *Pay dirt.* This was Quince's study, lined with bookcases and outfitted with expensive mahogany and what appeared to be a sophisticated computer system. She hurried to the keyboard, tapped it and watched the screen saver disappear. The idiot! He had files on his desktop.

She clicked the one that announced *Waste*. A list popped up with Jarad Al-Dayal's name second, beneath Carlotta's. There were ten names on his guest list, with only the first six recognizable to her. Her name was not included. Neither was Sean McCoy's.

What did those exclusions mean? She quickly committed the names to memory, closed the file and checked several others. Maintenance stuff. Frantic to finish her search, she checked the desk drawers.

Only one was locked. She forced it with a letter opener. Lo and behold, all by its lonesome, there lay a slender attaché, the portable flash drive, the same size and shape as a disposable cigarette lighter.

Hopefully this was the same thing she had seen stolen by Bergen at the Zelcon lab. No time to check it out. She stuck it in her pocket with the pistol, straightened everything else she had touched and got out of the room, closing the door behind her.

Quince's man lay where she had left him. Dawn unfastened the tightly woven cord from the attaché and used it to bind his hands behind him. He wasn't much bigger than she was, but no way could she drag him up those stairs. What could she do with him?

"I'll take him," Eric said from the stairway door.

"What are you doing here? You were supposed to—"

"You were gone too long. I was worried, okay?" he snapped.

Thank God he had followed. "Where will we put him?"

"The bathroom for the time being," he answered. He shouldered the body as if it were a sack of feathers.

It would be a tight squeeze getting back through the passageway carrying the computer tech, but they had little choice.

She closed the doors behind them with the remote and followed Eric's slow but steady progress back to their rooms.

With the man securely bound and gagged in the enormous marble tub, she and Eric collapsed in the sitting room to rest. No one was monitoring them now. She had fixed that for sure. "It's safe. No ears, no eyes," she reported.

"Good girl," Eric said.

"My boy, you have no idea *how* good," she replied. For the first time, Dawn allowed herself a self-satisfied grin. "I have the list of names." She paused to watch his surprise, then presented her next feat, adding, "and a gun, of course."

He nodded, pulling a face. "Of course."

She put the pistol away. "And the plans, I think." She drew the little flash drive out of her pocket and dangled it between her thumb and forefinger.

He laughed. "I'll be damned. You really think that's it?"

"It stands to reason. The one thing in the only locked drawer." At that moment, Dawn wanted to rush into his arms and do a little victory dance. She could see he felt the same way.

His excitement dimmed a little as she watched. "Now how do we keep Quince in the dark about your discovery until I can get the team in here to clean up?"

"Better call them in now. According to the list, there are only four who haven't arrived yet. Maybe they can be picked up on the mainland."

He rubbed his brow, frowning now. "If we can take them here, it would be better." He looked up at her. "Want to risk another day or two?"

Dawn shrugged. "I'm game, but Quince is gonna know

something's up. His guy is missing from the control room and somebody sabotaged his surveillance toys."

"We play dumb. Maybe Sean will take the heat for that since he's still out there running around," Eric reminded her.

Suddenly Dawn remembered. "Hey, I'd better get rid of this remote before Quince gets back. We can't lay *that* on McCoy."

"Downstairs," Eric suggested, getting up. "You can stick it between the cushions where he was sitting before we went on the house tour."

They hurried down to the lounge. Voices wafted up, alerting them that Quince and his other guests had already returned.

Eric stopped her on the stairs, tousled her hair and kissed her soundly on the mouth, smearing her lipstick. He grinned playfully when she tried to wipe it off and catch her breath at the same time. "We've been busy in bed, okay?"

"Don't you wish," she murmured.

"Absolutely, even if it is almost as nerve-racking as what we were really up to," he replied under his breath.

"Nerve-racking?" She couldn't help but smile.

Quince raised his eyebrows when they came in. "I trust you two have been entertaining yourselves while we were out."

Eric marched across the room to the bar without answering and helped himself to a glass of juice. "I tire of this incessant touring of yours, Quince. Shoot me if you will, but cease pretending this is some…" he windmilled one hand and scoffed "…house party."

"Ah, but that's precisely what it is, my friend," Quince said, turning away from Dawn, who moved surreptitiously toward the chair where she intended to drop the remote.

"Where is the American?" Eric demanded, looking around as if Cal Markham might appear out of nowhere.

"What do you have there, woman?" Boris demanded as soon as Dawn drew the remote from her pocket.

Dawn froze as all eyes turned to her, Eric's question about Cal Markham's absence forgotten.

She raised her chin and pinned the Russian with a haughty look. "You think I have a weapon?" She laughed mirthlessly. "I merely intend to watch television while you men argue." She pointed the remote at the big-screen TV housed in the entertainment center. "I will place it on mute."

"Wait!" Quince moved hurriedly and snatched the remote from her hand. "Where did you get this?"

Dawn pointed to the chair. "There."

"No television," he barked. "All of you, retire to your rooms immediately." He was suddenly sweating profusely.

He gave no explanation for his dismissal, nor did he have to. No one in residence was under the impression that they really were Quince's guests. They were captive here until he decided to hold the auction of the information and allowed them to leave.

The armed guards were just outside the door. As for Dawn and Eric, they both knew why Quince wanted everyone out of his way. He was going to check out his control room.

"Now you have angered our host, Aurora!" Eric accused Dawn as they marched up the stairs with the others. "I shall have to punish you."

Dawn hung her head, as if shamed and afraid. Boris grunted his approval and the African laughed. Men of a feather, she thought to herself, glad Eric didn't really fit that mold. If Quince wasn't careful, these jerks might actually bond into a new group instead of offing each other the way he planned.

She wondered where the other guy was. How would a

big, bad white supremacist have reacted to a Muslim man berating an uppity wife?

Eric herded her straight into the bathroom as soon as they reached their quarters. The computer weenie they had tied up in the bathtub was still there, wriggling uncomfortably, still secure. Dawn ignored him and addressed Eric. "What now?"

He was ripping off his shirt. "I need to contact Mercier. We can't wait. It's time for the showdown."

"For that you need to be naked? Somehow I expected you to close your eyes, go all woo-woo for a minute and that'd be it."

His lips quirked in a mirthless smile. "Better use something more concrete than a mind link. I don't seem to be functioning too well in that capacity, thanks to you."

"Me! What do I have to do with it?"

"Inadvertent interference. Not your fault." He tossed his shirt aside and reached for the back of his left shoulder with his right hand, feeling the skin there as if looking for something.

"What *are* you doing?" she demanded, moving around to see what was wrong with his shoulder.

"Get something sharp and remove this, will you?"

Dawn squinted at the mosquito bite he was touching with his forefinger. "What is it? Oh, the transmitter you mentioned?"

"It will be when I get it out and activate it. Right now, it's only emitting an infrequent pulse to give our location. Quince's scanner would have picked it up when he searched me if it emitted constantly. Not squeamish, are you?"

"No." She shrugged and went to search her makeup bag. She came up with a pair of nail scissors. "These should do."

He patiently sat on the lid of the commode while she

performed minor surgery, quickly slitting the skin that covered the tiny device. She noted the scattering of tiny freckles that lay beneath his fake tan, readily visible to anyone who looked closely. They reminded her how vulnerable he was, disguised this way. With one slipup, she could have punctured his plan as neatly as she had his skin and gotten them both killed. And yet, he had trusted her to become Aurora, who was the total opposite of her real self. How did anyone come by such trust, especially in someone they knew so little about?

"There," she muttered, handing him the instrument that proved to be about the size of a hearing-aid battery. She pressed a folded wad of toilet tissue over the incision and bore down on it to halt the bleeding.

He rolled off more tissue, cleaned the transmitter and took the nail scissors to it. She watched him poke it, then tap it lightly, using what was obviously a code. Not Morse, she realized. He repeated a pattern five times, then stopped. "That should do it."

"Are they near? Sextant, I mean?"

He nodded. "They should be just beyond the horizon, waiting for the signal."

Dawn bit her lips together, then suggested, "Could you maybe try that other method of contact, too, just to be on the safe side?"

He grinned up at her. "But you don't really buy into that. You said so."

She backed up a step, placing her free hand on her hips. "Any minute now, Quince is likely to come storming in here demanding what I took from his office. He has that bevy of trigger-happy guards with him and all we've got is a cheap pistol with four rounds in it. Anything you can do to hurry our backup along, I really want you to try." She frowned at the tiny transmitter. "That thing could be gunked up or something."

"All right. Then go in the other room. You distract me," he ordered.

"I want to watch," she argued.

His look turned serious as he placed a hand on her arm and squeezed it reassuringly. "Please."

She took his hand and placed it over the makeshift bandage. "Well, hold this while you *communicate* so you won't bleed to death."

"Thanks," he replied simply, then added, "I mean it. You've done a great job here, Dawn, however the mission ends. You remember that."

Dawn didn't reply. She might have asked him what he expected to go down now, why he looked so worried. He might have told her that their chances of surviving this had dropped to near zero because she had gotten caught with that remote control. The less said, the better, she guessed.

Eric was getting nothing back from Mercier. No confirming vibrations from the transmitter, none mindwise, either. Nada.

Okay, they would have to play this out as if backup was stuck out there with no wind for the sails. He checked the pistol again, as if that would help. Four rounds, not enough to take out the guards, much less the two terrorists left and Quince himself. Then there was the wild card, Sean McCoy.

Eric had tried to summon Clay. No response there, either. Maybe he was dead.

Dawn's yelp from the next room catapulted him into action. He cast a warning look at the man in the bathtub, then burst into the sitting room ready to fire.

Quince held up one hand. "Wait!"

Eric held his stance, the gun aimed directly at Quince's head. "I should shoot you," he rasped. "You came in here thinking my wife was alone."

"Not at all," Quince argued, sounding less than his debonair self. "I was…looking for someone…else." His eyes narrowed. "Where did you get that weapon?"

Eric didn't hesitate, banking on the hope that Quince was only searching for his missing computer tech. "Off the little man who was searching our room when we arrived."

"Where is he now?" Quince demanded, his fear obviously lessening with each second Eric allowed him to live.

Eric nodded toward the window. "He escaped. An eel, that one. If I see him again, he is dead."

Quince's jaw slid sideways in an expression of doubt. "It is three floors down to the terrace. Are you saying he survived such a drop and ran away?"

"Frankly, I don't care." Eric lowered the weapon marginally. "Should I assume his search was unauthorized? You should know by now that Aurora and I have nothing to hide from you."

"So I do," Quince agreed. "No, I gave no one permission to search these rooms or to be here for any other purpose. Now if you wish to stay in my good graces, Jarad, please give me the gun."

Eric laughed. "Be satisfied that I have not used it." He glanced again at the window and added, "Yet."

He added a smug chuckle. "I won't kill you, Quince. You have something I want and there is no way to get it if you're dead. However, I make no promises as to the others."

Quince stared at him for several seconds, then shrugged. "Very well. Keep it." With that, he turned and left the room by the hall door.

Dawn waited until Quince was gone, then turned to Eric. "He doesn't know we found the control room."

Eric agreed. He hurried her back into the bathroom. "We have a problem," he confessed.

She sighed. "They seem to be stacking up on us. What now?"

"I can't connect with Mercier," he admitted. "Or anyone else on the team. Looks like we'll have to wing it."

"You know what'll hit the fan when Quince discovers that flash drive is missing." She looked at their captive. "And if he finds Bozo over there and learns what happened, the jig's up. He'll kill us both."

"We could toss him out the window now," Eric suggested.

The man's eyebrows shot up and he began making whining noises.

Dawn caught on. She stood over the guy with her hands on her hips. "He's okay where he is *if* he'll stay quiet," she said pointedly. The whining stopped abruptly. "Better." She granted the man a smile. "Remain our little secret and you'll live. Understand?"

He nodded frantically.

Eric loosened the gag and removed it. "We need some answers. Help us and we'll help you. Who are you and where are you from?"

"Niko. From Ankros on the mainland. All I know is how to wire things. This is all I do. And listen and watch. This is my job."

"Stop hyperventilating, Niko," Eric advised. "Take a deep breath." He waited until the guy calmed down. "Now then. Tell me about the cameras located around the island and who else is watching the footage."

"Only I was to do that," Niko insisted. "The feed goes directly to the control room from all of them. I ate and slept there, only I was not to sleep except during specified hours of the early morning. If things of interest happened, I was to buzz Mr. Quince and advise him immediately. Everything is taped by day and to be saved."

"Why only you?" Eric asked, though he already knew. The questions were calming Niko, and they needed him to be calm.

"Because there are so few of us, and it is what he hired me to do. The others have their own tasks."

"When did he hire you, Niko? And for how long?"

"Six days ago. For two weeks, he said. No more and maybe less. A house party, he said, with guests he must watch closely. I think then that he intends blackmail and tell him no, but he promised me it was no such thing, only for his own protection."

"Were the others here when you arrived? The guards?"

"No. We came out together. Six guards, the butler, two servants and the chef. Quince brought us."

"Not the captain, but Quince," Eric stated, nodding. "Thank you, Niko. I'm going to replace your gag now. Don't be afraid. I promise we will not harm you unless you make noise. This will all be over soon and you'll go free, back home to your family in Ankros."

Dawn looked confused. "Six days ago? We were already on Leros then."

"Maybe that accounts for our delay there. Had to get things set up. But why issue the invitation before everything was ready to go?" He glanced around. "This place was already here, obviously, but is it Quince's usual lair or a recent buy?"

She sat down on the edge of the tub, her hands clasped in her lap. "Odd. What do you think it means?"

"That Quince is running with a skeleton crew that

probably knows nothing about what he's doing. Something's off about this. Way off."

Eric considered how the game had run this far. "It's almost as if he doesn't know what to do next and he's just hoping we'll bump one another off so he won't have to complete the deal." He scoffed. "He even let me keep the gun."

"Oh, he's saving you for me," Dawn said with a smirk. "He's sure I'm the bullied little wife who'll be damned glad to get rid of the big, bad overbearing husband. Probably means to slip me a ring full of poison for you or something like that."

"Exactly. He wants me to finish off the others, then you get to take care of me. But, the question is, how does he think he would profit by all that?"

"Maybe he plans to have another auction."

Eric shook his head. "But why? *We* are the primary buyers. The big money. If he eliminates all of us, he goes with the second-string. Plus, he's got all the big boys mad as hell because their prize negotiators are missing and presumed dead."

"Not a bad presumption in some cases. So what do we do now?"

"Find Clay and get him to call in the cavalry with his transmitter. We've done about all we can do here."

A shot rang out somewhere below. Eric rushed out into the hallway and headed for the stairs. "Something's going down now! C'mon!"

"What do you think…" She was almost running to keep up with his long strides, but he couldn't afford to slow down if they wanted Quince alive later to give them some answers.

Eric handed her the pistol. "Here, take this."

She huffed, speeding up as he did. "And what will you do, point your finger and go *bang?* Keep the damned gun."

"Won't need it," he assured her. "Wait here."

"Like hell," she muttered, staying right behind him as he pushed into Quince's study.

Chapter 14

Mohandra had the guard's automatic to Quince's head, apparently demanding access to the information they had come to bid on. Eric merely granted him an impatient look and marched directly over to Quince's desk and began opening drawers.

It had the desired effect. Mohandra redirected his weapon immediately, pointing it at Eric. "What are you doing?" he demanded in Arabic.

"What do you think? Ah, and here it is!" He lifted a disk out of the lower right-hand drawer and plunked it down on the desk. It was labeled a list of artworks, probably for insurance purposes. "You want to bid on it, Ali? Or will you simply take it and run? And if you run, where will you go to avoid my wrath? Kill me and even Bin Laden's best caves will not be deep enough in the ground to hide you. My people are everywhere and you know it. Put down that weapon and let us conduct business."

"I think not," Ali growled, shoving Quince away from him and approaching the desk.

Eric kept his gaze trained on the Arab, his peripheral vision noting Dawn's quiet moves. She was directly behind Ali now, her weapon drawn, almost touching the back of his head.

Could she fire? Eric knew she had never killed before. Shooting man-shaped targets was one thing; taking a life was quite another. He couldn't afford to doubt her now.

"Put down the weapon," she demanded, touching Ali's neck with the barrel. Surprised, he whirled, but she was faster, ducking the spray of bullets that took out several glass shelves lining the wall above her head. Eric leapt on him from the rear, pinching the nerve in Ali's wrist that controlled his gun hand. The weapon hit the floor and bounced. Dawn scooped it up and backed away.

But Ali didn't go down easily. Eric took a sharp blow to the ribs and a fist in the face before he clipped the Arab with a right cross that ended it all.

"Kill him!" Quince ordered in a near scream, pointing frantically at the unconscious man.

"No," Eric replied, catching his breath. "He will go home in disgrace. It is enough."

"No, no, it's not enough. He…he would have killed me!"

Eric turned on him. "Did that possibility never occur to you when you brought us here? That some might not hold to your fancy rules of etiquette?"

"But…but I have what all of you need and if you kill me you can never have it!"

"You are not dealing with mere greed here, Quince. Ali fights a holy war and you are his enemy. He takes what he wants. It's his way."

"And yours as well?" Quince asked, straightening his tie, brushing back his hair and recovering a little of his equilibrium.

"Mine as well," Eric agreed. "But I am a shade more civilized and a good deal more intelligent."

Heavy booted footsteps thundered down the corridor and two of the guards burst in. "Secure this man and confine him," Quince ordered.

Dawn had sunk into a crouch in the corner of the room, the two weapons on the floor behind her and out of sight. Eric stood and backed away while the two bound Ali and hauled him away. Odd, that Quince had not ordered *them* to kill the Arab, Eric thought.

Quince left soon after the guards, citing his need for a drink.

"Are you all right?" Eric asked Dawn.

"Fine," she said, getting up from her crouch and handing him the Uzi. She tucked the pistol back into her pocket. "We're building a little arsenal here and no one seems to care."

"You should have shot him," Eric said firmly. "You can't afford to hesitate."

She frowned and propped her free hand on her hip. "I didn't hesitate. I opted to take him alive."

Eric laughed at that. "He could have killed you with that volley. Or Quince. Or me, for that matter."

She worried her bottom lip with her teeth for a second, then admitted. "I couldn't shoot a man in the back of the head with no warning."

Eric blew out a frustrated breath. "Fair enough. You did fine." That's when he noticed her hands shaking, only a slight tremor. "Come here," he said softly and opened his arms.

She stepped into them and put her head on his shoulder. He caressed her hair and rested his hand on her neck, massaging it gently. "Will you be all right here if I go out for an hour?" he whispered.

She nodded. "I've got the pistol."

"Next time, don't think. Just shoot, okay?"

"A thousand pardons, *Jarad*," she said with a wry twist of her lips. "Be careful yourself."

"Stay out of everyone's way until I get back." Eric didn't like leaving her, but he needed to locate Clay and get the team in here. Things were falling apart fast and would collapse with a bang once Quince found out his prize was missing, but he was so shaken up right now, he'd be busy hitting the bottle. God only knew where the Russian or Cal Markham were, but they had no reason to bother Dawn.

Staying out of the way sounded good to Dawn. She'd had about all the excitement she could stand for the day. If she wasn't supposed to be converted, she'd be joining Quince in the lounge for a good stiff drink. Having your hair parted with a few Uzi rounds tended to make a girl pretty thirsty. Maybe she would go anyway and have a glass of juice or something and keep an eye on Quince.

She patted the pistol in her pocket and tried to walk without a betraying wobble in her knees.

Quince greeted her with more aplomb than she expected. Great recovery time, she had to give him that much. "Would you care for a brandy?" he asked, sipping his own.

She made a face. "I don't dare, but thank you for thinking of me." With a sigh, she helped herself to a bottled fruit juice from the small refrigerator behind the bar.

"Where is Jarad?" he asked. "And how is it he trusts you to wander around alone all of a sudden?"

Dawn took a deep draught of the juice and swallowed before answering. "He was upset and went out for a walk to cool his temper. He does that."

Quince nodded knowingly, his lips pinched in thought. Then he pointed to her with his snifter. "You handled yourself better than most women would under fire. How do you explain that?"

Dawn shrugged. "Jarad's training."

"I'm not certain I buy that explanation, Aurora," Quince told her frankly. "What you did seemed too…professional." He sighed, his gaze never leaving hers. "Perhaps you are not his wife at all."

Dawn laughed bitterly. "Believe it. He gives me lessons in self-defense. He's paranoid about some man accosting me and dishonoring him, you know that. Do you think for a moment Jarad would hire a *woman* to watch his back? Besides, if I were here for that, he would have me out there with him now." For a minute, Dawn was afraid she had overexplained, protested too much.

Quince shrugged. "Quite right." He smiled, toying with his drink, looking into its depths. "So, have you given any more thought to our plan to free you?"

"What do you have in mind?" Dawn decided to stop playing it coy. He had seen her in action and knew she was no shrinking violet. "It appears you are systematically eliminating all of those you asked to come here. One has to wonder why and whether *any* of us will be allowed to leave. Why should I trust you?"

He rolled the snifter between his palms. "I have eliminated no one."

"Then, let us say you have encouraged their elimination at every opportunity. Share with me why that is, and I might be inclined to trust you further."

He leaned forward then in an attitude of strict confidence. Dawn held her breath, certain he was about to give her his reasons. "These men, your husband included, represent the most evil elements of human society, Aurora. Whatever their reasoning, based on ideology or hunger for power, they are terrorists, bent on destruction. Why should you care—"

She interrupted. "And if I am not misinformed, you are providing them a means to do more of it," she reminded him, "for which you will be amply rewarded. Tell me I am wrong in this."

He assumed a wounded expression that looked sincere. "Rest assured, my motive is not fueled by greed. Look around you, woman! I have *enough*."

"Then why did you ask them here? Why would you offer them whatever it is they are so eager to get? I know it is something to further their respective causes, something valuable and secret."

"Something they must never put to use," he added succinctly, reaching across to take her hand in his. "Help me."

She tried to pull away, but he held her fingers fast in his. "This was a trap? You brought them here to kill them?"

Gunshots popped outside and the window of the lounge shattered. Dawn dived for the carpet, seeking shelter between their chairs. Quince fell on top of her, shielding her body with his.

"Let me up!" she cried, struggling to reach her pocket where she had hidden the pistol. But Quince held her immobile. Heavy as he was, she couldn't dislodge him. "Get off!"

He scrambled to one side and yanked her by her arm. "Stay on the floor. Crawl behind the bar!" he ordered. More shots rang out.

No fool, Dawn did as he suggested. The heavy mahogany structure offered the safest haven in the room. By the time they reached it, she had the pistol out and the safety off.

Had Eric's team arrived? She hoped to God that was the case and that this wasn't some other force attempting to take over the island. Especially since the thing everyone would be after was securely tucked between her breasts inside her lacy underwire bra. That gave a whole new meaning to Victoria's Secret.

The click of footsteps sounded on the tiles of the foyer, then on the stairs. No way could they exit the lounge without being seen by whoever was on the way up. Were there others waiting? She and Quince were trapped behind the bar with nowhere to run and only four rounds for defense. "Do you have another weapon?" she whispered.

"Not in here," he admitted. "You'd better give me that," he said, reaching for the gun. Dawn batted away his well-manicured hand and leaned to peek around the lower edge of the bar.

He tugged at her shoulder. "I said—"

"Shut up, Quince!" she snapped, her patience thin and her nerves on edge.

Eric had guessed right; Quince didn't know what to do next. He had gotten in over his head. How could that be? Given the rep Interpol credited him with, she didn't know. He was supposed to be the big deal maker, the mercenary even the baddest boys in the business bowed to. He had talked a good game up to a point, but she sensed he was shaking in his Italian leather mocs right now, too frightened to take the little peashooter away from a girl half his size.

"Back off and give me some room." She elbowed him out of her way. "And for God's sake, be quiet." Dawn realized she'd abandoned her Spanish accent along with her cover as a helpless little woman. Come to think of it, Quince's voice had changed, too, under pressure.

Someone was coming down the stairs now and in a hurry. "Dawn?" Eric called out.

She released a deep breath, only now aware she'd been holding it. "In here! Behind the bar," she answered.

He appeared then, a welcome sight as he dodged into the room, wheeling left, then right in a shooter's crouch, the AK-47 he carried braced to fire. He landed behind the bar with them. "Ali must have signaled a boatload of friends," he announced. "They just came ashore."

"Impossible!" declared Quince.

Eric shot him a dry look. "I didn't get a head count, but two are down outside."

Dawn's heart stuttered when she saw blood on his shirt. "You were hit?"

"No." He looked past her, his gaze focused on the open doorway. "They won't wait long to breach the house. They'll be coming in to find Ali. Among other things." He glanced at Quince. "Where'd your men take him?"

"There's a basement below the kitchen."

"With outside access?" Eric demanded.

"No."

"Any way out of this place without using the front or back door or the French doors onto the terrace?" The downstairs windows were barred, decoratively, but also efficiently.

Quince shook his head. Then he swallowed hard. "The place is wired to blow. If we can get out after they come in to search the house, we can get them all."

Eric sighed. "Where did you train, Quince, Utopia? They won't *all* come in. Some will be out there waiting for us to show. And they're armed to the teeth. Besides, you have employees in here. Conroy, the cook—"

"I'm blowing it anyway," Quince declared, muttering as

if to himself. "Ali's people can't be allowed to get what they're after."

Eric tossed Dawn a questioning look and she answered by patting her cleavage. He smiled. "I wouldn't worry about that."

"And if they shoot us?" Quince snapped. "What then? All they have to do is locate the safe and figure out how to crack it."

Eric's worried gaze locked with Dawn's as he repeated, "The *safe?*"

"Yes! It will only be a matter of time until they find the hidden office. It only took me two hours!"

Dawn's heart sank. The little aluminum device between her breasts suddenly felt cold, not comforting as it had moments ago. If the flash drive with the radar-shield plans was locked in Quince's safe, what was she carrying around in her bra?

Eric was glaring at Quince now. "Why would *you* have had to search for the office in your own house?"

Quince backed away in a crouch and looked behind him as if hoping to discover an escape route opening up.

"I'll get answers, Quince, but now's not the time," Eric said. "I locked the front door when I came in, but that won't keep them out for long. We need to set up a defense." He motioned to Dawn. "Make sure the kitchen entrance is locked. Find Conroy and the servants and put them in the walk-in fridge where they'll be safe. Quince and I will go for the weapons."

He turned to Quince. "Where are they?"

"The study," Quince answered. "Why are you doing this?"

"You have to wait for answers, too," Eric told him. "Just keep in mind that you aren't all that necessary to me, so your best bet is to cooperate. Let's go."

Dawn rushed down the hallway to the back of the house, her pistol ready. Conroy and the others weren't likely to follow her orders without it.

When she neared the kitchens, she approached the door with caution, edged up to it, then whirled into the opening in firing position. She sensed she wasn't alone, but saw no one. Carefully, she crept into the room, shifting the direction of her aim every couple of seconds.

This reminded her of a training exercise back at The Farm, where target villains appeared at random right along with pop-up friendlies. Conroy, the cook and the other servants were around somewhere, probably hiding behind something just as she, Eric and Quince had been doing in the lounge. She thought about calling out a warning.

"Drop it," said a quiet voice, devoid of its usual lilt.

"Sean?" she asked, turning. "Is that you?"

"Me and my Uzi, love. Lay down your gun."

She didn't do that, but she did lower the pistol, trying her best to look relieved to see him. "Where have you been? I am to find Mr. Conroy and the others and put them somewhere safe. Will you help me?"

He chuckled. "Appealing to my gentlemanly instincts, Aurora? I have so few of those. Put down the pistol or I will shoot you where you stand." She had to believe he meant it.

She placed the gun on the countertop. "There are men here on the island who intend to kill us all. Why are you treating *me* as the enemy?"

"Because everyone here *is* an enemy, love. Haven't you figured that out yet?"

She sighed and shrugged. "All I want is to board a boat and leave this cursed place. Why Jarad brought me here with him is a mystery."

He laughed. "Not to me. You handle a weapon like a

pro, which I always assumed you were. There are no innocents among us."

"Such bitterness, Sean," she said with a sugary smile. "What now? You'll get rid of me the way you did Carlotta?"

"Not yet. Let's go and find your husband and our friend, Quince, shall we?"

"All right," she agreed with one last longing look at the abandoned pistol on the counter. She was facing Sean and also the window near the back door where shadows moved quickly and quietly. Ali's men. In seconds, they would burst through the unlocked door and she and Sean would be cut down as surely as she stood there. "Sean, they're coming."

"Nice try," he said with a click of his tongue. Then a sound alerted him. He turned.

Dawn grabbed her pistol and dropped to the floor just as the back door flew open.

She heard them swarming in, shouting, firing. It sounded like a whole army. Sean had disappeared.

Two rounded the counter, and she squeezed the trigger. The sound of her shots was lost in the indiscriminate firestorm of the invaders—two more dashed past on the other side of the counter. They missed seeing her, hidden as she was. She aimed the pistol and pulled the trigger. Nothing happened. Damn. Useless. She laid it aside.

One man shouted in Arabic, probably to those outside. All she could do was watch from the shadows as the survivors headed out of the kitchen and down the hallway.

Dawn waited where she was, helpless to do anything at the moment. When no more shots were fired, she risked crawling to the edge of the counter and peeking around it. More men filed in.

The new wave immediately located the door to the cellar

and were trying to get it open. They broke it down and with a shout of success, headed downstairs.

Dawn scrambled over to the two men she had shot. One was writhing on the floor, holding his leg. Quick as a flash, she grabbed the heavy automatic he had dropped. The other man was obviously dead, his nine-millimeter pistol still clutched in his hand. She yanked it free and stuck it in her pocket. The first one recovered enough to make a clumsy grab for her. Dawn landed a butt-stroke to his head and knocked him cold.

For a moment, she considered shooting him again, but decided a shot might bring the others running. An excuse, maybe. Killing a man who was firing at you was definitely different than dispensing with one who was unconscious.

Eric was her first concern. She headed out the way the others had gone. She moved cautiously even though they were making enough noise to cover any sounds she might make.

She concentrated on her approach, so much so that she didn't realize anyone was directly behind her until an arm encircled her neck and a hand snatched her weapon away. She knew immediately it was McCoy. She recognized his scent.

"In there," he rasped, shoving her into a small storage room. He closed the door. "Now, let's have something straight, Aurora. I need to save Quince. I don't have to kill you. In fact, I could use your help. If you cooperate, I'll get rid of Jarad for you and get you back to the mainland today."

Right, like she would believe that? "Suppose I don't want to be rid of him?"

"It's you or him, love. Choose right now."

"I'll help you." If she could convince Sean she was no threat, at least she might have a chance to warn Eric. Maybe she could get the drop on Sean. She cleared her throat. "But the first order of business is to eliminate Ali's men, agreed?"

He nodded. "Go ahead of me. I want you where I can see you. Get out the Glock you took off the dead guy."

She pulled it out of her pocket, checked the load, clicked off the safety, then led the way back into the hall. The pistol was no match for the Uzi McCoy carried, but she felt a bit less vulnerable than she would have if he had made her his unarmed shield.

Dawn could hear Ali's men running up the stairs near the main entrance, making no attempt to conceal their presence. How many were there on the island? Ali obviously had used some method of contacting them similar to what Eric had brought. Or something even more sophisticated since they had known where to find him.

She stopped and turned. "Quince and Jarad were headed for the study where the weapons are kept."

He motioned down the hall to the left, then gave her a little shove when they neared the study door.

"Don't shoot! It's me!" she called softly, hoping no one would unload in her direction. "McCoy is here, too," she added in order to warn Eric.

Sean was right behind her. He pushed her through the doorway, using her for cover. The lights were off and the blinds were drawn.

"Quince? You there?" Sean called.

Quince stepped out from behind a tall bookcase. "Sean?" he asked softly. "Are you all right?"

"Where's Al-Dayal?" McCoy demanded.

Quince nodded to the opposite side of the room where Eric stood holding a fully automatic in the cradle of his arm, his finger on the trigger, the muzzle pointed up instead of at her.

Now that her eyes had adjusted to the dim light, Dawn

could see in Eric's eyes that he knew McCoy intended to kill him.

"If I were you," he said to Sean, "I'd eliminate the most immediate threat first. That is not me, by the way. Truce until we've cleared up this problem? Then we can haggle over the prize."

"Fair enough," Sean replied.

Dawn didn't trust him to keep his word, but realized there was no choice until she or Eric had a clear shot at him.

"Two of Ali's men are down in the kitchen. One dead and one unconscious," she informed Eric. "Five others have gone down to release Ali and more are searching upstairs. Four, I think."

"I didn't see them disembark," Eric said. "The entire island could be crawling with them for all we know."

Quince spoke up then. "We could try to make it to my boat and get off the island. I told you the place is wired. Why don't we get out and blow it?"

McCoy growled a protest. "Not until I get what I came here for. Get it, Quince. Now."

Dawn thought about giving Sean the attaché she had found in the locked drawer. He wouldn't have time to check the contents. Maybe she could fool him into thinking she had what he wanted, the same way Eric had bluffed Ali. But if she did, McCoy would probably shoot them all and take off. Damn.

However, if the information was locked in the safe, it needed to stay there until Eric's team arrived.

"I can't get it out of the safe," Quince admitted.

"What do you mean? How did you expect to… Never mind, I can get into it," Sean declared. "Haven't met a safe yet I couldn't crack. Let's go."

Quince was nodding, turning and pressing on one of the block designs beside the fireplace.

If they entered the secret passage and closed it behind them, they would be safe from Ali's men. But McCoy could also kill them all in there, get the plans out of the safe, then hide and wait out the small army that was after them. Without a lot of luck or a fortunate accident, those goons would never locate that hidden section of the house.

Dawn couldn't risk letting McCoy get whatever was in that safe. "No!" she cried. "Going there's not necessary. I have what he wants."

"Wait! Don't…" Eric said through gritted teeth. He was frowning at her, his frustration tangible.

Dawn offered him a wry grimace, an apology for probably sealing their doom, and reached inside the front of her blouse. She withdrew the small device. "Here. This is not worth dying for," she said, turning around and handing it to McCoy.

Sean took it in his left hand and gave it a cursory look. "And I'm supposed to believe this is what you say it is?"

Dawn shrugged. "Believe what you like. I followed the secret corridor from our rooms and found Quince's office. This was in a locked drawer beneath his computer station. The plans are on it. I checked." She reached for the device. "Of course, if you don't want it, then I'll…"

He snatched it back and shoved it into his pocket, then faced Quince. "What do you have to say about it, Quince? Is this what I'm looking for?"

Quince was already shaking his head. "No."

"Then let's go!" Sean commanded. "We're wasting time we don't have."

His words were nearly lost as bullets struck the door

frame behind him. Everybody dropped and scrambled for cover.

Ali's men were shouting now, running down the hallway, firing indiscriminately.

Eric popped one when he reached the doorway. The others obviously decided Allah didn't need them yet and stayed back.

Two seconds later, she watched a grenade bounce into the room. The windows were barred. The enemy was outside the door. There was no way out but the secret passage, and it would take too long for Quince to open the panel.

Chapter 15

Eric flipped the heavily padded sofa over the grenade, leapt over it, grabbed Dawn and threw her to the floor just as the grenade exploded. He rolled to his back, already aiming at the hall door when Ali's men came in shooting.

Dawn watched the scene unfold like something out of a silent movie, unable to hear it because the explosion had deafened her. While the action played out at full speed, her own reactions seemed to be in slow motion, her emotions temporarily numb. Then as suddenly as it had begun, the attack ceased.

Only when she saw Sean aiming directly at Eric did her autoresponse kick in. She finger-pointed her nine millimeter instead of taking time to aim and pulled the trigger repeatedly until the weapon emptied and she felt no recoil.

Sean fell flat on his back. Quince crawled out from behind a bookcase and bent over him. Dawn couldn't hear what he was saying, but his face had crumpled and he seemed to be begging McCoy not to die. Eric was checking the bodies of Ali's men. He turned to her. "You hurt?"

Dawn shook her head. She hadn't bothered to examine herself for wounds, but felt no pain anywhere. Her hands and arms were covered with plaster dust and residue from the gunshots. A small nick on her forearm began to sting, but it was only a minor scratch. "I'm okay," she muttered.

Another explosion outside the study rocked the room and collapsed the inner wall adjacent to the hall. Debris blocked their exit. The whole place was wired, Quince had said. It could go up any second.

Eric grasped her arm. "Reload," he ordered. She realized she was reading his lips and couldn't hear anything but a distant roaring.

She looked around and saw the shattered gun case with its drawers at the bottom hanging askew. Finding no clip for the empty nine millimeter, she grabbed another gun out of the shattered case and began to check and load it. A Walther PK, she noted. Dependable weapon.

Dawn forced thoughts to practical things like that, trying to ward off others she didn't want to have just yet. She had killed today. More than once.

Her hands shook. The odor of cordite made her gag. Or maybe it was the smoke that filled the room, almost obliterating her ability to see. Thank God she had seen Sean aim and…

No, she had to think about the gun. Get it loaded. Do what Eric ordered. Follow his lead. The only way out of this was to follow Eric. Her breath caught on a sob, but she held it in, willing her fingers to behave, to do what her brain demanded.

There. The clip was in. She had done it. She began to cough uncontrollably.

Eric's arms came around her from behind and lifted her to her feet. He guided her to a door in the wall, a door that shouldn't be there. The explosion must have triggered Quince's secret panel.

Eric reached into a niche just inside the tunnel door and procured two flashlights, handing her one.

Luckily, the grenade hadn't triggered the explosives Quince insisted were rigged to blow the entire place. Damn him and his stupid island villa anyway. Damn the whole island. Why hadn't the government sent a military team here to clear it? Why civilian Special Ops?

And why not? Things would be right on target if the gadget she had found were the real thing and Eric's transponder worked.

Dawn looked over her shoulder and saw that Eric had gone back to get Quince. He held him by the back of his collar and shoved him into the opening behind her.

She proceeded down the narrow tunnel until she came to a forked passage. When she stopped, Eric gestured to the right with his flashlight and she continued, hurriedly leading them God only knew where.

This was taking too long. Dawn sensed they were headed away from the main structure and that the path they were taking did not lead to Quince's office where he'd said the safe was located. Apparently, the study had had more than one secret panel or else they had taken the wrong fork. The whole place must be a rabbit warren underneath.

Her lungs cleared and she began to smell salt air. Dampness had invaded the poorly framed and unfinished corridor sometime after it had degenerated into a rough tunnel carved out of the lava stone.

She figured they had walked just under a quarter of a mile

since leaving the study and should be well away from the villa by now. In any direction, that should lead to a beach.

Her hearing had returned, at least some of it. Quince's breath huffed in and out right behind her. Their shoe soles scuffed against the irregular rock floor. Daylight loomed ahead.

"Wait," Eric said. "Stop here and wait until I see where we are." He stepped around Quince and came up beside her now that the tunnel had widened. "Keep him covered. If he tries to go back, shoot him."

"I *have* to go back!" Quince cried. "Sean might be…"

"McCoy is dead," Eric told him. "There's nothing you can do for him."

"Here. Hold on to this." He handed her the flash drive she had given to Sean. "I brought this. It might have something on it since it was locked up."

Dawn tucked it back between her breasts.

Quince had dissolved in tears, leaning against the wall of the tunnel with his face covered by his arms; he sobbed inconsolably. Sean had obviously been more to him than simply one of the bidders, but Dawn didn't want to know what, at least not now.

Eric had disappeared out the end of the tunnel. She heard his surprised laughter and another voice she thought she recognized. Clay Senate? Where the devil had he been all this time?

"Dawn? Come on out here," Eric called. "Bring Quince with you."

Thank goodness it was time to abandon their roles as the Al-Dayals. This kind of undercover work was not the fun she'd always imagined it would be. Surreptitious entry was one thing, but becoming someone else for days on end was quite another.

She prodded the weeping man until he staggered along in front of her. They exited the tunnel onto a wide, rocky ledge above the beach. Steps led down to a sandy, sheltered cove.

"Come with me," Clay said to them. "There's a cave over there with all the comforts of home." He smiled at her. "You could stand a little cleaning up."

She touched her face and winced. Her fingertips came away coated black with soot, cordite and dirt. The rest of her must look about the same as her hands. Nasty. Her hair felt as if it were standing on end and her clothes were a mess.

Dawn trudged along with the men, periodically urging Quince so she wouldn't step on his heels. He seemed to be in shock.

They entered Clay's cave. Someone had indeed made it a refuge, probably well before Clay ever arrived on the island. Bedding and blankets were neatly folded against one rough-hewn wall. A fire pit lay near the front, stacked with small lengths of driftwood.

"The prisoners are bound in the back there," Clay told them, pointing to a dark passage that led deeper into the rock.

"Prisoners?" Eric asked with a mirthless chuckle. "Who?"

Clay shrugged. "A really feisty woman I found hanging on to the rocks after she was pushed off the cliff's edge, a couple of guards I managed to disarm, a Russian and an American mercenary I would really like to choke personally."

"We need to contact Sextant and get this wound up," Eric announced. "Unfortunately one of Quince's bidders brought along a small army that seems determined to decimate the villa and everybody in it. See if your transponder's working. For some reason, mine's shot."

They watched as Clay removed a knife from his belt and quickly sliced the tracker from the top of his shoulder before she could think to offer her help.

He wiped it off on the leg of his pants, then tapped the point of his knife to it several times. "There," he said, pinching it between his thumb and forefinger for a minute. He frowned at Eric. "No response."

"You're bleeding." Dawn shook her head in exasperation and looked around for something to pad his wound.

"It's nothing," he replied "I'll go wash it off in a minute." Then he crouched near Eric. "Do you have what we came for?"

"It's still in the house, in the safe, so Quince says," Eric told him. "A safe he can't open. Oh, and the house is rigged with explosives, only he hasn't yet told us how that's set up. I can't read him."

Clay's dark brows drew together in a menacing look directed toward Quince. "Time for a few questions." He tapped the flat of his blade against his other palm. "Shall I?"

"Be my guest," Eric said with a negligent wave of his hand.

Quince seemed oblivious to the threat.

"You aren't going to try to scare it out of him, are you?" Dawn asked quietly. "He's pretty much zoned out. I don't think it would work."

"What's his problem?" Clay asked her.

Dawn considered the question before answering. "I think one of the bidders was more than that to him, maybe a co-conspirator. The guy was killed just before we came out." She had killed him. That was going to bother her, but she couldn't dwell on it now.

"McCoy," Clay declared with a nod.

"You've been keeping closer tabs than I thought," Eric said with a smile. As he spoke, he slid one arm around Dawn and drew her near, sharing his warmth. "Learn anything interesting?"

Clay looked from Eric to her and back again, one black eyebrow raised. "McCoy and the woman struggled and he shoved her off the cliff in an attempt to kill her. But they had a fascinating conversation before he did his worst." He paused, then looked curious. "You couldn't read them, could you?"

Eric glanced down at the floor of the cave, then raised his gaze to meet his friend's. "No."

"And you couldn't connect with me, either. Or Jack and the others? What's wrong, man?"

"Let it go for now, okay?" He released Dawn and stepped away from her, resting his hands on his hips. "Just tell me what you found out."

"Quince isn't Quince," Clay announced. "Or at least not the Quince we thought he was."

"That much I figured out on my own," Eric told them. He reached out to brush Dawn's hair off her brow and tuck the strands behind her ear with his finger. "You sensed that, too, didn't you, Dawn?"

She had, but not fully until they were in the study. "Let's ask him."

Quince was sitting cross-legged on the cave floor, his elbows on his knees and his face buried in his hands. Grieving?

Dawn knelt beside him and placed a hand on his shoulder. "Where is Quince?"

He raised his head slowly, as if he'd been sleeping. "My brother?" He swallowed hard. "Dead. And good riddance. The man was a monster. A traitor to the human race!" He sobbed once, then placed a hand over his mouth to hold it in.

"You took his place for the bidding. Why?"

"No. You don't understand. There was to be no bidding.

I can't even get to whatever it was he had for sale, don't you understand? I would never, ever sell it, even if I could!"

"But you wanted all of the bidders to come here to the island as planned, didn't you?" she asked.

"To die," he agreed. "I wanted to eliminate every one of them and I liked the irony of having them destroy one another." He slid his fingers through his hair and left them there, holding his head as if it hurt. "I have to make up for all Stefan did, all the terrible things he arranged, the terror he abetted." Then he looked directly at Dawn. "I wanted you to help me. You were like me, Aurora, caught up in something you couldn't control by yourself. Trapped."

She nodded and patted his shoulder. "I know. What is your name?"

"George. George Cydonia." He sniffed hard and ran a hand over his face, sighing as he did. "Sean is…was…my son."

"I'm sorry for your loss," Dawn said automatically, trying not to think how she was the one who emptied the pistol into McCoy. She'd had no choice really, and it was counterproductive to waste time sympathizing with a killer. "He was very clever," she offered. "I would have sworn he was Irish."

"He was," George said. "His mother raised him in Dublin. She and I parted ways when Sean was only two. He contacted me a few months ago in Athens. I have a business there," he said absently. "Real estate."

Dawn exchanged a look with Eric who was listening intently. They were dealing with a real estate agent?

"What happened to Stefan?" she asked, guiding the questioning away from Sean's death. She would come back to it, though. It seemed strange that Sean would look his father up after so many years. Maybe he wasn't Sean at all, but someone in league with Stefan. "Did your brother die here on the island?"

George nodded. "I acquired this property for him. He wanted something remote and isolated. Said he was retiring. I've known for years what he did, but was afraid I'd be implicated if I turned him in. Then two weeks ago, he insisted that Sean and I come out to the island with him. Then he wouldn't let me leave. He was afraid I would give away his location. Sean…he was…sympathetic to Stefan's plan. I thought I had dissuaded him, but…Stefan left for a few days last week and then returned."

"And he died here? Was he ill?" Dawn prompted.

George shook his head. "No. He was eating dinner. Choked to death on some calamari."

Or was poisoned? Dawn wondered. Sean's presence at the time made that a distinct possibility.

"He had already set up everything for the auction of the information, which he told me he had locked in his safe. Meeting the bidders face-to-face would give him the edge, he said. Stefan liked games."

"So you decided to follow through and get rid of the bad guys yourself," Dawn said, trying to sound approving so he would continue.

"It was a good idea. Sean said he was…helping me."

Or getting rid of his competition for acquiring the plans himself, Dawn thought. Canny.

Eric came and crouched down on George's opposite side. "Did you wire the place yourself?"

George shook his head. "Stefan did. The entire island. All but one of the boats. He told me that if anything happened to him after the guests arrived, if they betrayed him, that I was to get off the island and send them all to hell along with what they came after. I can do that." He looked up at Dawn, his eyes pleading for understanding. "But it seems such a waste, you know? It is a beautiful place. Worth millions."

"So we were all to kill one another and spare the property," Eric said.

"All but Sean. And Aurora, of course," George admitted. "As I said, she's merely a pawn to you, just as I was to Stefan." He swallowed hard.

"Okay, how were you to blow it?" Eric asked.

George seemed to snap out of his stupor as he glared up at Eric. "I won't tell you. But I still can do it at any time. I will before I let you—"

Eric leapt on George and grasped his arms before the words were out of his mouth. "Search him. The remote. Find it!"

Dawn was closest but not quite fast enough. George twisted free and had the thing out of his pocket and in his hand before she could get to it. He held it up and backed away from her, his back to the rock wall, a threat in his eyes. "I'll do it!"

"Do you really want Sean to end up under a huge pile of rubble, George?" she asked gently. "Wouldn't you rather have a ceremony of some kind? Say goodbye to him properly?" She glanced briefly at Eric, who nodded encouragement.

She reached out, trying to touch George's arm. "Please consider it, George. It is true we want what your brother took and intended to sell, but not for the reasons you think."

Again, she looked to Eric for permission to reveal why they were there. "You see, the three of us work for the American government. We came here to outbid the rest and to capture the terrorists' representatives sent here to buy it. We're on your side, George."

"I don't believe you! It's a trick!" He shook the remote as he pointed with it to Eric. "He…he's Arab, not American. And you…" He stopped, frowning. She figured he must have just realized her Spanish accent had disappeared.

"My name is Dawn Moon. I'm an agent with the National Security Agency," she explained. "This is Eric Vinland and Clay Senate. They are also agents."

George looked confused, but at least he was concentrating on them and not the remote he was holding. "It doesn't matter. If I destroy it, no one can have it."

Dawn sighed. "George, you don't even know what it is."

"It's important!" he insisted. "I know that much. It's vital to the terrorists!"

"Yes," she agreed, keeping her voice as calm as possible. "We need to make sure this gets back in the right hands. And to verify that Stefan brought it here and that it's not out there somewhere for someone else to discover. You never actually saw what he had, did you?"

"No." He slowly sank down to sit on the floor of the tunnel. With a gesture of resignation, he handed the remote to Dawn. "The code is 08-16-53. Stefan's birthday."

She sighed with relief and exchanged a look with Eric. He smiled at her and said a quiet, "Thank you."

She sat down next to George, careful to keep him covered in case he decided to reenergize suddenly and do something they didn't expect.

Clay was busy with the tiny device he had removed from beneath his skin. "This damned thing's definitely not receiving and probably not sending, either," he muttered. "Something must be blocking the signals."

Eric looked at Dawn with regret. "Then I guess we're on our own."

Surrounded by Arab terrorists, the most critical part of

their mission unaccomplished, Dawn wondered what they would do now. She could practically see the wheels turning in Eric's head as he assessed their predicament. That gave her hope. He was the one with all the experience. He would think of something. She watched him amble over to the mouth of the cave and step outside.

Clay crouched down near her and crossed his arms over his knees, his weapon dangling from one hand. He closed his eyes.

She hoped he was broadcasting mentally, trying his last-ditch method of contacting backup. Hadn't Eric said that each of the Sextant team had particular talents in that vein?

A few minutes passed in silence. Then Clay spoke. "I'm too tired to think. How about you?"

"Running on adrenaline," she admitted. "Trying not to crash." Now was a good time to satisfy some of her curiosity. She might not get another chance. "Can you do what Eric says he can do? Do you mind read or whatever?"

His full lips quirked down. "No. I'm supposed to have visions. Not that I can interpret them clearly until after the fact. Lot of good that does."

"Have you had any since we've been on the island?" she asked, only half believing him, but still wondering about the kind of men who thought they had these powers.

He made a sound in his throat, half grunt, half laugh. "I dreamed a bevy of demonic birds descended. Sort of like the old Hitchcock movie. Prophetic and pretty damn useless now, wouldn't you say?"

"You trust Eric's abilities, though, don't you?" she asked, reaching for hope.

Again that sound, this time more laugh than grunt. He opened his eyes and peered at her sideways. "The kid? That's what the team calls him, you know. *The kid.* And no, I don't think he can perform his parlor tricks any longer. Not since he met you."

"He said the same thing. So what'd I do?"

Clay sighed and leaned his head back against the rock, stretching his neck. "I don't know. Probably nothing. You just are who you are."

She reached out and touched his arm. "You mean I've screwed up his psychic abilities? That's what you're saying?"

He nodded and looked her full in the face. "He couldn't connect with you during the interrogation. Or since. I think maybe that's wrecked his confidence or something."

Had she done that? "How?"

"Again, I don't know. But maybe you can fix it," Clay suggested softly. "Try letting him in."

"In?" She almost croaked the word. She had let Eric in all right. Twice now. And that obviously hadn't helped him a lot, at least not in the way Clay meant. It had helped her, though. Or maybe not, now that she thought about it. She had trusted the man with her body, but she certainly didn't trust him with her heart. She hadn't let him in *there* yet and didn't dare.

The low rumble of Clay's chuckle broke her reverie. "Let him into your *thoughts* is what I meant, Moon. It might help." He watched her for a few seconds, looking deeply into her eyes, then added, "Send him a message. Think something to him. Try it."

"What?" she asked in a near whisper.

"Anything, doesn't matter what. Maybe he just needs to know he can still do it."

"And then he might be able to contact our backup?" she asked hopefully.

Clay shrugged, but his concern was evident. "It couldn't hurt to try, could it? But you need to believe in what you're doing when you do it."

Dawn wasn't sure she could, not fully anyway, but was willing to grasp at any straw right now. Eric needed to get his team here one way or another, and they weren't coming until he notified him that he was ready. If Clay thought she could help Eric do that, she would certainly try.

She tried to think of something to project to Eric that wouldn't involve anything personal or private. Revealing how she felt about him wouldn't be a good idea. Maybe a simple command to come back inside the cave would do for a start.

She took a deep breath, closed her eyes and repeated the phrase, Come to me, Eric. Over and over, she thought the words until they filled her mind completely.

To her surprise, she heard his hurried footsteps and opened her eyes.

"He came back in!" she crowed, shooting Clay a look of triumph.

"Damn right I did," he grumbled. "The beach out there is working alive with men. And they aren't ours. My guess is Sudanese. Ali's people. I figure we have less than five minutes before they climb up here and find this cave."

They all leapt to action except George. Clay grabbed him and half dragged him out of the cave. They hurried back into the tunnel that led to the house. There was nowhere else to go that didn't lead down to the beach and certain death.

"This way!" Eric ordered when they came to the passage that forked off the main corridor. "Where does this lead?" he asked George.

"To the roof," he answered when Clay jogged him with a firm shake.

They rushed onward and periodically climbed steps hewn into the rock. Dawn had visions of being trapped up there on top of the villa, besieged like knights in a medieval castle with the enemy crawling up the walls.

After an exhausting run, they reached a trapdoor that opened above them. Clay pushed his way next to Eric and they lifted it a few inches to look around.

"It's clear up here for now," Eric said. "Let's go."

They exited onto the flat rooftop that was, as she had hoped, deserted. A three-foot coping surrounded the edge like the battlements of a castle.

Below, outside the villa, they could hear shouts and thudding bootfalls. Definitely surrounded, she thought, and not as well armed as they needed to be.

"Only one door leading up here out of the house," Eric observed, inclining his head toward the small structure that looked sort of like a freestanding closet atop the roof near the middle.

He ordered George to lie down next to the balustrade and stay there. "Clay, you watch the doors. Dawn, check out the perimeter for access that way," he ordered, pointing to his right. "I'll go left."

They found no way that anyone could get to the roof unless they had brought grappling hooks or came through one of the two doors, the one main stairway from the house proper and the flat trapdoor from the tunnel.

However, there was no other way down for them, either. They were effectively trapped up here. The critical information was in the safe downstairs in Quince's office. That would have to be destroyed if it couldn't be reclaimed. Dawn realized they might have to die here in order to ensure national security.

Once they had reassembled, she felt she had to make a suggestion. "You have to try to summon the team again, Eric. Maybe from up here it'll be a clear shot with no interference. Straight across the water, right? They're out there waiting. Give it another shot."

His smile was wry. "I'm afraid it doesn't work that simply, sweetheart."

"It *might*," she argued, trying to ignore his use of the endearment. He probably called women that all the time. "Have you just given up?" She noted Clay's nod of encouragement and continued. "Give it a go, Eric. At least *try*. When I sent you a message to come back in the cave, you came. No hesitation. I think you were reading me then."

"She's right. You could have been, subconsciously," Clay added.

For a few seconds Eric studied her, then released a sigh. "Try your transponder again, Clay, and I'll do whatever I can, too. Maybe one of us will get through to Jack or Will. If we don't see our guys approach before we're overrun up here, we'll have to blow the house. We can't let anyone get off the island with what's in that safe."

Dawn experienced a chill, hearing him affirm out loud that they could die here. She moved closer and took Eric's hand. "You can still do it. I know you can."

He leaned down and kissed her, just a quick meeting of lips. Then he looked into her eyes. "Thanks, Dawn. For everything. You know how much I care, don't you?"

That near declaration sounded a lot like a goodbye. It made her realize she wanted more from Eric than she had admitted, even to herself. When he let go and started to turn away, she grabbed his sleeve. "Wait!"

"What?"

"Take out the contacts," she whispered. "Please. I'd...I'd like to see your eyes when you look at me for what might be the last... Do you mind?"

He reached up and hastily removed and discarded the tiny bits of brown that had disguised the vivid blue of his irises. Then he grinned at her, that same ingratiating expression that turned her all soft inside. "You never cease to amaze me, Dawn, you know that?"

Dawn couldn't speak; she was too caught up in the moment. Silently she brushed the dark hair off his brow with her fingers and wished it were streaky blond again. She would give nearly anything just to see him once more exactly as he had been before becoming Jarad.

"Now go over there, please," he suggested, pointing across the roof. "Keep watch. When you're this close, I can't think, much less project, okay?"

She let go of his hand and turned her back to him, not caring that Clay had witnessed what was between them or that he'd probably guessed how they'd crossed the line on the mission and become lovers.

What difference would his knowing make if they were all blown sky-high? And if they weren't, she would be glad to stand the consequences of fraternizing on the job.

But Clay wasn't watching. He was sitting down on the roof, his weapon resting across his legs as he used his knife to tap a message on the tiny disk.

She glanced back at Eric, who now crouched against the balustrade that surrounded the flat rooftop and looked out across the Aegean Sea. Was he doing it? Could he actually send thoughts out there and have them picked up by Jack Mercier or one of the others on his team? Apparently, he'd done it before, if they could be believed.

His broad shoulders and back were straight, his head tilted back a little.

God, she was in love with that man. Against her better judgment and all the rules governing what they were doing, she had fallen for him like a ton of bricks. Dawn wished to heaven she could see his face.

At that second, he turned and shot her a smile that made her breath catch. Had he read her thoughts at that moment?

Embarrassed to be caught with what was probably a sappy look on her face, she jerked around and hurried to the far side of the roof. Now was no time to go soft.

"Heads up!" Clay cried, a split second before his automatic spat a volley across the door he was guarding.

A scream, loud shouting and a garble of orders issued from inside the opening, now blocked by the bodies of several enemies.

Dawn crouched, weapon drawn, but held her fire.

Eric had assumed a similar stance across the roof. Every bullet counted now. And unless they could hold off Ali's men until help arrived, they would have to make the ultimate sacrifice.

Her gaze met Eric's, and his look said volumes. Frustration, regret and very little hope. Dawn had never wanted to live so badly in her life as she did right then.

"Any success?" Eric called to Clay.

"Nope. You?"

Eric shrugged. "How much ammo you got?"

"One extra clip."

"Dawn?" he asked.

She held up two fingers. Two clips. Thirty rounds.

He raised the machine gun. "Two clips here and a couple of rounds in a pistol," Eric said. "We'll be okay."

Right. Dawn wondered how many were out there and inside the house. Too many, she feared.

"Take cover," he said as he motioned for her to get behind the projection on the roof that housed the door leading down into the villa.

Dawn did that, careful to choose a spot where she wouldn't be in Clay's line of fire. "This okay?"

Eric nodded. "Watch the trapdoor from there. If it lifts, aim for the crack. Don't let them get it fully open or they could rush us."

"I'm on it," she assured him.

For nearly an hour, they held their positions, taking careful aim as they fired, to conserve ammunition.

But their ammo was slowly and surely running out. And, unfortunately, so was their time.

Chapter 16

Eric knew he'd have to blow the place if they were over-run. The remote in his pocket weighed heavy. He just didn't think he'd be able to punch in that code George had given them.

Sure, he could pay the ultimate price to keep that info out of terrorist hands. He tried to convince himself that going that way would be a better death for Dawn than leaving her at the hands of the enemy. Damn it, he couldn't kill her and he couldn't hand the job over to Clay, either! They had to hold out, somehow.

He crawled up to the side of the door where the bodies of the terrorists Clay had shot were lying. He managed to secure two of the weapons they had dropped as they fell. Almost full loads, he noted.

More men were filing up the stairs. He sent an Uzi sliding across the floor of the roof and watched Dawn grab it. Suddenly, the tunnel door raised, opened a crack and she fired. It slammed down.

Eric quickly scuttled away from the other door so he'd be out of Clay's line of fire when the next wave reached it. He aimed, too.

Both he and Clay were out in the open with no cover available. Dawn remained behind the raised structure, half-visible to Eric. He could see her in profile, every inch the agent she had trained to be. My God, how he admired her courage. Not many men would take this in stride the way she was doing.

She loved him. Eric had seen it in her eyes, maybe even heard her think it. He wasn't sure he had read her mind, but as soon as he'd ditched the contacts and looked into those liquid brown eyes of hers, he'd felt the same close connection as when they'd made love.

Maybe, just maybe, he had reached Jack with his thoughts and the team would get here in time. He tried again, as he had every time there was a lull so he could concentrate.

Come on, guys! Get here. We need backup. We're on the roof of the villa. Outmanned. Outgunned. Hurry!

Despite repeated attempts, Clay had had no success with his transponder and neither had Eric. Strange to get two faulty devices when they had been implanted at different times. They weren't even the same make or model. Could there be some sort of scrambler shield on the island?

Even that shouldn't have affected his own method of contact, though. No, he had lost that ability on meeting Dawn. He seriously regretted the loss, but only because it might now cost Dawn her life.

Doing without his lifelong ability to read the thoughts of others had forced him to rely on his instincts and powers of observation, things he had barely noticed he possessed and had never really needed much until this mission.

She made him a more complete person in spite of what he'd lost, maybe even because of that. For the first time in his life, he felt almost normal, but the price of that was too dear. He might lose her before they had a chance to declare their feelings for each other out loud. He had told her he cared, but it wasn't nearly enough. Eric wanted Dawn to know exactly how he felt.

I love you. His desperate inner shout, accompanied by an intense look, caused her to turn abruptly.

Or had it? Why did she wear that look of horror? Her features blurred even as the sound of shots registered. A flurry of action exploded near the door and rapid firing was the last thing Eric heard.

"Eric's down!" Dawn cried. Clay provided cover as she ran the dozen feet that separated her from Eric. Mindless with fear, she grabbed his feet to drag him to the area where she had been sheltered. She couldn't budge him.

"How bad?" Clay called.

"One hit, upper right chest!" she answered, pressing her hand over the wound. Eric was unconscious. She felt for an exit wound, found it and huffed a breath of relief. At least the bullet hadn't bounced around inside. Maybe it had missed anything vital. She prayed hard while doing all she could to stanch the bleeding.

So far none of the terrorists had made it onto the rooftop alive. The attacks came in waves, from the doorway and from the tunnel exit. Both means of access were blocked with bodies, which also acted as shields when the fresh troops appeared. Clay whipped his weapon back and forth, attempting to cover both the door and the hatch while Dawn checked on Eric. George moaned periodically, but wisely stayed where he was. The situation was rapidly degenerating.

She glanced out to sea. "Damn it, Mercier, get your boats in gear! And send us help! He could die!"

"We could all die if you don't cover that tunnel exit!" Clay snapped. He had changed position and now stood a couple of feet away, still watching the door. "A simultaneous attack could finish us off. How's your ammo?"

"Almost gone," she admitted, still pressing hard on both Eric's wounds.

"Get the remote out of his pocket and give it to me," Clay ordered. "Let me know when we're down to nothing. I'll have to blow it, Dawn."

"I know. Do it," she replied, handing him the remote, then resuming her pressure on Eric's wound. "Nice working with you, Senate."

"Same here, Moon, but we're not dead yet. Lay him on his back and use the floor for pressure on the exit wound while you lean on the entry with your forearm. That way you can still fire if you need to."

She took the suggestion, watching as Clay took the stubby little Uzi Eric had been using. "Empty," he muttered as he crawled away to a better position to fire on the doorway. Although no one else had tried to come out of the tunnel, she watched it like a hawk.

The warmth of Eric's body beneath her arm and against her hip felt reassuring. "I hope Mercier picked up something from you or Clay. We could sure use some company about now." Understatement of the year, she thought with an inner groan.

She felt more than heard Eric grunt, but couldn't look at him and effectively guard the trapdoor. At least he was moving a little and making sound.

"More coming up!" Clay said. "Get ready!"

She felt Eric shift her arm off his body and replace it

with his hand. The realization that he was conscious bolstered her hope like nothing else could.

She trained the Walther on the trapdoor and trusted Clay
to take care of the others. "Jeez, you'd think they'd have
run out of manpower by now. Must have unloaded a damn
troop ship."

"Coming," Eric said, his voice cracking with the effort to
speak. "Jack's coming…with the team. Don't let Clay—"

"Jack *better* come," she replied. "I sent him a mental
message myself. Told him to get his ass in gear. You just
rest and don't worry, honey. We'll be fine."

"Honey?" he croaked. She could hear the smile in his
word.

"Yeah, *honey*. Might as well start getting you domesti-
cated while I have some free time. You lead entirely too
wild a life, Vinland. Need to lighten up a little."

The trapdoor inched up even as she spoke. She fired at
it, cursing when it opened a bit wider. Whoever was in there
had a damn death wish. Okay with her. She fired again,
putting a few rapid rounds right into the dark space. It
slammed shut again as she heard a howl.

Eric was coughing. Or laughing. She risked a glance. A
pained smile stretched across his beautiful mouth wide
and she could see the gleaming white of his perfect teeth.
"Lighten up," he repeated in a croaking whisper. "Right."

She wanted so badly to kiss him. He'd realize it was
goodbye, though, and Dawn didn't want him to know it
was. "Go back to sleep until this is over," she told him.

It *was* nearly over. She reached in her pocket and felt
for the pistol, her last line of defense. The Walther was
empty now. If she counted correctly, the Glock had four
rounds left. Clay must be as low on ammo as she was since
he'd had to fire more often than she had.

Dutifully, she called Clay's name and held up the pistol with four of her fingers raised to show him how close she was to empty. He nodded and raised five fingers.

Great. Down to nine shots. Then he'd have no choice but to destroy the villa, everything and everyone in it, including themselves. Dawn looked down at Eric again, hoping he was asleep. He wasn't. He stared back at her. "Jack's…coming."

"I know," she said gently. "Just rest."

"Tell Clay," he ordered, sounding angry. "Now!"

Dawn wasn't sure what to do. Was Eric hallucinating? Delaying the inevitable? Or did he really feel something, maybe a response to his message to Mercier? She made a snap decision.

"Clay!" she shouted, trying to inject as much belief and excitement as possible into her voice. "Eric says the team's on the way!" She wanted to believe it more than anything ever.

Clay nodded, his eyes still trained on the open doorway littered with bodies. "About damn time," he shouted back. "Go have a look if you can leave him for a minute."

Again Eric moved her hand and replaced it with his own. "Go," he huffed, almost soundlessly.

She scrambled up and ran around the perimeter of the roof, looking out in every direction. When she reached the north side, she whooped and pointed. "There! There they are!" She whirled around and rushed back to Eric's side. "Hold on. They'll be here soon."

Then she remembered how low they were on ammo. Could they hold out until the team arrived? Or would Ali's men keep coming in bunches until they took the roof?

"Chopper," Eric said, his eyes closing. "Hear?"

The *whump-whump* of a distant aircraft gently vibrated the atmosphere. Dawn wanted to turn cartwheels.

"Down! Get down!" Clay shouted. Then all hell broke loose. Three of Ali's men poured out of the doorway, stumbling over their fallen comrades, spraying the rooftop with gunfire. Dawn dropped flat and returned fire just as she saw Clay crumple.

After the burst of activity, it seemed there was total silence. She couldn't even hear the *whump-whump* of the chopper now and wondered if it had veered away.

Clay stirred, then rolled to one side. Dawn blew out a breath of relief. He was down, but not dead.

She felt Eric's hand close over her calf and half turned to look at him. He raised a hand and pointed, reminding her to hurry and retrieve the guns. More ammo. She needed those weapons the new downed crew of enemy had on them.

She scuttled forward toward the door to gather what she could find. It was up to her now to keep Eric and Clay safe until backup arrived. For the first time, she remembered George. He was huddled in a corner by the coping, not moving, but there was no time to check and see whether he'd been hit. At this point, she didn't much care about that.

Dawn had almost reached the fallen terrorists in the doorway when a head appeared above the carnage. A head and a weapon. She pulled the trigger of the Glock and heard nothing but a click. Empty.

She prepared to duck. It was all she could do. The enemy's eyes narrowed as he smiled at her and aimed more carefully.

Dawn's life did not flash before her eyes as she'd heard happened at the moment of death. All she felt was horrible, crushing anger.

A single shot rang out. Had he missed at this range? Impossible. Then she saw the lethal wound in the center of his forehead. He crumpled onto the pile of dead that all but blocked the door.

Dawn grabbed the only weapon she could reach in a hurry, a top-of-the-line H&K automatic. Then she turned and saw Eric, propped on one elbow, pistol still clutched in his hand. He collapsed as she crawled back to him.

The confiscated H&K was nearly empty, a couple of rounds left, and there was no time to dig through the dead to find another gun. Footsteps were pounding on the stairs again.

Quickly she sat back facing the threat, bracing the weapon on her knee, aiming directly at the doorway. "C'mon, you bastards. Do your worst," she spat. She might go down, but she was taking somebody with her.

"Friendlies!" Eric shouted. She could hear the cost of that shout in the way he bit off the word with a groan.

Did she trust his instincts? Was that Mercier's bunch clattering up the stairs? How could they have gotten here that fast? And how could he know who it was? If he was wrong and she waited an instant too long to pull the trigger, they were all dead.

For a split second, she considered firing anyway. But she waited. Eric would never gamble with their lives. Unless he was damned sure of himself, rock-positive, he wouldn't have tried to stop her.

"Hold your fire!" someone on the inside called out. "Vinland? Senate? Moon?"

Dawn nearly collapsed with relief. "All clear!" she cried, tears running down her face, streaks of heat against her breeze-chilled cheeks. "We're clear." The last words rushed out on a sob that she caught and contained. Wouldn't do to get caught crying like a little girl.

A huge shadow with accompanying noise descended to the roof as the chopper set down twenty feet away from her. Dawn put down the weapons and crawled rapidly back to Eric. "Thank you, thank you, thank you," she murmured as she pressed her lips to the side of his face and her palm on top of his hand that clutched the wound.

"I love you, Eric," she added with feeling, knowing the sound was lost in the cacophony of sounds that surrounded them now. She just had to say it, though she knew he couldn't hear her, that he was too out of it with pain to read it in her mind if his ability had returned. He wouldn't die, and she had never been so glad of anything in her life.

Friendlies. What a marvelous word, she thought. They would whisk Eric and Clay to a hospital. They would be safe. They would live.

As for her, she would go back to NSA and do what she did best, identifying and illustrating security leaks. Her one big international anti-terrorist mission was all but over.

Mercier himself lifted her away from Eric as two guys with a stretcher hurriedly checked him out and began to load him up. The men were loading Clay's stretcher next, and another guy was assisting George toward the chopper. In a few moments, they would be gone. She had to go with Eric. "Wait!" she cried, but Mercier held her back. For a second, she struggled in protest, then realized she would only be in the way, and cooperated.

Eric's boss tugged her toward the stairs leading down. "Shake it off, Moon. Come with me," Mercier ordered in a loud voice.

After one last glance at the chopper, Dawn followed. She swallowed her tears and put on her agent's face.

If she did nothing else today, she would make Eric proud of how she followed through with their mission. There would be a lengthy debriefing, a chore he wouldn't be up to completing for some time. And there was still the flash drive to locate.

All she wanted right now was to get that over with and

find transportation to whatever medical facility was treating Eric. Before she went stateside again, she had to know he was recovering. Then she could say goodbye and get on with her life, such as it was.

Things would never be the same for her. Eric Vinland had turned her life upside down and inside out. She would always love him. Not that she intended to tell him so again.

If she did, that meant they would have to decide what to do about it. He might want them to be lovers for a while, she supposed. They were incredibly good together. But then it would end, and she didn't think she could face that.

She had before with the others, but Eric was different. His leaving her, even though she knew he would try to let her down easy when the time came, would be the end for her. Better not to get any more involved, end it now and convince herself that everything she felt for him had been due to forced proximity and hyped by adrenaline.

But not before she saw him once more and made sure he would be all right. Would he? Had the wound been worse than she imagined? What if he died? A chill shot through her.

"This way," Mercier directed as they reached the entrance to Quince's ruined study where the grenade had gone off. Sean McCoy's body lay covered with a blanket, as did the other terrorists' remains. He guided her through the rubble into the hallway and into the lounge, which remained virtually unchanged from the last time she'd seen it.

Once there, he sat her down on the silk striped divan and brought her a drink. Scotch. She drank it and made a face. Wicked stuff, and she hated the taste.

"Now then," he said gently. "We need to get to work."

A question occurred to her, and Dawn figured she might not get another chance to ask it. "Did Eric get through to you?"

"Telepathically, you mean?" Mercier smiled. "As a matter of fact, no."

"Then how…?"

He thumped the back of the divan near her shoulder. "What if I told you it was *you* who connected."

Her? Laughter welled up inside her and spilled out. Hysterical, unstoppable and totally inappropriate as it was, she couldn't stop it. She almost hoped he would slap her so she would stop, but he didn't.

Mercier let her laugh until she collapsed back against the divan with scotch spilled all over her lap and tears running down her face.

"Okay, now that you've got that out of your system…" He took the glass from her hand and set it aside. "Are you ready?"

Dawn sat up straight, wiped her face with her palms and composed herself.

"One of the bidders, a Russian, was under guard upstairs in one of the bedrooms," she told Mercier. She took another sip of the scotch and grimaced. "The one who brought all these guys to the party was locked in the kitchen basement. His men set him free, I'm sure."

"They'll be rounded up, don't worry," Mercier assured her. "No one's getting off this island without my say-so, depend on it."

She knew he meant her, as well as the perps involved.

She allowed herself one last glance out the window, sending a brief, silent and fervent prayer winging after the helicopter that had long disappeared. It was all she could do for Eric now. That, and finish what they had begun together. He would demand that of her and be right to do so.

She nodded succinctly and met Mercier's gaze with a steady one free of tears. "I'm ready."

Chapter 17

Eric railed against the tests that kept him isolated at the unnamed medical facility in the Poconos. Mercier had ordered him flown here directly after emergency surgery in Athens.

"For the hundredth time, I tell you I can't do it," he almost shouted. God, he was weary of making the attempts. "I don't want to do it. I'm sick of doing it, okay?"

"Not okay," Dr. Blumfeld declared. "This should be elementary for you, Eric. It's a simple guessing game. The subject in the other room is thinking one of these things," he said, pushing the large cards with pictures closer to Eric's side of the table. "You could do this with one hundred percent accuracy when you were five years old."

"And now I can't," Eric informed him yet again. "Call Mercier again. I want out of here. If he wants to fire me, fine, but I need to leave."

"You want to go and see that woman, don't you? But she's the one who did this, Eric. She took one of your senses from you. If she had blinded or deafened you, how would you feel then? This is even worse. Don't you understand that?"

Eric stood, trying not to kick his chair backward in a fit of fury. If he acted crazy, they just might throw a straight-jacket on him and put him somewhere even more secure. He forced a sigh. "I need to sleep for a while. My shoulder hurts like the devil. Hey, maybe that's interfering," he suggested, sounding quite reasonable, he thought. "The pain, you know." He rubbed the scar gently. It did still ache a little.

"Of course," the doctor said. "We'll try again tomorrow morning when you're more alert."

Sure they would, Eric thought, hiding his scowl. Damn the whole bunch of them. He was getting the hell out as soon as he could find a way. The trouble was, they expected him to try and were covering all possible exits. They wouldn't shoot him, of course. He was too valuable a subject for that. But they would restrain him.

Obviously Jack didn't realize the obsession these people had for ferreting out the intricacies of *gifts* like Eric's or he would never have sent Eric here for evaluation. Or perhaps he did. Maybe Dawn wasn't the only one who'd been betrayed by a superior.

The staff here were agents, too; even the docs were trained and badged. They weren't bad people, only overly dedicated. All the agencies had reps present while the research went on. They'd been at it too long. Eric had been brought here time and again since he was a child, giving them more data and answers to their questions than most of their subjects did. Funny how he had never minded before.

Now all he could think of was leaving, forgetting all this,

finding Dawn and thanking her for putting his life in better perspective.

Well, he hoped to do more than thank her, he thought with an inner smile.

He entered his room, a pleasant place even if it was a bit clinical. They had attempted to make him as comfortable as possible so he would be content and perform. Like hell.

The window was barred. There were four locked, guarded doors between him and the outside of the building. A high wall topped with concertina wire surrounded the property. For his protection against enemy agents who might come looking for him, so Dr. Blumfeld had said in a hushed voice. Did they think he was still five?

"Psssst!"

Eric looked around. His door was closed.

"Psssst! Here!"

He leaned back and looked up, astounded. "Dawn?"

"Get me a screwdriver," she whispered. "A flat-head. Mine broke."

He laughed, not bothering to lower his voice. "Where the hell would I get a screwdriver? They won't even let me have a dinner knife in this place. What are you doing here?"

"I came to bust you out. Or would you rather stay?"

"This is not a sanctioned insertion, I take it?"

"Are you kidding? Get me a damn screwdriver or neither one of us is going anywhere, and I don't plan to live in this freakin' maze of heating vents the rest of my life, okay?"

"Okay, hang on." He looked around the room for something that might do. "Ah, here we go." He lifted the thick folder Dr. Blumfeld had furnished of all Eric's former test results. Doc had let him read it to give him his confidence back. The pages were punched and held together with a flat metal clip and slide. He carefully removed it and tucked it up through the white painted vent.

He had tried the vents before, but they were securely screwed down from the inside where he couldn't get to them. Bless her heart, she had come for him. Wonders would never cease where that woman was concerned.

"How's your wound? Healed?"

"Fine," he answered.

"Clay's okay, too. I saw him last week. He told me where you were."

"Good man." Eric couldn't see Dawn through the slanted slots, but he could hear her shuffling around, grunting a curse now and then. "I hope you're quieter than this when you're really working," he said, unable to resist teasing her.

"Oh, shut up and push up on this thing, will you? Do I have to do everything?"

"Wind up one little mission by yourself and it goes straight to your head! How'd that turn out, by the way?" He bumped the vent with the heels of his hands and it popped out.

She peered down at him, grinning, her face streaked with dirt. "Good guys won, of course. Clay's recovering nicely and getting lots of TLC from your buds at Sextant. George is facing a conspiracy charge, but he's trying to cut some kind of deal by furnishing some of his brother's contacts. Sean was scamming George about being his son, just like we figured."

"I'm glad for George's sake."

"Yeah, he was, too. The radar info was on the flash drive I found in that drawer, by the way. It's now secure. Boris is on his way back to the Russian authorities and Ali bought it in the firefight along with most of his troops. The rest are in Uncle Sam's custody. Nothing left for you to do, Sport, but play Houdini and disappear from here."

She stuck out her hand and beckoned. "You coming or what?"

"Is Aristophanes Greek?" He dragged the desk chair over and climbed up on it, willing to follow her anywhere, the same way she had once followed him.

Moments later, she was leading him through the vents at a fast crawl. She hadn't paused to kiss him hello. Or tell him why she had come to his rescue. If discovered, her career would be over. His probably was anyway, since he'd lost the skill that made him valuable to Sextant.

Eric didn't care about that. What he had found was so much more than he'd ever had before. Dawn.

She had made him a normal person. Somehow, she had banished his enormous burden of carrying the dark secrets of others, of sometimes inadvertently invading the private thoughts of friends. His mind was his own now, the peace and quiet a blessed relief he had never expected and treasured above anything. Except Dawn.

"Did I ever tell you I love you, Moon?" he asked, huffing with exertion after six weeks of virtual inertia. He hurt, and the pain was exquisite.

"Not in so many words," she answered, still crawling forward. "Pick up the pace, will you? We don't have all day."

"How do we get over the wall unnoticed?"

"Leave it to me," she ordered. "We're coming up on the laundry area behind the kitchen. Just trust me and do what I do."

Trust her? She had placed her trust in him when trust should have been impossible for her. How could he do any less?

A moment later when she dived through a hole in the

ceiling, he had to question blind trust. Then he shoved forward and dropped headfirst, just as she had done.

He felt around. They landed in a bin of warm, recently dried bed linens ready for the morning pressing. The room was dark as pitch and smelled of detergent and bleach. Dawn lay beside him, but she wasn't moving.

When he ran his hands over her to see if she was all right, her hand grasped his neck and drew him closer. "We wait right here," she whispered. He watched her press the dial of her watch, which glowed green for a second. "For at least half an hour," she continued. "The workers in the next room will be leaving in precisely ten minutes, but we'd better stay put until we're sure the area's clear. Then we make our exit."

"Over the wall?" he asked, tracing her face with his fingers, dying to kiss her.

"Are you crazy? We change into whites like theirs and go out the service entrance."

"Well, how was I supposed to know your plans? What do you take me for, a mind reader?"

She pinched his cheek. Right through his jogging pants. "Don't get cute. I know you were telling the truth about that."

He pinched her back with both hands while pulling her flush against him and loving every subtle squirm she made. "A believer, are you?"

"I found the ring, right where you said it would be, stuck in the drain of the pool where I used to swim."

"So I can find things. That's not mind reading, Dawn. I can't do that any longer."

"Because of me?" she asked, sounding contrite. And a little defensive, he thought. "Clay said so, too."

"No, because I don't *want* to anymore," he answered truthfully.

Maybe Dawn hadn't been the primary cause of that loss, but only his motivation to ditch it. What did it matter? All he wanted, he had in his arms right now.

"I know what you're thinking," she said with a smile in her voice.

"Yeah? Want to do a little research in that area?" he asked, nipping at her neck. She tasted salty, a little dusty and pretty wonderful. "Tell me and let's see if you're on the money."

"You're thinking you'd like us to work a little late in the wash room, right?"

"God, Moon, you're good!"

"Damn straight I am." She kissed him soundly on the mouth. "You want to take me away from all this, keep me safe and make a wife out of me, that's what you're thinking now."

"Got it in one." He kissed her back until he had to come up for air.

"I'm not going to let you. You know that, don't you?" Her hands began to wander, driving every thought from his head except where they were going.

He reached for the hem of her shirt and began to lift it. "Okay, all but the wife part. Gotta insist on that."

"Fair compromise, I guess," she said, breathless. "Helluva proposal, Vinland."

Eric framed her face with his hands and wished with all his heart that he could see her right now, dirty face, wild red hair and all. "Hey, I don't mess around when it comes to romance. Privacy, a little sweet talk, total commitment, the works."

"Not to mention clean sheets," she added. "What more could a girl ask for?"

Epilogue

McLean, Virginia

"**I** now pronounce you man and wife. You may kiss your bride."

Dawn thought she had never heard more beautiful words in her life. She felt beautiful, dressed in ivory satin, hair red as before and gaining back its natural curl.

She couldn't say that her personality had changed all that much in the three months since their big adventure when she'd reverted to her former appearance. As she had informed Eric last night, she retained entirely too much of Aurora's meekness. He had laughed out loud.

But now, right now, Eric was kissing her more sweetly than ever, restraining the passion that usually raged between them every time they came together. Anyone watching the ceremony might think they were pretty conservative lovers, she guessed. Ha.

Eric led her down the aisle of St. John's chapel, beaming as if his dreams had all come true. Dawn knew that hers had. What a golden treasure he was in any guise he chose! So what if she couldn't figure him out. She'd just keep him guessing, too. He had risked everything for her, just as she had for him. Love was the ultimate risk, but she was taking it gladly.

Eric's parents didn't seem to know what to make of her, but then they didn't seem to know what to make of Eric, either.

They were a handsome couple, a bit older than she had expected and obviously uptight, which she *had* expected. Eric had said he didn't mind, that he loved them anyway. Dawn knew she would embrace them, too, whether they were comfortable with that or not.

She wondered if they knew him at all. He'd said he had spent more time in research facilities while growing up than he had at home. His grandmother had been the only one to offer much love and understanding after he began to exhibit his psychic gifts.

Well, he wouldn't lack for love and understanding from now on, she silently promised him.

Later, at the reception in the church's social hall, Jack Mercier, his wife Solange, Holly and Will Griffin, Joe and Martine Corda and Clay Senate were congregated at one of the tables. The Sextant team and spouses, Eric's work family. He danced her over to join them.

"Congratulations, you two," Jack said as he rose and kissed Dawn lightly on the cheek. "When can we expect him back at work, Mrs. Vinland?"

She noticed Eric's smile falter a little. He had misjudged Mercier's intentions in sending him to the clinic in the

Poconos. No one had any idea they would treat Eric the way they had.

He had also been mistaken about Jack's hiring him for the Sextant team only because of his ability to read minds. He'd been right about the loss. He couldn't do that anymore and seemed relieved about it. However, he still had other psychic tricks up his sleeve, like locating missing objects and people. Besides, his normal abilities as an agent far outweighed even those psychic tools.

The caring that his fellow agents had shown when he came home had humbled him as much as a guy like Eric could be humbled. She grinned at him just because he was who he was. Hers, with all his quirks.

"You can have him in three weeks, not a day sooner," Dawn told his boss, accepting a kiss from the rather stoic Clay Senate as she spoke. He offered her a rare smile. She felt a special affinity for the man who had shared the most dangerous day of her life, so she kissed him back. That earned her a comical frown from her new husband and laughter from the others.

"Eric says he needs to show me Greece the way it should be seen. No bullets, no bad guys, no secret plans hidden in my Wonderbra." She patted her bodice and made a face. George had been wrong. All along, the radar info had been on the flash drive she'd found and was now safely back where it belonged.

Eric slid his arms around her waist from behind and rested his chin on her shoulder. "Nope, no derring-do on this trip. Just sea, sand and…sightseeing." He hesitated a full second before the last word and it came out in a flat tone unlike the others.

"Well, I should hope so. Jack says the mission was an unqualified success," Solange said. "How fortunate that it brought you two together. Jack and I met on a mission, too. So did Joe and Martine."

"I'll be forever grateful we did, too. But I never want to participate in one like it again!" It was enough that Eric had agreed she should continue her work at NSA. She was suited for that, and he would continue to work for Sextant.

"Time to go," Eric reminded her, pointing at his watch and tugging on her elbow. "We fly in two hours."

"Cutting it close," Jack said, reaching out to shake his hand. "Have a great honeymoon, you two."

Eric nodded his thanks to each of them, looking very serious.

"Are you all right?" Dawn asked him as soon as they got into the limousine. He didn't seem his usual happy-go-lucky self, certainly not the beaming bridegroom he'd been earlier. He had changed while they were talking to the team. "What's wrong?"

"I felt something," he told her. "Back there, when I touched you, put my hands on your waist. For a minute there, I sensed…something. Rapid, like a heartbeat, but too fast. *Way* too fast." He bit his lips together, then turned to her and grinned. "For an adult, it was too fast. Hey, I know it's probably too soon to tell for sure, but, do you think…?"

Dawn gasped, meeting his gaze with wonder. "Wow, Vinland, you're amazing! You just might have located something a lot more precious than my grandmother's ring!"

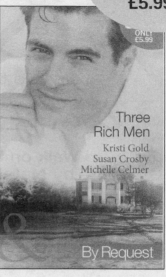

Her Not-So-Secret Diary
by Anne Oliver
Sophie's fantasies stayed secret—until her saucy dream was accidentally e-mailed to her sexy boss! But as their steamy nights reach boiling point, Sophie knows she's in a whole heap of trouble...

The Wedding Date
by Ally Blake
Under no circumstances should Hannah's gorgeous boss, Bradley, be considered her wedding date! Now, if only her disobedient legs would do the *sensible* thing and walk away...

Molly Cooper's Dream Date
by Barbara Hannay
House-swapping with London-based Patrick has given Molly the chance to find a perfect English gentleman! Yet she's increasingly curious about Patrick himself—is the Englishman she wants on the other side of the world?

If the Red Slipper Fits...
by Shirley Jump
It's not *unknown* for Caleb Lewis to find a sexy stiletto in his convertible, but Caleb usually has some recollection of how it got there! He's intrigued to meet the woman it belongs to...

On sale from 4th March 2011
Don't miss out!

Available at WHSmith, Tesco, ASDA, Eason and all good bookshops

www.millsandboon.co.uk

One night with a hot-blooded male!

18th February 2011

18th March 2011

15th April 2011

20th May 2011

www.millsandboon.co.uk

THE Royal
HOUSE OF NIROLI

The richest royal family in the world—united by blood and passion, torn apart by deceit and desire

The Royal House of Niroli: Scandalous Seductions
Penny Jordan & Melanie Milburne
Available 17th December 2010

The Royal House of Niroli: Billion Dollar Bargains
Carol Marinelli & Natasha Oakley
Available 21st January 2011

The Royal House of Niroli: Innocent Mistresses
Susan Stephens & Robyn Donald
Available 18th February 2011

The Royal House of Niroli: Secret Heirs
Raye Morgan & Penny Jordan
Available 18th March 2011

Collect all four!

M&B

Nora Roberts' *The O'Hurleys*

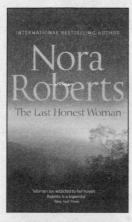

4th March 2011

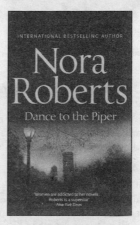

1st April 2011

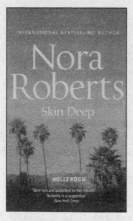

6th May 2011

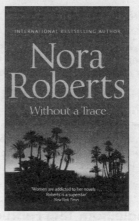

3rd June 2011

A STORMY SPANISH SUMMER
by Penny Jordan

Duque Vidal y Salvadores hated Fliss Clairemont—but now he must help her claim her inheritance! As their attraction takes hold, can Vidal admit how wrong he's been about her...?

NOT A MARRYING MAN
by Miranda Lee

Billionaire Warwick Kincaid asked Amber Roberts to move in, but then became distant. Is her time up? The chemistry between them remains *white-hot* and Amber finds it hard to believe that her time with Warwick is *really* over...

SECRETS OF THE OASIS
by Abby Green

After giving herself to Sheikh Salman years ago, Jamilah Moreau's wedding fantasies were crushed. Then Salman spirits her off to a desert oasis and Jamilah discovers he still wants her!

THE HEIR FROM NOWHERE
by Trish Morey

Dominic Pirelli's world falls apart with the news that an IVF mix-up means a stranger is carrying his baby! Dominic is determined to keep waif-like Angelina Cameron close, but who will have custody of the Pirelli heir?

On sale from 18th February 2011
Don't miss out!

*Available at WHSmith, Tesco, ASDA, Eason
and all good bookshops*
www.millsandboon.co.uk

MODERN

TAMING THE LAST ST CLAIRE
by Carole Mortimer

Gideon St Claire's life revolves around work, so fun-loving Joey McKinley is the sort of woman he normally avoids! Then an old enemy starts looking for revenge and Gideon's forced to protect Joey—day *and* night…

THE FAR SIDE OF PARADISE
by Robyn Donald

A disastrous engagement left Taryn wary of men, but Cade Peredur stirs feelings she's never known before. However, when Cade's true identity is revealed, will Taryn's paradise fantasy dissolve?

THE PROUD WIFE
by Kate Walker

Marina D'Inzeo is finally ready to divorce her estranged husband Pietro—even a summons to join him in Sicily won't deter her! However, with his wife standing before him, Pietro wonders why he ever let her go!

ONE DESERT NIGHT
by Maggie Cox

Returning to the desert plains of Kabuyadir to sell its famous *Heart of Courage* jewel, Gina Collins is horrified the new sheikh is the man who gave her one earth-shattering night years ago.

On sale from 4th March 2011
Don't miss out!

EXPECTING ROYAL TWINS! *by Melissa McClone*

Mechanic Izzy was shocked when a tall handsome prince strode into her workshop and declared he was her husband! Now she's about to face an even bigger surprise...

TO DANCE WITH A PRINCE *by Cara Colter*

Royal playboy Kiernan's been nicknamed Prince Heartbreaker. Meredith knows, in her head, that he's the last man she needs, yet her heart thinks otherwise!

HONEYMOON WITH THE RANCHER *by Donna Alward*

After Tomas' fiancée's death, he sought peace on his Argentine ranch. Until socialite Sophia arrived for her honeymoon...*alone*. Can they heal each other's hearts?

NANNY NEXT DOOR *by Michelle Celmer*

Sydney's ex left her with nothing, but she needs to provide for her daughter. Sheriff Daniel's her new neighbour who could give Sydney the perfect opportunity.

A BRIDE FOR JERICHO BRAVO *by Christine Rimmer*

After being jilted by her long-time boyfriend, Marnie's given up on love. Until meeting sexy rebel Jericho has her believing in second chances...

Cherish

THE DOCTOR'S PREGNANT BRIDE?
by Susan Crosby

From the moment Ted asked Sara to be his date for a Valentine's Day dinner, the head-in-the-clouds scientist was hooked; even if she seemed to be hiding something.

BABY BY SURPRISE
by Karen Rose Smith

Francesca relied on no one but herself. Until an accident meant the mother-to-be was forced to turn to fiercely protective rancher Grady, her baby's secret father.

THE BABY SWAP MIRACLE
by Caroline Anderson

Sam only intended to help his brother fulfil his dream of having children, but now, through an IVF mix-up, enchanting stranger Emelia's pregnant with his child!

Medical Romance™

SUMMER SEASIDE WEDDING
by Abigail Gordon

Dr Amelie Benoir plans to spend the summer healing her bruised heart—not falling for the impossibly handsome Dr Leo Fenchurch!

REUNITED: A MIRACLE MARRIAGE
by Judy Campbell

GP Sally Lawson is shocked that her ex, Dr Jack McLennan, still makes her pulse race… But Jack is a changed man and he's fighting for a second chance. It might take a miracle, but he wants Sally as his bride!

THE MAN WITH THE LOCKED AWAY HEART
by Melanie Milburne

There's definitely chemistry between the mysterious new cop Marc Di Angelo and local doctor Gemma Kendall. But can Gemma release his tightly guarded emotions before he leaves town for good…?

SOCIALITE…OR NURSE IN A MILLION?
by Molly Evans

Spanish doctor Miguel Torres isn't convinced new nurse Vicky has what it takes. Vicky is determined to show him that behind her socialite reputation lies a heart of gold—a heart that's rapidly falling for her gorgeous new boss!

**On sale from 4th March 2011
Don't miss out!**

*Available at WHSmith, Tesco, ASDA, Eason and all good bookshops
www.millsandboon.co.uk*

0211/03b

ST PIRAN'S: THE BROODING HEART SURGEON
bY Alison Roberts

Everyone at St Piran's hospital has fallen under Dr Luke Davenport's spell, except Anna Bartlett, who is certain the ex-army medic is hiding something. She should remain professional, but Anna's longing to be the one to save Luke from his nightmares—if only she can reach out to the man behind the brooding mask…

PLAYBOY DOCTOR TO DOTING DAD
by Sue MacKay

Arriving in Nelson to run the A&E department temporarily, gorgeous Kieran Flynn is greeted with a few life-changing bombshells—including Abby Brown, the woman he spent a magical night with two years ago…

On sale from 4th March 2011
Don't miss out!

Available at WHSmith, Tesco, ASDA, Eason and all good bookshops
www.millsandboon.co.uk